THE GENEVA DECEPTION

Also by James Twining

The Double Eagle
The Black Sun
The Gilded Seal

JAMES TWINING

The Geneva Deception

HarperCollins*Publishers*

HarperCollins*Publishers*
77–85 Fulham Palace Road, London W6 8JB

www.harpercollins.co.uk

Published by HarperCollins*Publishers* 2009

1

Copyright © James Twining 2009

James Twining asserts the moral right to
be identified as the author of this work

A catalogue record for this book
is available from the British Library

ISBN: 978-0-00-723042-6 (hbk)
ISBN: 978-0-00-727818-3 (tpbk)

Set in Meridien by Palimpsest Book Production Limited,
Grangemouth, Stirlingshire

Printed in Great Britain by
Clays Ltd, St Ives plc

Mixed Sources

Product group from well-managed
forests and other controlled sources
www.fsc.org Cert no. SW-COC-1806
© 1996 Forest Stewardship Council

FSC

FSC is a non-profit international organisation established
to promote the responsible management of the world's forests.
Products carrying the FSC label are independently certified
to assure consumers that they come from forests that are managed
to meet the social, economic and ecological needs
of present and future generations.

Find out more about HarperCollins and the environment at
www.harpercollins.co.uk/green

To Jack, Jill and Herbie. Vegas, baby.

'There is a house in New Orleans
They call the Rising Sun
It's been the ruin of many a poor boy
And me, Oh Lord! was one'

Traditional American folk song

ACKNOWLEDGEMENTS

My thanks to my fantastic agent, Jonathan Lloyd, and the whole team at Curtis Brown in London, who have done such a fantastic job of supporting me and promoting my work both here and abroad.

Thank you also to my editor Wayne Brookes, whose skill and endless energy and passion for my books has made me a better (I think!) writer. My thanks, of course, also go to the rest of the team at Harper Collins in the sales, editorial, marketing and creative departments, who have continued to work wonders for me.

In researching this novel I owe a debt of gratitude to two excellent books: *The Medici Conspiracy* by Peter Watson and Cecilia Todeschini, and *Stealing History* by Roger Atwood. I would also like to thank the Arlington National Cemetery in Washington DC, the Galleria Doria Pamphilj, the Palazzo Barberini and the Cimitero Acattolico in Rome, the Geneva Freeport and the Société des Bains de Mer in Monaco.

As ever, many people helped in the original conception and writing of this novel, but special thanks go to Jessica Hughes who first aroused my interest in the international trade in looted antiquities and Francesco Russo, Gemma

J'Auria and Flavia Ruffini. Thanks also to Ann, Bob and Joanna Twining and Roy and Claire Toft for their continued guidance and encouragement.

Victoria, Amelia, Jemima and now Felix! – I love you all.

London, April 2009

HISTORICAL BACKGROUND

This story was inspired by a Carabinieri raid on a warehouse in the Geneva Freeport in 1995 and their discovery within it of over ten thousand illegally excavated antiquities worth over $35 million. The resulting investigation implicated the mafia and raised questions over the role of some of the world's largest museums, collectors and auction houses in the multi-million-dollar international trade in illicit cultural artefacts.

All descriptions and background information provided on works of art, artists, thefts, antiquities smuggling, 'orphans', illegal excavation practices, and architecture are accurate, apart from the Desposito Eroli in Rome, which I have altered to suit my purpose.

For more information on the author and on the fascinating history, people, places, art and artefacts that feature in *The Geneva Deception* and the other Tom Kirk novels, please visit www.jamestwining.com

Extract from the Amherst Papyrus, original court records from the reign of Ramses IX (–1110 BC); translated by J. H. Breasted, *Ancient Records of Egypt*, Book IV (1904)

We opened their coffins and their coverings in which they were. We found this august mummy of this king . . . Its coverings were wrought with gold and silver, within and without; inlaid with every splendid costly stone.

We stripped off the gold, which we found on the august mummy of this god, and its amulets and ornaments which were at its throat, and the coverings wherein it rested. [We] found the King's wife likewise; we stripped off all that we found on her likewise. We set fire to their coverings. We stole their furniture, which we found with them, being vases of gold, silver, and bronze.

We divided, and made the gold which we found on these two gods, on their mummies, and the amulets, ornaments and coverings, into eight parts.

Extract from letter written by Thomas Bruce, the seventh Earl of Elgin, to Giovanni Lusieri, 1801

I should wish to have, of the Acropolis, examples in the actual object of each thing, and architectural ornament – of each cornice, each frieze, each capital of the decorated ceilings, of the fluted columns – specimens of the different architectural orders and of the variant forms of the orders – of metopes and the like, as much as possible. Finally everything in the way of sculpture, medals and curious marbles that can be discovered by means of assiduous and indefatigable excavation.

PROLOGUE

'I see wars, terrible wars, and the Tiber foaming
with blood'

Virgil, *The Aeneid*, Book VI, 86

Ponte Duca d'Aosta, Rome
15th March – 2.37 a.m.

The cold kiss roused him.

A teasing, tentative embrace, it nibbled playfully at his ear and then, growing in confidence, slipped down to nuzzle against his naked throat.

Eyes screwed shut, cheek pressed against the wooden decking, Luca Cavalli knew that he should enjoy this moment while it lasted. So he lay there, cradled by the darkness, the gentle swell of the river rocking him softly, concentrating on keeping the steady cadence of his breathing constant. So they wouldn't notice he was awake.

Ahead of him, near the bow, a small pool of rainwater had gathered. He could hear it sloshing from side to side under the duckboards as the boat swayed, smell the rainbow shimmer of engine oil dancing across its surface, the heady scent catching in the back of his throat like an exotic perfume. He had a strange, uncontrollable urge to swallow, to taste the raw truth of this moment while he still could.

The momentary stutter in his breathing's rhythmic beat was all it took. Immediately, the thin lips resting against his skin parted with a snarl, and the sharp teeth of the knife's serrated edge bit into him savagely. He was hauled upright, eyes blinking, shoulders burning where his wrists had been zip-locked behind his back.

There were three of them in all. One at the helm, his slab hands gripping the wheel. One perched on the bench opposite, a gun wedged into the waistband of his jeans and a cigarette balancing on his lip. One hugging him close, the knife he had caressed his cheek with only a few moments before now pressed hard against his belly.

They were silent, although there was something noisily boastful about their lack of disguise, as if they wanted him to know that they would never be caught, never allow themselves to be picked out from some Questura line-up. Perhaps because of this, the longer he gazed at them, the more featureless they appeared to become, their cruel faces melting into black shadows that he imagined travelled on the wind and lived in dark places where the light feared to go.

Instead, he was struck by their almost monastic serenity. Mute, their eyes fixed resolutely on the horizon, it was as if they had been chosen to complete some divinely ordained quest. Part of him envied their solemn determination, their absolute certainty in their purpose, however base. These were not people whose loyalty could be bought or trust swayed. They were true believers. Perhaps if he'd shared their unswerving faith, he might have avoided his present damnation.

Cavalli gave a resigned shrug and glanced over the side. The river was engorged and running fast, the sharp ripples on the water's ebony surface betraying the occasional patches of shallower ground where the current tripped and dragged against the muddy bed. Above them the streetlights glowed through the trees that lined the embankments on both sides, casting their skeletal shadows down on to the water. The roads

appeared quiet, the occasional yellow wash of a car's headlights sweeping through the gloom overhead as it turned, like
a distant lighthouse urging him to safety.

Cavalli realised then that the engine wasn't running, and
that this whole time they had been carried forward noise-
lessly on the river's powerful muscle as it flexed its way
through the city. Peering behind them, he could see that
because of this, and like some infernal, enchanted craft, they
had left no wake behind them, apart from a momentary fold
in the river's dark velvet that was just as soon ironed flat
again.

The gallows creak of the trees as they passed under the
Ponte Cavour interrupted his thoughts. He glanced up fear-
fully and caught sight of the cylindrical mass of the Castel
Sant'Angelo up ahead, the blemishes in its ancient walls
concealed by the sodium glare of the lighting that encircled it. To its rear, he knew, was the Passetto, the corridor
that had for centuries served as a secret escape route from
the Vatican to the castle's fortified sanctuary. For a moment,
he allowed himself to imagine that he too might yet have
some way out, some hidden passage to safety. If only he
could find it.

Still the current carried them forward, steering them
towards the Ponte Sant' Angelo and the carved angels lining
its balustrades, as if gathering to hear his final confession. It
was a strangely comforting thought, although as they drew
closer, he realised that even this harmless conceit was to be
denied him. The pale figures all had their backs to the river.
They didn't even know he was there.

Abruptly, the helmsman whistled, violating the code of
silence that had been so religiously observed until now. Up
ahead a light flashed twice from the bridge. Someone was
expecting them.

Immediately the engine kicked into life as the helmsman

wrestled control from the current and steered them towards the left-hand arch. The two other men jumped up, suddenly animated, one of them readying himself with a rope, the other tipping the fenders into place along the port gunwales. As they passed under the arch, the helmsman jammed the throttle into reverse and expertly edged the boat against the massive stone pier, the fenders squealing in protest, the rattle of the exhaust echoing noisily off the vaulted roof. He nodded at the others and they leapt forward to secure the boat to the rusting iron rings embedded in the wall, leaving just enough play for the craft to ride the river's swell. Then he switched the engine off.

Instantly, a bright orange rope came hissing out of the darkness, the excess coiling in the prow. The helmsman stepped forward and tugged on it to check it was secure, then found the end and held it up. It had already been tied into a noose.

Now, as he understood that there was to be no last-minute reprieve, that this was how it was really going to end, Cavalli felt afraid. Desperate words began to form in his mouth, screams rose from his stomach. But no sound came out, as if he had somehow been bound into the same demonic vow of silence that his captors seemed to have taken.

Hauling him out of his seat, the two other men dragged him over to where the helmsman was looping the surplus rope around his arm, and forced him on to his knees. Cavalli gave him a pleading look, gripped by some basic and irrational need to hear his voice, as if this final and most basic act of human communion might somehow help soften the ordeal's cold, mechanised efficiency. But instead, the noose was simply snapped over his head and then jerked tight, the knot biting into the nape of his neck. Then he was silently lifted to the side and carefully lowered into the freezing water.

He gasped, the change in temperature winding him. Treading water, he looked up at the boat, not understanding why they had tied the rope so long, its loose coils snaking through the water around him. The three men, however, hadn't moved from the side rail, an expectant look on their faces as if they were waiting for something to happen. Waiting, he realised as he drifted a few feet further away from the boat, for the current to take him.

Without warning, the river grabbed on to him, nudging him along slowly at first and then, as he emerged out from under the bridge, tugging at his ankles with increasing insistence. He drew further away, the rope gently uncoiling in the water, the steep angle of the cord where it ran down from the bridge's dark parapet getting closer and closer to him as the remaining slack paid out.

It snapped tight. Choking, his body swung round until he was half in and half out of the water, the current hauling at his hips and legs, the rope lifting his head and upper body out of the river, the tension wringing the water from the fibres.

He kicked out frantically, his ears flooding with an inhuman gurgling noise that he only vaguely recognised as his own voice. But rather than free himself, all he managed to do was flip himself on to his front so that he was face down over the water.

Slowly, and with his reflection staring remorselessly back up at him from the river's dark mirror, Cavalli watched himself hang.

PART ONE

'The die has been cast'
Julius Caesar (according to Suetonius,
Divus Julius, paragraph 33)

ONE

Arlington National Cemetery, Washington DC
17th March – 10.58 a.m.

One by one, the limousines and town cars drew up, disgorged their occupants on to the sodden grass, and then pulled away to a respectful distance. Parked end-to-end along the verge, they formed an inviolable black line that followed the curve of the road and then stretched down the hill and out of sight, their exhaust fumes pinned to the road by the rain as they waited.

A handful of secret service agents were patrolling the space between the burial site and the road. Inexplicably, a few of them were wearing sunglasses despite the black clouds that had sailed up the Potomac a few days ago and anchored themselves over the city. Their unsmiling presence made Tom Kirk feel uncomfortable, even though he knew it shouldn't. After all, it had been nearly two years now. Two years since he'd crossed over to the other side of the law. Two years since he'd teamed up with Archie Connolly, his former fence, to help recover art rather than steal it. Clearly it was going to take much longer than that to shake off instincts acquired in a lifetime on the run.

There were three rows of seats arranged in a horseshoe around the flag-draped coffin, and five further rows of people standing behind these. A pretty good turnout, considering the weather. Tom and Archie had stayed back, sheltering under the generous spread of a blossoming tree halfway up the slope that climbed gently to the left of the grave.

As they watched, the ceremony's carefully choreographed martial beauty unfolded beneath them. The horse-drawn caisson slowly winding its way up the hill, followed by a single riderless horse, its flanks steaming, boots reversed in the stirrups to symbolise a fallen leader. The immaculate presenting of arms by the military escort, water dripping from their polished visors. The careful securing and transport of the coffin to the grave by a casket party made up of eight members of the 101st Airborne, Tom's grandfather's old unit. The final adjustments to the flag to ensure that it was stretched out and centred, the reds, blues and whites fighting to be seen through the tenebrous darkness.

From his vantage point, Tom recognised a few of the faces sheltering under the thicket of black umbrellas, although most were strangers to him and, he suspected, would have been to his grandfather too. That figured. Funerals were a vital networking event for the DC top brass – a chance to talk to the people you normally couldn't be seen with; a chance to be seen with the people who normally wouldn't talk to you. Deals were done, handshakes given, assurances provided. In this city, death was known to have breathed life into many a stuttering career or stalled bill.

There was perhaps, Tom suspected, another, more personal reason for their presence too. After all, like them, Trent Clayton Jackson Duval III had been an important man – a senator, no less. And as such it was in their shared interest to ensure that he got a proper send off. Not because they cared about him particularly, although as a war hero, 'Trigger' Duval commanded more respect than most. Rather because they knew, as if they were all party to some secret, unspoken pact, that it was only by reinforcing these sorts of traditions that they could safeguard their prerogative to a similarly grand send off when their own time came.

'Who's the bird?' Archie sniffed. In his mid-forties, about five foot ten and unshaven with close cropped blond hair, Archie had the square-shouldered, rough confidence of someone who didn't mind using their fists to start or settle an argument. This was at odds with the patrician elegance of his clothes, however; a three-buttoned, ten-ounce, dark grey Anderson & Sheppard suit, crisp white Turnbull and Asser shirt, and woven black silk Lewin's tie hinting at a rather more considered and refined temperament. Tom knew that many struggled to reconcile this apparent incongruity, although the truth was that both were valid. It was only a short distance from the rain-lashed trestle tables of Bermondsey Market to Mayfair's panelled auction rooms, but for Archie it had been a long and difficult journey that had required this expensive camouflage to travel undetected. Tom rather suspected that he now deliberately played off the contradiction, preferring to keep people guessing which world he was from rather than pin him down to one world or the other.

'Miss Texas,' Tom answered, knowing instinctively that his eye would have been drawn to the platinum blonde in the front row. 'Or she was a few years ago. The senator upgraded after meeting her on the campaign trail. He left her everything.'

'I'll bet he did, the dirty old bastard.' Archie grinned. 'Look at the size of those puppies! She'd keel over in a strong wind.'

The corners of Tom's mouth twitched but he said nothing, finding himself wondering if her dark Jackie O glasses were to hide her tears or to mask the fact that she had none. The chaplain started the service.

'You sure you don't want to head down?' Archie was holding up a Malacca-handled Brigg umbrella. A gold identity bracelet glinted on his wrist where his sleeve had slipped back.

'This is close enough.'

'Bloody long way to come if all we're going to do is stand up here getting pissed on,' Archie sniffed, peering out disconsolately at the leaden skies. 'They invited you, didn't they?'

'They were being polite. They never thought I'd actually show. I'm not welcome here. Not really.'

The empty caisson pulled away, the horses' hooves clattering noisily on the blacktop, reins jangling.

'I thought he liked you?'

'He helped me,' Tom said slowly. 'Took me in after my mother died, put me through school, recommended me to the NSA. But after I left the Agency . . . well. We hadn't spoken in twelve years.'

'Then tell me again why the bloody hell we're here?' Archie moaned, pulling his blue overcoat around his neck with a shiver.

Tom hesitated. The truth was that, even now, he wasn't entirely sure. Partly, it had just seemed like the proper thing to do. The right thing to do. But probably more important was the feeling that his mother would have wanted him to come. Expected it. Insisted on it. To him, therefore, this was perhaps less about paying his respects to his grandfather than it was a way of remembering her.

'You didn't have to come,' Tom reminded him sharply.

'What, and miss the chance to work on my tan?' Archie winked. 'Don't be daft. That's what mates are for.'

They stood in silence, the priest's faint voice and the congregation's murmured responses carrying to them on the damp breeze. Yet even as the service droned mournfully towards its conclusion. 'Let us pray'.

As people lowered their heads, a man stepped out from the crowd and signalled up at them with a snatched half-wave, having been waiting for this opportunity, it seemed Tom and Archie swapped a puzzled look as he clambered up towards them, his shoes slipping on the wet grass.

'Mr Kirk?' he called out hopefully as he approached. 'Mr Thomas Kirk?'

Short and worryingly overweight, he wore a large pair of tortoiseshell glasses that he was forever pushing back up his blunt nose. Under a Burberry coat that didn't look as though it had fitted him in years, an expensive Italian suit dangled open on each side of his bloated stomach, like the wings on a flying boat.

'I recognised you from your photo,' he huffed as he drew closer, sweat lacquering his thinning blond hair to his head.

'I don't think . . .?' Tom began, trying to place the man's sagging face and bleached teeth.

'Larry Hewson,' he announced, his tone and eagerly outstretched hand suggesting that he expected them to recognise the name.

Tom swapped another look with Archie and then shrugged.

'Sorry, but I don't . . .'

'From Ogilvy, Myers and Gray – the Duval family attorneys,' Hewson explained, almost sounding hurt at having to spell this out. 'I sent you the invitation.'

'What do you want?' Archie challenged him.

'Meet Archie Connolly,' Tom introduced him with a smile. 'My business partner.'

Below them, the chaplain had stepped back from the casket, allowing the senior NCO and seven riflemen to step forward and turn to the half right, their shoulders stained dark blue by the rain, water beading on their mirrored toecaps.

'Ready,' he ordered. Each rifleman moved his safety to the fire position.

'It's a delicate matter,' Hewson said in a low voice, throwing Archie a suspicious glance.

'Archie can hear anything you've got to say,' Tom reassured him.

'It concerns your grandfather's will.'

'Aim,' the NCO called. The men shouldered their weapons with both hands, the muzzles raised forty-five degrees from the horizontal over the casket.

'His will?' Archie asked with a frown. 'I thought he'd left the lot to Miss 32F down there?'

'Fire.'

Each man quickly squeezed the trigger and then returned to port arms, the sharp crack of the blank round piercing the gloom, the echo muffled by the rain. Twice more the order to aim and fire came, twice more the shots rang out across the silent cemetery. Hewson waited impatiently for their echo to die down before continuing.

'The senator did indeed alter his will to ensure that Ms Mills was the principal beneficiary of his estate,' he confirmed in a disapproving whisper. 'But at the same time, he identified a small object that he wished to leave to you.'

A bugler had stepped forward and was now playing Taps, the mournful melody swirling momentarily around them before chasing itself into the sky. As the last note faded away, one of the casket party stepped forward and began to carefully fold the flag draped over the coffin, deliberately wrapping the red and white stripes into the blue to form a triangular bundle, before respectfully handing it to the chaplain. The chaplain in turn stepped over to where the main family party was seated and gingerly, almost apologetically it seemed, handed the flag to the senator's wife. She clutched it, rather dramatically Tom thought, to her bosom.

'I believe it had been given to him by your mother,' Hewson added.

'My mother?' Tom's eyes snapped back to Hewson's, both surprised and curious. 'What is it?'

'I'm afraid I don't know,' Hewson shrugged as the ceremony ended. The congregation rapidly thinned, most hurrying back to their cars, a few pausing to conclude the business they had come there for in the first place, before they too were herded by secret service agents towards their limousines' armour-plated comfort. 'The terms of the will are quite strict. No one is to open the box and I am to hand it to you in person. That's why . . .'

'Tom!' Archie interrupted, grabbing Tom's arm. Tom followed his puzzled gaze and saw that a figure had appeared at the crest of the hill above them. It was a woman dressed in a red coat, the headlights of the car parked behind her silhouetting her against the dark sky in an ethereal white glow.

'That's why I sent you the invitation,' Hewson repeated, raising his voice slightly as Tom turned away from him. 'I've taken the liberty of reserving a suite at the George where we can finalise all the paperwork.'

'Isn't that . . .?' Archie's eyes narrowed, his tone at once uncertain and incredulous.

'Otherwise I'm happy to arrange a meeting at our offices in New York tomorrow, if that works better,' Hewson called out insistently, growing increasingly frustrated, it seemed, at being ignored. 'Mr Kirk?'

'Yes . . .' Tom returned the woman's wave, Hewson's voice barely registering any more. 'It's her.'

TWO

Via del Gesù, Rome
17th March – 5.44 p.m.
Ignoring her phone's shrill call, Allegra Damico grabbed the double espresso off the counter, threw down some change and stepped back outside into the fading light. Answering it wouldn't make her get there any quicker. And if they wanted her to make any sense after the day she'd just had, she needed the caffeine more than they needed her to be on time. Shrugging with a faint hint of indignation, she walked down the Via del Gesù then turned right on to the Corso Vittorio Emanuele, cupping the coffee in both hands and blowing on it, her reflection catching in the shop windows.

She owed her athletic frame to her father, an architect who had met her mother when he was working as a tour guide in Naples and she, a Danish student, was backpacking across Europe. As a result, Allegra had contrived to inherit both his olive skin and quick temper and her mother's high cheekbones and the sort of curling strawberry blonde hair that the rich housewives who stalked the Via dei Condotti spent hundreds of euros trying to conjure from a bottle. Nowhere was this genetic compromise more arrestingly reflected than in her mismatched eyes – one crystal blue, the other an earthy brown.

Lifting her nose from the cup she frowned, suddenly aware that despite the time of day, dawn seemed to be breaking ahead of her, its golden glow bronzing the sky. Sighing, she quickened her pace, taking this unnatural event and the growing wail of sirens as an ominous portent of what lay in wait.

Her instincts were soon proved right. The Largo di Torre Argentina, a large rectangular square that had once formed part of the Campo Marzio, had been barricaded off, a disco frenzy of blue and red lights dancing across the walls of the surrounding buildings. A swollen, curious crowd had gathered on one side of the metal railings, straining to see into the middle of the square, some holding their mobile phones over their heads to film what they could. On the other side loomed a determined cordon of state police, some barking at people to stay back and go home, a few braving the baying masses in a valiant attempt to redirect the backed-up traffic along the Via dei Cestari. A police helicopter circled overhead, the bass chop of its blades mingling with the sirens' shrill treble and the raw noise of the crowd to form a deafening and discordant choir. A single searchlight shone down from its belly, its celestial beam picking out a spot that Allegra couldn't yet see.

Her phone rang again. This time she answered it.

'*Pronto*. Yes sir, I'm here . . . I'm sorry, but I came as soon as I could . . . Well, I'm here now . . . Okay, then tell him I'll meet him at the north-east corner in three months . . . *Ciao*.'

She extracted her badge from her rear jeans pocket and, taking a deep breath, plunged into the crowd and elbowed her way to the front, flashing it apologetically in the vague direction of the muffled curses and angry stares thrown her way. Once there, she identified herself and an officer

unhooked one of the barriers, the weight of the crowd spitting her through the gap before immediately closing up behind
her.

Catching her breath and pulling her jacket straight, she
picked her way through a maze of haphazardly parked squad
cars and headed towards the fenced-off sunken area that
dominated the middle of the square. She could see now that
this was the epicentre of the synthetic dawn she had witnessed
earlier, a series of large mobile floodlights having been
wheeled into place along its perimeter, the helicopter frozen
overhead.

'Lieutenant Damico?'

A man had appeared at the top of a makeshift set of steps
that led down to the large sunken tract of land. She nodded
and held out her ID by way of introduction.

'You're a woman.'

'Unless you know something I don't?'

'I know you're late,' he snapped.

About six foot three, he must have weighed seventeen
stone, most of it muscle. He was wearing dark blue trousers,
a grey jacket and a garish tie that could only have been a
gift from his children at Christmas. She guessed he was in
his late fifties; his once square face rounding softly at the
edges, black hair swept across his scalp to mask his baldness
and almost totally grey over his ears. A scar cut across his
thick black moustache, dividing it into two unevenly sized
islands separated by a raised white ribbon of skin, like a path
snaking through a forest.

For a moment she thought of arguing it out with him.
Not the fact that she was late, of course: she was. Which,
to be honest, she always was. Rather that she had an in-
tray full of reasons to be late. He should be grateful she
was there at all, in fact. But for once she held back,
suspecting from his manner that he wouldn't be interested

in her excuses. If anything, his anxious tone and the nervous twitch of his left eye suggested that he was wasn't so much angry, as afraid.

'So everyone keeps telling me.'

'Major Enrico Salvatore –' he grudgingly shook her hand – 'Sorry about . . . we don't see too many women in the GICO.'

She just about managed to stop herself from rolling her eyes. GICO – properly known as the Gruppo di Investigazione Criminalità Organizzata – the special corps of the Guardia di Finanza that dealt with organised crime. And by reputation an old-school unit that frequented the same strip joints as the people they were supposedly trying to lock up.

'So what's the deal?' she asked. Her boss hadn't told her anything. Just that he owed someone a favour and that she should get down here as soon as she could.

'You know this place?' he asked, gesturing anxiously at the sunken area behind him.

'Of course.' She shrugged, slightly annoyed to even be asked. Presumably they knew her background. Why else would they have asked for her? 'It's the "Area Sacra".'

'Go on.'

'It contains the remains of four Roman temples unearthed during an excavation project ordered by Mussolini in the 1920s,' she continued. 'They were built between the fourth and second centuries BC. Each one has a different design, with . . .'

'Fine, fine . . .' He held his hands up for her to stop, his relieved tone giving her the impression that she had just successfully passed some sort of audition without entirely being sure what role she was being considered for. He turned to make his way back down the steps. 'Save the rest for the boss.'

The large site was enclosed by an elegant series of brick archways that formed a retaining wall for the streets some fifteen or so feet above. Bleached white by the floodlights' desert glare, a forensic search team was strung out across it, inching their way forward on their hands and knees.

Immediately to her right, Allegra knew, was the Temple of Juturna – a shallow flight of brick steps leading up to a rectangular area edged by a row of travertine Corinthian columns of differing heights, like trees that had been randomly felled by a storm. They were all strangely shadow-less in the artificial light. Further along the paved walkway was the Aedes Fortunae Huiusce Diei, a circular temple where only six tufa stone Corinthian columns remained standing, a few surviving bases and mid-sections from the other missing pillars poking up like rotting teeth.

But Salvatore steered her past both of these, turning instead between the second and third temples and making his way over rough ground scattered with loose bits of stone and half-formed brick walls that looked like they had been spat out of the earth. Here and there cats, strays from the animal shelter located in the far corner of the Area Sacra, glanced up with disdainful disinterest or picked their way languidly between the ruins, meowing hopefully for food.

With a curious frown, Allegra realised that Salvatore was leading her towards a large semi-permanent structure made of scaffolding, covered in white plastic sheeting.

Wedged into the space between the rear of the second and third temples and the retaining wall, she immediately recog-nised it as the sort of makeshift shelter that was often erected by archaeologists to protect an area of a site that they were excavating or restoring.

'I'd stay out of the way until the colonel calls you over,' Salvatore suggested as he paused on the threshold to the shelter, although from his tone it sounded more like an order.

'The colonel?'

'Colonel Gallo. The head of GICO,' Salvatore explained in a hushed tone.

She recognised the name. From what she remembered reading at the time, Gallo had been parachuted last year in from the AISI, the Italian internal security service, after his predecessor had been implicated in the Mancini corruption scandal.

'He'll call you over when he's ready.'

'Great.' She nodded, her tight smile masking a desperate urge to make some pointed observation about the irony of having been harried halfway across the city only to now be kept waiting.

'And I'd lose that if I were you, too,' he muttered, nodding at her cup. 'It's probably better he doesn't know you were late because you stopped off for a coffee.'

Taking a deep breath, she theatrically placed the cup on the ground, then looked up with a forced smile. It wasn't Salvatore's fault, she knew. Gallo clearly orbited his waking hours like a small moon, the gravitational pull off his shifting favour governing the ebb and flow of Salvatore's emotions. But that didn't make him any less annoying.

'Happy now?'

'Ecstatic.'

Greeting the two uniformed men guarding the entrance with a nod, Salvatore held a plastic flap in the sidewall open and they stepped inside. It revealed a long, narrow space, the scaffolding forming a sturdily symmetrical endoskeleton over which the white sheeting had been draped and then fixed into place. In one place some of the ties had come loose, the wind catching the sheet's edges and snapping it against the metal frame, causing it to chime like a halyard striking a mast.

Salvatore motioned at a crumbling pediment, his gesture suggesting that he wanted her to sit there until she was called forward, then made his way towards a small group of people standing in a semi-circle fifteen or so feet in front of her – all men, she noted with a resigned sigh. Making a point of remaining standing, she counted the minutes as they ticked past – first one, then three, then five. Nothing. In fact no one had turned round to acknowledge that she was even there. Pursing her lips, she decided to give it another few minutes and then, when these too had passed, she made an angry clicking noise with her tongue and set off towards them. Busy was one thing, rude was another. She had better things to do than sit around until Gallo deigned to beckon her over like some sort of performing dog. Besides, she wanted to see for herself whatever it was they were discussing so intently.

Seeing her approaching, Salvatore frantically signalled at her to stay back. She ignored him, but then stopped anyway, the colour draining from her face as a sudden gap revealed what they had been shielding from view.

It was a corpse. A man. A half-naked man. Arms spread-eagled, legs pinned together, he had been lashed to a makeshift wooden cross with steel wire. Allegra glanced away, horrified, but almost immediately looked back, the gruesome scene exercising a strange, magnetic pull. For as if drawn from some cursed, demonic ritual, the cross had been inverted.

He had been crucified upside down.

THREE

Arlington National Cemetery, Washington DC
17th March – 11.46 a.m.

'You sure about this?' Special Agent Bryan Stokes stepped out of the car behind her, his tone making his own doubts clear.

'Absolutely,' Jennifer Browne nodded, surprised at the unforced confidence in her voice as she watched Tom set off towards them, his short brown hair plastered down by the rain. He had seemed pleased to see her, his initial surprise having melted into a warm smile and an eager wave. That was something, at least.

'So what's the deal with you two?' Stokes wedged a golf umbrella against his shoulder with his chin and flicked a manilla file open. Medium height, about a hundred and seventy pounds, Jennifer guessed that Stokes had been born frowning, deep lines furrowing a wide, flat forehead, bloodless lips pressed into a concerned grimace. In his early forties, he was dressed in a severe charcoal suit and black tie that had dropped away from his collar, revealing that the button was missing.

'There is no deal,' she said quickly, looking away in case he noticed her smile.

'Then how do you know him?'

'We've worked a couple of cases together, that's all.'

Tom was navigating his way towards them through the blossom scatter of white gravestones like a skiff through a storm, tacking first one way and then the other as he plotted a route up the hill. Not for the first time she noted that despite his tall, athletic frame, there was something almost feline about the way he moved – at once graceful and fluid and yet strong and sure-footed.

'It says here he was Agency?'

'Senator Duval was on the Senate Intelligence Committee and recommended him,' she explained, picking her words carefully. FBI Director Jack Green had made it crystal clear that the specific circumstances in which Tom had joined and left the CIA were highly classified. 'They recruited him into a black op industrial espionage unit. When they shut it down five years later, Kirk went into business for himself, switching from technical blueprints and experimental formulas to fine art and jewellery.'

'Was he any good?'

'The best in the business. Or so they said.'

'And the guy with him?'

'Archie Connolly. His former fence. Now his business partner. And his best friend, to the extent he allows himself to have one.'

There was a pause as Stokes consulted the file again. It had been Jennifer's idea to come here, of course. INS had flagged Tom's name up when he'd landed at Dulles and it hadn't taken her much to figure out where he'd be headed. But now that she was actually here, she was surprised at how she was feeling. Excited to be seeing Tom again after almost a year, certainly. But there was also a nagging sense of nervousness and apprehension that she couldn't quite explain. Or perhaps didn't want to. It was always easier that way.

'And now they've gone straight?' There was the suggestion of suppressed laughter in Stokes's voice.

'I'm not sure that someone like Tom can ever go straight,' she mused. 'Not in the way you and I mean it. The problem is, he's seen too many supposedly straight people do crooked things to think those sorts of labels matter. He just does what he thinks is right.'

'And you're sure about this?' Stokes pressed again, her explanation seeming to have, if anything, heightened his initial misgivings.

She didn't bother replying, hoping that he would interpret her silence in whichever way made him most comfortable. Instead she stepped forward to greet Tom, who had reached the final incline that led up to where they were waiting. Tom, however, hesitated, his eyes flicking to Stokes and then back to her. He was clearly surprised that she hadn't come alone.

'Tom –' She held out her hand. It felt all wrong, too formal, but with Stokes hovering she didn't exactly have much choice. Besides, what was the alternative? A hug? A kiss? That also didn't seem right after eleven months.

'Special Agent Browne,' Tom shook her hand with a brief nod, having clearly decided to ape her stilted greeting. He looked healthier than when she had last seen him, his handsome, angular face having lost some of its pallor, his coral blue eyes clear and alive.

'This is Special Agent Stokes.'

'Agent Stokes,' Tom nodded a greeting.

Stokes grunted something indistinct in reply and glanced nervously over his shoulder, as if he was worried about being seen out in the open with him.

'Come to pay your respects?'

'We need some help on a case,' Jennifer began hesitantly.

'You mean this wasn't a coincidence?'

Despite his sarcastic tone, she sensed a slight tension lurking behind his smile. Annoyance, perhaps, that she was only there because she wanted something. Or was that just her projecting her own guilty feelings?

'*I* need your help,' she said.

There was a pause, his smile fading.

'What have you got?'

'Why don't we get in . . .' She held the Suburban's rear door open. Tom didn't move. 'There's something I want to show you. It'll only take a few minutes.'

Tom hesitated for a moment. Then, shrugging, he followed Jennifer into the back, while Stokes climbed into the driver's seat.

'Recognise this?'

She handed him a photograph sealed inside a clear plastic evidence bag. Tom smoothed the crinkles flat so that he could see through it. It showed a nativity scene, an exhausted Mary clutching her belly and staring blankly at the Christ child lying on the straw in front of her, an angel plunging dramatically overhead. Unusually, in the foreground a spiky-haired youth, his back to the viewer and one foot touching the baby, has turned to face an aged Joseph, his face tortured by a mischievous disbelief.

Tom looked up, a puzzled smile playing across his lips. Outside, the sky had darkened even further, the rain thrashing the roof, the water running off the windscreen in sheets like rolled steel off a mill.

'Where did you get it?'

'Do you recognise it?' Stokes repeated, although Jennifer could already tell from Tom's face that he did.

'Caravaggio. *The Nativity with San Lorenzo and San Francesco,*' he pointed at the two other men in the painting gazing adoringly at the infant. 'Painted in 1609 for the Oratory of San Lorenzo in Palermo, Sicily. Missing since 1969. Where did you get it?'

It was Tom's turn to repeat his question.

Jennifer looked to Stokes and took his muted sigh and faint shrug as agreement to continue.

'Special Agent Stokes is from our Vegas field office,' she explained. 'A week ago he took a call from Myron Kezman.'

'The casino owner?' Tom asked in surprise.

'The photo arrived in his personal mail.'

'It had a New York City post mark,' Stokes added. 'We've checked the envelope for prints and DNA. It was clean.'

'There was a cell-phone number on the back of the photo,' Jennifer continued; Tom turned it over so he could see it. 'When Kezman called it there was a recorded message at the other end. It only played once before the number was discon- nected.'

The windows had started to fog up. Stokes started the engine and turned the heating on to clear them, a sudden blast of warm air washing over them.

'What did it say?'

'According to Kezman it made him a simple offer. The painting for twenty million dollars. And then a different cell- phone number to dial if he was interested in making the trade.'

'That's when Kezman called us in,' Stokes took over. 'Only this time we taped the call. It was another message setting out the instructions for the exchange. The denominations for the cash. The types of bags it should be in. The meet.'

'And then they called you?' Tom turned to Jennifer.

'The Caravaggio is on the FBI Art Crime team's top ten list of missing art works, so it automatically got referred our way,' she confirmed. 'I got pulled off a case to help handle it. I've been camping out in an office here in DC, so when I saw that you'd been flagged up at Dulles . . .'

'You thought that maybe I could handle the exchange for you.'

'How the hell did you . . .?' Stokes eyed him suspiciously.

'Because you've never dealt with anything like this before.' Tom shrugged. 'Because you're smart and you know that these types of gigs never go down quite like you plan them. Because you know I might spot something you won't.'

There was a pause as Stokes and Jennifer both swapped a look, and then laughed.

'That's pretty much it, I guess.' Stokes nodded with a grudging smile.

'When's this happening?'

'Tonight in Vegas. On the main floor at the Amalfi.'

'Kezman's joint?'

'Yep,' Stokes nodded.

'That's smart. Busy. Exposed. Plenty of civilian cover. Multiple escape routes.'

'So you'll do it?' Jennifer asked hopefully.

There was a sharp rap on the window. Tom lowered it and Archie peered in, the rain dripping off his umbrella.

'Very bloody cosy,' he observed with a wry smile. 'Not interrupting anything, am I?'

'I don't think you two have ever actually met before, have you?' Tom asked, sitting back so Jennifer could lean across him and shake his hand.

'Not properly.' She smiled.

'What do you want with my boy this time?' Archie sniffed, eyeing her carefully.

'The *Nativity* has turned up,' Tom answered for her. 'They want me to fly to Vegas with them to help handle the exchange.'

'I'll bet they do. What's our take?'

Tom looked searchingly at Jennifer and then at Stokes, who shrugged sheepishly.

'Looks like the usual fee,' he said with a smile. 'Attaboys all round.'

'Well, bollocks to that, then,' Archie sniffed. 'You and I are meant to be meeting Dom in Zurich tomorrow night to see a real client. One that pays and doesn't try and lock you up every five seconds.' He gave first Jennifer, then Stokes, a reproachful glare.

Tom nodded slowly. Having given up on the Swiss police, the curator of the Emile Bührle Foundation wanted their help recovering four paintings worth a hundred and eighty million dollars taken at gunpoint the previous month. Archie had a point.

'I know.'

A pause. He turned back to Jennifer.

'Who'll handle the exchange if I don't?'

'Me, I guess,' she replied with a shrug. 'At least, that was the plan until you flashed up on the system.'

There was a long silence, Tom looking first at Jennifer, then Stokes. He turned back to Archie.

'Why don't I just meet you in Zurich tomorrow.'

'Oh, for fuck's sake, Tom,' Archie protested. 'I don't know why I bother sometimes.'

'One night. That's all,' Tom reassured him. 'I'll be on the first flight out.'

'Fine,' Archie sighed. 'But you can deal with Hewson.' Archie stepped back and pointed down the slope towards a lonely figure who appeared to be patiently waiting for them to return. 'He's doing my bloody head in.'

'Whatever he's got for me, it's waited this long –' Tom sat back with a shrug – 'it can wait a day longer.'

FOUR

Largo di Torre Argentina, Rome
17th March – 6.06 p.m.
Allegra could just about make out one of the men's low voices. A pathologist, she guessed.

'Cause of death? Well, I'll only know when I open him up. But at a guess, oedema of the brain. Upside down, the heart continues to pump blood through the arteries, but because the veins rely on gravity, his brain would have become swollen with blood. Fluid would then have leaked out of his capillaries, first causing a headache, then gradual loss of consciousness and finally death, probably from asphyxiation as the brain signals driving respiration failed. Terrible way to go.'

'How long has he been here?' the man next to him asked. From his flinty, aggressive tone, Allegra knew immediately that this had to be Gallo.

'All day. Possibly longer. It was a cold night and that would have slowed decomposition.'

'And no one saw him until now?' Gallo snapped, his voice both angry and disbelieving. She could just about detect the vestiges of a Southern accent, presumably carefully discarded over the years. After all, provincial roots were not exactly something you advertised if you wanted to get ahead. Not in Rome.

'No one works here at the weekend,' Salvatore explained in an apologetic tone. 'And you couldn't see him from the street.'

'Terrible way to go,' the pathologist repeated, shaking his head. 'It would have taken hours for him to die. And right until the end he would have been able to hear people walking around the site and the cars coming and going overhead, and not been able to move or call for help.'

'You think I give a shit about how this bastard died?' Gallo snorted dismissively. 'Don't forget who he was or who he worked for. All I want to know is who killed him, why they did it here and why like this. The last thing I need is some sort of vigilante stalking the streets of Rome re-enacting Satanic rituals.'

'Actually, Colonel, it's Christian, not Satanic,' Allegra interrupted with a cough.

'What?' Gallo rounded on her, looking her up and down with a disdainful expression. He was six feet tall and powerfully built, with a strong, tanned face covered in carefully trimmed stubble. About forty-five or so, she guessed, he was wearing the full dress uniform of a colonel in the Guarda di Finanza and had chin-length steel-grey hair that parted down the centre of his head and fell either side of his face, forcing him to sweep it back out of his eyes every so often. He also had on a pair of frameless glasses with clear plastic arms. From the way he adjusted them on his nose, she sensed that these had only recently been prescribed and that he still resented wearing them, despite having done what he could to make them as unobtrusive as possible.

'The inverted crucifixion,' she explained, ignoring the horrified look on Salvatore's face. 'It's taken from the Acts of Peter.'

'The Acts of Peter?' Gallo snorted. 'There's no such book in the Bible.'

'That's because it's in the Apocrypha, the texts excluded from the Bible by the church,' she replied, holding her temper in check. 'According to the text, when the Roman authorities sentenced Peter to death, he asked to be crucified head down, so as not to imitate Christ's passing.'

Gallo said nothing, his eyes narrowing slightly as he brushed his hair back.

'Thank you for the Sunday school lesson, Miss . . .'

'Lieutenant. Damico.'

'The antiquities expert you asked for, Colonel,' Salvatore added quickly.

'You work at the university, then?' It sounded like a challenge rather than a question.

'I used to be a lecturer in art and antiquities at La Sapienza, yes.'

'Used to be!' he spluttered, glaring at Salvatore.

'The university passed me on to the Villa Giulia. One of the experts there recommended her,' Salvatore insisted.

'Now I'm in the TPA,' she added quickly, spelling out the acronym for the Nucleo Tutela Patrimonio Artistico, the special corps within the Carabinieri tasked with protecting and recovering stolen art. He looked her up and down again, then shrugged.

'Well, you'll have to do, I suppose,' he said, to Salvatore's visible relief. 'I take it you know who I am?'

She nodded, although part of her was itching to say no, just to see the look on his face. Ignoring the other two men standing there, which she assumed meant that he did not consider them important enough to warrant an introduction, Gallo jabbed his finger at the man next to him.

'This is Dottore Giovanni la Fabro from the coroner's office, and this is, or was, Adriano Ricci, an enforcer for the De Luca family.'

Allegra nodded. The GICO's involvement was suddenly a lot clearer. The De Luca family were believed to run the Bande della Magliana, one of Rome's most notorious criminal organisations. Gallo clearly thought this was some sort of professional hit.

He stepped back and introduced the corpse with a sweep of his hand. Even dead, she could tell that Ricci had been overweight, loose skin sagging towards the ground like melted wax on the neck of a bottle. He was bare-chested with a large Lazio football club tattoo on his left shoulder, and was still wearing a striped pair of suit trousers that had fallen halfway down his calves. His wrists and ankles were bleeding where the chicken wire used to bind him to the cross had bitten into his flesh.

'Why am I here?' she asked with a shudder, glancing back to Gallo.

'This –' He led her forward to the body and snapped his flashlight on to illuminate its face.

For a few moments she couldn't make out what he was pointing to, her attention grabbed by Ricci's staring, blood-shot eyes and the way that, from the shoulders up, his skin had turned a waxy purple, like marble. But then, trapped in the light of Gallo's torch, she saw it. A black shape, a disc of some sort, lurking in the roof of Ricci's mouth.

'What is it?' she breathed.

'That's what you're meant to be telling me,' Gallo shot back.

'Can I see it, then?'

Gallo snapped his fingers and la Fabro handed him a pair of tweezers. To Allegra's horrified fascination, he levered the object free as if he was prising a jewel from an ancient Indian statue and then carefully deposited it inside an evidence bag,

holding it out between his fingertips as if it contained something mildly repellent.

'Knock yourself out,' he intoned.

'I thought it might be some sort of antique coin,' Salvatore
suggested eagerly over her shoulder as she turned it over in
the light. 'It seems to have markings etched into it.'

'The ancient Romans used to put a bronze coin in the
mouths of their dead to pay Charon to ferry their souls across
the Styx to the Underworld' she nodded slowly. 'But I don't
think that's what this is.'

'Why not?'

'Feel the weight. It's lead. That's too soft to be used in
everyday coinage.'

'Then what about the engraving?' Gallo asked impatiently.

She traced the symbol that had been inlaid into the coin
with her finger. It showed two snakes intertwined around a
clenched fist, like the seal from some mediaeval coat of arms.

'I don't know,' she said with an apologetic shrug. 'But
whatever this is, it's not an antique nor, I would say, particularly valuable.'

'Well, that was useful.' Glaring angrily at Salvatore, Gallo
turned his back on Allegra as if she had suddenly vanished.

'I'm sorry,' Salvatore stuttered. 'I thought that . . .'

'We've wasted enough time. Let's just get him bagged up
and out of here so the forensic boys can move in,' Gallo
ordered as he turned to leave. 'Then I want a priest or a
cardinal or somebody else in sandals down here to tell me
more about . . .'

'It can't be a coincidence though, can it, Colonel?' Allegra
called after him.

Gallo spun round angrily.

'I thought you'd gone?'

'It can't be a coincidence that they killed him here?' she
insisted.

'What the hell are you talking about?'

'In Roman times, this entire area was part of the Campus Martius, a huge complex of buildings that included the Baths of Agrippa to the north, the Circus Flaminius to the south and the Theatre of Pompey to the west,' she explained, pointing towards each point of the compass in turn. 'The Senate even met here while the Curia was being rebuilt after a fire in 54 BC –' she pointed at the floor – 'in a space in the portico attached to the Theatre of Pompey.'

'Here?' Gallo looked around him sceptically, clearly struggling to reconcile the fractured ruins at his feet with the imagined grandeur of a Roman theatre.

'Of course, the one drawback of this spot was that the Campus Martius stood outside the sacred *pomerium*, the city's official boundaries, meaning that, although it was quieter than the Forum, it was not subject to the same restrictions against concealed weapons.'

'What's your point?' Gallo frowned wearily, and she realised that she was going to have to spell it out for him.

'I mean that Ricci isn't the first person to be killed here,' she explained, a tremor of excitement in her voice. 'I mean that in 44 BC, Julius Caesar was assassinated on almost this exact same spot.'

FIVE

The Getty Villa, Malibu, California
17th March – 10.52 a.m.

Verity Bruce had been looking forward to this day for a while. For nearly three years, to be precise. That's how long it had been since she had first been shown the dog-eared Polaroid in a smoky Viennese café, first been winded by the adrenaline punch of excitement at what was on offer and chilled by the fear of possibly losing out.

She'd shaken on the deal there and then, knowing that the director would back her judgement. The trustees had taken a little more convincing, of course, but then they didn't know the period like she did. Besides, once they'd understood the magnitude of the find, they'd bitten and bitten hard, sharing her mounting frustration at the years lost to the scientists as test upon test had heaped delay upon deferral until she was sure they must have finished and started all over again. And then, of course, the lumbering and self-perpetuating wheels of international bureaucracy had begun to turn, a merry-go-round of sworn affidavits, authentication letters, legal contracts, bank statements, money transfer forms, export and import licences and Customs declarations that had added months to the process. Still, what was done was done. Today, finally, the waiting ended.

She positioned herself in front of the full-length mirror she'd had bolted to the back of her office door. Had the intervening years between that first breathless, absinthe-fuelled encounter and today's unveiling aged her? A little, perhaps, around her fern-green eyes and in the tiny fissures that had begun to fleck her top lip like faint animal tracks across the snow. Ever since she'd turned forty-five, the years seemed to weigh a little heavier on her face, as if they were invisibly swinging from grappling hooks sunk into her skin. She could have had surgery, of course – God knows everyone else her age in LA seemed to have had work done – but she hated anything fake or forced like that. Highlights in her long, coiled copper hair were one thing, but needles and knives . . . Sometimes, nature had to be allowed to run its course.

Besides, she reminded herself as she put the finishing touches to her makeup, it wasn't as if she'd lost her looks. How else to explain the fact that that gorgeous thirty-two-year-old speech writer she'd met at a White House fund-raiser the other month was pestering her to travel up to his place in Martha's Vineyard next fall? And she still had great legs, too. Always had. Hopefully always would.

'They're ready for you.'

One of the Getty PR girls had edged tentatively into the room. Verity couldn't remember her name, but then all these girls looked the same to her – blonde, smiley, skinny, jutting tits that would hold firm in a 6.1 – as if the city was ground zero in some freakish cloning experiment. Even so, the girl's legs still weren't as good as hers.

'Let's do it,' she said, grabbing her leather jacket off the chair and slipping it over a black couture Chanel dress that

she'd bought in Paris last year. It was an unlikely combination, but one deliberately chosen to further fuel the quirky
image that she'd so carefully cultivated over the years. It
was simple really. If you wanted to get ahead in the hushed
and dusty corridors of curatorial academia without waiting
to be as old as the exhibits themselves, it paid to get noticed.
She certainly wasn't about to tone things down now,
despite the occasion, although she had at least upgraded
from flats to a vertiginous pair of scarlet Manolos that
matched her lipstick. After all, this was a ten-million-dollar
acquisition and the *Los Angeles Times* would be taking
pictures.

The small group of donors, experts and journalists that
she and the director had hand-picked for this private
viewing to guarantee maximum pre-launch coverage was
already gathered expectantly in the auditorium. The figure
had been draped, rather melodramatically she thought, in
a black cloth and then placed in the middle of the floor so
that people had to circle, brows furrowed in speculation,
around it. Snatching up a glass of Laurent-Perrier Rosé
from a tray at the door, Verity swept inside and began to
work the room, shaking the hands of some, kissing the
cheeks of others, swapping an amusing anecdote here and
clutching at a shared memory there. But she was barely
aware of what she was saying or what was being said to
her, her excitement slowly building as the minutes counted
down until she could hear only the pregnant thud of her
heart.

'Ladies and gentlemen . . .' The director had stepped into
the middle of the room. 'Ladies and gentlemen, if I could
have your attention please,' he called, ushering the audience closer. The lights dimmed. 'Ladies and gentlemen,
today marks the culmination of a remarkable journey,' he

began, reading from a small card and then pausing for effect.
'It is a journey that began over 2,500 years ago in ancient
Greece. And it is a journey that ends, here, in Malibu.
Because today, I am delighted to unveil the Getty Villa's
latest acquisition and, in my opinion, one of the most
important works of art to enter the United States since the
Second World War.'

With a flourish, the cloth slipped to the floor. Under a lone
spotlight stood a seven foot tall marble sculpture of a young
boy, his left foot forward, arms at his sides, head and eyes
looking straight ahead. There was a ripple of appreciative,
even shocked recognition. Verity stepped forward.

'This uniquely preserved example of a Greek kouros has
been dated to around 540 BC,' Verity began, standing on the
other side of the statue to the director and speaking without
notes. 'As many of you will undoubtedly know, although
inspired by the god Apollo, a kouros was not intended to
represent any one individual youth but the *idea* of youth
itself, and was used in Ancient Greece both as a dedication
to the gods in sanctuaries and as a funerary monument. Our
tests show that this example has been hewn from dolomite
marble from the ancient Cape Vathy quarry on the island of
Thassos.'

Talking in her usual measured and authoritative style, she
continued her description of the statue, enjoying herself more
and more as she got into her stride: its provenance from the
private collection of a Swiss physician whose grandfather had
bought it in Athens in the late 1800s; the exhaustive scien-
tific tests that had revealed a thin film of calcite coating its
surface resulting from hundreds, if not thousands of years
of natural lichen growth; the stylistic features linking it to
the Anavysos Youth in the National Museum in Athens. In
short, a masterpiece that was yet further evidence of the

Getty's determination to build the pre-eminent American collection of classical antiquities.

Her speech drew to a close. Acknowledging the applause with a nod, she retreated to allow people forward for a closer look, anxiously watching over the figure like a parent supervising a child in a busy playground.

At first all went well, a few people nodding appreciatively at the sculpture's elegant lines, others seeking her out to offer muted words of congratulations. But then, without warning, she sensed the mood darkening, a few of the guests eyeing the statue with a strange look and whispering excitedly to each other.

Thierry Normand from the Ecole Française d'Athène was the first to break ranks.

'Doesn't the use of Thassian marble strike you as rather . . . anomalous?'

'And what about the absence of paint?' Eleanor Grant from the University of Chicago immediately added. 'As far as I know, all other kouroi, with the possible exception of the Melos kouros, show traces of paint?'

'Well, of course we considered . . .' Verity began with a weak smile, forcing herself not to sound defensive even though she could hardly not feel insulted by what they were implying.

'I'm sorry, Verity,' Sir John Sykes, the highly respected Lincoln Professor of Classical Archaeology and Art at Oxford University interrupted with an apologetic cough. 'It just isn't right. The hair is pure early sixth-century BC, as you say, but the face and abdomen are clearly much later. And while you can find similarly muscular thighs in Corinth, I've only seen feet and a base like that in Boeotia. The science can only tell you so much. You have to rely on the aesthetics, on what you can see. To me, this is almost verging on the pastiche.'

'Well, I'm sorry, Sir John, but we couldn't disagree more
. . .' Verity began angrily, looking to the director for support
but seeing that he appeared to have retreated to the periphery
of the group.

'Actually, Sir John, the word I'd use,' Professor Vivienne
Foyle of the Institute of Fine Arts at New York University
added, pausing to make sure everyone was listening, 'is
fresh.'

The loaded meaning of the word was clear. Foyle was
suggesting that the statue was in fact a forgery, that it had
been knocked up in some backstreet workshop and never
been in the ground at all. Verity was reeling, but the mood
in the room was now such that she knew she had no chance
of sensibly arguing her case.

The interrogation continued. Why didn't the plinth have
a lead attachment like other kouroi? Couldn't the degrada-
tion of the stone have been caused deliberately by oxalic
acid? How was it that such an exceptional piece had only
surfaced now? What due diligence had been carried out on
its provenance?

She barely heard them, her ears filled with the dull pulse
of her mounting rage. Her face white and cold as marble,
she nodded and smiled and shrugged at what seemed oppor-
tune moments, not trusting herself to open her mouth
without swearing. A further ten minutes of this torture had
to be endured before the director, perhaps sensing that she
might be about to erupt, finally saw fit to bring an end to
her ordeal.

'Fresh? I'll give that senile old bitch fresh,' she muttered
angrily as she stalked back to her office. 'Sonya?'

'I'm Cynthia,' the PR girl chirped, skipping to keep up with
her.

'Whatever. Get me Faulks on the phone.'

'Who?'

'Earl Faulks. F-A-U-L-K-S, pronounced like folks. I don't care where he is. I don't care what he's doing. Just get him for me. In fact, I don't want just to speak to him. I want to see him. Here. Tomorrow.'

SIX

Over Nebraska
17th March – 8.43 p.m.

Normally used to scoop whales into the casino's deep-throated net, Kezman's private jet was a potent introduction to the Vegas experience: snow-white leather seats with a gilded letter 'A' embroidered into the head-rests, leopard-skin carpets, polished mahogany panelling running the length of the cabin like the interior of a pre-war steamer, a small glass bar lit with blue neon. At the front, over the cockpit door, hung a photo of Kezman, all teeth and tan, gazing down on them benevolently like the dictator of some oil-rich African state.

Tom, lost in thought, had immediately settled back into his seat, politely declining the offer of a drink from the attentive stewardess whose skirt seemed to have been hitched almost as high as her top was pulled low. Head turned to the window, gaze fixed on some distant point on the horizon, he barely noticed the plane take off, let alone Jennifer move to the seat opposite him.

'You're still wearing it, then?' she asked, head tilted to one side so that her curling mass of black hair covered the top of her right shoulder.

He glanced down at the 1934 stainless steel 'Brancard' Rolex Prince on his wrist. It had been a gift from the FBI for Tom's help on the first case he'd worked on with Jennifer, although Tom suspected that the decision to offer it to him, and the choice of watch, had been all hers.

'Why?' He turned to face her with a smile. 'Do you want it back?'

Five feet nine, slim with milky brown skin, she had a lustrous pair of hazel eyes and was wearing her usual office camouflage of black trouser suit and cream silk blouse. Her 'Fuck You' clothes, as she'd once described them, as opposed to the 'Fuck Me' outfits that some of the other female agents favoured, only to wonder why they got asked out all the time but never promoted. The truth was that the odds of a woman succeeding in the Bureau, let alone a black woman, were stacked so heavily against her, that she had to load the dice any way she could just to be given a fair spin of the wheel. Then again, from what he'd seen, Jennifer knew what it took to play the game, having risen from lowly field agent in the Bureau's Atlanta Division to one of the most senior members of its Art Crime Team. That didn't happen by accident.

'Not unless you're having second thoughts.'

'Should I be?'

'You just seem a bit . . . distracted,' she ventured.

'Not really.' His gaze flicked back to the window. 'I guess I was just thinking about today.'

'About your grandfather?'

'About some of the people there. About my family, or what's left of it. About how little I know them and they know me.'

'You're a difficult person to get to know, Tom,' she said gently.

'Even for you?' He turned back to her with a hopeful smile.

'Maybe especially for me,' she shot back, an edge to her voice that was at once resigned and accusing.

He understood what she meant, although she had got closer to him than most over the years. Not that things had started well between them when they had first met, necessity strong-arming their initial instinctive mutual suspicion into a grudging and fragile working relationship. And yet from this unpromising beginning a guarded trust, of sorts, had slowly evolved which had itself, in time, built towards a burgeoning friendship. A friendship which had then briefly flowered into something more, their growing attraction for each other finding its voice in one unplanned and instinctive night together.

Since then, the intervening years and a subsequent case had given them both the opportunity at different times to try and revive those feelings and build on that night. But for whatever reason, the other person had never quite been in the same place – Tom initially unwilling to open up, Jennifer subsequently worried about getting hurt. Even so, the memory had left its mark on both of them, like an invisible shard of metal caught beneath the skin that they could both feel whenever they rubbed up against someone else.

'How have you been?' Tom asked, deliberately moving the focus of the conversation away from himself. Jennifer glanced over his shoulder before answering, prompting Tom to turn in his seat and follow her wary gaze. Stokes was asleep, his legs stretched out ahead of him, his head lolling on to his shoulder, two empty whisky miniatures on the table in front of him. The stewardess had retreated into the limestone-floored toilet cubicle with her make-up bag.

'Were you annoyed I came?' Jennifer answered with a question of her own.

'I was disappointed you didn't come alone,' he admitted, almost surprising himself with his honesty.

'This is Stokes's case,' she explained with an apologetic shrug. 'I couldn't have come without him.'

'That's not what I meant.'

A pause.

'You should have told me you were coming.'

'I didn't know I was until I was on the plane,' he protested.

'You could have called,' she insisted.

'Would you have called me if you hadn't needed my help?'

Another, longer pause.

'Probably not,' she conceded.

It was strange, Tom mused. They weren't dating, hadn't spoken in almost a year, and yet they seemed to be locked into a lover's awkward conversation, both of them fumbling around what they really wanted to say, rather than risk looking stupid.

There was a long silence.

'Why did you agree to come?' Jennifer eventually asked him, her eyes locking with his.

'Because you said you needed my help,' he said with a shrug.

'You were going to say no,' she pointed out. 'Then something changed.'

'I don't really . . .'

'It was because I said I would handle the exchange myself if you didn't, wasn't it?'

A smile flickered across Tom's face. He'd forgotten how annoyingly perceptive she could be.

'What do you know about this painting?' Tom picked up the photo from the table between them and studied it through the plastic.

'It was one of four that Caravaggio completed in Sicily in 1609 while he was on the run for stabbing someone to death,' she said. 'We have it down as being worth twenty million dollars, but it would go for much more, even in today's market.'

'What about the theft itself?'

'October sixteenth, 1969,' she recited from memory. 'The crime reports say that the thieves cut it out of its frame over the altar of the Oratory of San Lorenzo in Palermo with razor blades and escaped in a truck. Probably a two-man team.'

'I'd guess three,' Tom corrected her. 'It's big – nearly sixty square feet. I'm not sure two men could have handled it.'

'At the time, people blamed the Sicilian mafia?' Her statement was framed as a question.

'It's always looked to me like an amateur job,' Tom replied with a shake of his head. 'Couple of local crooks who'd thought through everything except how they were going to sell it. If the Sicilian mafia have got it now, it's because no one else was buying or because they decided to just take it. The Cosa Nostra don't like people operating on their turf without permission.'

'And no one's ever seen it since?'

'I've heard rumours over the years,' Tom sighed. 'That it had surfaced in Rome, or maybe even been destroyed in the Naples earthquake in 1980. Then a few years ago, a mafia informer claimed to have rolled it up inside a rug and buried it in an iron chest. When they went to dig it up, the chest was empty.'

'What do you think?'

'If you ask me, it's been with the Cosa Nostra the whole time. Probably traded between *capos* as a gift or part payment on a deal.'

'Which would mean that the mafia are behind the sale now?'

'If not the mafia, then someone who has stolen it from them,' Tom agreed. 'Either way, they'll be dangerous and easily spooked. If we're lucky, they'll just run if they smell trouble. If we're not, they'll start shooting.' A pause. 'That's why I came.'

'I can look after myself,' she said pointedly; irritated, it seemed, by what he was implying. 'I didn't ask you here to watch my back.'

'I'm here because I know how these people think,' Tom insisted. 'And the only back that will need watching is mine.'

SEVEN

Amalfi Hotel and Casino, Las Vegas
17th March – 9.27 p.m.
Ever since going freelance, Kyle Foster had never met or even spoken to his handler. It was safer that way. For both of them. Besides, what would have been the fucking point? All he needed was a name, a photograph and fifty per cent of his fee in his Cayman Islands account. Why complicate things with a face or a voice when he could just email the details through and save them both the trouble? Assuming the handler was a guy, of course. There was no real way of knowing. A broad in this line of business? Not unheard of, but rare. Maybe he should suggest a meet after all?

His PDA vibrated on the glass table in front of him, breaking into his thoughts. Swinging his feet to the floor he sat forward, muting the TV so he could concentrate on the message rather than the squeals of the girl being screwed by her twin sister wearing a strap-on.

It was the photo he noticed first, his boulder-like face breaking into something resembling a smile at life's occasional burst of comic irony; he knew this person, or rather he'd come across them before on a previous job. Beneath it was a simple message:

Target confirmed arriving LAS tonight. Terminate with extreme prejudice.

Good, he thought, climbing on to the bed. He hated being kept waiting, especially now the mini-bar was running dry and he'd cycled through both the porn channels.

Unscrewing the ceiling grille, he lifted down a black US Navy Mark 12 Special Purpose Rifle from where he'd hidden it inside the AC duct and began to disassemble it. This weapon was a recent issue to US Special Forces in the Middle East and he liked what they had done with it, producing a rifle with a greater effective range than an M4 Carbine, while still being shorter than a standard-issue M16. He especially appreciated that although it had been chambered for standard NATO rounds, it performed much better with a US-made Sierra Bullets MatchKing 77-grain hollow-point boat-tail bullet, although for jobs like this he preferred using his own bespoke ammunition.

Stripped down, the dismembered weapon parts lay on the crisp linen sheets like instruments on a surgeon's tray. Laying a white hand-towel down next to them, he carefully arranged the pieces on it and then rolled it into a tight bundle that he secured shut by wrapping duct tape around it several times. Shaking the trussed-up towel hard to make sure nothing rattled, he placed it in his backpack.

Draining the last of the whisky, he turned his attention to his uniform, pulling on his red jacket and ensuring that his buttons were straight and done up right under his chin. Not quite as smart as the Army Green hanging in his wardrobe back in Charlotte, carefully positioned so you could see the gold flash of his Rangers badge through the plastic, but it would serve its purpose. He doubted the dry-cleaning company had even noticed that it had been taken from its storeroom, and as for the waiter whose security pass he'd stolen and doctored . . . well, he wouldn't be missing anything anytime soon.

Finally, he smoothed down his light brown hair, almost not recognising himself without his straggly beard. That was one thing that had thrown him about Vegas. You could walk around in an Elvis suit or with a twelve-foot albino python around your neck and nobody would give you a second look. But wander more than twenty feet down the strip with a beard and people would stare at you like you were a freak in a circus side-show.

In the end, he'd had no choice but to shave it off. How else to blend in with the casino staff? How else to get where he needed to be, to take the shot?

EIGHT

McCarran International Airport, Nevada
17th March – 10.37 p.m.

'Kezman's laying it on pretty thick,' Tom observed as the plane taxied to a halt and the stairs folded down. A stretched white Hummer emblazoned with a gilded letter 'A' was waiting to greet them, its neon undercarriage staining the apron blue. 'First the jet. Now this. What does he want?'

'A friendly word with the Nevada Gaming Control Board,' Stokes growled, as he pushed past Tom and stepped through the doorway. An unmarked FBI escort vehicle was drawn up behind the limo and he gestured at them to follow. 'One of his pit bosses was caught dealing ecstasy to some college kids out here on spring break and he doesn't want to lose his gaming licence.'

An envelope was waiting for them on the white leather seat, together with three glasses and a bottle of Cristal on ice. To Jennifer's surprise, it was addressed to her. She opened it with a puzzled frown which relaxed into a slow nod as she realised what it was.

'Status update from my other case,' she explained as she

flicked through it, guessing that someone in the escort vehicle must have been entrusted with it to pass on to her. Nodding, Stokes shuffled further along the seat towards the driver and reached for his phone.

'Bad news?' Tom asked eventually, his question prompting her unconscious scowl to fade into a rueful smile.

'Isn't it always?' she replied, placing the typed pages down next to her.

'Anything I can help with?'

She paused, her eyes locked with his. Discussing a live investigation with a civilian, let alone a civilian with Tom's flawed credentials, wasn't exactly standard procedure. Then again, her case wasn't exactly standard either, and she had learned to value his opinion. Besides, who would know? Certainly not Stokes, whom she could overhear noisily checking on the money and making sure that Las Vegas Metro weren't playing their usual jurisdictional games.

'A few weeks ago the Customs boys over in Norfolk got a tip-off about a shipment of car parts out of Hamburg,' she began in a low voice, leaning in closer. 'When they opened the container everything looked fine, but something weird showed up on the X-ray.'

'A marzipan layer?' Tom guessed.

'Exactly. Car parts stacked at the front and round the sides. A smaller crate hidden in the middle filled with furniture.'

'Furniture?' Tom frowned.

'Eileen Gray. Ten to fifteen million dollars' worth.'

Tom whistled, echoing her own surprise when she'd first understood what they were dealing with. Eileen Gray art deco furniture was apparently as rare as it was expensive.

'They boxed it back up and then followed the shipment via a freight-forwarding service to an art dealer in Queens, an Italian who moved here in the seventies. He started squealing the minute they kicked down the door. He thought they were a hit squad. I don't think anyone's ever been so relieved to see a badge.'

'Who did he think had sent them?'

'It turns out that he's been smuggling pieces for a high-end antiquities trafficking ring for years. The furniture was a little side-deal he'd cooked up for himself. He thought they'd found out.'

'What sort of antiquities?' Tom asked.

'Statues, vases, plates, jewellery, even entire frescoes. Most of it illegally excavated from Roman and Etruscan tombs. One of their favourite tricks was to cover objects in liquid plastic and then paint them so that they looked like cheap souvenirs. That's when they called me in.'

'My mother used to be an antiquities dealer,' Tom sighed. 'I remember her once describing grave-robbing as the world's second oldest profession.

'You're talking about tomb robbers?'

'In Italy they call them *tombaroli*, in Peru *huaceros*,' Tom nodded. 'Mexico, Cambodia, China, Iraq – The truth is that as long as there are people prepared to buy pieces without asking difficult questions about where they've come from, there'll be others only too happy to dig them up.' But Italy is ground zero, the *Terra Santa* of the tomb-robbing world. It's got over forty UNESCO World Heritage Sites and the remains of about five different civilisations.' A pause. 'Did your guy ID any of his buyers?'

She gave a firm shake of her head.

'His job was just to get the stuff through Customs. He never had any idea where it was coming from or going to. But he did give us another name. Someone from within the organisation who had apparently broken cover a few weeks before, looking to bring something across. We passed it on to the Italians and they said they'd check him out.' She tapped the file next to her in annoyance. 'The State Department's been working on them to make sure they keep us in the loop, but so far they're playing hard to get.'

'Does this outfit have a name?'

'We're not sure. Have you ever heard of the Delian League?'

Tom frowned.

'League as in club?'

'When we went through his trash, we found two bags of shredded paper,' she explained. 'Most of it was unusable, but the lab were able to piece together one yellow sheet, because the coloured strips stood out from everything else. It was mainly covered in doodles and practice runs of his signature; the sort of thing you do when you're on the phone to someone. But in one corner he'd written the words Delian League and then sketched out a sort of symbol underneath. Two snakes wrapped around a clenched fist.'

'Means nothing to me,' Tom shook his head.

'Well, it means something to him because he's clammed up since we showed it to him. Won't even talk to his attorney. But we found his bank records too and I think that the Delian League is –'

She broke off as Stokes ended his call and shuffled back down towards them.

'The money's ready and Metro are playing ball. Looks like we're all set.'

They turned on to Las Vegas Boulevard, a grinning cowboy on an overhead billboard welcoming them to the home of the seven-day weekend, the streets teeming with nocturnal creatures who, like vampires it seemed, were only now venturing outside to feed.

It was Jennifer's first time in Las Vegas, and even as they'd circled prior to landing she'd found herself struck by the almost unnatural way that this concrete oasis seemed to have been cut out of the desert's soft belly, its neon heartbeat pulsing hungrily, its wailing lungs breathing expensively chilled air.

The view from the ground wasn't much better, the different hotel resorts galloping past in a single garish streak of light, like an overexposed photograph of a merry-go-round. The Pyramids, Arthurian England, New York, Paris, Lake Como, Venice – she had the sudden, disorientating sensation of travelling without moving, of time and space having been folded in on itself so as to meet at this one point in the universe.

The strange thing was that while there was something undeniably intoxicating, perhaps even gorgeous, about the multi-million-dollar light shows, the balletic fountain displays and the smell of sulphur from the half-hourly volcanic eruptions, she had the strong sense that if she were to reach out and try to grasp anything, it would dissolve under her touch. She realised then that this was a city of hyper-reality, of carbon-fibre monuments, plastic trees and contrived experiences. A copy of everywhere and yet nowhere all at once, the desperate striving for authenticity only serving to reveal its essential falsehood. A non place. She hoped they wouldn't have to stay here long.

'We're here,' Stokes called as the limo turned in under a monumental arch topped by two rearing lions.

Despite its name, the Amalfi seemed to have been inspired by Florentine rather than Neapolitan architecture, although rendered on such a scale as to make the Duomo look like a concession stand. It was the Palazzo Strozzi on steroids, a massive, fortress-like structure made from Indiana limestone and Ohio sandstone, the soaring arched windows covered with portcullis-like iron grilles that only added to its impregnable appearance.

Rather than pull round to the covered main entrance, their car headed to the left and then dipped into an underground car park.

'The high-rollers' entrance,' Stokes explained. 'Some of these guys don't want to risk getting jumped between the car and hotel.'

Tom laughed.

'They're more likely to be robbed inside than out there.'

NINE

The Pantheon, Rome
18th March – 6.58 a.m.

Different day. Different place. And yet it seemed to Allegra that there was something strangely familiar about the way things were playing out – the unexpected, and unwelcome, phone call. The barked summons. The police barricades across the streets. The swelling crowd. The fevered wailing of the sirens. The helicopter wheeling overhead. The TV crews prowling like hyenas around a kill. Her being late.

Even so, there was a subtle difference from the previous evening's events too. For if yesterday she had seen shock and curiosity on her way to the Area Sacra, today she had sensed outrage from the officers manning the barriers and mounting anger from the swelling crowd.

Returning her ID to her bag, she crossed the Piazza della Minerva and made her way on to the Piazza della Rotunda. Compared to the zoo she had just walked through, the square seemed eerily peaceful to her – the gentle chime of the fountain echoing off the massed walls, the hushed conversations of the officers and the muted fizz of their radios generating a faint hum that sounded like electricity on a power line on a wet day.

There was also a sense of dignified order here, perhaps even respect. For rather than being casually abandoned on the cobbles as appeared to have happened last night, the assembled police and other emergency service vehicles had been neatly parked next to each other along one side of the square.

As she walked it started to spit with rain, the sky huddling beneath a thick blanket of grey clouds, as if it didn't want to be woken. The Pantheon loomed ahead of her, the classical elegance of the three rows of monolithic granite columns which supported its front portico compromised by the hulking, barrel-shaped building behind it. Squat and solid, it appeared to sit in a small crater of its own invention, the streets encircling it as if it had fallen, meteor-like, from the sky, and buried itself between the neighbouring buildings.

Allegra walked up to the portico, stooping under the police tape that had been strung between the columns, and made her way inside the rotunda, her shoes squeaking on the ancient marble. Almost immediately she paused, her eyes drawn to the pale beam formed by the searchlight of the helicopter hovering overhead as it was funnelled through the circular opening at the apex of the coffered dome. A slanting column of light had formed between the ceiling and the altar, sparks of rain fluttering around it like fireflies trapped in a glass jar. It was a beautiful and unexpected sight.

'Are you coming in, or just going to stand there like a retard?' Salvatore crossed through the beam of light, sounding even more put upon than he had yesterday.

'"Hello" would be nice.'

'You're late.'

'Believe me, it takes years of practice to be this unreliable.'

'Gallo's not happy.'

'He doesn't exactly strike me as the happy type.'

He eyed her unblinkingly, looking both appalled and yet also slightly envious of her brazen tone. He gave a resigned shrug.

'Suit yourself.'

There were about fifteen, maybe even twenty people inside, some in uniform interrogating the security guards who'd been covering the night shift, others in hooded white evidence suits taking photographs or examining the floor around the altar, which itself was obscured by some makeshift screens. Gallo, in a suit this time, was waiting for her next to Raphael's tomb, his hands folded behind his back like a teacher readying himself to hand out a punishment. As Salvatore had warned her, he was in a dark mood, and she found herself wondering if the angry atmosphere she'd noticed on the other side of the barricades was in some strange way linked to his own emotional barometer.

'Nice of you to show up.'

'Nice of you to ask me.'

Gallo paused, lips pursed, as if he couldn't quite decide if he found her insolent or amusing.

'Where did you say you were from?' he asked, taking his glasses off and polishing them on his tie.

'I didn't. But it's Naples,' she stuttered, his question taking her by surprise.

'An only child?'

It was a simple question, but she could tell from his tone that it was loaded with meaning – difficult, spoilt, selfish, stubborn. Pick your stereotype.

'That's none of your business.'

He paused again, then gave an apologetic nod.

'You're right. I'm sorry.'

Salvatore made a strangled noise next to her. She wondered if this was the first time he'd ever heard Gallo apologise.

'You say what you think, don't you?'

'Pretty much.'

'The difference between you and me is that you can get away with it because you're a woman,' Gallo sniffed. 'When I do it, I get called a rude bastard.'

'I wouldn't say you were rude, sir.' The words were out of her mouth before she even knew she was saying them.

His smile faded. Salvatore looked faint.

'What can you tell me about this place?' he snapped, motioning at her to follow him over to the altar.

'What do you mean?'

'The Pantheon. Is there anything I should know about it? Anything that might tie it to where we found Ricci's body last night?'

She ran her hand through her hair, desperately trying to dredge up the highlights of some long-forgotten lecture or text book.

'It was built by Hadrian in about 125 AD, so there's no obvious connection to Caesar, if that's what you mean?' she began with a shrug. 'Then again, although it's been a church since the seventh century, the Pantheon did used to be a pagan temple, just like the ones in the Area Sacra.'

'Hardly conclusive,' Gallo sniffed, patting his jacket down as if he was looking for cigarettes and eventually finding a packet of boiled sweets. 'I'm trying to give up,' he admitted as he popped one into his mouth. She noticed that he didn't offer her one.

'No,' she agreed with a firm shake of her head.

'Then what do you make of this?'

At a flick of his wrist, two forensic officers rolled away the screens. A body was lying on the altar, naked from the waist up. His bearded face was turned towards them, eyes gaping open with shock. Two gleaming white shop mannequins were standing at his head – one small and hunched, the other taller – staring down at the corpse with cold, vacant expressions. Both were unclothed, with moulded blank features and no hair, although the smooth hump of their breasts marked them out as female.

The taller mannequin had been carefully arranged so that her left hand was gripping the man's hair and the right holding a short sword. The sword itself was embedded in a deep gash in the victim's neck that had almost decapitated him. The blood had gushed from his wound, covering the altar and cascading to the floor where it had pooled and solidified into a brackish lake.

It was a carefully arranged, almost ritualistic scene. And one that, for a reason Allegra couldn't quite put her finger on, seemed strangely familiar to her.

'Who is it?'

'Don't you recognise him?' Salvatore, looking surprised, had ventured forward to her side. 'His brother's always on TV. He looks just like him.'

'Why, who's his brother?' she asked, wanting to look away and study the man's tortured features at the same time.

'Annibale Argento,' Salvatore explained. 'The Sicilian deputy. The stiff is his twin brother Gio, otherwise known as Giulio.'

'Hannibal and Julius,' Gallo nodded. 'There's your damn Caesar connection.'

'What's any of this got to do with me?' she interrupted, wondering if she still had time to untangle herself from this mess before the media got wind of it.

'We found this in his mouth —'

Gallo held up a clear plastic evidence bag. She knew, almost without looking, what it contained.

TEN

Amalfi Hotel and Casino, Las Vegas
17th March – 11.02 p.m.

Kezman's private elevator opened on to a tennis court-sized room, rainbows cloaking the lush tropical gardens that could be glimpsed through the open windows where the flood-lights shimmered through a permanent cooling mist.

Glancing up, Tom could see that the soaring ceilings had been draped in what looked like black satin, three huge chandeliers flowering from within their luxuriant folds as if they were leaking glass. The only furniture, if you could call it that, was a 1926 Hispano-Suiza H6. Parked about two-thirds of the way down, it was a mass of gleaming chrome and polished black metal, the wheel arches soaring up over the front wheels and then swooping gracefully down towards the running boards, two dinner plate-sized headlights perched at the end of a massive bonnet like dragon's eyes.

'You're here. Good.'

A man had come in off the balcony, a radio in one hand, a mobile phone in the other. Short and wiry, his olive skin was pockmarked by acne scars, his black hair shaved almost to his skull. Rather than blink, he seemed to grimace every few seconds, his face scrunching into a pained squint as if he had something in his eye.

'Tom, this is Special Agent Carlos Ortiz.' They shook hands as she introduced them. 'I've borrowed him from my other case for a few days to help out.'

'Welcome.'

Ortiz's expression was impenetrable, although Tom thought he glimpsed a tattoo just under his collar – the number fourteen in Roman numerals. Tom recognised it as a reference to the letter 'N', the fourteenth letter of the alphabet, and by repute to the *Norteños*, a coalition of Latino gangs from Northern California. Ortiz had clearly taken a difficult and rarely trodden path from the violent street corners of his youth to the FBI's stiff-collared embrace.

'I hope you're half as good as she says you are,' Ortiz sniffed. Tom glanced questioningly at Jennifer, who gave him an awkward shrug. 'Did you get the envelope from the State Department?'

'Yeah.' She nodded. 'Let's talk about that later. How long have we got?'

'It's set for midnight so . . . just under an hour,' he replied, checking his watch – a fake Rolex Oyster, Tom noted, its second hand advancing with a tell-tale staccato twitch rather than sweeping smoothly around the dial as a real one would.

'Everyone's already in place,' Stokes added. 'I got six agents on the floor at the tables and playing the slots, and another four on the front and rear doors. Metro and SWAT are holding back two blocks south.'

'What about the money?' Tom asked.

'In the vault in two suitcases,' Stokes reassured him. 'Unmarked, non-sequential notes, just like they asked. They'll bring it out when we're ready.'

'Let's get you mike'd up.'

Ortiz led Tom over to the car, which Tom suddenly realised had been turned into a desk, the seats ripped out and the roof and one side cut away and replaced with a black marble slab.

'I guess rich people are always looking for new ways to spend their money, right?' Ortiz winked.

'Some just have more imagination than others,' Tom agreed.

Ortiz removed a small transmitter unit from the briefcase and, as Jennifer turned away with a smile, helped Tom fix it to his inner thigh, hiding the microphone under his shirt.

'If anyone finds that, they're looking for a date not a wire,' Ortiz joked once he was happy that it was secure and working. He checked his watch again. 'Let's go. Kezman asked to see you downstairs before we hit the floor.'

'Any reason we didn't just meet down there in the first place?' Jennifer asked with a frown.

'He thought you might like the view.'

They stepped back inside the elevator and again it headed down automatically, stopping at the mezzanine level, close to the entrance to the Amalfi's private art gallery.

'He suggested we wait for him inside,' Ortiz said, nodding at the two security guards posted either side of the entrance as he walked past.

The gallery consisted of a series of interlinked rooms containing maybe twenty or so paintings, as well as a number of small abstract sculptures on glass plinths. It was an impressive and expensively assembled collection, bringing to mind the recent newspaper headlines when Kezman had broken his own auction record for the highest amount ever paid for a painting. Tom's eyes sought out the Picasso he'd bought on that occasion in amongst the works by Cézanne, Gauguin, van Gogh, Manet and Matisse.

'Impressive, isn't it?' Jennifer said in a low voice, echoing his own thoughts. 'Although, I don't know, it feels a bit . . .'

'Soulless?' Tom suggested.

'Yes.' She nodded slowly. 'Soulless. Perhaps that's it.'

Tom's sense was that Kezman had been less concerned with the paintings themselves than by who had painted them. To him these were trophies, specimens of famous names that he'd only bought so that he could tick them off his list, much as a big-game hunter might set out on safari intent on adding a zebra's head to the mounted ante-lope horns and elephant tusks that already adorned his dining-room walls.

'What do you know about him?'

'He's rich and he's smart. In thirty years he's gone from running a diner in Jersey to being the biggest player on the Strip.'

'He buys a place that's losing money, turns it around or knocks it down, and starts over,' Stokes added, having been listening in. 'As well as the Amalfi, he owns three other places in Vegas, two in Atlantic City and one in Macau.'

'And he's clean?' Tom asked.

'As anyone can be in this town,' Stokes replied with a smile. 'He mixes with a pretty colourful crowd, which always gets people talking, but so far he seems to check out.'

'He used to collect cars, but art is his new passion now,' Jennifer added. 'He's become a major donor to both the Met and the Getty.'

'Which is your favourite?'

Kezman had breezed into the room wearing sunglasses, a gleaming white smile and a tuxedo. He was closely flanked by an unsmiling male assistant clutching a briefcase in one hand and two gold-plated mobile phones in the other. From the way his jacket was hanging off his thin frame, Tom guessed that he was armed.

Kezman was in his mid-fifties or thereabouts, and shorter than Tom had expected. Although he was still recognisably the same person, the photo on his jet had clearly been taken several years before, his brown hair now receding and greying at the temples, the firm lines of his once angular face now soft and surviving only in the sharp cliff of his chin. The energy in his voice and movements, however, was undimmed, his weight constantly shifting from foot to foot like a boxer, his head jerking erratically as he looked around the room, as if it pained him to focus on any one thing for longer than a few seconds. He answered his own question before anyone else had a chance to respond.

'Mine's the Picasso, and not just because I paid a hundred and thirty-nine million dollars for it. That man was a genius. A self-made man. A true visionary.'

Tom smiled, the machine-gun rattle of Kezman's voice making it hard to know whether he was talking about himself or Picasso.

'Mr Kezman, this is . . .'

'Tom Kirk, I know.' He grinned. 'Luckily the FBI doesn't have a monopoly on information. At least not yet. I like to know who's on my plane.'

Tom stepped forward to shake his hand, but Kezman waved him back.

'Stay where I can see you, goddammit,' he barked.

Tom suddenly understood why Kezman was wearing sunglasses and moving his head so erratically – he was clearly blind, or very nearly so, his aide presumably there to help steer him in the right direction as he navigated through the hotel.

'Retinitis pigmentosa,' Kezman confirmed. 'The closer I get to things, the less I can see. And one day even that . . .'

His voice tailed off and Tom couldn't stop himself wondering if this explained Kezman's insistence that they should go up to his private apartment first, before meeting him down here. It was almost as if he'd wanted to give them some small insight into his shrinking world. A world where there was little point in furnishing a room he could barely see, but where a view was still there to be enjoyed. At least for now.

'I'm sorry,' Tom said. He didn't know Kezman, but he meant it all the same.

'Why? It's not your fault,' Kezman shrugged. 'Besides, in a way, it's a gift. After all, would I have started my collection if I hadn't known I was going blind? Sometimes, it's only when you are about to lose something that you really begin to understand what it's worth.'

There was a long silence, which Ortiz eventually broke with a forced cough.

'As I have discussed with your head of security, the plan is for Mr Kirk to take the money down on to the casino floor and wait there for them to make contact.'

'It's unlikely they'll bring the painting with them,' Jennifer added. 'So we expect them to either provide us with a location, which we will then check out before handing over the money, or lead us to it so that we can make the exchange there.'

'Either way, we'll follow them to make sure we grab them, the painting and the money,' Stokes said confidently.

'Once again, Mr Kezman, the federal government is very

grateful for your co-operation in this matter. We'll do what we can to ensure that your staff and customers . . .'

'Don't mention it,' Kezman waved Jennifer's thanks away with a sweep of his hand. 'You just make sure no one gets hurt.'

ELEVEN

Amalfi Casino and Hotel Resort, Las Vegas
17th March – 11.22 p.m.

It was funny how people conditioned themselves to only ever see what they wanted to, Foster mused. Ask anyone who wears a watch with Roman numerals how the number four is written on it and they'll say IV. All those years that they've been looking at it, checking the time, the numbers only a few inches from their stupid dumb-ass faces, and they've never actually noticed that it's IIII. That it's always IIII on a watch, because IV would be too easily confused with VI. That their brains have tricked them into seeing what they expect to, or rather not seeing what they should. It was pathetic really.

Like tonight. The security detail at the staff entrance had barely glanced at his badly fitting uniform and tampered badge before waving him through. He looked the part, so why see something that you've convinced yourself isn't there? That's why the beard had had to go in the end; that might have been the one thing that could have triggered a response.

He, on the other hand, had immediately picked out the FBI agents, uncomfortable in their civilian clothes as they loitered near the entrance, or perched unconvincingly in front of the slot machines. It was the half-hearted way they were feeding the money into the machine that was the killer tell – either you played the slots, or they played you.

He stopped next to an anonymous-looking red door. How many people had walked past it, he wondered, without ever asking themselves why, out of all the doors that lined this service corridor, this was the only one that warranted two locks. Without ever asking themselves what might possibly lie behind it that demanded the extra security. But then, that's what he'd noticed in civilians: a lack of basic human curiosity, a slavish, unquestioning acceptance of a life dropped into their lap like a TV dinner.

Quickly picking the locks, he opened the door on to a dimly lit stairwell that he slipped into, wedging a fire extinguisher between the base of the door and the bottom step of the metal staircase to stop anyone coming in after him. The staircase led up several flights to the observation deck – a series of cramped, interconnecting gantries hidden in the ceiling void that stretched over the entire casino floor.

Although in theory these were to allow maintenance staff to invisibly service the casino's complex lighting grid and vast network of A/C ducts, the careful positioning of two-way mirrors and air vents also allowed casino security to spy on people without being seen. Dealers watching the gamblers, boxmen watching the dealers, supervisors watching the boxmen, pit bosses watching the supervisors, shift managers watching the pit bosses . . . the entire set-up functioned on the assumption that everyone was on the make and on the take.

Not that the deck was used as often as it used to be – video cameras and advances in biometric technology that could flag-up suspicious changes in body heat and pupil dilation had seen to that. But Kezman was famously old-school and had insisted on having it there anyway, both as a low-tech back-up, and because he knew that sometimes you needed to get up there and sniff the floor to get a feeling for where the trouble was brewing.

As Foster had expected, the gantries were empty. He took up his position, removed the towel from his back-pack, and unrolled it. Piece by piece he began to reassemble his rifle, the parts sliding into place with a satisfying click echoed by the sound of the roulette ball skipping on the wheel below. With the infrared sight fitted he hesitated momentarily, toying with the suppressor before slipping it into his top pocket like a good cigar he was saving for the right moment.

No suppressor. Not tonight. He wanted everyone to hear the shot, to be paralysed by its angry roar, and then to run. To run screaming.

TWELVE

The Pantheon, Rome
18th March – 7.41 a.m.
Allegra was sheltering in the portico, grateful for the coffee Salvatore had conjured up for her and for the fresh air – there had been a strange, curdled atmosphere inside that she had been glad to escape.

The storm had now tethered itself directly overhead, rain lashing the square, lightning cleaving the stygian sky only for the clouds to crash thunderously back together. But it was the more powerful storm brewing on the other side of the barricades that worried her now. Rising out of the warm waters of political scandal and feeding on the lurid details of these murders, it would quickly spin out of control, blowing them violently towards the rocks until either the media lost interest or they had all been dashed into pieces, whichever came sooner. She wondered if Gallo's men all knew this, and whether what she could sense inside, what she could almost taste, was their fearful anticipation of the hurricane that lay ahead.

'So it's the same coin?' Gallo had materialised at her side, lighting a cigarette.

'I thought you'd given up?'

'So did I.'

She was reassured that she wasn't the only one feeling the pressure.

'It's the same.' She nodded, not bothering to repeat that it wasn't a coin but a lead disc.

'So it's the same killer?'

'Are you asking me or telling me?'

'I'm asking.' As earlier, the hint of a smile was playing around his lips, as if she somehow amused him.

'There are some obvious similarities,' she began hesitantly, surprised that Gallo even cared what she thought. 'The lead discs. The proximity of the two murder scenes. The pagan temples. The connection to Caesar. But . . .'

'But what?'

'It's . . . the way they were killed. I'm not a profiler, but there's no consistency between the two murders. They look different. They feel different.'

'I agree. Two murders. Two killers.' Gallo held up photographs of the two crime scenes side by side as if to prove his point.

Allegra glanced at the photos and jumped. There was something in the crime scenes, something she'd not noticed before, but which, when framed within the photographs' white borders, was now glaringly obvious.

'Where's your car?'

'Over there –' He pointed out a dark blue BMW.

'Come on!' She stepped out into the rain, then turned and motioned impatiently at him to follow when she realised he hadn't moved.

'Where to?'

'The Palazzo Barberini,' she called back, her hair darkening. 'There's something there you need to see.'

A few moments later, Gallo gunned out of the square down

the Via del Seminario, the Carabinieri clearing a path for him through the crowd, Allegra shielding her face as the photographers and TV crews pressed their lenses up against their windows. As soon as they were clear, he accelerated through the Piazza San Ignacio and out on to the busy Via del Corso, his siren blazing as he carved his way through the rush-hour traffic. Reaching the Via del Tritone he turned right, racing down to where the palazzo loomed imposingly over the Piazza Barberini and then cutting up a side street to the main entrance at the top of the hill. The drive was chained off, although the museum was clearly open, those foreign tourists still able to swallow the euro's inexorable climb over the past few months already filtering through the gates.

'Damn these peasants,' Gallo muttered, leaning on his horn, until a guard appeared and let them through.

They lurched forward, the gravel spitting out from under their tyres as they shot round to the far side of the fountain.

'First floor,' Allegra called as she jumped out and headed through the arched entrance, not pausing on this occasion to admire the monumental Bernini staircase that led up to the Galleria Nazionale d'Arte Antica, the museum that now occupied this former papal residence.

'Police,' Gallo called, waving his badge at the astonished museum staff as they burst through the entrance and bypassed the queue waiting patiently at the ticket desk.

Allegra sprinted through first one room, then another, her eyes skipping over the paintings, not entirely sure where it was, but knowing it was here somewhere. Filippo Lippi, Piero de Cosimo . . . no, not here. Next room. Tintoretto, Bronzino . . . still nothing. Carry on through. Guercino . . .

'There,' she called triumphantly, pointing at the wall.

'*Ammàzza!*' Gallo swore, stepping past her for a closer look.

The large painting showed a bearded man being decapitated

by a woman, a sword in her right hand, his hair firmly gripped in her left. He was naked, his face contorted into an inhuman scream, his body convulsed by pain, the blood spurting on to a white sheet. Next to the woman stood an old woman, her wrinkled face hungrily absorbing the man's death, her hands gripping the hem of her mistress's dress to keep it clear of the blood.

Gallo held the photograph of the Pantheon crime scene up next to it. There was no question it had been staged to mirror the painting's composition.

'It's the same.'

'*Judith and Holofernes,*' Allegra said slowly. 'It was only when I saw the photos that I made the connection.'

'And Ricci?'

'*The Crucifixion of Saint Peter* in the Cerasi Chapel in Santa Maria del Popolo,' she confirmed. 'That's what links your two murders, Colonel. The killers are re-enacting scenes from Caravaggio paintings.'

THIRTEEN

Amalfi Casino and Hotel Resort, Las Vegas
17th March – 11.56 p.m.

Tom had insisted on getting down on to the floor early, guessing that whoever had been sent to meet him would already be in position and that it would help if it looked as though he was keen to do the deal. More importantly, it gave them a chance to see the money, to see that this was for real. It was at Tom's feet now – twenty million in cash, neatly packed into two aluminium suitcases.

Twenty million dollars.

There was a time, perhaps, when he might have considered . . . But those days were behind him now, although you wouldn't have guessed it from the obvious reluctance with which Stokes had entrusted the cases to him, and his pointed reminder that they were electronically tagged. Then again, maybe Tom was naïve to have expected anything else. All Stokes had to go on was his file, and that told its own, damning story.

He looked around the blinking, cavernous floor to get his bearings, momentarily disoriented by the tumbrel-clatter of the roulette wheels, the dealers' barked instructions and the machines' remorseless chuckling. The place was packed. If Vegas was suffering from the economic slowdown that the press had been so gleefully reporting for the past few months, then it was hiding it well. Either that or it was still in denial.

He spotted Jennifer at the bar to his left, nursing a coke. Ortiz, meanwhile, was to his right, pretending to play video poker and losing badly. Stokes, he knew, was in the back with the casino's head of security, watching the screens and co-ordinating the other agents who had been posted around him. In front of him was a roulette table, the animated abandon with which a noticeably younger crowd were merrily flinging chips on to the baize contrasting with the silent, mesmerised application of the older people on the slots.

On cue, a woman wearing an *'I love Fort Lauderdale'* T-shirt waddled over to the machine next to him, the stool screeching under her weight. Resting a bucket full of quarters on her lap, she bowed her head briefly as if offering up a prayer, and then began to feed it with metronomic precision, the tips of her fingers stained black by the coins. A kaleidoscope of changing colours immediately skipped across her rapt face, her eyes gazing up at the spinning wheels with a mixture of hope and expectation.

Tom wondered if she knew that her faith was unlikely to be rewarded. In here, chance danced to the casino's tune. The roulette tables that paid out thirty-five to one, when the odds of winning were one in thirty-seven. The deliberate location of the premium slots next to the main aisles and blackjack tables, to lure people in. The lack of clocks and the suppression of natural light, so that everyone lost track of time. The careful variation in ceiling heights, lighting levels and music zones to trigger different emotional responses. The strategic location of the bathrooms, to minimise time off the floor. The purposefully labyrinthine layout, so that the sight-lines provided neither a glimpse of a possible way out, nor allowed a potentially overwhelming view of the entire space. In this broad church, you were damned from the moment you walked through the door.

There. A man with his back to him at the neighbouring blackjack table, his head snapping back a little too fast to suggest the glance he had just given him had been accidental. And again, only this time he didn't break eye contact. He knew Tom had seen him. He was tipping the dealer, getting up. This was it.

'Blackjack table,' Tom muttered into his mike, hoping the others could hear him over the noise. 'White hair, black . . .' His voice tailed off as the man turned round and nodded.

Dressed in a black suit, he was about five feet ten with a curling mop of white hair and a farmer's sun-blushed cheeks that echoed the red handkerchief peeking out of a trouser pocket. But it was the white band encircling his neck that had drawn Tom's attention, its unexpected glare seeming to cast a bleaching wash over everything at the periphery of his vision.

'He's a priest,' Tom breathed in disbelief, as much to himself as anyone.

The man advanced towards him, Tom reassured that as Jennifer had predicted to Kezman earlier, he wasn't carrying anything that might have contained the painting. That would have marked him and whoever he was working for as amateurs, and amateurs were unpredictable and more easily spooked. Instead, slung over his left shoulder was a tired leather satchel.

They met in the middle of the main aisle. Saying nothing, the priest reached into his bag and handed Tom a series of photographs. They showed the *Nativity*, but in more detail this time, with close-ups of the faces and hands, always the hardest things to paint. From what Tom could tell, the brush-work looked genuine, and although the canvas had been slightly damaged over the years, overall the condition was very good, the faint reflection of a camera flash in a couple of the photos suggesting that it was being kept behind glass.

There was no sign of a signature, but Tom took that as further proof of the painting's probable authenticity. As far as he knew, Caravaggio had only ever signed one painting, *The Beheading of the Baptist*, where he had marked an M for Merisi, his family name, in the blood spilling from John the Baptist's neck.

'Is it close?' Tom asked.

'Close enough,' the priest replied, Tom detecting an Italian accent.

'I need to see it.'

'Is that the money?'

'Twenty million dollars,' he confirmed, tapping the case nearest to him with his foot. 'Unmarked, non-sequential bills, as requested.'

'*Bene, bene.*' The priest nodded. 'Good.' There was an anxious edge to the man's voice that surprised Tom. For a pro he seemed a little tense, although twenty million was enough to make most people tighten up.

'I need to see the painting first,' Tom reminded him.

'Of course,' the priest said. 'You have a car?'

'The painting's not here?'

'It's not far. Where's your car?'

'The money's going nowhere until I see the painting,' Tom warned him.

'Don't worry,' the priest immediately reassured him. 'We have a deal, see –' He reached for Tom's hand and shook it energetically. 'You have the money, I have the painting, we have a deal, yes?'

'We have a deal,' Tom agreed.

'You want this painting, yes?'

'As much as you want the money,' Tom answered with a

puzzled smile. It was a strange question to ask. Why else would he be there? 'My car's in the garage.'

'It has been a long time. You will be the first, the first in many years to see it.' His eyes flicked over Tom's shoulder as he spoke and then back again. 'It is beautiful, still beautiful, despite everything it has been through.'

Tom felt his stomach tightening. Something wasn't right. First a hint of nervousness. Now an abrupt shift from urgency to an almost languid calm as if . . . as if he was trying to waste time so that somewhere else . . .

A shot rang out, its whiplash crack cutting through the casino's raucous din. Tom staggered back, the world suddenly slowing, as if someone was holding the movie projector to stop the reel from turning – the individual frames crawling across the screen; a roulette ball, frozen in mid-flight; the soundtrack stretched into a low, slurring moan as words folded into each other.

Then, almost immediately, everything sprang forward, only sharper, louder and faster than before, as if time was over-compensating as it tried to catch up with itself. The ball landed, the winner cheered. But their celebration was drowned out by a terrified scream, one voice triggering another and that one two more until, like a flock of migrating birds wheeling through a darkening sky, a sustained, shrieking lament filled the air.

Tom glanced instinctively to his left. Jennifer was lying on the floor. Her blouse was blotted poppy red.

FOURTEEN

Institute for Religious Works, Via della Statzione Vaticana, Rome
18th March – 8.08 a.m.

As the six men opposite him bowed their heads, Antonio Santos picked up his spoon and studied the hallmarks. To the left he recognised the symbol of the Papal State, and next to it the initials NL – Lorenzini Nicola, an Italian silversmith active in the mid eighteenth century, if he wasn't mistaken.

'*Nos miseri homines et egeni, pro cibis quos nobis ad corporis subsidium benigne es largitus, tibi Deus omnipotens, Pater cælestis, gratias reverenter agimus . . .*' Archbishop Ancelotti intoned grace, his voice rising and falling as if he was reciting some mediaeval incantation. Turning the spoon over, Santos smiled at the way its polished surface distorted his reflection.

'*Simul obsecrantes, ut iis sobries, modeste, atque grate utamur. Per Iesum Christum Dominum nostrum. Amen.*'

'Amen,' Santos agreed enthusiastically, carefully returning the spoon to its proper place before anyone had opened their eyes.

Ancelotti looked up and nodded at the two young priests standing near the door to serve breakfast. He was wearing a

black simar with amaranth-red piping and buttons together
with a purple fascia and zuchetto. A large gold pectoral cross
dangled from his neck. The other five men sitting either side
of him were similarly dressed, although, as cardinals, their
buttons, sashes and skull-caps were scarlet.

'Thank you for coming, Antonio,' Ancelotti said, motioning
with his finger to indicate that he wanted one, two, three
spoonfuls of sugar. 'I apologise for the short notice.'

'Not at all, Your Grace,' Santos said with a generous shrug,
holding his hand over his coffee as one of the priests went
to add cream. 'I apologise for being late. The Carabinieri seem
to have closed off half the city.'

'Nothing too serious, I hope,' Ancelotti enquired, brushing
his hands together over his plate to dust some crumbs from
his fingers.

'My driver told me that they've found a body in the
Pantheon,' Cardinal Simoes volunteered, pushing his gold-
rimmed glasses back up his nose.

'Dear, dear,' Ancelotti tutted, licking some jam from his
thumb with a loud sucking noise. 'We live in such wicked
times. Jam?'

'No, thank you.' Santos gave a tight smile. 'I don't eat
breakfast.'

'You should, you should,' Ancelotti admonished him. 'Most
important meal of the day. Now, does everyone have what
they need?'

Seeing that they did, he waved at the two priests to retire
to the outer room, then turned back to face Santos.

'I believe you know everyone here?'

He nodded. Cardinals Villot, Neuman, Simoes, Pisani and
Carter. The Oversight Commission of the Istituto per le Opere
di Religione. The Vatican Bank.

'Your eminences,' he said, bowing his head. Their
murmured greetings were muffled by fresh croissants.

'Antonio, we asked you here today in our capacity as the largest shareholder in the Banco Rosalia,' Ancelotti began, sipping his coffee.

'Largest and most important shareholder,' Santos added generously. 'We are, after all, working to help finance God's work.'

'Ah yes, God's work.' Ancelotti clasped his hands together as if in prayer, pressing them against his lips. 'Which is, as I'm sure you understand, why we need to be especially vigilant.'

'I'm not sure I do understand, Your Grace,' Santos said with a frown, placing his cup back down on the table. 'Vigilant for what?'

'For anything that could harm the reputation of the Catholic Church, of course.'

'I hope you are not suggesting that –'

'Of course not, Antonio, of course not,' Ancelotti reassured him warmly, 'But after what happened before . . . well, we have to go through the motions, be seen to be asking the right questions.'

He was referring, Santos knew, to the huge scandal that had engulfed the Vatican Bank in the 1980s, when it had been implicated in laundering billions of dollars of mafia drug money. It was partly in response to this that the Oversight Commission had been set up in the first place.

'I fail to see how . . .'

'Your year-end accounts are almost a month overdue,' Cardinal Villot said in an accusing tone.

'As I've already explained to Archbishop Ancelotti, there are a number of small, purely technical matters that the auditors have . . .'

'We've also heard your liquidity position's deteriorated,' Cardinal Carter added, his voice equally sharp.

'Not to mention the provisions on your real estate portfolio,' Cardinal Neuman chimed.

Santos took a deep breath. So much for casting the money lenders out of the temple, he thought ruefully. Instead, armed with an MBA and a bible, the Oversight Commission seemed to be setting up shop right next to them.

'A number of banks have withdrawn their funding lines, yes, but that's to be expected with the squeeze that the whole market is feeling. We still have more than enough headroom, given our deposit and capital base. As for our real estate book, we've seen a slight uptick in bad debts like everyone else, but the provisions we took last year should be more than . . .'

'I think what we're suggesting is that a short, sharp financial review would help allay our concerns, in light of the extreme volatility of the markets and the rather bleak economic outlook,' Ancelotti said in a gentle tone.

'What sort of a financial review?'

'We'd probably start with a quick canter through your latest management accounts, bank statements and ALCO reports,' Ancelotti said breezily. 'We have a small team of accountants we like to use for this sort of thing. They'll be in and out in a few weeks. You won't even notice they're there.'

A pause. It wasn't as if he had any choice.

'When would you like them to start?'

'Is the day after tomorrow too soon?' Ancelotti asked with a casual shrug, although Santos noticed that the archbishop's eyes were locked on to his, as if to gauge his reaction.

'Of course not,' Santos replied with a confident smile. 'That gives me enough time to brief the team so that we can make sure that we have a room set aside and all the documentation prepared.'

'Excellent, excellent.' Ancelotti stood up to signal that the meeting was over and leant across the table to shake his hand. 'I knew you'd understand. By the way, I'm hosting a Mozart recital in Santa Sabina next month. You should come.'

'It would be my pleasure, Your Grace,' Santos smiled. 'Please forward on the details. Your Eminences . . .'

A few minutes later he was down on the street in the rain, angrily loosening his collar as he flicked a tin open and pushed one, then two pieces of liquorice into his mouth. Then he reached for his phone.

'We're fucked,' he barked into it the moment it was answered. 'Ancelotti and his performing monkeys want to audit the bank . . . I don't know what they know, but they must know something, and even if they don't, it won't take more than a few days for them to figure everything out . . . I need to bail. How much would I have if I liquidated everything? . . . No, not the property. Just whatever I can get out in cash by the end of the week . . . Is that it?' He swore angrily, earning himself a disapproving look from two nuns walking past. 'That's not enough,' he continued in an angry whisper. 'That's not even halfway to being enough . . . Hold on, I've got another call.' He switched lines, '*Pronto?*'

'It's done,' a voice rasped.

'Are you sure?' Santos stepped out of the rain and sheltered inside a doorway.

'It's done,' the voice repeated. The line went dead.

Smiling, Santos went to switch back to the first caller before pausing, a thought occurring to him. He helped himself to some more liquorice as the idea slowly took shape. It had only ever been part of the set-up, but why not? Why the hell not? The trick was getting to it, but if he could . . . the Serbians would take it off his hands. They were always in the market for that sort of thing.

'Spare some change?'

A beggar wearing a filthy army surplus overcoat, his face masked by a spade-like beard studded with raindrops, was holding a creased McDonald's cup up to him. Santos glanced up and down the street behind him. It was empty. With a flick of his wrist he knocked the cup into the air, the few, pathetic coins it contained scattering across the pavement. The beggar dropped moaning to his knees, his blackened fingernails scrabbling in the gutter.

'Spare *you* some change?' Santos spat. 'I'm the one who needs a handout.'

FIFTEEN

Amalfi Casino and Hotel Resort
18th March – 12.08 a.m.

Kicking their stools out from under them, people began to run, half-drunk cocktails collapsing to the floor and neatly stacked piles of chips swooning on to the baize as gamblers clambered over each other like calves trying to escape a branding pen.

Tom fought his way across to Jennifer's side, Ortiz only a few feet behind him. She was still alive, thank God, her eyes wide with shock, but still alive. He ripped her blouse open, saw the blood frothing from under her left breast.

'It's okay,' Tom reassured her, leaning close so she could hear him. She nodded, lifted her head as if to speak, then fell back.

'Where's she hit?' Ortiz fell on to his knees next to him as the fire alarm sounded.

'Get an ambulance here,' Tom shouted back over the noise, ripping his jacket off and folding it into a makeshift pillow. 'Press down –' He grabbed Ortiz's hand and jammed it hard against the wound, then leant across and snatched his Beretta out from under his arm.

'Where the hell are you going?' Ortiz called after him.

'To find the shooter.'

He leapt up on to the roulette table, knowing from the location of her wound and the direction she'd been facing that the gunman must have been positioned somewhere ahead of her. Scanning the floor, he suddenly noticed an unexpected shimmer of glass under the stampeding crowd's feet. He glanced instinctively up at the ceiling and saw that a single mirrored panel was missing from its reflective surface, the empty black square as obvious as a decaying tooth in an otherwise perfect smile.

'He's in the ceiling void,' Tom breathed.

He leapt down and grabbed a passing security guard who seemed more intent on saving himself than in stewarding anyone else to the exit.

'The observation deck,' Tom shouted. 'How do I get up there?'

The guard paused, momentarily transfixed by the gun gripped in Tom's left hand, then pointed unsteadily at a set of double doors on the other side of the floor.

'Through there,' he stuttered.

Snatching the guard's security pass off his belt, Tom fought his way through to the doors he had indicated and swiped them open. He found himself in a long white service corridor lit by overhead strip lighting and lined on both sides by a series of identical red doors. Cowering under the fire alarm's strident and persistent echo, a steady stream of people were half walking, half running towards him – casino staff ordered to evacuate the building, judging from their identical red Mao jackets and the confusion etched on to their faces.

Tom walked against the flow, scanning for a pair of shoes, or a uniform, or a face that didn't quite fit. Ahead of him, about two thirds of the way down the corridor, a door opened and a man wearing a baseball cap stepped out. Tom noticed him immediately. It was his studied calmness that gave him away. His calmness and the detached, almost curious expression on his face, as if he was taking part in some bizarre sociological experiment that he couldn't quite relate to.

He seemed to notice Tom at almost the same time because, grimacing, he turned and retreated back inside, locking the door behind him. Tom sprinted down the corridor after him, tried the handle and then stepped back and pumped four shots into the locks. With a firm kick, the door splintered open.

Carefully covering the angles above him, Tom made his way up the stairs into the shadows of the observation deck, his eyes adjusting to the darkness. He felt the shooter before he saw him, the metal walkways shuddering under his heavy step as he sprinted along the gantries away from him. Tom took aim and fired three times, then twice more, a couple of the bullets sparking brightly where they struck the steel supports. But the man barely broke his stride, turning sharply to his left and then to his right.

Tom set off after him, trying to guess where he'd turned, so that he wouldn't end up stranded in a different section of the deck. Up ahead the gunman paused and then in an instant was over the side of the gantry and dangling down over the suspended ceiling below. Tom again took aim, and fired twice, this time catching him in his shoulder. With a pained yell he let go, crashing through the mirrored ceiling and vanishing from sight.

Tom sprinted across to the same point and then lowered himself down as far as he could before letting go and dropping through the hole on to a blackjack table scattered with chips and fresh blood.

'Where did he go?' Tom asked the dealer, who was staring up at him open-mouthed.

The man pointed dumbly towards the exit. Tom looked

up and saw the gunman almost at the doors, his jacket burst open at the shoulder where the bullet had passed through him. Tom again pulled the trigger, the bullet skimming the man's head and shattering a slot machine deliberately positioned to tempt people into one final roll of the dice before heading outside. Next to it a bearded man in a *'Remember Pearl Harbour'* baseball cap carried on playing, gazing at the wheels as if he hated them.

Tom leapt down and followed the gunman outside, determined not to lose him. But rather than melt away into the panicked crowd that had swamped the forecourt, the man seemed to be waiting for him, backpack hitched over one arm. For an instant, no longer, they stood about twenty feet apart, their eyes locked, the swollen human flow parting around them like a river around two rocks. The gunman, clutching his shoulder, studied Tom with a detached curiosity; Tom, his gun raised, finger tested the trigger spring's resistance. But before he could take the shot, a powerful hand gripped his arm and pulled him back.

'Not here, for Chrissake,' Stokes yelled. 'Are you fucking crazy? You'll hit someone.'

Tom angrily shook him off, took aim and fired. The gun clicked, empty. With a wink, the killer turned and dived into the frothing sea of people.

In an instant, he was gone.

SIXTEEN

18th March – 12.23 a.m.

'Where's the backup? They need to set up a perimeter,' Tom ordered angrily.

'It's a little late for that,' Stokes shrugged helplessly at the untamed mob that had already spilled out on to the Strip, bringing the traffic to a standstill as they surged across the road, trying to get as far away from the Amalfi as they could.

Tom glared resentfully at the crowd, wanting Stokes to be wrong but knowing he wasn't. What made it worse was that the gunman had played him. He'd seen Tom was carrying a Beretta, counted the shots until he'd known it was empty then waited for him. Then taunted him.

With a violent jolt, Tom's thoughts snapped back to Jennifer.

'How is she?'

'The paramedics are with her now,' Stokes reassured him, before lowering his gaze. 'She's lost a lot of blood.'

'Where is she?'

'They're taking her up on to the roof for a medevac to UMC.'

'Get me up there,' Tom barked.

They ran back into the casino and, using the card Tom had taken from the security guard, rode up to the top floor.

'What happened to the priest?' Tom asked as the levels pinged past.

'We lost him too,' Stokes admitted. 'Soon as everyone started running, he vanished. The money's safe, though.'

'You think I give a shit about the money?' Tom hissed.

The doors opened and they sprinted up the final two flights of the service staircase to a metal door that Tom swiped open. The helicopter was already there, its rotors buffeting them with a wash of hot, dusty air. Jennifer was lifted in into the rear by two paramedics, a drip attached to her arm and an oxygen mask over her face. Ortiz was crouching on the ground, his shirt covered in her blood, his head in his hands.

'I'm going with her,' Tom shouted over the throb of the engines.

'No way,' Stokes called back. 'You're the only person who can ID the gunman. I need you here.'

'I wasn't asking for your permission.'

Keeping his head down, Tom sprinted across the pad and hauled himself in behind the stretcher, slamming the door shut after him. The pitch of the engines deepened as the pilot throttled up and with a lurch they rose into the sky.

'How is she?' Tom called to one of the medics as they hooked her up to a mobile ECG, her pulse registering with a green blip on the screen and a sharp tone – Beep . . . beep . . . beep. Around them power and warning lights from other machines flashed and sounded intermittently.

'Who are you?'

'A friend.'

'She's lost a lot of blood . . . we need to get her into theatre ASAP.'

'Is she conscious?'

'In and out. Try talking to her. Keep her awake.'

Tom shuffled forward until he was sitting next to Jennifer's head. The glow of the ECG screen was staining her skin green. Her eyes flickered open and he was certain that he saw a smile of recognition tremble across her face.

'Hold on, Jen,' he whispered, pressing his lips to her ear. 'We'll be there soon.'

She nodded weakly. He brushed the hair out of her eyes, speaking almost to himself.

'You're going to be okay. I'll make sure you're okay.'

Beep . . . beep . . . beep.

He smiled at her reassuringly, glad that she couldn't see the paramedics' grim-faced expression as they worked on the wound, the blood still oozing from her chest. He felt her hand reach for his, press something hard and rectangular into it, her grip tightening as she pulled him closer, her mouth moving under the oxygen mask.

He bent over her, straining to hear her voice against the chop of the rotors and the rhythmic pinging of the heart monitor. He caught something, the fragment of a word, perhaps more, and then her eyes closed again and her grip loosened, allowing him to slip what she had given him into his pocket.

'Come on, Jen,' Tom called, shaking her arm gently at first and then with increasing urgency. 'We're nearly there now. You're going to be okay. You just need to keep listening to me. Listen to my voice.'

He shook her again, more roughly this time. But there was no reaction and all he could hear was the gradual, almost imperceptible lengthening of the gaps between each tone of the ECG.

Beep . . . beep. Beep ...... beep. Beep .... beep.

'Help her,' Tom shouted angrily to the paramedics. 'Do something.'

They swapped a glance, one of them wiping the back of his hand across his brow, smearing blood.

'We've done what we can.'

Far below, the city's neon carpet unravelled into the distance. But from up here, Tom could see that it ended, that a black line had been drawn across the desert at the city's limits, and that beyond that was only darkness.

He leaned forward, his lips brushing against her cheek. He knew now that it was just him and her. Him and her and the hiss of the respirator and the unfeeling pulse of the ECG's electronic heart.

'Stay with me,' he whispered.

For a second he could have sworn that her breathing quickened. Then the machine gave a piercing shriek. The monitor showed a perfectly flat line.

PART TWO

'It is from the greatest dangers that the greatest glory is to be won.'

Thucydides, *History of the Peloponnesian War* – Book 1, 144

SEVENTEEN

Via Galvani, Testaccio, Rome
18th March – 3.12 p.m.

The speaker crackled into life.

'Mitto tibi navem prora puppique carentem.'

Allegra hesitated, her mind racing. She understood the Latin, of course – I send you a ship lacking stern and bow. But what did it mean? How could a ship not have a stern and a bow? Unless . . . unless it was referring to something else. To the front and the back? The beginning and the end? The first and the last? Latin for ship was *navem*, so if it was missing its beginning and its end, its first and last letters perhaps . . .

'Ave,' she replied with a smile. Latin for hello.

'Ave, indeed,' the voice replied with a chuckle. 'Although I can't claim the credit this time. That was one of Cicero's.'

The door buzzed open and Allegra made her way to the lift, smiling. She'd first met Aurelio Eco at La Sapienza before heading off to Columbia for her masters where he'd been a visiting professor in the university's antiquities department. Before that, he'd spent fifteen years as the Director of the Villa Giulia, Rome's foremost Etruscan museum, during ten of which he had also headed up the Ufficio Sequestri e Scavi Clandestini, the Office of Clandestine Excavations and Seized Objects. Unfortunately for her, these posts seemed to have provided him with an inexhaustible supply of riddles, which he delighted in asking her as a condition of entry to his apartment. A latter-day Sphinx to her Odysseus.

As usual the door was open and the kettle boiling. She made herself a strong black coffee and Aurelio an Earl Grey tea with lemon, an affectation of his from a brief stint at Oxford in his twenties that he had never been able, or wanted, to shake off.

He was waiting for her in his high-backed leather chair, the split in the seat cushion covered by a red-and-white *keffiyeh* purchased during an exchange posting to Jordan. His dusty office was full of such mementoes – photographs of him at various digs over the decades, framed maps and faded prints, prayer beads and inlaid boxes picked up in dusty Middle-Eastern souks, fragments of inscribed Roman tablets, shards of Etruscan pottery, carved remnants of Greek statues. At times it seemed to Allegra that his entire life was held in this small room, each piece invested with a particular meaning or memory that he only had to glance at or hold to live all over again.

And yet this primitive mental filing system was as chaotic as it was effective, pictures hanging askew, books stacked any which way on the shelves with dirty cups and glasses squeezed into the gaps, the floor covered in a confetti trail of newspaper cuttings and half-read books left face-down, alongside a stack of index cards inscribed with notes for a forthcoming lecture. And while a favoured few of his artefacts had been placed in a glass display cabinet, the rest were scattered indiscriminately around the room, some squeezed on to his desk and the marble mantelpiece, others lining the edges of the bookshelves like paratroopers waiting for the order to jump.

Despite his cheerfulness on the intercom, Aurelio now seemed to have sunk into what Allegra could only describe as a sulk, his bottom lip jutting out, brows furrowed. Funny, she thought, how old age seemed to have given him an almost childlike ability to flit between moods on a whim.

'Maybe you shouldn't come any more,' he sighed. 'Spend time with your real friends, instead, people your own age.'

'Don't start that again,' she sighed. 'I've told you, I'm too busy to have any friends. Besides, I like old things.' She winked. 'They smell more interesting.'

Approaching seventy, Aurelio had no family left now, apart from a distant cousin who only seemed to show up when he needed a handout. As they had got to know each other, therefore, Allegra had taken it upon herself to look in on him whenever she knew she would be in the area. And sometimes, like today, when she knew she wouldn't.

'But you said you'd be here for lunch,' he continued in a hurt tone, although she could sense that her reply had pleased him. 'You're late.'

'And whose fault is that?'

He grinned, his sulk vanishing as quickly as she suspected it had appeared. He had a kindly face, with large light brown eyes, a beaked nose and leathered skin that spoke of too many long summers spent hunched over an excavation trench. He was dressed in an open-necked shirt and a yellow silk cravat, another hangover from his Oxford days. As ever, he was wearing a moth-eaten grey cardigan for warmth, his refusal to pay the 'extortionate' prices demanded by 'piratical' energy companies condemning his apartment to a Siberian permafrost for at least three months of the year.

'So they did call you?' he crowed.

'I knew it!' she remonstrated angrily. 'Who did you speak to? What did you tell them?'

'The GICO wanted an antiquities expert. They called the

university. The university put them on to me. I told them
I'd retired and recommended you instead.'

'Did they tell you what they wanted?'

'Of course not. It's the GICO. They never tell you anything.'
He paused, suddenly concerned. 'I thought you'd be pleased.
Is there a problem?'

With a deep breath, Allegra recounted the events of the
past twenty-three hours. The inverted crucifixion at the site
of Julius Caesar's assassination. The carefully staged beheading
in the Pantheon. The apparent link to two Caravaggio master-
pieces. Aurelio listened intently, shaking his head at some of
the more gruesome details, but otherwise remaining silent
until she had finished.

'So the man they found in the Pantheon . . .?'

'Was Annibale Argento's twin brother, Gio.'

'*Merda*,' he swore, for what could well have been the first
time since she'd known him. '*They* must be lapping it up.'

They, she knew, referred to the media, an industry he
despised, having been tricked a few years ago into authen-
ticating a forged Etruscan vase by an investigative reporter.
He gave a contemptuous wave of his hand towards an imagined TV set in the corner of his room, as if trying to further
distance himself from an object he had already demonstrably
banished from his life.

'I've spent half the day trying to see if there's anything else
that links the two sites or any of Caravaggio's other works.
Gallo is trying to get me seconded on to the case full time.'

'I'm sorry, Allegra. I didn't know . . . I didn't mean to get
you involved in anything like this.'

She shrugged. It was hard to be angry with him. It was
Aurelio after all who, guessing that she would quickly tire
of academia, had encouraged her to apply to the art and
antiquities unit of the Carabinieri in the first place. He'd only
been trying to help.

'I know.'

'Anything to go on?' he asked hopefully.

'Plenty to go on. Just no idea where to start,' she sighed. 'Which reminds me. There's something I wanted to ask you.'

'Anything, of course.'

'Both victims had what looked like an antique coin in their mouths.'

'To pay Charon,' Aurelio guessed immediately.

'That's what I thought. Except it wasn't a coin. It was a lead disc.'

'Lead?' Aurelio frowned. 'That's unusual.'

'That's what I thought. I seem to remember that Roman forgers used to fake coins by casting them in lead and covering them in gold leaf, but I wondered if there was some other reference to the Classical world that I might have –'

'Unusual, but not unprecedented,' he continued, interrupting her. 'Can you reach that red book down for me.'

She extricated the book from between the fifteen or so other academic texts he had written and handed it to him. He held it for a few seconds, his eyes closed, fingers resting lightly on the leather cover as if he was reading braille. Then, opening his eyes, he leafed through it, the brain haemorrhage that he'd suffered some fifteen years before betraying itself in his slow and deliberate movements.

'Here,' he fixed her with a knowing smile, about halfway in.

'Here what?'

'*Threatened by the Persian empire, several Greek states came together in the fifth century BC to form a military alliance under the leadership of the Athenians,*' he read. '*Members had to contribute ships or money, and in return the alliance agreed to protect their territory. Symbolically,*' he paused, Allegra remembering that he used to employ the same theatrical technique in lectures when he was about to make a particularly compelling point. *'Symbolically, upon joining, representatives of the member states had to throw a piece of metal into the sea.'*

'Lead,' Allegra breathed. He nodded.

'Normally a piece of lead. The alliance was to last until it floated to the surface again.'

There was a pause, as she reflected on this.

'And you think . . .?'

'You asked about a link between lead and the Classical world.' He smiled. 'Thinking's your job.'

'What was the name of this alliance?'

Aurelio pretended to consult the book, although she could tell it was just an excuse for another of his dramatic pauses.

'They called themselves the Delian League.'

EIGHTEEN

J. Edgar Hoover Building, FBI headquarters, Washington DC
18th March – 9.37 a.m.

The door buzzed open. Tom didn't bother to look round. He could tell from Ortiz's shuffling steps and Stokes's heavier, wider stride, who it was.

'How long are you going to keep me here?' he demanded angrily.

'A federal agent's been killed, Mr Kirk,' Stokes replied icily, no longer even attempting to mask his instinctive hostility. He dragged a chair out from under the table and extravagantly straddled it. 'So we're going to keep you here pretty much as long as we like.'

'You don't have to tell me she was killed, you pompous bastard,' Tom hissed, holding out a sleeve still flecked with Jennifer's blood. 'I was holding her hand when she died, remember?'

In a way he was glad that Stokes was acting like this. It gave him a reason to be angry, to give himself over to his rage, to feel its intoxicating opiate course through his veins and his pulse quicken. Better that than allow his sadness to envelop him, feel the paralysing arms of grief tighten around him as he subjected himself to a Sisyphean analysis of what he could and should have done to save her.

Even as this thought occurred to him, he felt Jennifer's image forming in his mind. An image he'd tried to suppress ever since he'd seen the gurney disappear into the bowels of the hospital, and then been escorted back on to Kezman's jet and flown to this windowless interview room. But there she was, bloodied, her face shrouded by an oxygen mask, arms pierced by wires. A martyr? A sacrifice? But if so, for what and by whom?

'If we're going to catch the people who did this, we're going to need your help.' Ortiz, standing to his right, had adopted a more conciliatory tone which Tom sensed was genuine, rather than some clumsy attempt at a good cop, bad cop routine. His cheeks were shadowed by stubble, his eyes tired.

'You're not going to catch anyone, stuck down here,' Tom retorted. 'The longer we talk, the colder the trail. We should be in Vegas.'

'SOP says we pull back and let an IA team step in when an agent falls in the line of duty,' Stokes intoned, sounding as though he was reciting from some sort of manual. 'They're on the ground there already, reporting directly to FBI Director Green.'

'Green?' Tom asked, momentarily encouraged. He knew Jack Green, or at least had met him a few times when working with Jennifer. He had first-hand experience of the help Tom had given the Bureau in the past. 'I want to talk to him. Does he know I'm here?'

Ortiz's eyes flickered questioningly towards the large mirror that took up most of the left-hand wall. Tom's heart sank. Not only did Green know he was here, but, judging from the uncomfortable expression on Ortiz's face, he was probably watching. Jennifer's death had clearly reset the clock. Until they knew exactly what had happened, he wasn't going to qualify for any special treatment.

'You can talk to us instead,' Stokes snapped. 'Tell us what happened.'

'You know what happened. You were there. You saw the whole damn thing.'

'All I know is that twelve hours after Browne brought you into the case, she was dead.'

'You think I had something to do with it?' Tom's anger was momentarily overwhelmed by incredulity.

'Twenty million dollars is a lot of money.' Stokes's eyes narrowed accusingly. 'Even for you.'

'So that's your theory? That this was some sort of botched heist?' Tom wasn't sure whether Stokes was being deliberately provocative, or just plain stupid.

'I think that shooting a federal agent is a pretty good diversion. If one of our agents hadn't secured the suitcases, who's to say –'

'If all they'd wanted was a diversion, they could have shot anyone in that place,' Tom countered. 'They could have shot me.'

'Exactly.' Stokes raised his eyebrows pointedly, as if Tom had somehow proved his point.

'Except they didn't. They chose Jennifer. Maybe you should be asking yourselves why,' Tom insisted.

'What are you talking about?' Stokes said with an impatient shrug.

'Jennifer told me that two weeks ago she'd stumbled across an antiquities smuggling ring,' Tom said, looking to Ortiz who acknowledged this point with a nod. 'Then, out of the blue, a long-lost Caravaggio shows up. One of the few works in the world guaranteed to ensure that Jennifer gets the call. You think that's a coincidence?'

'You don't?' Ortiz asked him with a frown.

'I did until last night.' Tom shrugged. 'But now I'm thinking that there never was any Caravaggio; never was any exchange. That it was all a set-up. That that's why the priest started stalling. Because he was expecting Jennifer, not me. Because he wanted to give the gunman enough time to find her.'

'This was about the money, and you know it,' Stokes said with a dismissive wave of his hand. 'We just got to it before you or anyone else could.'

'Jennifer told me that the dealer you arrested in Queens had given you a name. Someone in Italy,' Tom said to Ortiz, still ignoring Stokes. 'Who was he? Did he have any ties to the mafia?'

'Why? What do you . . .?'

'That's classified,' Stokes interrupted angrily before Ortiz could answer. 'Browne trusted you with too much, and *you* shouldn't be encouraging him.' He jabbed his finger at Ortiz.

'The mafia control the illegal antiquities business in Italy,' Tom explained. 'They decide who can dig where, and take a cut on everything that comes out of the ground. It's worth millions to them. The same mafia who, if you believe the rumours, have been holding the Caravaggio all these years.'

'What are you saying?' Ortiz breathed, ignoring Stokes's venomous gaze.

'I'm saying it was a professional hit. I'm saying that something she'd stumbled across had made her a threat and that the painting was just a way of flushing her out into the open.'

'If you're right . . .' Ortiz said slowly.

'If I'm right, then we're already too late to catch the killer. You can run a DNA test on the blood traces, but people like that are ghosts. You'll get nothing. But I might still be able to find whoever ordered the hit.'

'*You* might be able to find them?' Stokes gave a hollow laugh. 'We've got a long way to go yet before we'll even let you take a piss without someone holding your dick for you.'

'Let me see her files.' Tom turned to Ortiz. 'I can go places you can't, speak to people you don't know. But I need to move fast. I need to move now.'

Ortiz went to say something, but then hesitated, his eyes again flickering towards the mirror.

'Yeah, sure!' Stokes gave a rasping laugh. 'Get a load of this guy. Our necks are already on the line and now he wants us to bend over and drop our pants too?'

'Then either charge me with something, or let me go,' Tom shouted angrily, rising to his feet. 'Right now you're just wasting my time.'

'Like I said, Kirk, you're going nowhere,' Stokes said coldly, standing up and swiping the door open.

'I'm sorry, man,' Ortiz shrugged, joining him in the doorway. 'But he's right. This is how it's got to be.'

The door sealed shut behind them and the electronic reader flashed from green to red. Saying nothing, Tom reached into his trouser pocket and felt the hard outline of the swipe card Jennifer had pressed into his hand in the helicopter.

Even then, as she lay dying, she'd known how this would play out. Even then, she'd known what he would have to do.

NINETEEN

Ospedale Fatebenefratelli, Isola Tiberina, Rome
18th March – 3.51 p.m.

Allegra had left Aurelio in yet another of his sulks. She had arrived late and was now leaving early, he had complained as she hurriedly saw herself out. She had pointedly reminded him that she was only leaving so she could follow up on a case that he was responsible for her being involved with in the first place. But by then he had turned the radio on and was pretending he couldn't hear her. No matter. All would be forgiven and forgotten by tomorrow, she knew, his moods breaking and clearing as quickly as a summer storm.

Allegra wasn't sure whether the link between the lead discs and the Delian League was meaningful or not, but one thing that she was almost certain about was that Gallo would want to know about it ASAP, so he could make that decision for himself. Normally she would have called him, but his phone appeared to have been switched off. According to his assistant, this was because there was no reception in the mortuary, where she would still catch him if she hurried.

Having signed in, she headed down to the cold store in the basement. A young man wearing a white lab coat – a medical student, she guessed, judging by his age – was manning the reception desk and glaring at a monitor.

'Colonel Gallo?' she asked, flicking her wallet open. He jumped up, deftly minimising a game of solitaire.

'You just missed him,' he replied anxiously, leaning over the top of the counter and peering down the corridor behind her as if he still might be able to see him. 'Signor Santos is still here, though.'

'Who?'

'He came in for the formal ID on Argento. Colonel Gallo thought it better that they leave separately.'

She glanced at the door he had indicated and with a curious frown stepped towards it. Peering through the port-hole she could see that it opened on to a large and resolutely featureless rectangular room, the only splash of colour coming from a few moulded blue plastic seats that were huddled for warmth around a water cooler bolted to the right-hand wall. Opposite these were a series of evenly spaced square aluminium doors, perhaps eight across and three high, each with a large levered handle and a name-tag slot. One of the doors was open; the drawer had been pulled out. A man was standing to one side of it, his back to her.

'Signor Santos?'

She pushed the door open and announced herself with a warm smile and an outstretched hand. Santos turned slowly at the sound of her voice. He was in his late forties and looked slim and fit, with a tanned face and teeth the colour of polished ivory. His close-cropped dark hair was sprinkled with silver and started high up his head where his hairline had begun to recede a little. He was immaculately dressed in a Cesare Attolini navy blazer and white flannel trousers that had been cut to crease at just the right place to slightly ride up over a pair of brown Church's. His creamy pink shirt

was from Barba in Naples, his striped tie from Marinella, and
his belt by Gucci, although given the obvious excellence of
the tailoring, this last item was clearly worn for sartorial
effect rather than to keep his trousers up.

He gave her a wary, even suspicious look that prompted
her into an explanation.

'Lieutenant Allegra Damico,' she introduced herself,
holding out her ID. 'I'm working with Colonel Gallo.'

'I see.' He smiled, returning her wallet with a nod.
'Apologies. I thought you might be from the press.'

'They're looking for you?'

'They're looking for an opportunity to snatch a photograph of an elected official grieving over his dead brother's
butchered corpse. I'm here to make sure they don't get that
chance.'

'Deputy Argento asked you to identify his brother's body
instead of him?' she guessed.

'Actually, Colonel Gallo suggested it,' he corrected her. 'He
thought it might help . . . simplify matters.'

'How did you know the victim?'

'My apologies –' Santos stepped forward with an
apologetic shrug, his hand rising to meet hers – 'I haven't
introduced myself. I am Antonio Santos, President of the
Banco Rosalia.'

He handed her his business card, the way he held it out
with both hands suggesting he had lived, or at least done a
lot of business in the Far East. It was stiff and elaborately
engraved with a sweeping copperplate script that identified
him as:

Antonio Santos
President & Director-General
Banco Rosalia

'Gio used to work for me.'

Allegra moved over to stand on the other side of the open drawer, her ghostly form reflecting indistinctly in the adjacent door's dull aluminium surface.

Giulio Argento was lying in between them, naked and shrouded by a white sheet apart from his uncovered face and where it had fallen away from his left arm, revealing a bar-coded tag fixed to his wrist like a supermarket label. She barely recognised his waxen and hollow features but there was no mistaking the ugly welt of the sword strike where it had opened up his neck like a second smile.

'Liquorice?'

She refused. There seemed something strangely inappropriate about the way Santos was shaking the ornate tin over Argento's body.

'I read that Roman soldiers could go for ten days without eating or drinking with liquorice in their rations,' he said, popping two pieces into his mouth and then slipping the tin back into his pocket. Allegra, deciding against mentioning that she had read somewhere else that too much liquorice could reduce a man's testosterone levels. 'So? Any leads? Any clues as to who did it? Why they did it?'

'I'm sorry, sir, but I can't . . .'

'I understand.' He shrugged. 'Due process, jeopardising a live investigation, respect for the victim's family . . . Gallo spun me a similar line.'

'It's for your own protection,' she insisted.

A pause. Santos looked back down at the body.

'You know, the traffic was terrible the day they found the body,' he said eventually, a strangely vacant expression on his face, as if he couldn't quite see Argento and yet knew he was there. 'Half the streets seemed to have been barricaded off. I remember being angry that it had made me late for a meeting. I never realised that . . .'

'What did Signor Argento do for you?'

'God's work.'

'In a bank?' The words came out sounding more sceptical than she had intended.

'The Vatican Bank is our largest shareholder,' he explained with the weary patience of someone who had had to give this explanation many times before. 'We take deposits in the normal way and then lend money at subsidised rates to worthy projects that might not otherwise get funding. Gio had responsibility for managing the relationships with some of our larger accounts.'

'So no reason to think that anyone would want to –'

'This?' Santos gestured with disgust. 'This is the devil's work.'

'The devil?' she asked, not sure from his expression if he meant it literally or had someone in mind.

'I trained as a priest in Rio before I realised that my true calling lay in financing God's will rather than trying to live by it.' He fiddled with the buckle of his belt, aligning it with his shirt buttons. 'But I still recognise the hand of evil when I see it.'

'Yes.' She nodded. 'Of course.' With the memory of Ricci's staring eyes and Argento's congealed scream still fresh in her mind, it was hard not to agree with him.

'The irony, of course, was that, despite working for us, poor Gio was not a true believer.' Santos glanced up at Allegra with a rueful smile. 'He used to say that life was too short to waste it worrying about what might happen when he was dead. At times like this, when it almost seems that God might have deserted us, I almost understand what he meant.'

Folding the sheet back over Argento's face, Santos made the sign of the cross and then eased the drawer back into the wall and swung the door shut. It closed with a hollow metal clang, the echo reverberating around them as if a stone slab had been dropped over a tomb. Allegra turned to leave, then paused.

'I wonder, did he ever mention an organisation or group called the Delian League?'

'The Delian League? Not as far as I remember.' Santos shook his head, frowning in thought. 'Why, who are they? Do you think they . . .?'

'It's just a name I've come across,' she reassured him with a smile. 'It probably means nothing. Shall I see you out?'

A large Mercedes with diplomatic plates was waiting for Santos on the street outside. The chauffeur jogged round and held the rear door open for him.

'A small perk of the job,' Santos smiled as he shook her hand. 'Saves me a fortune in parking tickets.'

He slipped inside and peered up at her through the open window, an earnest look on his face.

'Gio had many faults, but he was a good man, Lieutenant Damico. He deserved better. I hope you catch whoever did this to him.'

'We'll do our best,' she reassured him with a nod.

The window hummed shut and Santos settled back into his seat. As the car drew away, he reached for his phone.

'You know who it is. Don't hang up – ,' Santos said carefully when the number he had dialled was answered. 'I need a favour. And then I'm gone. For good this time, you have my word.'

TWENTY

Hotel Bel-Air, Stone Canyon Road, Los Angeles
18th March – 7.12 a.m.

Verity always sat at the same table for breakfast. In the far left corner, under the awning, behind a swaying screen of bamboo grass. It was close enough to the entrance to be seen by anyone coming in, sheltered enough not to be bothered by anyone walking past.

'Good morning, Ms Bruce.' Philippe, the maître d', bounded up to her, his French accent so comically thick that she wondered if he worked on it at home. 'Your papers.'

He handed her meticulously folded copies of the *Washington Post* and the *Financial Times*, both still warm from being pressed. Politics and money. The cogs and grease of life's little carousel, even if the deepening global economic downturn had rather slowed things recently.

'Your guest is already here.'

She pushed her sunglasses back on to her head with a frown and followed his gaze to where Earl Faulks was sitting waiting for her, absent-mindedly spinning his phone on the tablecloth.

'He tried to sit in your seat,' Philippe continued in an outraged whisper. 'I moved him, of course.'

Faulks had just turned fifty but was still striking in a gaunt, patrician sort of way, his dark hooded eyes that seemed to blink in slow motion looming above a long oval face and aquiline nose, silver hair swept back off a pale face. He was wearing a dark blue linen suit, white Charvet shirt with a cut-away collar, Cartier knot cufflinks and one of his trade-mark bow-ties. Today's offering was a series of garish salmon pink and cucumber green stripes that she assumed denoted one of his precious London clubs.

'Verity! Looking gorgeous as always.'

He rose with a smile to greet her, leaning heavily on an umbrella, an almost permanent accessory since a riding acci-dent a few years ago. She ignored him and sat down, a waiter pushing her chair in for her, the maître d' snapping her napkin on to her lap.

'Muesli with low-fat yogurt?' he asked, his tone suggesting he already knew what her answer would be.

'Yes please, Philippe.'

'And a mineral water and a pot of fresh tea?'

'With lemon.'

'Of course. And for monsieur?' He turned to Faulks, who had sat back down and was observing this ritualistic exchange with a wry smile.

'Toast. Brown. Coffee. Black.'

'Very well.' The maître d' backed away, clicking his fingers at one of the waiters to send him running to the kitchen.

Verity reached into her handbag and took out an art deco silver cigarette case engraved with flowers. Opening it care-fully, she tipped the thirty or so pills it contained into a small pile on her side plate. They lay there like pebbles, an assort-ment of vitamins and herbal supplements in different shapes and sizes and colours, some of the more translucent ones glinting like amber.

'Verity, darling, if you go on being this healthy, it'll kill you,' Faulks warned as their drinks arrived.

He was American, a shopkeeper's son from Baltimore, if you believed his detractors – of which he had amassed his fair share over the years. Not that you could detect his origins any more; his affected accent, clipped way of speaking and occasional Britishisms reminded her of a character from an Edith Wharton novel. She'd always thought it rather a shame that he didn't smoke – she imagined that a silver Dunhill lighter and a pack of Sobranies would have somehow suited the casual elegance of his slender fingers.

'I mean, what time did your trainer have you up this morning for a run? Five? Six? Only tradesmen get up that early.'

'I'm still not talking to you, Earl,' she replied, watching carefully as the waiter strained her tea and then delicately squeezed a small piece of lemon into it.

'You were the one who wanted to meet,' he reminded her. 'I was packing for the Caribbean.'

She ignored him again, although she couldn't help but feel a pang of envy. Faulks seemed to ride effortlessly in the slipstream of the super rich as their sumptuous caravan processed around the world: Gstaad in February, the Bahamas in March, the La Prairie clinic in Montreux in April for his annual check-up, London in June, Italy for the summer, New York for the winter sales, and then a well-earned rest before the whole gorgeous procession kicked off again.

She began to sort her pills into the order in which she liked to take them, although she had long since forgotten the logic by which she'd arrived at this particular sequence. Satisfied, she began to take them in silence, washing each one down with a mouthful of water and a sharp jerk of her head.

'Fine, you win,' Faulks said eventually, throwing his hands up in defeat. 'What do you want me to do? Apologise? Wear a hair shirt? Walk up the Via Dolorosa on my knees?'

'Any of those would be a start.' She glared at him.

'Even when I come bearing gifts?' He unfolded his napkin to reveal three vase fragments positioned to show that they fitted cleanly together. 'The final pieces of the Phintias *calyx krater* that you've been collecting for the past few years.' He smiled at her. 'In our profession, patience truly is a necessity, not a virtue.'

'The same fragments I seem to remember you wanted a hundred thousand for last year,' Verity said archly. 'Are you feeling generous or guilty?'

'If I had a conscience I wouldn't be in this business,' he replied with a smile, although there was something in his voice that suggested that he was only half joking. 'Let's call it a peace offering.'

'Have you any idea of the embarrassment you've caused me?'

'You have nothing to be embarrassed about,' he assured her.

'Tell that to Thierry Normand and Sir John Sykes. According to them, I paid you ten million dollars for something that was at best "anomalous", at worst a "pastiche".'

'Pastiche?' Faulks snorted. 'Did you tell them about the test results? Don't they know it's impossible to fake that sort of calcification?'

'By then they weren't listening.'

'You mean they didn't want to hear,' he corrected her. 'Don't you see, Verity, darling, that they're all jealous. Jealous of your success. Jealous that while their donors have pulled back as the recession has begun to bite, the Getty remains blessed with a three-billion-dollar endowment.'

'Sometimes I think it's more a curse than a blessing,' she

sniffed. 'Do you know we have to spend four and a quarter per cent of that a year or lose our tax status? Have you any idea how hard it is to get through one hundred and twenty-seven million dollars a year? Of the pressure it puts us under?'

'I can only imagine,' he commiserated, shaking his head. 'That's why the kouros was a smart buy. After all, don't you think the Met would have made a move if they'd been given even half a chance? But you beat them to it.'

'Vivienne Foyle *is* close to the Met.' She nodded grudgingly, remembering how she had twisted the knife right at the end. 'She's never liked me.'

'The problem here isn't the kouros,' Faulks insisted, his full baritone voice taking on the fervent conviction of a TV evangelist. 'The problem is people's unwillingness to accept that their carefully constructed picture of how Greek sculpture developed over the centuries might need to be rewritten. They should be thanking you for opening their eyes, for deepening their understanding, for extending the boundaries of their knowledge. Instead, they're seeking to discredit you, just as the church did with Galileo.'

She nodded, rather liking this image of herself as an academic revolutionary that the establishment was desperate to silence at all costs. The problem was, she didn't have the time or the temperament to become a martyr.

'I agree with you. If I didn't, the kouros would already be on its way back to Geneva. But the damage is done. Even if they're wrong, it'll take years for them to admit it. Meanwhile the director can't look me in the eye, the trustees have asked for a second round of tests, and the *New York Times* is threatening to run a piece at the weekend. I mean, what if something else comes out?'

'Nothing else will come out,' Faulks said slowly, his voice suddenly hard. 'Not unless someone's planning to talk. And nobody's planning to talk, are they, Verity?'

It was phrased as a question, but there was no doubting that he was giving her a very clear instruction. Maybe even a warning.

'Why would I risk everything we've achieved together?' she said quickly.

'You wouldn't,' he said, his eyes locked unblinkingly with hers. 'But others . . . well. I don't like to be disappointed.'

There was an icy edge to his voice and she gulped down a few more pills, wishing that she'd packed some Valium as well. Almost immediately, however, Faulks's face thawed into a warm smile.

'Anyway, let's not worry about that now. I understand that you're upset. And I want to make it up to you. What are you doing tomorrow?'

'Tomorrow?' She frowned. 'Tomorrow I'll be in Madrid. The US ambassador is hosting a two-day cultural exchange. We fly out this afternoon. Why?'

'There's something I want to show you.' He reached inside his jacket and handed her a Polaroid. 'I was hoping you might come to Geneva.'

'Do you really think that, after what happened yesterday, the director is going to let me buy anything from you again?' she asked, taking the photo from him with an indifferent shrug.

'You won't have to. It'll come to you as a donation.'

She glanced down at the photo, then heard herself gasp.

'Is it . . .?' she whispered, her mouth suddenly dry, her hands trembling, her chest tight.

'Genuine? Absolutely,' he reassured her. 'I've seen it myself. There's no question.'

'But no one has ever found . . .'

'I know.' He gave her a schoolboy's wide grin. 'Isn't it wonderful?'

'Who's it by?'

'Come now, Verity – 450 BC? Can't you guess?'

There was a pause, her eyes still not having lifted from the photograph.

'Where is it now?'

'On its way to me.'

'Provenance?'

'Private Lebanese collection since the 1890s. I have all the documentation.'

Another pause as she carefully placed the photograph on the table, sipped some water and then looked up hungrily.

'I have to see it.'

TWENTY-ONE

Headquarters of the Guarda di Finanza, Viale XXI Aprile, Rome
18th March – 4.25 p.m.

The headquarters of the Guarda di Finanza was located to the north-east of the city centre, just beyond the Porta Pia. It occupied a Spanish-looking building, with shutters at every window and its walls painted a dusty yellow and rich ochre colour. The main entrance was surmounted by the Italian and European Union flags, but these were sagging limply, the light breeze that was chasing the rain clouds away registering only in the rustling fronds of the palm tree that stood to the left of the door.

In a way, Allegra reflected as she stepped out of her taxi, it was perhaps better for her to catch up with Gallo here, rather than at the mortuary. This, after all, was where the physical evidence from the two murders was being kept, giving her the opportunity to have another look at the lead discs in the light of what Aurelio had told her and to get her story straight before seeing him.

Not that the decision to house the evidence here would have been a simple one, given all the different law enforcement

agencies with a potential stake in this case. The Guarda di
Finanza, for one, was a sprawling empire, covering not only
Gallo's organised crime unit but a variety of money-related
crimes such as tax evasion, Customs and border checks, money
laundering, smuggling, international drugs trafficking and counterfeiting. A military corps, it even had its own naval fleet and
air force.

Allegra's art and antiques unit, meanwhile, was part of the
Arma dei Carabinieri, a paramilitary force with police duties
that also oversaw counter-terrorism operations, the forensic
bureau, the military police, undercover investigations and,
bizarrely, sanitary enforcement.

Then, of course, there was the state police, a civilian
force that, as well as having responsibility for routine
patrolling, investigative and law enforcement duties, also
oversaw the armed, postal, highway and transport police
forces. And this was not to forget the various layers of
provincial, municipal and local police, prison officers, park
rangers and the coast guard who further crowded the
picture.

In fact, Allegra seemed to remember from one of the
induction lectures she had had to endure upon first joining
up, any one area in Italy could theoretically be under the
jurisdiction of up to thirty-one different police or police-
type forces. Unsurprisingly, this resulted in a sea-fog of
overlapping responsibilities, unclear accountabilities and red
tape that more often than not led to the different agencies
competing against each other when they should have been
collaborating.

Allegra's temporary secondment from the Carabinieri to
their fierce rivals at the Guarda di Finanza was, therefore, a
relatively unusual request on Gallo's part, as proved by the
raised eyebrows of the duty officer who buzzed her in and
directed her towards the basement.

Following the signs, she found the evidence store next to the armoury. It was secured by a steel door with a lock but no handle, suggesting that it could only be opened from the inside. Next to it, a low counter had been chopped out of the reinforced concrete wall. An elderly officer in a neatly pressed grey uniform with gold buttons and a green beret was sitting on the other side behind a screen of bullet-proof glass. Allegra knocked on the window and then placed her ID flat against it.

'You're a long way from home, Lieutenant.' The man gave her a quizzical look over the top of his glasses, his feet up and the newspaper resting across his knee. His badge identified him as Enrico Gambetta.

'I've been seconded on to the Argento case,' she explained.

'You're working with Colonel Gallo!' Gambetta struggled to his feet, anxiously peering out into the corridor as if he half expected Gallo to jump out of the shadows.

'Until he decides he doesn't need me any more,' she said, unable to stop herself wondering what strange gravitational anomaly was securing Gambetta's trousers around his enormous waist.

'So he got my message?' he asked excitedly. 'He sent you to see me.'

'Your message?' She frowned.

'About the other murder.'

'I haven't spoken to him all afternoon,' she said with a shrug. 'I was just hoping to take another look at the lead discs from the Argento and Ricci killings before I see him.'

'The lead disc – exactly!' He beamed, looking like he might break into a lumbering jig. 'Like the ones you found in their mouths, right?'

'How do you know that?' Allegra asked sharply.

'When you've been around as long as I have, you get to hear about most things.' He winked. 'Now, I can't really let you sign it out, but . . .' He paused, clearly trying to decide what to do. 'Wait there.'

A few moments later there was the sound of bolts being thrown back and the steel door opened. Gambetta stuck his head out into the corridor and, having checked that it was empty, ushered her inside.

'Are you sure I'm allowed to . . .?' she began, frowning.

'I won't tell if you won't,' he whispered, as if afraid of being overheard. 'But I need to show somebody. Are you carrying?'

'Yes.' She swept her jacket back to reveal the gun holstered to her waist.

'Pick it up on your way out.' He tapped his desk, the determined look on his face telling her that this was one rule he clearly wasn't prepared to turn a blind-eye to.

'Of course.'

The room was divided into five narrow aisles by a series of floor-to-ceiling metal shelving units. Waddling unsteadily, Gambetta led her down the second aisle. Allegra blinked as she followed him, her eyes adjusting to the anaemic glow of the overhead strip lighting that was competing for ceiling space with a snaking mass of heavily lagged water pipes and colour-coded electrical cabling. Even so, she could see that the shelves were crammed with hundreds, if not thousands, of cardboard boxes and plastic evidence bags, each one sealed and diligently identified by a white tag.

'They think that all we do down here all day is sit on our arses and read the paper,' Gambetta moaned, grabbing hold of a small set of steps and wheeling them ahead of him, one of the wheels juddering noisily on the concrete. 'They forget that we have to check every piece of evidence in, and every piece out.'

'Mmm.' Allegra nodded, wondering how on earth he managed to bend down to tie his shoes every day, until she realised that he was wearing slip-ons. Not that that accounted for his socks.

'Most of the time they barely know what the people in their own teams are doing, let alone the other units,' he called back excitedly over his shoulder. 'That's why they missed it.'

The neon tube above where he had stopped was failing, the light stuttering on and off with a loud buzzing noise, creating a strange strobing effect. Climbing up the steps, he retrieved a box that Allegra could see was marked *Cavalli* and dated the fifteenth of March.

'It's the Ricci and Argento cases I'm interested in,' she reminded him impatiently, but he had already placed the box on the top step and ripped the seal off.

'Three murders in three days. They may have me stuck down here in the dark with the rats and the boiler, but I'm not stupid.' He tapped the side of his head with a grin.

'Three murders?' She frowned.

'I left the details on Gallo's answer machine: Luca Cavalli. A lawyer from Melfi they found hanging from the Ponte Sant'Angelo with this in one of his pockets –'

He reached into the box and handed her a clear evidence bag. It contained a small lead disc, the plastic slippery against its dull surface as if it had been coated with a thin layer of oil. And engraved on one side, just about visible in the flickering light, was the outline of two snakes and a clenched fist.

TWENTY-TWO

J. Edgar Hoover Building, FBI headquarters,
Washington DC
18th March – 10.31 a.m.

Tom had given them half an hour or so before making his move. Long enough for Ortiz, Stokes and whoever else had been lurking on the other side of the two-way mirror to have dispersed, but not so long for them to feel the need to check up on him again.

Stepping quickly to the door he flashed Jennifer's pass through the reader. The device beeped, its light flashing from red to green as the magnetic seal was released. The FBI was good at many things but, as he had suspected, operational efficiency wasn't one of them. News of Jennifer's death would still barely have reached the Bureau's higher grades, let alone filtered down to the foot soldiers who manned the IT and security systems. That gave him a small window of opportunity that would last until someone joined the dots and triggered whatever protocol disabled her access rights and log-ons.

Tom found himself momentarily clinging to this thought. In a way, it was almost as if she wasn't really dead yet, kept alive instead in a sort of digital limbo. Not that it would last, he realised with a heavy heart. Soon a remorseless and faceless bureaucracy would see to it that the delicate electronic threads to Jennifer's life were severed. One by one, bank accounts, driver's licence, social security number, email addresses would all lapse or be cancelled, each heavy keystroke and deleted file wiping a little more of her from the world, until all that would remain were his fading memories.

Swallowing hard and trying to clear his head, Tom ripped the fire evacuation instructions off the back of the door and stepped out into a white corridor. Not wanting to appear lost amidst the thin trickle of people making their way along it, he immediately turned to his right and followed the arrows on the map at the top of the laminated sheet towards what looked like the main fire escape stairwell.

Just before he reached it, however, he came across an open doorway. Glancing inside, he could see that it appeared to be some sort of storeroom – a photocopier idling in the corner, pens, paper and envelopes carefully sorted by type and size stacked on the shelves. More promising was the blue FBI jacket that someone had left hanging over the back of a chair and the internal phone screwed to the wall. Darting inside he slipped the jacket on as a rudimentary disguise, then dialled the operator.

'I'm trying to find Jennifer Browne's office,' He explained when the call was answered. 'She's normally based in New York with the Art Crime Team, but she's been spending some time here lately. I wanted to swing by and surprise her.'

'Let's see,' the voice came back, her fingernails tap-dancing noisily on her keyboard in the background. 'Browne, Jennifer. Oh yeah, she's got her calls diverting to Phil Tucker's office up on five while he's on leave.'

Memorising the room number, Tom slipped back out into

the corridor and headed for the stairwell. He knew that this was a long-shot, that the odds of him getting out of this building undetected and with what he needed were slim. But he'd rather take his chances out here, where he at least had some say in the outcome, than sit in a dark room while Jennifer's killer slipped even further over the horizon. He owed her that at least. He wouldn't allow her to fade away.

Clearing the call, the operator immediately dialled another extension.

'Yes, good morning, sir, it's the switchboard. I'm sorry to bother you, but you asked that we should let you know if anyone asked for the location of Special Agent Browne's office. Well, someone just did.'

TWENTY-THREE

Headquarters of the Guarda di Finanza, Viale XXI Aprile, Rome
18th March – 4.36 p.m.

'When was this?' Allegra asked, returning the bag containing the lead disc with a puzzled frown.

'The fifteenth,' Gambetta replied, placing it carefully back in the box.

'The fifteenth?' she shot back incredulously. 'He died on the fifteenth of March? Are you sure?'

'That's what it said in the case file,' he confirmed, looking startled by her reaction. 'Why?'

The fifteenth was the Ides of March, the same day that Caesar had been killed over two thousand years before. Cavalli and Ricci's murders weren't just linked by the lead disc. They were echoes of each other.

'What was he doing in Rome?' she asked, ignoring his question.

'He owned a place over in Travestere. Was probably up and down here on business.'

'Who found him?'

'River police on a routine patrol. He was hanging from

one of the statues on the bridge – the Angel with the Cross, from what I can remember. Their first thought was that it was a suicide, until some bright spark pointed out that his wrists were tied behind his back. Not to mention that the rope would have decapitated him if he'd jumped from that height.'

'You mean he was deliberately lowered into the water?' Allegra asked in a sceptical tone.

'The current there is quite strong. Whoever killed him clearly wanted to draw it out. Make sure he suffered.'

She detected the same hint of horrified fascination in Gambetta's voice that she'd noticed in herself when she'd first caught sight of Ricci's body.

'Why's the GDF involved? It sounds more like one for the local Questura.'

'It was, until they impounded his Maserati near the Due Ponti metro and found fifty thousand euro in counterfeit notes lining the spare wheel. Anything to do with currency fraud gets referred here.'

She nodded slowly, her excitement at this unexpected breakthrough tempered by the depressing thought that this was probably going to make an already difficult case even more complicated. Something of her concern must have shown in her face because Gambetta fixed her with a worried look.

'Is everything okay? I hope I haven't . . .'

'You did the right thing,' she reassured him. 'I'm sure Colonel Gallo will want to come down here in person to thank you.'

Gambetta beamed, a vain attempt to pull his stomach in and push his chest out making his face flush.

'Do you mind if I have a quick look through the rest of Cavalli's stuff?'

'Of course not. Here, I'll move it over there where you

can see properly.' He scooped the box up and led her a short way further down the aisle to where a battered angle-poise lamp decorated with the small stickers found on imported fruit had been arranged on a folding table. 'That's better.'

'Much,' she smiled. 'You've been incredibly –'

There was a rap against the counter window at the far end of the room. Gambetta placed his fingers against his lips.

'Wait here,' he whispered conspiratorially. 'I'll get rid of them.'

He lumbered back towards the entrance, leaving Allegra to go through the rest of the contents of the box. Much of it was what you'd expect to find in someone's pockets: a mobile phone – no longer working – some loose change, reading glasses, a damp box of matches and an empty pack of Marlboro Lights. His wallet, meanwhile, as loaded with the standard everyman paraphernalia of cash, bank cards, identity card and an assortment of disintegrating restaurant receipts.

There was a nice watch too – round and simple with a white face, elegant black Roman numerals and a scrolling date. Unusually, apart from the Greek letter Gamma engraved on the back of the stainless steel case, it seemed to have no make or logo marked anywhere on it, featuring instead a distinctive bright orange second hand which stood out against the muted background. Finally there was a set of keys – house and car, judging from the Maserati key fob.

An angry shout made her glance up towards the entrance. Gambetta seemed to be having an argument with the person on the other side of the window, his voice echoing towards her. As she watched, he stepped away from the window, unclipped his keys from his belt, and waved at her to get back.

Allegra didn't have to be told what to do. Still clutching Cavalli's keys, she retreated to the far end of the aisle and hid. Gambetta had done her a favour by letting her in here and the last thing she wanted to do was get him in trouble. Even so, she couldn't quite resist peering around the edge of the pier as he unbolted the door.

She never even saw the gun, the rolling echo of the shot's silenced thump breaking over her like a wave before she'd even realised what was happening. The next thing she knew, Gambetta was staggering back, his arms flailing at his throat, legs buckling like an elephant caught in a poacher's snare. He swayed unsteadily for a few moments longer, desperately trying to stay on his feet. Then, with a bellow, he crashed to the concrete floor.

TWENTY-FOUR

**J. Edgar Hoover Building, FBI headquarters,
Washington DC
18th March – 10.37 a.m.**

The fifth floor was much busier than the one he had just come from. Even so, Tom wasn't worried about being recognised. Of the eight thousand or so people who worked out of this building, he doubted whether any more than five knew who he was. And rather than hinder him, the floor's bustling, largely open-plan configuration made it easier for him to blend in and move around unchallenged.

What was immediately clear, however, was that here, news of what had happened last night in Vegas had already spread. There was a strained atmosphere, people going about their usual business with a forced normality, judging from their sombre faces and the irritable edge to their voices. Tom, it seemed, wasn't the only one who was finding comfort in anger's rough-hewn arms. And yet, amidst the bitterness, he detected something else in people's eyes, something unsaid but no less powerfully felt. Relief. Relief that it hadn't been them. He wondered how many people had called up their wives or boyfriends or children this morning upon hearing what had happened, just to hear the sound of their voice. Just to let them know that they were okay.

As the operator had suggested, Tom found the room Jennifer had been camping out in the north-eastern quadrant of the building. Like all the other offices that lined the perimeter of the floor, it was essentially a glass box, albeit one with a view of 9th Street and a nameplate denoting the identity of its rightful owner – Phil Tucker. Unlike the rooms which flanked it, however, its door was shut and all the blinds drawn in what Tom assumed was a subtle and yet deliberately symbolic mark of respect. Less clear was whether this was a spontaneous reaction to Jennifer's death or part of some well-defined and yet unwritten mourning ritual that was observed whenever a colleague fell in the line of duty. Either way, it suited him well, concealing him from view once he had satisfied himself that no one was watching him and slipped inside.

Almost immediately, Tom's heart sank. Perhaps without realising it until now, he had secretly been hoping to find a bit more of Jennifer here, even though he knew that this had only ever been a very recent and temporary home for her. Instead it boasted a sterile anonymity that was only partly lifted by Tucker's scattered photographs and random personal trinkets. Then again, he couldn't help but wonder if Jennifer's hand wasn't perhaps present in the clinical symmetry of the pens laid out on the desktop and the ordered stack of files and papers on the bookshelf, that he suspected had probably been littering the floor when she had first taken ownership of the room. And there was no debating who was responsible for the lipstick-smeared rim of the polystyrene cup that was still nestling in the trash. He gave a rueful smile. She had been here, after all. He was a guest, not an intruder.

The safe was in a cupboard under the bookshelf. With a weary sigh, he saw that it was protected by both a password and voice-recognition software, two red lights glowing ominously over the small input screen. Tricky. Very tricky, unless . . . He glanced up at her desk hopefully. The light on her phone was glowing red to indicate that somebody had left her a voicemail. With any luck, that also meant that she'd recorded a greeting.

He picked the phone up and dialled Jennifer's extension, the second line beeping furiously until it tripped over into the voicemail system.

'You've reached Special Agent Jennifer Browne in the FBI's Art Crime Team . . .' Tom's stomach flipped over at the sound of her voice, as if he'd just gone over a sharp hump in the road. She sounded so close, so real that for a moment it was almost as if . . . It was no use, he knew. This was an illusion that would dissolve the moment he tried to warp his arms around it. He needed to stay focused. 'Please leave a message . . .'

He replaced the handset. That would do. Now for the password. He bent down and opened each of the desk drawers, guessing that the lipstick on the cup was a sign that Jennifer, for all her refusal to play conventional sexual politics at work, had still occasionally worn make-up. He was right. The third drawer down yielded a small make-up bag and within that, a powder brush.

Kneeling next to the safe, he gently dusted the brush over the keys and then carefully blew away the excess. The result certainly wasn't good enough to lift prints from, but it did allow him to see which keys had been most recently and heavily used, the powder sticking more thickly to the sweat left there.

Reading from left to right, this highlighted the letters A, C, R, V, G, I and O. Tom jotted them down in a circle on a piece of paper, knowing that they formed an anagram of some other word, although there was no way of telling how many times each letter had been used. The key was to try and get inside Jennifer's head. She would have chosen something current, something relevant to what she had been working on. A name, a place, a person . . . Tom smiled, seeing that the last three letters had given him an obvious clue. G, I, O – Caravaggio, perhaps? He typed the word in and one of the two lights flashed green.

Reaching the phone down from the desk, he listened to Jennifer's greeting a few more times to get a feel for the timing of exactly when she said her name. Then, just at the right moment, he placed the handset against the microphone before quickly snatching it away again. The second light flashed green. With a whir, the door sprang open.

He reached inside and pulled out a handful of files and a stack of surveillance DVDs. Returning the discs to the safe, he flicked through the files, discarding them all apart from one that Jennifer had initialled in her characteristically slanting hand.

Sitting at the desk, he unsealed the file and scanned through it, quickly recognising in the typed pages and photographs the details of the case that Jennifer had laid out for him on their way to Vegas. The anonymous Customs tip-off. The discovery of the Eileen Gray furniture hidden in the container. The tracing of the container to a warehouse in Queen's. The raid on the warehouse and the discovery of an Aladdin's cave of illegally exported antiquities. The panic-stricken dealer's stumbling confession. A copy of his doodled sketch of the two snakes wrapped around a clenched fist, the symbol of the so-called Delian League that the forensic lab had reconstituted from strips of yellow paper recovered from his shredding bin. Bank statements. An auction catalogue. And, of course, the name provided by the dealer which Jennifer had passed on to the Italian authorities who had rewarded her with an address in Rome and a promise to follow-up: Luca Cavalli, Vicolo de Panieri, Travestere. It wasn't much, but it was a start.

Closing the file with a satisfied smile he stood up, only to brush against the mouse as he turned to leave. The log-on screen immediately flickered on, the cursor flashing tauntingly at him. He stared at it for a few moments and then, shrugging, sat down again. It was worth a try.

TWENTY-FIVE

**Headquarters of the Guarda di Finanza, Viale XXI
Aprile, Rome
18th March – 4.41 p.m.**

Allegra snatched her head back, heart thudding, fist clenched, the teeth of Cavalli's keys biting into her palm. Gambetta shot. No, executed. Executed here, right in front of her, in the basement of the Guarda di Finanza headquarters. It was ridiculous. It was impossible. And yet she'd seen it. She'd seen it and she only had to close her eyes to see it all over again.

Now wasn't the time to panic, she knew. She needed to stay calm, think through her options. Not that she had many, beyond staying exactly where she was. Not with her gun stranded on the edge of Gambetta's desk and only the length of the room separating her from the killer. Perhaps if she was quiet, she reasoned, he wouldn't even realise . . .

The sudden hiss of polyester on concrete interrupted her skittering thoughts. She frowned, at first unable to place the noise, until with a sickening lurch of her stomach she realised that it was the sound of Gambetta's corpse being dragged towards her.

She knew immediately what she had to do. Move. Move now while she still could; while the killer was still far enough away not to see or hear her. In a way, he'd made things easier for her. Now all she had to do was figure out which aisle he was coming down. As soon as she knew that, she'd be able to creep back to the entrance up one of the other ones. At least, that was the idea.

She shut her eyes and concentrated on the noise of the fabric of Gambetta's uniform catching on the tiny imperfections in the concrete, fighting her instinct to run as the tick-tock of the killer's breathing got closer and closer, knowing that she had to be absolutely sure. Then, when it seemed that he must be almost on top of her, she opened them again. The second aisle. She was sure of it. The one she'd been standing in a few moments before when looking through Cavalli's evidence box.

Taking a deep breath, she edged her head around the pier and peeked along the first aisle. It was empty. Her eyes briefly fluttered shut with relief. Then, crouching down, she slipped her shoes off and began to creep towards the exit, her stockinged feet sliding silkily across the cold floor. But she'd scarcely gone ten yards before suddenly, almost involuntarily, she paused.

She could see the killer.

Not his face, of course, but his back; through a narrow gap between the shelves as he dragged Gambetta towards her. Maybe if she . . .? No, she dismissed the thought almost as soon as it had occurred to her. It was stupid; she needed to get out of here while she still could. But then again, she couldn't help herself thinking, what if someone here was working with him? It would certainly explain how he had got in. What if they now helped him escape in the confusion once she raised the alarm? She couldn't risk that, not after what he'd done. A glimpse of his face, that was all she needed. Just enough to be able to give a description, if it came to that. If she was careful and stayed out of the light, he wouldn't even know she was there.

Her mind made up, she edged carefully forward, trying to find a place where she could stand up without being seen, occasionally seeing the blur of the killer's leg and his black shoes through cracks in the shelving as he backed towards her. Then, without warning, when he was almost parallel to her, Gambetta's feet fell to the floor with an echoing thud.

Sensing her chance, she slowly straightened up, occasional gaps and openings between the shelves giving her a first glimpse of a belt, then the arrow tip of a tie, followed by the buttons of his jacket and finally the starched whiteness of his collar and the soft pallor of his throat through a narrow slit between two boxes.

There. She could see his face, or rather the outline of it, the overhead neon tube having blinked off yet again. Holding her breath, she waited until, with a clinking noise, the light stuttered on again, the image strobing briefly across her retina until it finally settled.

It was Gallo.

She instinctively snatched her head back, but the sudden blur of movement must have caught his eye because he called out angrily.

There was no time to think. No time to do anything. Except run. Run to the door, throw the bolts back, tumble through it, stumble up the steps and stagger out into the street, gasping with shock.

The world on its head.

TWENTY-SIX

J. Edgar Hoover Building, FBI headquarters, Washington DC
18th March – 10.47 a.m.

Tom had found Jennifer's password taped to the underside of the stapler. No great mystery there. It was always the same in these large organisations. Obsessed by security, IT insisted on people using 'strong' passwords that had to be changed every five minutes, and then claimed to be surprised when people chose to write them down. What else did they expect when most people struggled to remember their wedding anniversary, let alone a randomly assigned and ever-changing ten-character alphanumeric code. The government was the worst offender of all.

He typed the password in and hit the enter key. Almost immediately the screen went blue. Then it sounded a long, strident beep. Finally it flashed up an ominously bland error message.

User ID and password not recognised. Please remain at your desk and an IT security representative will be with you shortly.

The phone started to ring. Tom checked the display and saw that it was Stokes, presumably tipped off by some clever piece of software that someone was trying to access Jennifer's account. The Bureau was clearly more nimble and joined up than Tom had given them credit for earlier.

Shoving the file under his jacket, he leapt across to the door and, gingerly lifting the blind, looked outside. To his relief, everything seemed normal, the people working in the open-plan team room on the other side of the corridor still gazing into their screens or talking on the phone. Checking that no one was coming, he slipped out of the office and headed back towards the stairs and swiped the door open.

Almost immediately he jumped back, the stairwell thundering with the sound of heavy footsteps and urgent shouts that he knew instinctively were heading towards him. He glanced around, looking for somewhere to hide and realising that he had only moments to find it. But before he could move, he felt a heavy hand grip his shoulder. He spun round. It was Ortiz, his chest heaving, eyes staring.

'This way,' he wheezed, urging him towards an open office. 'Quickly.'

Tom hesitated for a fraction of a second, but the lack of a better option quickly made up his mind for him. Following him inside, Tom watched as Ortiz shut the door behind him and let the blinds drop with a fizz of nylon through his fingers.

'Can you really find them?' he panted, peering through a narrow crack as a group of armed men, led by Stokes, charged past them towards Jennifer's office.

'What?' Tom asked, not sure he'd heard right.

'Jennifer's killers? Can you find them?' Ortiz repeated, spinning round to face him, his face glistening, the half-hidden tattoo on his neck pulsing as if it was alive.

'I can find them.' Tom nodded. 'If I can get out of here, I can find them.'

Ortiz stared at him unblinkingly, as if trying to look for the trap that might be lurking behind Tom's eyes.

'Where are you going to go?'

'It's probably better you don't know.'

'What will you do?'

'Whatever I have to,' Tom reassured him in a cold voice. 'What you can't. What Jennifer deserves.'

Ortiz nodded slowly and gave a deep sigh, Tom's words seeming to calm him.

'Good.' He stepped forward and pressed his card into Tom's hand, pulling him closer until their faces were only inches apart. 'Just call me when it's done.'

Releasing his grip, Ortiz reached out and with a jerk of his wrist, flicked the fire alarm switch. The siren's shrill cry split the air.

'Go,' he muttered, his eyes dropping to the floor. 'Get outside with everyone else before I change my mind.'

With a nod, Tom sprinted back towards the stairwell, the siren bouncing deliriously off the walls. Taking the steps two at a time, he raced down towards the ground floor, doors above and below him crashing open as people streamed on to the staircase, their excited voices suggesting that they knew this wasn't a drill.

As he cleared the first-floor landing, however, he was forced to slow to a walk, the crowd backing up ahead of him. Peering over their heads, he saw that a line of security guards was quickly checking everyone's ID before allowing them to leave the building. Had Stokes tipped them off, guessing that he might be using the alarm as cover? Either way, Tom had to do something and do something quickly, before the tide of people behind him swept him into the guards' waiting arms.

Waiting until he was almost at the bottom of the penultimate flight of stairs, Tom deliberately tripped the man ahead of him and, with a sharp shove, sent him crashing into the wall opposite. He smacked into it with a sickening crunch, a deep gash opening up in his forehead, the blood streaming down his face.

'Let me through,' Tom called, hauling the dazed man to his feet and throwing his arm around his shoulder. 'Let me through.'

'Get out the way,' somebody above him called.

'Get back,' someone else echoed. 'Man down.'

Seeing Tom staggering towards them, one of the guards stepped forward and supported the injured man on the other side. Together they lifted him along the narrow path that had miraculously opened through the middle of the crowd, people grimacing in sympathy at the unnatural angle of the man's nose.

'He needs a doctor,' Tom called urgently. 'He's losing a lot of blood.'

'This way, sir.'

The line of guards parted to let them through, another officer escorting them clear as he radioed for a medic. Reaching a safe distance, they sat the still groggy man down on the sidewalk, an ambulance announcing its arrival moments later by unnecessarily laying down three feet of rubber as it stopped. The paramedics jumped out, threw a foil blanket around the man's shoulders and pressed a wet compress against his nose to stem the flow. Tom stepped back, leaving the two guards to crowd round with words of advice and encouragement. Then, seeing that no one was watching, he turned and walked away.

Standing at a seventh-storey window, FBI Director Green watched Tom disappear down D Street with a smile. Smartly dressed with a crisp parting in his brown hair, plump cheeks and perfectly capped teeth, he was engaged in a running battle with his weight, the various scarred notches on his belt showing the yo-yo fluctuations of his waistline.

He knew Kirk well enough to guess that he'd find a way out of that room and that, when he did, he'd head straight for Browne's safe. That's why he'd ordered her swipe card not to be cancelled. That's why he'd briefed the operator to let him know if anyone called asking for directions to her office.

The truth was that Kirk was her best chance now. While the Bureau was holding its collective dick worrying about who was going to get blamed for one of its most promising young agents getting killed, Kirk would be out there making things happen. Browne had trusted Kirk with her life many times before now. It seemed only right to trust him with her death too.

TWENTY-SEVEN

Viale XXI Aprile, Rome
18th March – 4.51 p.m.

Panting, Allegra sprinted on to the Via Gaetano Moroni and then right on to Via Luigi Pigorini, the cars here parked with typical Roman indifference – some up on the kerb, others end-on to fit into an impossibly narrow gap.

Gallo . . . a killer? It made no sense. It was impossible. But how could she ignore what she'd seen? The shots fired from the doorway; Gambetta staggering backwards and toppling to the floor like a felled tree; Gallo's animal grunt as he had hauled the carcass across the concrete; his stony face and cold eyes.

She found her stride, her ragged breathing slowly falling into a more comfortable rhythm, her thoughts settling.

Had Gallo seen her face? She wasn't sure. Either way, it wouldn't take him long to pull the security footage. The only thing that mattered now was getting as far away from him as she could.

Seeing a taxi, she flagged it down and settled with relief into the back seat as she gave him her home address up on the Aventine Hill.

Whether Gallo had seen her or not, at least his motives seemed pretty clear. He'd killed Gambetta so that he couldn't tell anyone else about his discovery of the links between the murders. Why else would he have paused under the faltering neon light where Gambetta had taken Cavalli's evidence box down from its shelf. He'd been looking for the lead disc, so that no one else would think or know to make the connection. No one apart from her.

'What number?' the driver called back over his shoulder ten minutes later as they drew on to the Via Guerrieri.

'Drive to the end,' she ordered.

With a shrug, he accelerated down the street, tyres drumming on the cobbles as Allegra sank low into her seat and peered cautiously over the edge of the window sill.

There. About fifty yards past the entrance to her apartment. A dark blue Alfa with two men sat in the front, their mirrors set at an unnatural angle so they could see back up the street behind them. She didn't recognise the driver as they flashed past, but the passenger . . . the passenger, she realised with a sinking heart, was Salvatore. Not only had Gallo clearly seen her, but he had already unleashed his men on to her trail.

'Keep going,' she called, keeping her head down. 'I've changed my mind. Take me to . . . Take me to the Via Galvani,' she ordered, settling on the only other place she could think of. 'It's off the Via Marmorata.'

Making a face, the driver mumbled something about women and directions, only to roll his eyes when they reached the Via Galvani ten minutes later and she again asked him to drive down it without stopping.

'Do you even know where you're going?' he called back tersely over his shoulder.

'Does it even matter as long as you get paid?' she snapped as she warily scanned the street. This time there was no sign of Gallo or any of his men. 'Here, this will do.'

Paying him, she got out and walked back up the street towards Aurelio's apartment.

'*Ego sum principium mundi et finis sæculorum attamen non sum deus,*' came the voice from the speaker.

'Not now, Aurelio,' Allegra snapped. 'Just let me in.'

There was the briefest of pauses. Then the door buzzed open. She made her way to the lift. Aurelio was waiting for her on the landing, a worried look on his face.

'What's happened?' he asked as she stepped out.

'I'm in trouble.'

'I can see that. Come in.'

He led her silently into his office and perched anxiously on one arm of his leather chair rather than settling back into his seat as usual. Pacing from one side of the room to the other and speaking in as dispassionate a tone as she could, she described what she'd seen and heard: the Cavalli murder; the engraved discs; Gambetta's shooting; the flickering shadow of Gallo's pale face. Aurelio listened to all this while turning over a small piece of broken tile in his hands, studying it intently as if looking for something. When she eventually finished, there was a long silence.

'It's my fault.' He spoke with a cold whisper. 'If I'd known . . . I should never have got you involved with any of this.'

'If you want to blame someone, blame Gallo,' she insisted with a hollow laugh.

'I know someone. A detective in the police,' Aurelio volunteered. 'I could call him and –'

'No,' she cut him off with a firm shake of her head. 'No police. Not until I understand what's going on. Not until I know who I can trust.'

'Then what do you need?'

'A place to stay. A coffee. Some answers.'

'The first two I can help with. The third . . . well, the third we might have to work on together.'

'Two out of three's a good start.' She bent down and planted a grateful kiss on his forehead.

'I should offer to make the coffee more often.' He grinned. 'Here, sit.' Aurelio stood up and pulled her towards his chair. 'Rest.'

She shut her eyes and tried to clear her mind, finding the familiar smell of Aurelio's aftershave and the merry clatter of pans and clink of crockery as he busied himself in the kitchen strangely comforting. For a few seconds she imagined herself back at home, perched on the worktop, eagerly telling her mother about what had happened that day at school while she prepared dinner. But almost immediately her eyes snapped open.

Rest? How could she rest, after what she'd just seen? How could she rest, with Gallo out there somewhere, looking for her.

She jumped up and padded cautiously to the window, standing to one side so she could check the street below without being seen. It was empty. Good. As far as she knew, she'd never spoken to Gallo or anyone else on the team about her friendship with Aurelio, so there was no reason to think they would come looking for her here. Not that she was in a position to put up much of a fight if they did, given that she was unarmed.

The realisation made her feel strangely vulnerable, and she patted her hip regretfully, missing her weapon's reassuring solidity and steadying ballast. If only . . . she had a sudden thought and glanced across at Aurelio's desk. Somewhere inside it, she seemed to remember, he had a gun. It was completely illegal, of course – a Soviet Makarov PM that he'd picked up in a souk to protect himself from the local bandits while working on a dig in Anatalya. But right now, she wasn't sure that mattered.

She crossed over to the desk, noticing the closely typed notes for a lecture that according to the cover page Aurelio was giving at the Galleria Doria Pamphilj the following day. Crouching down next to it, she tried each of the overflowing drawers in turn, her fingers eventually closing around the weapon at the back of the third drawer, behind some cassette tapes and a fistful of receipts.

She slid out the eight-round magazine. It was full and she tapped it sharply against the desk in case the spring was stiff and the bullets had slipped away from the front of the casing. The gun itself was well maintained and looked like it had recently been oiled, the slide pulling back easily, the hammer firing with a satisfyingly solid click. It wasn't much, she knew, but it was certainly better than nothing. Satisfied, she slapped the magazine home.

Deriving a renewed confidence from her find, she sat down again in Aurelio's chair and tried to clear her head. But she soon found her thoughts wandering again. To Gambetta and what he'd told her; to Gallo and her escape; to Salvatore and how close she'd come to falling into his grasp; to Aurelio and the sanctuary he was providing. And annoyingly, to the riddle that she had ignored earlier, but which had now popped back into her head.

'I am the beginning of the world and the end of ages, but I am not God.' She repeated the line to herself with a frown.

The beginning of the world – Genesis, dawn, a baby? But then how were any of these the end, she asked herself. And who else but God could claim to be at the beginning and end of time? Maybe she needed to be more literal, she mused – the Latin for world was *mundi* and for ages was *sæculorum*, so the beginning of mundi was . . . her eyes snapped open.

'It's the letter M,' she called out triumphantly. 'The beginning of *mundi* and the end of *sæculorum* is the letter M.'

Grinning, she walked into the kitchen. To her surprise it
was empty, the kettle boiling unattended on the stove.
Frowning, she turned the hob off and then stepped back into
the hall.

'Aurelio?' she called, reaching warily for the gun.

There was no answer, although she thought she heard the
faint echo of his voice coming from his bedroom. She stepped
over to it, a narrow slit of light bisecting the worn floor-
boards where the door hadn't quite been pulled to. Not
wanting to interrupt, she pressed her ear against the crack
and then froze. He was talking about her.

'Yes, she's here now,' she heard him say in an urgent
voice. 'Of course I can keep her here. Why, what do you
need her for?'

She backed away, the gun raised towards the door, her
face pale, heart pounding, the blood screaming in her ears.
First Gallo. Now Aurelio too?

Her eyes stinging, she turned and stumbled out of the
apartment, down the stairs and on to the street, not knowing
if she was crying from sadness or anger. Not sure if she even
cared.

Not sure if she cared about anything any more.

TWENTY-EIGHT

Villa de Rome apartment building, Boulevard de Suisse, Monte Carlo, Monaco
18th March – 5.23 p.m.

It was earlier than usual, but then Ronan D'Arcy figured he'd earned it. After a bloodbath in the first few months of the year, some of his shorts were finally beginning to pay off and the latest round of Middle Eastern sabre rattling had pushed his oil futures back to historic highs. If that didn't warrant a drink, what did?

A helicopter droned overhead, circling low over the palace up on the hill, and then swooping back around to perch gracefully on the deck of one of the larger yachts lying at anchor in the harbour, the sea glittering like gold in the sinking sunlight. D'Arcy gave a rueful smile. It didn't matter how good the market was or how well you thought you were doing, someone else, somewhere, was always doing better. It was a lesson that this place seemed to take a sadistic pleasure in beating into him at every opportunity. Still, he wasn't going to let it spoil his little celebration.

He stepped off the balcony back into his office and quickly scanned the six trading screens that formed a low, incandescent wall on his desk to check that some random market sneeze hadn't wiped out a good month's work. Reassured, he picked up the phone and dialled the internal extension to the kitchen. If it had been a beer he could have fixed it himself, of course – he wasn't that lazy. But celebrations called for cocktails, and cocktails called for mojitos, and Determination was the mojito-master.

Determination. He'd never get used to that name. It was from Botswana, or some other spear-chucking African country that he'd never been able to find on a map. He'd heard of names such as Hope and Faith and Temperance. Even a Chastity, if you could believe that. But Determination . . .?

Maybe it wasn't the name but the irony of it that jarred, D'Arcy reflected, his tanned forehead creasing in annoyance as the phone rang unanswered. Indolence. That would have been a more appropriate name. Lethargy. Torpidity. Yes, that was a good one. Where was the shiftless bastard now?

He slammed the phone down and clicked his mouse to bring up the apartment's internal closed circuit TV system. The kitchen, laundry room, gym and billiard room were all empty. So too were the sitting rooms and the dining room. Which only left the . . .

D'Arcy paused, having suddenly noticed that, according to the camera in the entrance hall, the front door was wide open.

'For fuck's sake,' he swore. What was the point of flying in a specialist security company from Israel to fit armoured doors if the stupid fucker was going to leave them wide open?

Muttering angrily under his breath, he turned to leave, and then paused. The lights were on in the corridor outside, the travertine marble floor reflecting a narrow strip of light under his office door. But the pale band was broken by several dark shapes. Someone was standing outside, listening.

He punched the emergency shut-down button on his trading

system and then sprang across to the bookcase. In the same instant the door burst open and two men came tumbling through the gap, guns raised. D'Arcy hit the panic-room release button. A section of the bookcase slid back and he leapt inside. The men started firing, the silenced shots searing the air with a fup-fupping noise. He slammed his hand against the 'close' switch, the door crashing shut with a hydraulic thump, leaving him in a strange deadened silence that echoed with the rasping gasps of his adrenaline-charged breathing.

'Fuck, fuck, fuck . . .' Frantically he scrabbled in the sickly light for the phone. It was dead, his clammy fingers sliding on the moulded plastic as he stabbed at the hook switch. There was no dial tone, the line presumably cut at the junction box downstairs.

'Mobile,' he breathed, patting his jacket and trouser pockets excitedly until, his heart sinking, his eyes flicked to the monitor which showed a picture of his office. His phone was still where he'd left it on his desk.

He quickly reassessed his situation. Without a phone, there was no way of letting anyone know he was in here. That meant he'd have to wait until someone came looking for him. The chances were that his brokers in London would raise the alarm when he missed their usual morning call. That would be in – he checked his watch – less than sixteen hours' time. In the meantime he was quite safe. After all, he'd had this place installed by a Brazilian firm who specialised in kidnap prevention. It had five-inch-thick steel walls, forty-eight hours of battery life if they cut the power, access to the CCTV system and a month's worth of supplies. He might as well make himself comfortable and enjoy the show.

He sat back, his pulse slowing, and watched the men with an amused expression. They were arguing, he noticed with a smile. Probably trying to figure out which of them would carry the can for him having got away. At least he only planned to fire Determination, he thought to himself. Judging by their brutal methods, he doubted whether whoever had sent these two would be as forgiving when they learnt of his escape.

Suddenly he sat forward, his face drawn into a puzzled frown. The arguing had stopped, the men now intent on emptying the bookcase on to the floor and arranging its contents into a large uneven mound that pressed up against the panic room's concealed entrance. Seemingly satisfied, they turned their attention to the walls, ripping the paintings down and tossing them on to the pile. They reserved special treatment for his Picasso, one of the men punching his fist through the *Portrait of Jacqueline* that had found its way to D'Arcy after being stolen a few years before from Picasso's granddaughter's apartment in Paris. Then he sent it spinning through the air to join the others.

D'Arcy shook his head, swearing angrily. Did they think he would come charging out to save a few old books and a painting? He valued his life far more dearly than that. Their petty vandalism was as pointless as it was . . .

He lost his train of thought, noticing with a frown that one of the men seemed to be spraying some sort of liquid over the jumble of books and canvases and wooden frames, while the other had lit a match. Glancing up at the camera with a smile, as if to make sure D'Arcy had seen them, the man with the match stepped forward and dropped it on to the pile. The screen flared white, momentarily blinded by a whoosh of fire.

D'Arcy was gripped by a chilling realisation. His eyes rose slowly from the screen to the small metal grille positioned in the right-hand corner of the panic room. To the thin tendrils of acrid smoke that were even now snaking through its narrow openings. To the acid taste at the back of his throat as he felt his lungs begin to clench.

TWENTY-NINE

Vicolo de Panieri, Travestere, Rome
19th March – 7.03 a.m.
Tom had booked himself on to the afternoon flight out of
DC, taking the obvious precaution of using another name.
He never travelled without at least two changes of identity
stitched into his bag's lining and luckily the FBI had not
thought to check whether he had left anything with the
concierge at the hotel he'd been staying in the previous night.

There had been a relatively low-key police presence at
Reagan International. Understandable, given that the FBI
would probably be focusing all their efforts on the Vegas area
if they were serious about catching him. After all, he'd
dropped a pretty strong hint to Stokes that that was where
he'd head in the first instance to pick up the killer's trail.

He'd managed to snatch a few hours' sleep, recouping a
little of what he'd lost over the past two days, and then spent
the rest of the flight reading through Jennifer's file in a bit
more detail. Most of it was by now familiar to him, although
he had paused over the witness statements, bank records and
various other documents that the FBI had seized in their raid
on the art dealer's warehouse in Queen's which he hadn't

seen before. One, in particular, stood out and had triggered the call he was making now as his taxi swept into the city along the A91, accompanied by the dawn traffic and the chirping tones of the driver's sat-nav system.

'Archie?' he said, as soon as he picked up.

'Tom?' Archie rasped, jet lag and what Tom guessed had probably been a heavy night at the hotel bar combining to give his voice a ragged croak. 'What time is it? Where the hell are you?'

'Rome,' Tom answered.

'Rome?' he repeated sleepily, the muffled noise of something being knocked to the floor suggesting that he was groping for his watch or the alarm clock with one hand while digging the sleep out of his eyes with the other. 'What the fuck are you doing in Rome? You're meant to be in Zurich. What number is this?'

'Jennifer's dead,' Tom said sharply. 'It was a set-up. The Caravaggio. The exchange. They were waiting for us.'

'Shit.' Any hint of tiredness had immediately evaporated from Archie's voice. 'You all right?'

'I'm fine.'

'What the fuck happened?'

'Sniper,' Tom said, trying not to think about what he'd seen or heard or felt, concentrating on just sticking to the facts. 'Professional job.'

'You're sure she was the target?'

'Pretty sure. Have you ever heard of an antiquities-smuggling operation called the Delian League?'

'No. Why? Is that who you think did it?'

'That's what I'm in Rome to find out. That's why I need you in Geneva.'

'Of course,' Archie replied instantly. 'Whatever you need, mate.'

'There's a sale at Sotheby's this afternoon,' Tom said,

glancing down at the circled entry in the Geneva auction catalogue that had been included in the file. 'One of the lots is a statue of Artemis. It looks like Jennifer thought it was important. I want to know why.'

'No worries,' Archie reassured him. 'What about you? What's in Rome?'

'A name. Luca Cavalli. He was fingered by someone Jennifer arrested in New York. I thought I'd start with him and work my way back up the ladder.'

A pause.

'Tom . . .' Archie spoke haltingly, for once lost for words. 'Listen, mate, I'm sorry. I know you two were . . . I'm really sorry.'

Tom had thought that sharing the news of Jennifer's murder with Archie might help unburden him in some way. But his hesitant awkwardness was so unusual that it was actually having the opposite effect, forcing Tom to reflect yet again on the events that had brought him here, rather than focus on the immediate task at hand.

'Are you going to be all right?'

'I'll be fine,' Tom said. 'Just call me on this number when you get there.'

About fifteen minutes later the taxi pulled up and Tom stepped out.

It was a wide, cobbled street largely populated by neat four-storey buildings with symmetrical balconies and brightly coloured plaster walls. Cavalli's house, by contrast, was a feral, hulking shape. Long and only two storeys high, its stonework was grey and wizened by age, the roof sagging under a red blister of sun-cracked tiles, the flaking green shutters at its upstairs windows betraying years of neglect. An old horse block stood to the right of the front door, while to the left, a large dilapidated arched gate suggested that the building had once served as some sort of workshop or garage.

For a moment, Tom wondered if he'd been misled by the sat-nav's confident tone and been dropped off in the wrong place. But the seals on the door and the laminated notice declaring the premises a court-protected crime scene removed any lingering doubts. He was definitely in the right place. It just looked as though he was too late.

Hitching his bag across his shoulders and checking that the street was empty, Tom clambered quickly up the drainpipe, glad that he had changed out of his suit. Reaching across to the window, he could see that although it had been closed shut, the frame was warped and the latch old and loose. Pushing a knife into a narrow gap, he levered the blade back and forth, shaking the window so that the latch slowly worked itself free, until it popped open and he was able to clamber inside.

He found himself in what he assumed was a bedroom, although it was hard to be sure, the contents of the wardrobe having been swept on to the floor, the bed propped against the wall and the chest flipped on to its back, its emptied drawers lying prostrate at its side. It struck Tom that there was a deliberate violence in the way that the room had been upended. The police, for all their clumsiness, usually searched with a little more restraint. The people who had done this, however, hadn't just been looking for something. They'd been trying to make a point.

He exited the bedroom on to a glass and stainless steel walkway that ran the length of the building and looked down on to a wide, double-height living space. Here the décor was as modern as the outside had been neglected, the back wall made of folding glass panels and looking out on to a small walled garden, the floor a dull mirror of polished concrete, the galley kitchen a mass of stainless steel that looked like it might double as an operating theatre.

Tom stepped along the walkway past a bathroom and another bedroom that had been similarly turned upside down. Then he made his way down a glass staircase to the ground floor, its icicle-like glass treads protruding unsupported from the wall. Down here, the brutality of the assault was, if anything, even more marked – the large plasma screen lifted off its brackets and broken almost in two across a chair; the seats and backs of the leather furniture slashed open, their innards ripped out in handfuls through the deep gashes; the coffee table overturned and its metal legs stamped on so that they were bent into strange, deviant shapes; the bookcase forced on to its front, crushing its contents underneath. There was a distinctive and unpleasant aroma too, and it was a few moments before Tom was able to guess at its meaning – not content with defeating these inanimate foes, the assailants had, it seemed, chosen to mark their victory by urinating on them.

A sudden noise from the front door made Tom look up. Someone was coming in, the bottom lock clunking open, the key now slipping into the top one. He knew immediately he wouldn't have enough time to make it back upstairs.

They only left him one option.

THIRTY

19th March – 7.22 a.m.
The seal ripped as the door opened. Someone stepped inside
and then quickly eased it shut behind them. They paused.
Then, with careful, hesitant footsteps, they walked down the
small entrance hallway towards him.

Tom, his back pressed to the wall, waited until the intruder
was almost level with him and then leapt out, sending their
gun spinning across the floor with a chop to the wrist. Rather
than press his advantage, however, Tom paused, surprised
by the sudden realisation as he caught sight of their dark
hair, that it was a woman. But this momentary hesitation
was all the invitation she needed to turn and crash her right
fist into his jaw, the force of the blow sending him staggering
back with a grunt. Spinning round, she stretched towards
the gun, but Tom stuck out a leg and tripped her, sending
her sprawling headlong into an upturned chair. In a flash he
was on top of her, digging his knee into the small of her
back, trying to pin her arms to her sides. But with surprising
force, she reached behind and, grabbing his arm, flipped him
over her head and on to the floor, winding him.

Again she turned and scrambled towards the gun, but Tom,

still coughing and trying to get his breath just managed to grab one of her ankles and drag her back, her leg thrashing wildly until she was able to kick herself free. Struggling to her feet, she reached down and grabbed one of the dislocated struts from the coffee table and then lunged at him with it, her face contorted with rage. Tom sidestepped the first downward swipe aimed at his head, but the second wild swing struck him with a painful thump at the top of his right arm, momentarily numbing it. Her attack provided him with an opening, however, because with his other hand he reached out and grabbed the end of the metal rod, and then yanked it sideways. The woman went with it, tripping over a small pile of books and collapsing on to her knees. By the time she was on her feet, the gun was in Tom's hands and aimed at her stomach.

'*Trovisi giù,*' he wheezed. Her chest heaving, she gave him a long, hateful look and then lay face down on the floor as he'd ordered. Tom quickly patted her down, finding her wallet in her jeans pocket.

'*Siedasi là,*' he ordered as he opened it, waving the gun at a chair. Her eyes burning, she pulled herself to her feet, righted the chair he had indicated, and then sat in it.

'*Siete un poliziotto?*' he asked in surprise, the sight of her ID made him feel a little less embarrassed about his sore chin and throbbing arm. Tall and obviously strong, she was wearing jeans, a tight brown leather jacket and red ballet-style pumps. She was also very striking, with olive skin, a jet-black bob that was cut in a square fringe around her face and mismatched blue and brown eyes embedded within a smoky grey eye shadow. There was something odd about her appearance, though. Something that Tom couldn't quite put his finger on yet, that didn't quite fit.

'Congratulations,' she replied. 'You've managed to assault a police officer and trespass on a crime scene before most people have got out of bed.'

'Where did you learn your English?' Tom's Italian was good, but her English, while slightly accented, was almost faultless.

She ignored him. 'Put the gun down.'

'You tell me what you're doing here and I'll think about it,' he offered unsmilingly.

'Who are you working for? Gallo?'

'Who's Gallo?'

'He didn't send you?' There was a hint of hope as well as disbelief in her voice.

'Nobody *sent* me,' he said. 'I work for myself. I'm looking for Cavalli.'

A pause.

'Cavalli's dead.'

'Shit,' Tom swore, pinching the top of his nose and shutting his eyes as he gave a long, weary sigh. Cavalli had been his main hope of working his way back up the Delian League to whoever had ordered the hit. 'How?'

She shook her head, eyeing him blankly, refusing to be drawn.

'What does it matter, if he's dead?' Tom insisted.

Another pause as she considered this, before answering with a shrug.

'He was murdered. Four days ago. Why?'

'I wanted to talk to him.'

'About what?'

'This for a start –' Tom held up the photocopied page showing the sketch of the symbol of the two snakes wrapped around a clenched fist. 'I hoped he might . . .'

'Where did you get that?' she gasped.

'You've seen it before?'

'C-Cavalli,' she stammered. 'They found a lead disc in his pocket. That was engraved on it!'

'Do you know what it means?' Tom pressed, hoping that

her obvious surprise might cause her to momentarily lower her guard to his advantage. But she quickly regained her composure, again glaring at him defiantly.

'It means that you've got about five minutes to get out of here before someone comes looking for me.'

Tom studied her face for a few moments. She was bluffing.

'Why wait?' he said, offering her his phone. 'Call it in.'

She gazed at the handset for a few moments, then lifted her eyes to his.

'What are you doing?'

Tom smiled.

'No one even knows you're here, do they?'

She ignored his question, although the momentary flicker of indecision across her otherwise resolute face effectively answered it for him.

'Just let me go,' she repeated. 'You're in enough shit as it is.'

Tom went to reply and then paused, having suddenly realised what it was about her appearance that had been troubling him earlier. It was her hair, or rather the ragged way it had been cut, especially around the back, which seemed at odds with the rest of her. She'd clearly cut it herself. Recently. Probably dyed it too, given its unnaturally deep lustre.

'Where did you put the bottles?' he asked.

'What?' She shook her head, as if she wasn't sure she'd heard him properly.

'The empty dye bottles and the hair you cut off. Did you lose them somewhere safe? Because if you didn't and whoever's looking for you finds them, it won't take them much to figure out what you look like now.'

Allegra gave him a long, curious look.

'Who are you?'

'Someone who can help,' Tom said with a tight smile. 'Because right now, I'm guessing you're in a lot more shit than me.'

Leaning forward, he offered the gun to her, handle first.

THIRTY-ONE

Headquarters of the Guarda di Finanza, Viale XXI Aprile, Rome
19th March – 7.22 a.m.
'Colonel? We've got her.'

'About time!' Gallo grabbed his jacket off the back of his chair, pausing in front of the mirror to do up the silver buttons and centre his tie. 'Her phone?'

'She switched it on about ten minutes ago,' Salvatore nodded, still standing in the corridor and leaning into the office.

'How long for?'

'Long enough. The signal's been triangulated to a street in Travestere.'

'Cavalli's house?' Gallo snapped, looking up into the mirror to seek out Salvatore's eyes over his left shoulder.

'Could be.'

Salvatore flinched and then relaxed into an uneasy smile as Gallo turned and raised his hand and gave him a sharp clap on the back.

'Well done.'

Fixing his peaked cap on his head, he strode towards the lift.

Twenty seconds later they stepped outside and walked towards two waiting cars. They climbed in, but just as Gallo was about to turn the key in the ignition, Salvatore's phone rang. Gallo paused, glancing across questioningly as he took the call.

'We know where she stayed last night,' Salvatore explained, still listening, but with his hand shielding the microphone.

'A hotel?' Gallo guessed.

'Out near the airport. The manager saw her picture this morning and called it in.'

'They ran the story?'

Salvatore reached across to the back seat and handed Gallo a copy of that morning's *La Repubblica*. Allegra's face dominated the front page under a single shouted headline:

Killer cop on the run.

'Apparently she checked in late last night and paid in cash. I guess we got lucky.'

'Funny how much luckier you get when you load the dice,' Gallo growled as he scanned through the article. He wouldn't normally have leaked the details of a case, but he'd seen enough of Allegra to realise that, for all her inexperience, she was smart. And in a city of 2.7 million people, that was more than enough to hide and stay hidden. The more people who knew what she looked like, the better. As long as he found her first.

Salvatore ended his call. Gallo turned the key.

'Who else is running it?'

'Everyone.'

'What about the old man?'

'Professor Eco?'

'Is that what he calls himself?' Gallo shrugged as he checked his mirrors and swung out, tyres shrieking.

'According to him, she took off before telling him anything.'

'I want him watched anyway,' Gallo insisted. 'Just in case she tries to contact him again.'

'She's probably armed now, by the way. Eco had a gun. Illegal. Says he can't find it any more.'

'Even better.' Gallo gave a satisfied nod. 'Gives us an excuse to go in heavy.'

Smiling, he punched the siren on.

THIRTY-TWO

Vicolo de Panieri, Travestere, Rome
19th March – 7.27 a.m.
Allegra wasn't about to take any chances. Snatching the gun from Tom's grasp, she immediately turned it back on him. Unflustered, he settled into his chair.

'Who are you running from?' he asked.

The easy thing, the smart thing, she knew, would be to walk away right there and then. She had enough of her own problems already, without getting swept up into his.

But it wasn't that simple. For a start, it was hard to ignore that, whoever this man was and whatever dark secret had drawn him to this place, it seemed to involve Cavalli and the mysterious symbol that had been linked to three different corpses. What's more, he'd just placed his fate in her hands by handing her the gun. It was, she knew, a rather unsubtle attempt to win her trust. But it was a powerful gesture all the same, and one that had, if nothing else, earned him the right to be heard.

'How can you help me?' she demanded, answering his question with one of her own.

There was a pause, and she guessed from the slight twitch

of his left eye that he was debating how much he should tell her.

'Thirty-six hours ago a friend of mine was murdered,' he said eventually. 'Shot by a sniper in a casino in Vegas. I think they were killed because they were closing in on someone.'

'"Closing in"? What was he, a cop?' Allegra guessed with a surprised frown. This guy didn't look or feel like any policeman she'd ever met.

'*She* was FBI,' he corrected her. 'Special Agent Jennifer Browne. Cavalli was fingered by a man she arrested in New York. A dealer for a tombaroli smuggling ring. She found a drawing of the symbol I showed you in his trash. I've got the case file, if you want to see it,' he offered, leaning forward to reach into his bag.

'Wait,' she said sharply. 'Kick it over here.'

With a shrug, he placed his bag on the floor and slid it towards her with his foot. Keeping her eyes fixed on him, she felt inside it, her fingers eventually closing around a thick file that she pulled on to her lap. Seeing the FBI crest, she shot him a questioning, almost concerned look.

'Don't tell me you're FBI too?'

'No,' he admitted.

'Then where did you get this?'

A pause.

'I borrowed it.'

'You borrowed it?' She gave him a disbelieving smile. 'From the FBI?'

'When one agent gets killed, another one gets blamed,' he said, an impatient edge to his voice for the first time. 'Everyone was too busy covering their own ass to worry about finding Jennifer's killer. I did what I had to do.'

'And came here? Why? What were you hoping to find?'

'I don't know. Something that might tell me why Jennifer

was murdered, or what this symbol means, or who the Delian League is.'

'The Delian League?' she shot back. 'What do you know about them?'

'Not as much as you, by the sound of things,' he replied with a curious frown.

'I just know what it used to be,' she said, his story so far and the reassuring weight of the gun in her hand convincing her she wasn't risking much by sharing a little more of what she knew.

'What do you mean, "used to be"?'

'There was an association of city states in Ancient Greece. A military alliance, formed to protect themselves from the Spartans,' she explained. 'The members used to throw lead into the sea when they joined, to symbolise that their friendship would last until it floated back to the surface.'

'Lead. Like the engraved disc you found on Cavalli?'

'Not just on Cavalli,' she admitted, trying not to think of Ricci's sagging skin and Argento's tortured smile. 'There have been two other murders. The discs were found with them too.'

'Did Cavalli know them?'

'I doubt it,' she said, shaking her head. 'Cavalli was an attorney based in Melfi. Adriano Ricci was an enforcer for the De Luca crime family. While Giulio Argento worked for the Banco Rosalia, a subsidiary of the Vatican bank. A priest would have more in common with a prostitute than those three with each other.'

'But the same killer, right?'

Allegra's eyes snapped to the door before she could answer, the sound of approaching sirens lifting her to her feet.

'You must have been followed,' Tom glared at her accusingly.

She ignored him, instead picking up a chair and swinging it hard against one of the sliding glass doors. It fractured on the third blow, the safety glass falling out in a single, crazed sheet. They leapt through the frame as they heard three, maybe four cars roar up the street outside.

'Here –'

Tom cradled his hands and gave Allegra a boost, then reached up so she could help haul him up on to the garden wall beside her.

'You'll slow me down,' she said with a firm shake of her head.

'You need me,' Tom insisted.

'I've done okay so far.'

'Really? Then how do you explain that?' Tom glanced towards the muffled sound of the police banging on the front door.

'They got lucky,' she said with a shrug, readying herself to jump down.

'You mean they got smart. Let me guess. You turned your phone on just before you got here, right?'

'How did you know . . .?' she breathed, Tom's question pulling her back from the edge. She had briefly switched it on. Just long enough to see if Aurelio had left her a message. Something, anything, that might explain what she had overheard. But all there had been was a series of increasingly frantic messages from her boss to turn herself in.

'It only takes a few seconds to triangulate a phone signal. You led them straight here.'

She took a deep breath, a small and increasingly insistent voice at the back of her head fighting her instinct to just jump down.

'Who are you?'

'Someone who knows what it's like to be on the run,'

he shot back. 'Someone who knows what it takes to keep running fast enough to stay alive.'

Sighing heavily, she reached down, her hand clutching on to his.

THIRTY-THREE

Verbier, Switzerland
19th March – 7.31 a.m.
It had snowed last week – recently enough for the village's blandly functional concrete heart to still be benefiting from its decorative touch, long enough ago for the briefly pristine white streets to have been turned into a dirty river of slush and mud-stained embankments.

Faulks had never seen the point of skiing, never understood the attraction of clamping his feet into boots that in another age would have likely been in the hands of the Spanish Inquisition, and then hurling himself off a mountain on two narrow planks, just to get to the bottom so that he could queue and pay for the privilege of repeating the whole infernal experience again. And again.

Glancing up from his phone as they drove past, he almost felt sorry for them, a few early starters clomping noisily down the street trying not to break their necks on the ice, skis balancing precariously on their shoulder, their edges sawing down to the bone. It seemed a heavy price to pay to ensure you could able to hold your own at the school gates with the other parents or be able to join in with the dinner party circuit chit chat.

Still, if there was one thing he'd learnt over the years it was that there was no limit to people's ingenuity when it came to devising irrational ways to spend their money. And the richer they were, the more irrational and ingenious they seemed to become. It was a status symbol. A badge of honour. In fact, compared to some things he'd witnessed over the years, skiing was almost sane.

Chalet Septième Ciel was perched in an isolated spot high above the village, facing westward and with a breathtaking view over the valley below. Converted from an old school, its name meant Seventh Heaven; strangely inappropriate, given that most of its occupants, Faulks was fairly sure, were fated for a far warmer destination when their time came. Maybe that was why they chose here, Faulks mused. The prospect of an eternity roasting in the fires of Hell was perhaps all the incentive they needed to pay the extortionate fees this place charged. Anything to spend their final days somewhere cold.

Faulk's silver 1963 Bentley S3 Continental pulled up and Logan got out to open his door for him. A former paratrooper from the outskirts of Glasgow, he'd done two tours in Afghanistan before realising that he could make more in a year as a private bodyguard than ten being shot at for Queen and country. Wearing a suit and his regimental tie, he had straw-coloured hair and a wide, round face, his nose crooked and part of one earlobe missing. His jaw was permanently clenched, as if he was chewing stones.

A female voice answered the intercom.

'I'm here to see Avner Klein,' Faulks announced in French.

The door buzzed open and he stepped inside, a dark-haired nurse in a white uniform rushing forward to greet him, a stern expression on her face.

'Visiting hours aren't until nine,' she informed him icily.

'I know, but I've just flown in from Los Angeles,' he

explained apologetically. 'And I have to be back in Geneva mid morning. I knew that if I didn't at least try to see him now . . .'

'I understand,' she relented, her face softening as she placed a comforting hand on his sleeve. 'In this case . . . well, time is short. I'm sure he'll see you. He's not been sleeping well recently. Follow me.'

She led him downstairs and down a long, dark corridor, Faulks marking every third step with the sharp clip of his umbrella against the wooden floor. Reaching the last door she knocked gently. From the other side came a faint call that seemed barely human to Faulks, but which the nurse clearly took as permission to enter, nodding at him to go in.

'Mrs Carroll is having breakfast on the terrace,' she called as she retreated back along the corridor before he could stop her. 'I'll let her know you're here.'

The curtains had been partly drawn, throwing a narrow ribbon of light across the otherwise dark room. This had unravelled along the floor and then spooled up and across the bed, revealing the pale hands of the person lying in it, his face wreathed in darkness.

'Avner?' Faulks said, his eyes straining to adjust to the sepulchral half light.

'Earl, is that you?' a thin voice rasped from the bed.

'How are you doing, sport?' Faulks stepped across to the bed with what he hoped was an encouraging smile.

Klein looked barely alive, his cheeks hollowed out, eyes sunk into the back of his head, hair missing, skin wrinkled and sagging. Wires from several machines disappeared under the white bedclothes that shrouded his body, their monitors flashing up a hieroglyphic stream of numbers and graphs and pulsing dots. There was a drip too, Faulks noticed, the line seeming to vanish somewhere in the direction of Klein's groin, the livid purple patches along his wizened forearm suggesting that they couldn't find a vein there any more.

'I'm dying,' Klein replied, the very effort of blinking seeming to make him wince in pain.

'Rubbish,' Faulks assured him breezily. 'You'll be back on your feet in time for the Triple Crown. I've got a killer tip on the Derby this year. A guaranteed winner!'

Klein nodded weakly, although his empty smile told Faulks that they both knew he was lying.

'Thank you for visiting,' Klein wheezed. 'I know you're busy.'

He nodded at the drink next to the bed and Faulks reached across and held it for him, trying not to wrinkle his nose in disgust as Klein's cracked lips sucked at it greedily, a drop escaping from the corner of his mouth and trickling down his chin like a tear.

'Never too busy for an old friend.' A pause. 'And there is something I wanted to show you.'

'Oh?'

Rather than curiosity, there was a resigned sadness in Klein's voice, as if Faulks had somehow confirmed a rumour that he'd been hoping wasn't true.

'I knew you wouldn't want to pass up a chance like this,' Faulks enthused, opening his wallet and extracting a small Polaroid. 'Look –'

Klein lifted himself forward and then almost immediately collapsed back on to his pillow, convulsing under the grip of a sudden hacking cough.

'Verity Bruce wants it,' Faulks continued through the noise, glancing lovingly at the picture. 'I've brought all the paper-work ready for you to sign. All you need to do is authorise the payment and –'

Faulks broke off as Deena Carroll, Klein's second wife, stormed into the room behind him, gold bangles and earrings clanging like a Passing Bell.

'What the hell are you doing here?' she said, roasted coffee bean eyes blazing out of a leathered face crowned by a swooping wave of dyed platinum blonde hair.

'Visiting an old friend,' Faulks shrugged. 'I mean, old friends,' he added with a small bow of his head.

'You're no friend,' she hissed contemptuously, snatching the photograph from him and waving it in his face. 'Friends don't try and hawk their grimy trinkets to a dying man.' She flicked the photograph to the floor. 'You make me sick, Earl.'

'Those grimy trinkets have made the Klein–Carroll collection one of the greatest in the world,' he reminded her tersely as he knelt down stiffly to retrieve the photograph. 'And now that you've donated it to the Met, a permanent monument to your taste and generosity.' He spat these last two words out, as if he'd just bitten into a bar of soap.

'We both know what that collection is and where it came from,' she said with a hollow laugh. 'And if it's a monument to anything, it's to your greed.'

'Be careful, Deena,' Faulks said sharply, still smiling. 'I've buried a lot of bodies for Avner over the years and dug up even more. And I can prove it. You should think about how you want him to be remembered.'

She went to answer but said nothing, glancing instead at Klein. Hands clasped together on the crisp sheets, grinning lovingly at her, he had quite clearly not followed a word of their exchange. She walked over to his side and smiled, tears welling as she stroked the few wisps of hair that clung stubbornly to his scalp.

'Just go, Earl,' she said in a toneless voice. 'Find someone else to dig for.'

THIRTY-FOUR

Lungotevere Gianicolense, Rome
19th March – 7.37 a.m.

They had found a battered old Fiat a few streets from Cavalli's house, Tom preferring it to the Mercedes parked just behind it. It was a suggestion that Allegra was already rather regretting, the rusted suspension jarring with every imperfection in the road as they headed north along the river. And yet she couldn't fault his logic – the Fiat was coated in a thick layer of rain-streaked dirt that suggested that it hadn't been used for weeks, and so was less likely to be missed.

'What are you doing?' he asked as she suddenly cut across the Ponte Principe Amedei di Savoia and pulled in on the Largo dei Fiorentini. 'We can't stop here. We're still too close. If anyone's seen us . . .'

'If you want to get out, now's your chance,' she snapped, leaning across him and pushing his door open. 'Otherwise, I want some answers.'

'What sort of answers?'

'How about a name?'

He sighed, then slammed the door shut.

'It's Tom. Tom Kirk.' He made a point of holding out his

hand so that she had to shake it rather formally. 'Can we do the rest of the Q and A somewhere else?'

'You said you knew what it was like to be on the run. Why? Who are you?' she demanded.

'You really want to do this here?' he asked, his face screwed into a disbelieving frown. She returned his stare, jaw set firm. 'Fine,' he said eventually with a resigned sigh. 'I . . . I used to be a thief.'

'A thief?' She smiled indulgently before realising that he wasn't joking. 'What sort of thief?'

'Art mainly. Jewellery too. Whatever paid.'

She nodded slowly. It was strange, but it was almost as if she'd been expecting him to say something like this. It certainly seemed to fit him better than being police or FBI.

'And now?'

'Now I help recover pieces, advise museums on security, that sort of thing,' he replied.

'What's any of that got to do with Cavalli?'

'I told you. Jennifer had asked me to help her on a case before she was killed. Cavalli was the best lead I had as to who might have ordered the hit.'

'So we both went there looking for answers,' Allegra said with a rueful smile.

'Why – what's Cavalli to you?'

'It's what he is to Gallo that I care about.' She turned back to face the front, her hands clutching the wheel.

'Who's Gallo?' Tom frowned. 'The person you're running from?'

'Colonel Massimo Gallo,' she intoned in a bitter voice. 'Head of the GICO – the organised crime unit of the Ministry of Finance – and the officer in charge of the two Caravaggio killings.'

'What?'

'Ricci and Argento,' she explained impatiently. 'The other

murders I told you about. Their deaths had been staged to mirror two Caravaggio paintings.'

'Jennifer was lured to Las Vegas to help recover a Caravaggio stolen in the 1960s,' Tom explained with the triumphant finality of someone laying down a winning poker hand.

'You think . . .?'

'Don't you?'

There was a pause as she let this sink in. First the symbol. Then the mention of the Delian League. Now Caravaggio. Perhaps he was right. These surely couldn't all be coincidences?

Speaking fast and confidently, she plunged into an account of the past few days – the murders of Ricci and Argento; the choice of locations; the references to Caesar; the Caravaggio staging of the murder scenes; what she knew about Cavalli and his death; Gallo's cold-blooded execution of Gambetta. It was only when she got to describing Aurelio's treachery that her voice faltered. The memory of his betrayal was still too fresh, too raw for her to share anything more than the most basic details. Instead she quickly switched to her tortured flight from his apartment and the restless night that she had spent in the grimy airport hotel until, unable to sleep, she had decided to visit Cavalli's apartment for herself and see what she could find there.

Tom listened to all this without interrupting and she realised when she had finished that it had been strangely calming to talk things through, even if she barely knew him. There had been so much going on, so many thoughts tripping over each other inside her head, that it had been surprisingly cathartic to lay all the different elements together end to end.

'Somehow, it's all linked,' he said slowly when she had finished. 'The murders, Caravaggio, the symbol . . . we just need to find out how.'

'Is that all?' she said with a bitter laugh.

'Sometimes you just need to know who to ask.'

'And you do?' she asked in a sceptical tone.

'I know someone who might be able to help.' He nodded.

'Someone we can trust?'

Tom took a deep breath, then blew out his cheeks.

'More or less.'

'What sort of an answer's that?' she snorted.

'The sort of answer you get when you're out of better ideas.'

There was a pause. Then with a resigned shrug she started the engine.

'Where to?'

THIRTY-FIVE

Fontana di Trevi, Rome
19th March – 8.03 a.m.

Allegra heard the fountain before she saw it, a delirious, ecstatic roar of water that crashed and foamed over gnarled travertine rocks and carved foliage, tumbling in a joyful cascade into the open embrace of the wide basin below. This was no accident, Allegra knew, the Trevi having been deliberately positioned so that, no matter what route was taken, it could only be partially seen as it was approached, the anticipation building as the sound got louder until the monument finally revealed itself.

Despite the relatively early hour, the tourists were already out in force, some seated like an eager audience on the steps that encircled the basin's low stage, others facing the opposite direction and flinging coins over their shoulders in the hope of securing their return to the Eternal City. Oblivious to their catcalling and the popcorn burst of camera flashes, the statues ranged above them silently acted out an allegorical representation of the taming of the waters. Centre stage loomed Neptune's brooding figure, his chariot frozen in flight, winged horses rearing dramatically out of the water and threatening to take the entire structure with them.

'Was there a Trevi family?' Tom asked as they paused briefly in front of it.

'Trevi comes from Tre Via, the three streets that meet here,' she corrected him in a curt voice. 'Are we here for a history lesson or to actually see someone?'

'That depends,' he said with a shrug.

'On what?'

'On whether you can keep a secret.'

She gave a dismissive laugh.

'How old are you, ten?'

Tom turned to face her, face set firm.

'You can't tell anyone about what you see.'

'Oh come on,' she snorted impatiently.

'Yes or no?' he insisted.

There was a pause. Then she gave a grudging nod.

'Yes, fine, whatever.'

'No crossed fingers?'

'What?' she exploded. 'If this is some sort of . . .'

'I'm only joking.' He grinned. 'Come on. It's this way.'

He led her round to the right to the Vicolo Scavolino where a small doorway had been set into the side wall of the building directly behind the fountain. A flock of pigeons rendered fat and tame by years of overfeeding, barely stirred as they waded through them.

'Here?' she asked with a frown, glancing up at the carved papal escutcheon suspended over the entrance.

'Here.' He nodded, knocking sharply against the door's weather-worn surface.

A few moments later it opened to reveal a young Chinese man dressed in black, his hair standing off his head as if he had been electrocuted. From the way he was awkwardly holding one hand behind his back, Allegra guessed that he was clutching a gun.

'I'm here to see Johnny,' Tom announced. 'Tell him it's Felix.'

The man gave them a cursory look, then shut the door again.

'Felix?' Allegra shot him a questioning look.

'It's a name people used to call me when I was in the game,' he explained. 'I try not to use it any more, but it's how a lot of people still know me.'

'The game?' She gave a hollow laugh. 'Is that a word people like you use to make you feel better about breaking the law?'

The door reopened before Tom had a chance to answer, the man ushering them inside and then marching them along a low passageway, through a second door and then up a shallow flight of steps into a narrow room, with a stone stair-case leading both up and down.

'Where are we?' Allegra hissed.

'Listen,' Tom replied.

She nodded, suddenly realising that the dull ringing in her ears was no longer the angry echo of the shot that had killed Gambetta but the muffled roar of water through the thick walls.

'We're behind the fountain,' she breathed.

'The Trevi was pretty much tacked on to the façade of the Palazzo Poli when they built it,' Tom explained as the man ordered them up the stairs with a grunt. 'This space was bricked off as a maintenance shaft, to provide access to the roof and the plumbing in the basement. Johnny cut a deal with the mayor to rent the attic.'

'You're kidding, right?'

'Why? How else do you think he paid for his re-election campaign?'

They climbed to the first floor, then to the next, the fountain's low rumble slowly fading, until it was little more than a distant hum. In its place, however, Allegra was increasingly aware of a whirring, rhythmical clattering noise. She glanced at Tom for an explanation, but he said nothing, his expression suggesting that he was rather enjoying her confusion.

Another man was waiting to greet them on the second-floor landing, a machine gun slung across his oversized Lakers shirt, in place of the rather less threatening Norinco Type 77 handgun that their escort was sporting. The higher they climbed, the more lethal the weaponry, it seemed.

The second man signalled at them to raise their arms and then quickly patted them down, confiscating Tom's bag and Allegra's gun and keys. Then he nodded at them to follow him to the foot of the next flight of stairs, where an armoured steel door and two more guards blocked their way. Unprompted, the door buzzed open.

Swapping a look, they made their way upstairs.

THIRTY-SIX

19th March – 8.12 a.m.

The staircase led to a long, narrow attic room that seemed to run the width of the entire building. A line of squat windows squinted down on to the square below, their view obscured in places by the fountain's massive stone pediment. And running down the centre of the room, hissing and rattling like an old steam engine under the low ceiling, was a huge printing press.

'The sound of the fountain masks the noise of the machine,' Tom called to her over the press's raucous clatter as she approached it. 'It's actually five separate processes, although the machines have been laid out end to end. A simultan machine to print the background colours and patterns. An intaglio machine for the major design elements. A letterpress for the serial numbers. An offset press for the overcoating. And obviously a guillotine right at the end to cut the sheets to size.'

Allegra stepped closer to the press, trying to catch what was coming off the machine's whirling drum, then looked back to Tom in shock.

'Money?'

'Euros.' He nodded. 'Johnny runs one of the world's biggest counterfeiting operations outside of China. He used to print dollars, but no one wants them any more.'

'Johnny who?' she asked, looking back along the room and noticing the small army of people in blue overalls tending silently to the press.

'Johnny Li. His father is Li Kai-Fu. Runs one of the most powerful Triad gangs in Hong Kong,' Tom explained in a low voice. 'A couple of years ago he posted his five sons around the world, via Cambridge, to help grow the family business. Johnny's here, Paul's in San Francisco, Ringo's in Buenos Aires . . .'

'He moved to Rio,' a voice interrupted him. 'Better weather, cheaper women.'

'Johnny!' Tom turned to greet the voice with a warm smile.

Li was young, perhaps only in his late twenties, with long dark hair that he was forever brushing from his eyes, a pierced lip, and a dotted line tattooed around his neck as if to show where to cut. He was also the only person on this floor not in overalls, dressed instead in a white Armani T-shirt, red Ferrari monogrammed jacket, expensively ripped Versace jeans with a stainless steel key chain looping down one leg, and Prada trainers. Flanked by two unsmiling guards and balancing Allegra's gun in his hand as if trying to guess its weight, his face was creased into an unwelcoming scowl.

'What do you want, Felix?' He had an unexpectedly strong English accent.

'Bad time?' Tom frowned, clearly surprised by his tone.

'What do you expect when you turn up at my place with a cop?' Li snapped, stabbing a rolled-up newspaper towards him. 'Even she is bent.'

Tom took the paper off him and scanned the front page, then handed it to Allegra with an awkward, almost apologetic look. She didn't have to read much beyond the headline to understand why. Gallo was pinning Gambetta's death on her. There she was, looking slightly arrogant in her crisp Carabinieri uniform, she had to admit. Beneath it was an article describing her 'murderous rampage', the text scrolling around her, as if the words themselves were worried about getting too close. She felt suddenly dizzy, as if the floor was moving under her, and was only vaguely aware of Tom's voice.

'She's with me, now,' he said.

'Why, what do you want?' Li shot back, flashing Allegra a suspicious glance.

'Your help.'

'I thought you'd retired?' Li's question sounded more like an accusation.

'A friend of mine has been killed. We're both after the people who did it.'

Li paused, glancing at Tom and Allegra in turn. Then he handed Allegra her gun back with a grudging nod.

'What do you want to know?'

Tom handed Li the drawing of the symbol.

'What can you tell me about this?'

Li took it over to an architect's desk on which he had been examining a sheet of freshly printed notes under a microscope and angled it under the light. He glanced up at them with a wary look.

'Is this who you think killed your friend?'

'You know what it means?' Allegra asked excitedly.

'Of course I do,' he snorted. 'It's the symbol of the Delian League.'

Allegra gave Tom a look. As they had both suspected, far from being a footnote in some dusty textbook, the Delian League, or rather some bastardised version of it, was clearly alive and well.

'Who runs it?' Tom pressed.

Li sat back.

'Come on, Tom. You know that's not how things work.' He smiled indulgently as if gently scolding a child. 'I'm running a business here, not a charity. Even for deserving causes like you.'

'How much?' Tom asked wearily.

'Normally twenty-five thousand euro,' Li said, picking at his fingernails. 'But for you and your friend I'm going to round it up to fifty. A little . . . five-o surcharge.'

'Fifty thousand!' Allegra exclaimed.

'I can get it.' Tom nodded. 'But it's going to take some time.'

'I can wait.' Li shrugged.

'Well, we can't,' Tom insisted. 'I'll have to owe you.'

'No deal.' Li shook his head. 'Not if you're going up against the League. I want my money before they kill you.'

'Why don't you just pay yourself?' Allegra tapped her finger angrily against the sheet of uncut notes on the desk.

'This stuff is like dope,' Li sniffed. 'You never want to risk getting addicted to your own product.'

'Come on, Johnny,' Tom pleaded. 'You know I'm good for it.'

Li took a deep breath, clicking his front teeth together slowly as he considered them in turn.

'What about a down-payment?' he asked. 'You must have something on you?'

'I've told you, we don't . . .'

'That watch, for example.' Li nodded towards Tom's wrist.

'It's not for sale,' Tom insisted, quickly pulling his sleeve down.

'Think of it as a deposit,' Li suggested. 'You can have it back when you bring me the cash.'

'And you'll tell us what we need to know?' Allegra asked in a sceptical tone.

'If I can.'

'Tom?' Allegra fixed Tom with a hopeful look. Unless they wanted to wait, it seemed like a reasonable deal. Tom said nothing, then gave a resigned shrug.

'Fine.' Sighing heavily, he took the watch off. 'But I want it back.'

'I'll look after it,' Li reassured him, fastening it carefully to his wrist.

'Let's start with the Delian League,' Allegra suggested. 'Who are they?'

'The Delian League controls the illegal antiquities trade in Italy,' Li answered simply. 'Has done since the early seventies. Now, nothing leaves the country without going through them.'

'And the tombaroli? Where do they fit in?'

'They control the supply,' Li explained. 'Most of them are freelance. But since all the major antiquities buyers are foreign, the League controls access to the demand. The tombaroli either have to sell to them, or not sell at all.'

'And the mafia?' Tom interrupted. 'Don't they mind the League operating on their turf?'

'The League *is* the mafia,' Li laughed, before tapping his finger on the symbol. 'That's what the two snakes represent – one for the Cosa Nostra. One for the Banda della Magliana.'

'The Banda della Magliana is run by the De Luca family,' Allegra explained, glancing at Tom. 'They're who Ricci worked for.'

'The story I heard was that the Cosa Nostra was getting squeezed out of the drugs business by the 'Ndrangheta. So when they realised there was money to be made in looting antiquities, they teamed up with the Banda della Magliana who controlled all the valuable Etruscan sites around Rome, on the basis that they would make more money if they operated as a cartel. The League's been so successful that most of the other families have sold them access rights to their territories in return for a share of the profits.'

'Who runs it now?' Tom asked. 'Where can we find them?'

Li went to answer, then paused, crossing one arm across his stomach and tapping his finger slowly against his lips.

'I can't tell you that.'

Tom gave a hollow laugh.

'Can't or won't?'

'It's nothing personal, Felix,' Li said with a shrug. 'I just want my money. And if I give you everything now, I know I'll never see it.'

'We had a deal,' Allegra said angrily. Li had tricked them, first reeling them in to show them how much he knew and then holding out when they'd get to the punchline.

'We still do,' Li insisted. 'Come back tomorrow with the fifty k and I'll tell you what side of the bed they all sleep on.'

'We need to know now,' Allegra snapped.

Another pause, Li first centring Tom's watch on his wrist and then wiping the glass with his thumb.

'What about the car?' he asked without looking up.

'What car?' Tom frowned.

'Cavalli's Maserati,' Allegra breathed, as she recognised the set of keys that Li had produced from his pocket as the ones that had been confiscated from her on the way in.

'Do you have it?' Li pressed.

'No, but I know where it is,' she replied warily, his forced indifference making her wonder if he hadn't been carefully leading them up to this point all along. 'Why?'

'New deal,' Li offered. 'The car instead of the cash. That way you don't have to wait.'

'Done,' Allegra confirmed eagerly, sliding the keys over to

him with a relieved sigh. 'It's in the pound, but it should be easy enough for you to get to.'

Smiling, Li slid the keys back towards her.

'That's not quite what I had in mind.'

THIRTY-SEVEN

Via Principesa Clotilde, Rome
19th March – 8.35 a.m.

Ten minutes later and they were skirting the eastern rim of the Piazza del Popolo, Tom catching a glimpse of the Pincio through a gap in the buildings.

'Who gave it to you?' Allegra asked, finally breaking the silence.

'What?' Tom looked round, distracted.

'The watch? Who gave it to you?'

There was a brief pause, a pained look flickering across his face.

'Jennifer.'

A longer, more awkward silence.

'I'm sorry. I didn't realise . . .'

'We didn't have much choice,' Tom said, sighing. 'Besides, as long as we can get him the car, he'll give it back.'

'It shouldn't be too hard,' she reassured him. 'Three, four guards at most.'

'It's worth taking a look,' he agreed. 'It's that or wait until I can get him the cash tomorrow.'

'Why does he even want it?' She frowned, checking her

mirrors as she turned on to the Lungotevere Arnaldo da Brescia.

'He collects cars,' Tom explained. 'Has about forty of them in a sealed and climate-controlled private underground garage somewhere near Trajan's Column. None of them paid for.'

They followed the river in silence, heading north against the traffic as the road flexed around the riverbank's smooth contours, the sky now bright and clear. Tom caught Allegra glancing at herself in the mirror, her hand drifting unconsciously to her dyed and roughly chopped hair, as if she still couldn't quite recognise herself.

'Tell me about the Banda della Magliana,' he said eventually.

'There are five major mafia organisations in Italy,' Allegra explained, seeming to welcome the interruption. 'The Cosa Nostra and Stidda in Sicily, the Camorra in Naples, the Sacra Corona Unita in Apulia and the 'Ndrangheta in Calabria. The Banda della Magliana was a smaller outfit based here in Rome and controlled by the De Luca family.'

'Was?'

'You might remember that they were linked to a series of political assassinations and bombings between the seventies and the nineties. But since then they've been pretty quiet.'

She leaned on her horn as she overtook a three-wheeled delivery van that was skittering wildly over the worn tarmac.

'And Ricci worked for them?'

'Gallo said he was an enforcer,' she nodded. 'As far as I know the family's still controlled by Giovanni De Luca, although no one's seen him for years.'

'What about the Cosa Nostra, the Banda della Magliana's partner in the Delian League? Who heads them up?'

'Lorenzo Moretti. Or at least that's the rumour. It's not the sort of thing you put on your business card.'

The car pound occupied a large, anonymously grey

multi-storey building at the end of a tree-lined residential street. Two guards were stationed at each of the two sentry posts that flanked the entry and exit ramps. Seeing them walking up to the counter, the officers manning the entrance jumped up and tried to look busy, one of them having been watching TV inside their small office, the other sat outside reading the paper, tipped back on a faded piece of white garden furniture.

'*Buongiorno*.' Allegra flashed a broad smile and her badge in the same instant, snapping it shut before they could get a good look at her name or the picture. 'Sorry to disturb you,' she continued. 'But my friend has had his car stolen.' The two men glanced at Tom accusingly, as if this was somehow his fault.

'It's probably in a container halfway to Morocco by now,' one of them suggested gloomily.

'That's what I told him,' Allegra agreed. 'Only one of his neighbours says they saw it being towed. And this is the closest pound to where he lives.'

'If it's been towed it will be on the database,' one of the officers said to Tom, 'Pay the release fee and you can have it back.'

'He's already looked and it's not there,' she said with a shrug before Tom could answer. 'He thinks that someone might have made a mistake and entered the wrong plates.'

'Really?' The men eyed him like they would a glass of corked wine.

'He's English,' she murmured, giving him the sort of weary look a mother might give a naughty child. The officers nodded in sudden understanding, a sympathetic look crossing their faces. 'Is there any chance we can go up and take a quick look to see if it's here? I'd really appreciate it.'

The two men glanced at each other and then shrugged their agreement.

'As long as you're quick,' one of them said.

'When did it go missing?' the other asked her, ignoring Tom completely now.

'Around the fifteenth of March.'

'We store all the cars in the order they get brought here,' the first officer explained, pointing at a worn map of the complex that had been crudely taped to the counter. 'Cars for that week should be around here – in the blue quadrant on the third floor.' He pointed at a section of the map. 'The lift's down there on the right.'

A few moments later the doors pinged shut behind them.

'You enjoyed that, didn't you?' Tom said in a reproachful tone.

'It could have been worse,' she said with an amused smile. 'I could have told them you were American.'

The lift opened on to the southern end of the third floor. It was a dark, depressing place, most of the neon tubes missing or broken, the walls encrusted with a moulding green deposit, the ceiling oozing a thick yellow mucus that hung in cancerous clumps. The floor was divided by lines of decaying concrete pillars into three long aisles, with cars parked along both sides and a spiralling up-and-down ramp at one end linking it to the other levels like a calcified umbilical cord.

They made their way over to the area pointed out by the guard, dodging around oily lakes of standing water, until they were about halfway down the left-hand aisle. Jennifer took out the keys and pressed the unlock button. Cavalli's car eagerly identified itself with a double flash of its indicators – a souped-up Maserati Granturismo, worth almost double what Johnny was asking for. No wonder he'd pushed them into this.

'What are you doing?' Tom called in a low voice as Allegra opened the boot and leaned inside. 'It must have been searched already.'

'That doesn't mean they found anything,' she replied, her voice muffled.

'Let's just get out of here before they . . .'

She stood up, triumphantly holding a small piece of pottery that had been nestling in a fold in the muddy grey blanket that covered the boot floor. About the size of her hand, it featured a bearded man's face painted in red against a black background.

'It's a vase fragment. Probably Apullian, which dates it to between 430 and 300 BC.'

'Dionysius?' Tom ventured.

'Yes,' she said, looking impressed. 'I'd guess it was part of a *krater*, a bowl used . . .'

'For mixing wine and water,' Tom said, grinning at her obvious surprise. 'My parents were art dealers. My mother specialised in antiquities. I guess I was a good listener.'

'Notice anything strange?' she asked, handing it to him with a nod.

'The edges are sharp.' He frowned, gingerly drawing his finger over one of them as if it was a blade.

'Sharp and clean,' she agreed. 'Which means the break is recent.'

'You mean it was done after it was dug up?' Tom gave her a puzzled look, still holding the fragment.

'I mean it was done on purpose,' she shot back, Tom detecting a hint of anger in her voice. 'See how they've been careful not to damage the painted area so they can restore it.'

'You mean it's been smashed so it can be stuck back together again?' he asked with a disbelieving smile.

'It makes it easier to smuggle,' she explained with a despairing shake of her head. 'Unfortunately, we see it all the time. The fragments are called orphans. The dealers can sometimes make more money selling them off individually than they would get for an intact piece, because they can raise the price as the collector or museum gets more and more desperate to buy all the pieces. And of course, by the time the vase is fully restored, no one can track where or who they bought each fragment from. Everyone's protected.'

'Then Cavalli must have been working either with or for the League,' Tom said grimly as she dropped the boot lid. 'Perhaps they found out that the FBI had his name and killed him before he could talk?'

The noise of an engine starting echoed up to them from one of the lower floors, and drew a worried glance from Tom towards the exit.

'We should go.' He opened the passenger door to get in, but then immediately staggered back, coughing as a choking chemical smell clawed at his throat.

'You okay?' Allegra called out in concern.

'It's been sprayed with a fire extinguisher,' he croaked, pointing at the downy white skin which covered most of the car's interior, apart from where it had been disturbed by the police search. 'Old trick. The foam destroys any fingerprint or DNA evidence.'

'Which Cavalli's killers would only have done if they'd been in the car,' Allegra said thoughtfully, opening the driver's side door and standing back to let the fumes clear.

'Where did they find the car keys?' He asked, rubbing his streaming eyes.

'In his pocket, why?'

'I'm just wondering if he was driving. Based on that I'd guess he was.'

'How do you work that out?'

'Because I doubt his killers drove him out to wherever the car was dumped and then planted the keys on him before killing him.' Tom shrugged.

'What does it matter either way?'

Taking a deep breath, Tom disappeared inside the car. Leaning over the passenger seat, he plunged his hand down the back of the driver's seat, wisps of foam fluttering like ash caught by the wind. Feeling around with his fingertips, he pulled out first some loose change, then a pack of matches, and finally, pushed right down, a folded Polaroid. He stood up, brushing the sticky white paste from his clothes.

'If Cavalli was driving, that's about the only place he would have been able to hide something once he realised what was going on,' he explained, enjoying the look on Allegra's face. 'Here.' He leant over the roof and handed the photo to her. 'Any ideas?'

'Some sort of statue fragment,' she said slowly. 'Greek, I'd guess, although –'

She was interrupted by a shout.

'*Rimanga dove siete*!' Stay where you are!

THIRTY-EIGHT

19th March – 8.51 a.m.

Spinning round, Allegra immediately recognised the two officers they had talked their way past downstairs. One was hunched over the wheel of the blue Fiat squad car that had ghosted up the ramp behind them, its headlights now blazing through the darkness. The other was standing next to it, his voice echoing off the car park's low ceilings, gun drawn.

'We found the car after all,' Allegra stepped towards him with a smile, switching back into Italian. 'My friend just needs to pay . . .'

'I said stay where you are,' the officer barked again, his trigger finger twitching.

'I don't think he's buying it any more,' Tom whispered out of the corner of his mouth.

'No,' she agreed. 'Get in!'

Diving through the open doors, she jammed the key in the ignition, fired up the engine and selected reverse. Tom jumped in alongside her, the crack of a gun shot whistling overhead. The car leapt backwards and swung out, swiping the rear wing of the car parked next to them and setting off the harsh shriek of its two-tone alarm.

'You're facing the wrong way,' Tom shouted, their windscreen now engulfed by the glare of the squad car's headlights as it accelerated, wheels-spinning, towards them.

'Don't tell me how to drive,' she retorted indignantly, turning to look back over her shoulder. 'If I'd tried to reverse out the other way I'd have wrapped it around the pillar.'

She stamped on the pedal, the car springing backwards and then yawing wildly as she fought to keep it straight, traces of foam making the wheel slick in her hands. Tyres screaming, they rounded the corner and then doubled back on themselves, the engine protesting with an angry whine as they sped down the central aisle, the revs climbing steeply.

Another shot rang out. They both flinched. One of their headlights exploded.

'Head down a floor,' Tom suggested. 'Try and get far enough ahead of them to flip it around.'

She cannoned the wrong way on to the up-ramp, the gloom suddenly lit by a blaze of sparks as she glanced off the concrete and used the ramp's curved walls to guide herself down to the second level.

'Someone's coming up the other way,' Tom warned her as a second squad car, siren pulsing, stormed up the ramp towards them, the sweep of its headlights circling beneath them as it rose, like a shark closing in on a seal.

She steered them off the ramp on to the flat, the floorpan slapping the concrete with a heavy bang. From behind them came the angry squeal of brakes as the squad car chasing them fish-tailed to avoid colliding with the second police car coming up the other way. Allegra sensed her opportunity. Leaning on the clutch, she yanked on the handbrake and jerked the wheel hard to spin them round so that they were facing forward, then shoved the car into gear and accelerated away along the left-hand aisle, tyres smoking.

'You've got one right behind, one to the right,' Tom shouted over the engine noise, pointing to where the second car was now speeding down the central aisle, roughly parallel to them.

'They're going to try and cut us off at the end,' she guessed, before glancing down at her lap. 'What the hell are you doing?'

Tom had leant forward and was feeling under the dashboard between her knees.

'Looking for something,' he said, straining to reach.

'I can see that,' she hissed through gritted teeth, his head almost resting on her lap.

'There –' he sat up, 'the front air-bag switch. They put it down there in case you want to disable them.'

She nodded in immediate understanding.

'Hold on.'

Checking in her mirror to see how close the car behind her was, she stamped on the brake. The ABS immediately kicked in, the car juddering to a halt and forcing their pursuers to run into the back of them, the impact knocking them five or six feet forward and wrenching their boot open, so that it was flapping around like a half-opened tin can. What damage they had sustained was as nothing compared to the Fiat, however, which had, unsurprisingly come off second best with both front tyres burst, the engine block almost in the front seat, and the bonnet concertinaed back on itself.

Allegra glanced across at Tom with a satisfied grin, but he was pointing at the second police car, which was already at the far end of the second aisle and rounding the corner towards them.

'Here comes the cavalry.'

Dropping the Maserati into gear, she pulled forward and cut through a gap in the parked cars to her right to reach the central aisle and then spun round, so that she was facing back towards the exit ramp.

'What are you doing?' he asked with a frown.

'Enjoying myself,' she breathed.

Gunning the motor hard, she took off, glancing across at the squad car racing down the adjacent aisle to make sure she was far enough ahead, its surging shape strobing across her eyes as she caught glimpses of it through gaps between the cars and the concrete pillars.

'Now!' Tom called, pulling his seat belt tight across himself and hanging on to the grab handle.

She steered away from the line of cars to her right and then carved back in, ramming an Alfa square on. It jumped forward as if it had been fired from a cannon, colliding with the front of the VW parked only a few inches opposite it, which in turn T-boned the squad car as it came past, sending it ploughing into the line of parked cars on the far side of the aisle.

There was an abrupt, empty moment of calm, the squad car's blue light pulsing weakly in the gloom. Then a jarring chorus of car alarms kicked in, each singing in a different key and to a different tempo, roused by the force of the crash.

'Where did you learn to drive like that?' Tom asked with an approving nod.

'Rush hour in Rome.' She smiled, breathing hard.

'Do you think Johnny will notice the damage?'

She glanced in the mirror and saw the boot lid flapping around behind them like a loose sail, then looked along the crumpled bonnet at the cloud of steam rising from the cracked radiator.

'It'll polish out.' She grinned.

Reversing out, the steering pulling heavily to the right, she nursed the car down the exit ramp and then made her way out on to the street.

THIRTY-NINE

Desposito Eroli, Via Erulo Eroli, Rome
19th March – 9.23 a.m.

'I thought you told these idiots to hold off until we got here when they called?' Gallo said in an accusing tone as Salvatore hurried towards him, his notebook clutched to his chest.

Misfortune was snapping at his heels like one of those annoying handbag dogs, it seemed. First the triangulation of Allegra's mobile phone signal, only for her to have vanished by the time they got there. Then a sighting reported by the officers here, only for her to slip through his fingers a second time, it now seemed.

'I did,' Salvatore sighed wearily. 'Apparently they were trying to lockdown the area in case they drove off.'

'Lockdown the area? The stupid bastards have been watching too much TV,' Gallo glowered at the two men in neck braces being stretchered past him into a waiting ambulance. 'It's just as well she's put them in hospital. She's saved me the trouble.' Cursing under his breath, he lit a cigarette.

'You mean *they* saved you the trouble,' Salvatore corrected him.

'She wasn't alone?' Gallo glanced up, surprised, brushing his long silvery hair back behind each ear.

'There was a man.'

'What man?'

'Not sure yet.'

A pause, as Gallo let this sink in. He'd not banked on her teaming up with someone. Certainly not this soon.

'What were they doing here?'

'They were seen opening up a black Maserati. Registration number . . . JT149VT,' Salvatore read from his notebook.

'Presumably not hers? Not on a lieutenant's salary.'

'Cavalli's.'

Gallo span round to face him.

'Cavalli's?' he spat. 'What the hell was she looking for?' He glared at the building behind him as if it was somehow at fault and owed him an answer. To his surprise, it gave him one.

'There must be a camera up there.' He pointed at the lens fixed above the entrance. 'Get me the disc.'

A few minutes later they were seated around a small monitor in the sentry post, Salvatore forwarding to the time of the last entry in the log. For ten, maybe twenty seconds, the grainy black-and-white footage showed nothing but parked cars and the wet concrete floor, but then, just as Gallo was about to hit the fast forward button again, two people appeared in the shot.

'That's not her,' Salvatore said with a shake of his head.

'Yes it is,' Gallo breathed, reluctantly putting his glasses on so he could see properly. 'She's cut her hair. Dyed it, too. Clever girl.' His face broke into a grudging smile. 'And who are you?' He leaned forward and hit the pause button, squinting to try and make out the face of the man walking next to her.

'Never seen him before,' Salvatore shrugged.

'Get a print of this off to the lab when we've finished,' Gallo ordered, starting the disc again. 'Get them to run it through the system. Interpol too.'

'Where did she get his car keys?' Salvatore asked with a frown as they watched Allegra beep the car open and then step round to the boot.

'Evidence room. They were probably on the same set as . . .' Gallo broke off with a frown as he saw Allegra retrieve something from the boot. He paused the footage again. 'What the hell is that?'

'Christ knows.' Salvatore shrugged. 'The picture's too dark. I'll ask the lab to see what they can do with it.'

'I thought you said that car had been searched?' Gallo barked angrily.

'I . . . I thought it had,' Salvatore stammered. Coughing nervously, he restarted the film only to pause it himself a few moments later.

'He's got something too,' he said, squinting as he tried to make out the image. 'Looks like . . . a piece of paper. Or maybe a photo?'

'I want the names of whoever searched that car,' Gallo said through gritted teeth. 'Their names and their fucking badges.'

A squad car suddenly appeared at the top edge of the screen and one of the guards Gallo had just seen being loaded into the ambulance stepped out. He ejected the disk, lip curled in disgust.

'Put out a revised description of Damico and get something worked up for this guy, whoever he is,' he ordered. 'Then –'

'Colonel, we've found the car!' A young officer had appeared at the door, breathing hard. 'Abandoned in the Borghese Gardens.'

'And Lieutenant Damico?'

'No sign of her I'm afraid.'

Salvatore stood up, giving Gallo an expectant look.

'Go.' He nodded. 'Take whoever you need. Find her. She can't have got far if she's on foot.'

Gallo waited until the room was empty and then dug his phone out of his pocket and dialled a number.

'It's me.' He lit another cigarette and took a long drag. 'We just missed her again.'

He listened, making a face.

'She came looking for Cavalli's car . . . I don't know why, but she found something he'd hidden in it . . . If I had to guess, a photograph.'

Another pause as he listened, his expression hardening.

'How should I know what was on it?' he said angrily. 'I was rather hoping you could tell me.'

FORTY

The train galloped into the station, its metal flanks elaborately embroidered with graffiti – the angry poetry of Rome's disenfranchised youth delivered at the point of an aerosol can. In a few places, the authorities had scrubbed the carriages clean, no doubt in the hope of protecting the wider population from these dangerously subversive voices. Their efforts, however, had largely been in vain, the ghostly outline of the censored thoughts still clearly visible where the chemicals had bleached them, like a scar that refused to heal.

The doors hissed open and a muscular human wave swept Tom and Allegra through the tunnels and up the escalators, until it broke as it reached the street above, beaching them in the shadow of the Spanish Steps.

'Let's head into the centre,' Tom said, shaking off the street hawkers tugging at his sleeve and pointing himself towards the seductive windows of the Via Condotti. 'Stick with the crowds.'

'I know a good place for a coffee,' Allegra suggested with a nod.

Ten minutes later and they were opposite each other in a small cubicle at the rear of a bar on the Piazza Campo Marzio, tucking into pastries and espressos.

'Too strong for you?' Allegra asked with a smile as Tom took a sip.

'Just right.' He grimaced, licking the grit from his front teeth as he glanced round.

The place didn't look as though it had been touched in thirty years, its floor tiles cracked and lifting, the brick walls stained yellow by smoke and festooned with faded Roma flags, tattered banners and crookedly framed match-day programmes. Pride of place, behind the battle-scarred bar, had been given to a signed photograph of a previous Roma club captain who, in what looked like more prosperous times, had clearly once stopped in for a complimentary Prosecco. Apart from Tom and Allegra, it was more or less deserted, a few construction workers loitering at the bar. One had his foot resting on his hardhat, like a hunter posing for a photo with his kill.

'Did you choose this place on purpose?'

'What do you mean?'

'Caravaggio killed a man near the Campo Marzio.'

'I'd forgotten.' She frowned. 'Some sort of a duel, wasn't it?'

'An argument over the score during a game of tennis,' Tom explained, emptying another sugar into his coffee to smooth its bitter edge. 'Or so the story goes. Swords were drawn, and in the struggle . . .'

'Which is how he ended up in Sicily?'

'Via Naples and Malta,' Tom confirmed. 'He painted the *Nativity* while he was still on the run.' A pause. 'That's the wonderful thing about Caravaggio. That he could be so deeply flawed as a person, and yet capable of such beauty. They say his paintings are like a mirror to the soul.'

'Even yours?' she asked, Tom detecting the hint of a serious question lurking behind her teasing smile.

'Perhaps. If I had one.' He smiled back.

Allegra ordered another round of coffees.

'So what are we going to do about Johnny?' she asked as the waiter shuffled away.

'What can we do?' Tom shrugged. 'Even if we hadn't trashed the car, the cops will be all over it by now. We're just going to have to wait until Archie calls and then pay him the cash instead.'

'Archie?'

'My business partner,' Tom explained. 'He's on his way to Geneva, but he knows people here. The sort of people who can lend us fifty grand without asking too many questions. It might take until tonight but as soon as we have it we go back to Johnny, hand it over and see what he knows.'

One of the workers made his way past them, returning a few moments later wiping his hands on his trousers and fastening his fly, the toilet flushing lustily behind him.

'Show me that photo again,' Allegra said, when he was out of earshot.

Reaching into his pocket, Tom laid the Polaroid down between them. It showed a sculpted man's face against a black background, a jagged edge marking where part of his chin and left cheek had broken off.

'It looks like marble. A statue fragment,' she said slowly, turning it to face her. 'Beautifully carved . . .' She ran her fingers across the photo's surface, as if trying to stroke its lips. 'Almost certainly looted.'

'How can you tell?'

'Tomb-robbers always use Polaroids. It avoids the risk of sending negatives off to be developed. And they can't be as easily emailed around as digital photos, allowing you to keep track of who has seen what.'

'Are you sure it's marble?' Tom frowned. 'It looks pretty thin. Almost like some sort of mask.'

'You're right,' she said, peering at the image. 'Strange. To be honest, I've never really seen anything like it before.'

'Then we need to find someone who has. The photo was pushed too far down that seat to have fallen there accidentally. Cavalli must have hidden it for a reason.'

'Well the obvious person is . . .' Allegra began, breaking off as she realised what she was saying.

'Your friend, the professor?' Tom guessed.

'I wasn't thinking.' She shook her head. 'There's no way I'm –'

'You won't have to, I'll do the talking,' Tom reassured her. 'Where can I find him?'

'Forget it,' she sighed impatiently. 'Gallo will have someone watching his apartment.'

'He must go out?'

'Not if he can avoid it,' she said with a shake of her head. 'Bad hip and a completely irrational fear of weeds.'

'Weeds?'

'He's old. It's a long story.'

Tom noticed that, for the briefest of moments, she allowed herself to smile. Then, just as quickly, her face clouded over again.

'Then I'll have to find a way in. There must be –'

'What time is it?' she interrupted, gripping Tom's arm.

'What?'

'The time?'

He glanced up at the pizza-inspired clock tethered to the wall over the toilet.

'Just after ten. Why?' Tom asked as she excitedly stuffed the photograph into her pocket.

'He's giving a lecture this morning,' she exclaimed, sidling along the bench so that she could stand up. 'I saw his notes yesterday. Eleven o'clock at the Galleria Doria Pamphilj.'

Tom jumped up, throwing a handful of change down. 'That doesn't give us much time.'

FORTY-ONE

Hotel Ritz, Madrid, Spain
19th March – 9.48 a.m.

'Oh. It's you.'

Director Bury's face fell, either too jet-lagged or annoyed to conceal his disappointment. It was hard to tell.

'Yes, sir.' Verity Bruce nodded, trying to sound like she hadn't noticed. 'It's me.'

There was a long pause, and he looked at her hopefully, as if she might suddenly remember that she needed to be somewhere else, or that she had accidentally knocked on the wrong door. But she said nothing, playing instead with the silver locket around her neck in the knowledge that it would draw his eyes towards the bronzed curve of her breasts.

'Yes, well,' Bury coughed nervously, his eyes flicking to his feet and then to a point about three inches above her head. 'You'd better come in.'

To say that he had been deliberately avoiding her since the unveiling of the kouros would have been going too far. They'd both had lunch with someone from the mayor's office the previous day, for example, both sat in the first-class cabin together on the flight over and both been guests at that morning's cultural exchange breakfast at the embassy. But to say that he had been avoiding being *alone* with her would have been entirely accurate. He had sought safety in numbers, inventing a reason to leave the lunch early so they wouldn't have to share a taxi back to the museum, arriving at the breakfast late to avoid getting trapped over muffins and orange juice. That's why she'd followed him back to his hotel suite now. She'd known he would be alone and out of excuses.

He walked over to the desk and perched on its edge, indicating that she should sit in one of the low armchairs opposite. She recognised this as one of his usual tricks; a clumsy attempt, no doubt picked up from some assertiveness training course, to gain the psychological advantage by physically dominating the conversation.

'I'll stand, if that's all right,' she said, enjoying his small flicker of anxiety.

'Good idea.' He jumped up, clearly not wanting to get caught out at his own game. 'Too much sitting around in this job.'

'Dominic, I thought it was time we talked. Alone.'

'Yes, yes.' Bury seemed strangely pleased that she'd said this, like someone who was desperate to break up with their partner, but too chicken to bring it up first. He gave a nervous laugh. 'Drink?'

The offer appeared to be directed more at himself than her. She shook her head, her eyebrows raised in surprise.

'It's a little early, isn't it?'

'Not in Europe,' he said quickly. 'When in Rome and all that, hey?'

There was another strained silence as he busied himself over a bottle of scotch and some ice, the neck of the bottle chiming against the glass's rim as his hand trembled while he poured.

'Cheers!' he said, with a rather forced enthusiasm.

'About the other day . . .' she began.

'Very unfortunate,' he immediately agreed, refilling his glass. 'All those people, all those questions . . .' He knocked back another mouthful, swallowing it before it had touched the back of his throat. 'It doesn't look good, you understand.'

'The kouros is genuine,' she insisted. 'You saw the forensic tests.'

'Yes, of course.'

'Only sometimes it's easier for people to attack us than it is for them to accept that their fixed views on the evolution of Greek sculpture might be wrong,' she said, paraphrasing Faulks's rather more eloquent argument from the previous day.

'I know, I know.' Bury sat down wearily, momentarily forgetting his usual mind games, it seemed. 'But the trustees . . .' he said the word as if they were a local street gang who he suspected of vandalising his car. 'They get nervous.'

'Building a collection like ours isn't risk free,' she observed dryly. 'Their canapés and cocktails come with some strings attached.'

'They don't understand the art world,' he agreed. 'They don't understand what it takes to play catch-up with the Europeans and the Met.'

'They're out of their depth,' she nodded. 'And they're dragging us under with them.'

He shrugged and gave a weak smile, not disagreeing with her, she noted.

'They just want to wake up to the right sort of headlines.'

'Then I have just the thing for them,' she jumped in, sensing her moment. 'A unique piece. Impeccable provenance. I'm flying to Geneva tomorrow to see it.'

'Verity –' he stood up again, as if he sensed a negotiation looming and therefore the need to physically reassert himself once more '– I have to tell you that it's going to be a while before the trustees, or me, for that matter . . .'

She thrust the Polaroid Faulks had entrusted her with towards him. He sat down again heavily, his face pale. 'That's . . .'

'Impossible? Wait until I tell you who I think carved it.'

FORTY-TWO

Piazza del Collegio Romano, Rome
19th March – 10.49 a.m.

This was Aurelio's Eco's favourite art gallery. Quite an accolade, when you considered the competition. Yes, the Capitoline Museum was richer, the Vatican Museum bigger, the Galleria Borghese more beautiful. But their fatal flaw was to have been crudely sewn together from larger collections by different patrons over time, leaving ugly and unnatural scars where they joined and overlapped.

The Doria Pamphilj, on the other hand, had been carefully built over the centuries by a single family. In Aurelio's eyes this gave it a completely unique integrity of vision and purpose that stretched unbroken, like a golden thread, back through time. It was a sacred flame, carefully tended by each passing generation and then handed on to the next custodian to nurture. Even today, the family still lived in the palazzo's private apartments, still owned the fabulous gallery that sheltered within its thick walls. He rather liked this – it appealed to his sense of the past and the present and the future and how they were inexorably wedded through history.

He paused on the entrance steps and snatched a glance over his shoulder, tightening his scarf around his neck. Gallo's men weren't even trying to pretend they weren't following him now, two of them having parked up near where he'd been dropped off by his taxi and following on foot about thirty feet behind. He felt more like a prisoner than protected, despite what they'd told him. With a helpless shrug, he placed his hand on the door and heaved it open.

'*Buongiorno, Professore,*' the guard on reception welcomed him cheerily.

He was early, but then he liked to leave himself enough time to check the room and have a final read through his notes. It was funny, but even at his age, after doing this for all these years, he still got nervous. That was the problem with an academic reputation. It was brittle, like porcelain. All those years of care could be shattered in one clumsy moment. And even if you managed to find all the pieces and reassemble them, the cracks invariably showed.

'Expecting a big turnout today?'

'An interpretation of the archaeological remains of the Etruscan bridge complex at San Giovenale,' Aurelio recited the title of his lecture in a deliberate monotone. 'I almost didn't come myself.'

'In other words, I'll be turning people away as usual.' The guard's laughter followed him along the entrance hall.

The one thing Aurelio didn't like about this place was the lift. It was ancient and horribly cramped and seemed to rouse a latent claustrophobia that years of archaeological excavations had never previously disturbed. Still, it was only one floor, he thought to himself as the car lurched unsteadily upwards, and with his hip the way it was, it wasn't as if he had much choice.

Stepping out, he limped though the Poussin and Velvets rooms to the ballroom, where two banks of giltwood and red velvet chairs had already been laid out. Enough seating for fifty, he noted with a smile. Perhaps the turnout wouldn't be so bad after all.

'Are you alone?'

He turned to see a man closing the door behind him, the key turning in the lock.

'The lecture doesn't start until eleven,' he replied warily.

'Are you alone, Aurelio?' A woman stood framed in the doorway to the small ballroom, her face stone, her voice like ice.

FORTY-THREE

Galleria Doria Pamphilj, Rome
19th March – 10.57 a.m.

'Allegra?' Aurelio gasped. 'Is that you? What have you done to yourself?'

'How many?' Tom growled in Italian.

'What?' Aurelio's eyes flicked back to him.

'How many men followed you here?'

'Two,' he stuttered. 'Two, I think. Gallo's. They've been watching me ever since . . .'

'Ever since you betrayed me?' Allegra hissed. It was strange. She'd felt many things for Aurelio since yesterday afternoon. Sadness, disbelief, confusion. But now that he was actually standing in front of her, it was her anger, instinctive and uncontained, that had come most naturally.

'We haven't got time for that now,' Tom warned her, bolting shut the door that gave on to the adjacent ballroom. 'Just show it to him.'

'I'm sorry, Allegra. I'm so sorry,' Aurelio whispered, reaching pleadingly towards her. 'I should have told you. I should have told you everything a long time ago.'

'Save it,' she snapped, stony faced, then pressed the photo into his hands. 'What is it?'

He gazed down at the picture, then looked up, open mouthed.

'Is this real?' he croaked.

'What is it?' Tom repeated.

'It looks Greek,' Allegra prompted. 'I thought the marble could be from Pentelikon.'

'Greek, yes, but that's not marble.' He shook his head excitedly, his eyes locking with hers. 'It's ivory.'

'Ivory?' she repeated breathlessly. It was obvious, now he'd mentioned it. Obvious and yet impossible.

'It's a mask from a chryselephantine statue,' Aurelio confirmed. 'Circa 400 to 500 BC. Probably of the sun god Apollo.' A pause. 'Are you sure this is real?' he asked again.

'Chryselephantine means gold and ivory in Greek,' Allegra quickly explained in English, seeing the confused look on Tom's face. 'They used to fix carved slabs of ivory on to a wooden frame for the head, hands and feet and then beat sheets of gold leaf on to the rest to form the clothes, armour and hair.'

'It's rare?'

'It's a miracle,' Aurelio replied in a hushed tone, almost as if they weren't there. 'There used to be seventy-four of them in Rome, but they all vanished when it was sacked by the Barbarians in 410 AD. Apart from two fire-damaged examples found in Greece and a fragment in the Vatican Museum, not a single piece has survived. Certainly nothing of this size and quality.'

Their eyes all shot to the door as someone tried the handle, rattling it noisily.

'Time to go,' Tom said firmly, snatching the photo from his grasp. 'The private apartments should still be clear. We can go out the same way we came in.'

'Wait,' Aurelio called after them. 'Don't you want to know who it's by?'

'You can tell that from a photo?' Allegra frowned, something in his voice making her pause.

There was a muffled shout and then a heavy drum roll of pounding fists.

'Not definitively. Not without seeing it,' he admitted. 'But if I had to guess . . . there's only one sculptor from that period that we know of who was capable of something of that quality. The same person who carved the statue of Athena in the Parthenon. The same person who carved the statue of Zeus at Olympia, one of the Seven Wonders of the Ancient World.'

'Phidias?' Allegra guessed, her mouth suddenly dry. No wonder Aurelio had turned pale.

'Who else?' He nodded excitedly. 'Don't you see, Allegra? It's a miracle.'

'Let's go,' Tom repeated, grabbing Allegra's arm, the door now shaking violently. But she wrestled herself free, determined to ask the one question that she most wanted answered.

'Why did you do it, Aurelio?' she snapped. 'Has Gallo got something on you?'

'Gallo? I'd never even heard of him until yesterday,' he protested.

'Then who were you on the phone to?'

There was a long pause, Aurelio's lips quivering as though the words were trapped in his mouth.

'The League.'

'The Delian League?' she breathed, not sure which was worse – Aurelio working with Gallo, as she'd first assumed, or this?

'They said they wouldn't hurt you. That they just wanted to see what you knew,' he pleaded. 'I wanted to tell you everything. Have done for a long time. When you told me about the lead discs and the killings . . . I tried to point you in the right direction. But I was afraid.'

Abruptly, the noise outside stopped.

'They'll be back with a key,' urged Tom. 'Come on!'

'You could have trusted me,' she insisted, ignoring Tom. 'I could have helped you.'

'It was too late for that. It's been twenty, thirty years. They'd kept records of everything I'd ever done for them. The false attributions, the inflated valuations, the invented provenances. I needed the money. You see that, don't you? I needed the money to finance my work. Who else was going to pay? The university? The government? Pah!'

'Who are they?' she pressed. 'Give me a name.'

'Th-there was a dealer who I met a few times,' he muttered. 'An American called Faulks who used to fly in from Geneva. He was with them, I'm sure of it. But everyone else was just a voice on the phone. Believe me, Allegra, I tried to get out so many times. Tried to give it up. But the older I got, the harder it became to throw everything away.'

'Throw what away?'

'Oh, you don't understand. You're too young.' He gave an exasperated sigh, throwing his hands up as if she had somehow let him down. 'You don't know what it means to be old, to be out of breath from tying your shoelaces, to not be able to take a piss without it hurting.'

'What's that got to do . . .?'

'My books, my research – everything I'd ever worked for . . . my whole life. It would all have been for nothing if they'd leaked my involvement.'

'Your books?' she repeated with an empty laugh. 'Your books!'

'Don't you see?' he pleaded, a desperate edge to his voice now. 'I had no choice. My reputation was all I had left.'

'No,' she said, with a broken smile. 'You had me.'

FORTY-FOUR

Quai du Mont Blanc, Geneva
19th March – 11.16 a.m.
There was a definite spring in Earl Faulks's step that morning,
despite the slightly bitter taste left by Deena Carroll's sermon-
ising earlier. After everything he'd done for them over the
years . . . the ungrateful bitch. The truth was that, having
thought about it, he was rather glad she'd turned him down.
With Klein as good as dead, he was no use to him any more
anyway, so why do her any favours? Better to give someone
else a sniff of the action.

Besides, he could afford to take a small risk. Things were
going well. Much better, in fact than he had anticipated. His
courier had cleared the border at Lake Lugano that morning
and was due down at the Free Port any time now. In Rome,
meanwhile, events were unfolding far more quickly and
dramatically than he had ever dreamt would be possible.
That was the beauty of the Italians, he mused. They were
an amaretto paper of a race – ready to ignite at the faintest
spark.

There had been that unhelpful little episode with the
kouros at the Getty, of course, although for the moment at

least, tempers seemed to have cooled. Having seen the ivory mask, Verity had understood that there was a far greater prize at stake here than a dry academic debate over a statue's marble type and muscle tone. Barring any last-minute disaster, she was due in from Madrid around lunchtime the following day.

Until then he had an auction to prepare for, lots to examine, commission bids to place . . . On cue, his car drew up outside Sotheby's. He sat back, waiting for his chauffer to jog round and open his door, but then waved him away when his phone began to ring. An American number that he didn't recognise. A call he wanted to take.

'Faulks.'

'This is Kezman,' the voice replied.

'Mr Kezman . . .' Faulks checked his watch in surprise – a classic fluted steel Boucheron. 'Thank you for returning my call. I wasn't expecting to hear from you so late.'

'I'm in the casino business. This is early,' he growled.

'Mr Kezman, I don't know if you know . . .'

'Yeah, I know who you are,' he shot back. 'Avner Klein's a personal friend. He told me about you.'

'And he told me about you,' purred Faulks. 'Said you were a shrewd collector.'

'Don't blow smoke up my ass. I pay people for that and I guarantee they've all got bigger tits than you. If you've got something to sell, sell it.'

'Fair enough. Here's the pitch: seven and a half million and your name in lights.'

'My name's in ten foot neon out on the Strip already.' Kezman gave an impatient laugh. 'Tell me about the money.'

'Seven and a half million dollars,' Faulks repeated slowly. 'Risk free.'

'Why don't you leave the odds to the experts?' Kezman snapped.

'How would you price a federal government guarantee?'

There was a pause.

'Go on.'

Faulks smiled. He had his attention now.

'An . . . item has come into my possession. An item of immense historical and cultural significance. I want you to buy it off me for ten million dollars.'

'Sure. Why not make it twenty?' Kezman gave a hollow laugh. 'The global economy's on its knees, but let's not let small details like that get in the way.'

'Then, you're going to donate it to Verity Bruce at the Getty,' he continued, ignoring the interruption. 'She will value it at fifty million, its true price. This will lead the IRS . . .'

'To give me a seventeen and a half million tax credit for having made a fifty-million-dollar charitable donation,' Kezman breathed, his flippant tone vanishing.

'Which, subtracting the ten you will have paid me, nets out at a seven and a half million profit, courtesy of Uncle Sam. Not to mention the PR value of the coverage that will be triggered by your generosity,' Faulks added. 'Hell, they'd probably name a wing after you, if you asked.'

'How firm is the valuation?'

'Do you know Verity Bruce?' Faulks asked.

'I had breakfast with her two weeks ago.'

'She's due here tomorrow to authenticate the piece. Something this rare isn't affected by short-term economic factors. The value will hold.'

Kezman was silent for a few moments. Faulks waited, knowing that his next question would reveal how well he'd played his hand.

'When would you need the money?'

Blackjack.

'A few days. A week at most.'

'If Verity okays it, I'm in,' Kezman confirmed. 'You have my private number now. Just get her to call me when she's seen it.'

'Wait! Don't you even want to know what it is?' Faulks asked with a frown.

A pause.

'Will I make any more if I do?'

'No,' Faulks conceded.

'Then why should I care?'

FORTY-FIVE

Via del Governo Vecchio, Rome
19th March – 11.32 a.m.

The streets were dark and narrow here, the buildings seeming to arch together over Tom and Allegra's heads like trees kissing over a country lane. It was busy too; people carefully picking their way along the narrow pavements, dodging around the occasional dog turds and an elderly woman who was furiously scrubbing her marble doorstep. The traffic, meanwhile, was backed up behind a florist's van which had stopped to make a delivery. Alerted by the relentless sounding of impatient car horns, a few people were leaning curiously over their balconies, some observing events with a detached familiarity, others hurling insults at the van driver for his selfishness. Glancing up, he made an obscene gesture, and pulled away.

Allegra was silent, her eyes rarely lifting from her shoes. She was hurting, Tom knew, probably even blaming herself for Aurelio's betrayal, as if his selfishness and pride was somehow her fault. He tried to think of something to say that might comfort her and relieve her imagined guilt. But he couldn't. Not without lying. The truth was that in time the floodwaters of her anger and confusion would recede, leaving behind them the tidemark of their lost friendship. And whatever he said, that would never fade. He, of all people, bore the fears of betrayal.

'What other Phidias pieces are there?' he asked, stepping to one side to let past a woman holding on to five yapping dogs, the leashes stretching from her hands like tentacles.

'There's a torso of Athena in the École des Beaux-Arts in Paris that's been attributed to him,' she replied without looking up. 'And they found a cup inscribed with his name in the ruins of the workshop at Olympia where he assembled the statue of Zeus.'

'But nothing like the mask?'

'Not even close.' She shook her head. 'If Aurelio's right, it's priceless.'

'Everything has a price,' Tom smiled. 'The trick is finding someone willing to pay it.'

'Maybe that's what Cavalli was doing the night he was killed,' she said, grimacing as an ancient Vespa laboured past, its wheezing engine making the windows around them rattle under the strain. 'Meeting a buyer. Or at least someone he thought was a buyer.'

'It would explain why he had the Polaroid on him,' Tom agreed. 'And why he hid it when he realised what they really wanted.'

'But not where he got the mask from in the first place.' She paused, frowning, as the road brought them out on to the Piazza Ponte Sant'Angelo. 'What are we doing here?'

'Isn't this where you said Cavalli was killed?' Tom asked.

'Yes, but . . .'

'I thought we should take a look.'

A steady two-way traffic of pedestrians was streaming over the bridge's polished cobbles, the hands and faces of the statues lining the parapet seeming strangely animated under the sun's flickering caress, as if they were waving them forward. For Tom, at least, the wide-open vista was a welcome relief from the narrow street's dark embrace.

'Where did they find him?' he asked, hands shoved deep into his coat pockets.

'In the river. Hanging from one of the statues.'

'Killed on the anniversary of Caesar's murder, only for Ricci to be murdered on the site of Caesar's assassination,' he said thoughtfully.

'With both Ricci's and Argento's deaths staged as a re-enactment of a Caravaggio painting.' She nodded impatiently. 'We've been through all this.'

'I know.' He shrugged. 'It's just that everything about these murders has been so deliberate. The dates, the locations, the arrangement of the bodies, the careful echoing of some element of the one that had preceded it. It's almost as if . . . they weren't just killings.'

'Then what were they?'

Tom paused before answering. In the distance the glorious dome of St Peter's rose into the sky, massive and immutable. Around it swarmed a flock of pigeons, their solid mass wheeling and circling like a shroud caught in the wind.

'Messages,' he said eventually. 'Maybe someone was trying to have a conversation.'

'If you're right, it started with Cavalli,' she said slowly, her eyes narrowing in understanding.

'Exactly. So, why kill him here? Why this bridge? They must have chosen it for a reason.'

Allegra paused a few moments before answering, her face creased in thought.

'It was originally built to connect the city to Hadrian's mausoleum. Before becoming a toll road for pilgrims who wanted to reach St Peter's. And in the sixteenth and seven-

teenth centuries, of course, they used to display the bodies
of executed prisoners along it as a warning.'

'A warning to who?' Tom frowned, then nodded at the
weathered shapes looming over them. 'What about the
statues? Do they mean anything?'

'Commissioned from Bernini by Pope Clement IX. Each
angel is holding an object from the Passion. Cavalli's rope
was tied to the one holding a cross.'

'Which was then echoed by Ricci's inverted crucifixion and
Argento being found in a church.' Tom clicked his fingers as
two more small pieces of the puzzle fell into place.

'That's not the only thing,' Allegra added excitedly, a
thought having just occurred to her. 'Cavalli's not the first
person to have been killed here.'

'What do you mean?'

'A noblewoman called Beatrice Cenci was tortured and
put to death on the Piazza Ponte Sant'Angelo in 1599,' she
explained. 'It was one of Rome's most notorious public execu-
tions.'

'What had she done?'

'Murdered her father.'

Tom nodded slowly, remembering the deliberate violence
with which Cavalli's house had been ransacked.

'Patricide. Treason. Maybe that's it. Maybe Cavalli had
betrayed the League and this was his punishment?' He gave
a deep sigh, then turned to her with a shrug. 'Your guess is
as good as mine. Come on, let's try and call Archie. He should
have landed by now.'

They turned and walked to the end of the bridge, Tom
reaching for his phone as they waited for a break in the
traffic. But before they could cross, a large armoured truck
gunned down the road towards them. Two men jumped down
holding what Tom recognised as what the Sicilian mafia called
a Lupara – a traditional break-open design shotgun, sawn off

a few inches beyond the stock to make it more effective at close range and easier to manoeuvre and hide. The weapon of choice in old-school vendettas.

A woman screamed and Tom could hear the fumbling scramble of panicked feet behind him as people scattered.

'Get in,' one of the men barked.

FORTY-SIX

Lungotevere Vaticano, Rome
19th March – 11.53 a.m.

Looking around him, Tom could see that the truck's interior had been furnished like an expensive office, the floor laid with thick carpet, the sides lined with a cream wallpaper decorated with tropical birds. To his left a red leather sofa abutted what he assumed was a toilet cubicle, its door latched shut. In the far right-hand corner, meanwhile, stood an elegant cherrywood desk on which a brass banker's lamp illuminated a laptop and a police scanner spitting static. Overhead were four flat-panel screens, each tuned to a different news or business channel. Most telling, perhaps, was the gun rack opposite the sofa, which contained four MP5s, half a dozen Glock 17s and a pair of Remington 1100s. Neatly stacked on the shelves below were two dozen grenades and several boxes of ammunition. Enough to start and win a small war.

The gears crunched and the truck swayed forward with a determined snarl. The gunman who had followed them inside waved at them to sit down and then instructed them to hand-cuff themselves to the hoop bolted to the wall above them so that their arms were held above their heads. Stepping forward, he made sure that the ratchets were tight against their wrists and then emptied their pockets and Tom's bag, pausing over the FBI file and the Polaroid of the ivory mask. In the background, Tom could make out the opening aria of the *Cavalleria Rusticana*.

There was the muffled sound of the toilet flushing. The latch clicked open and a man walked out, placing a folded newspaper down on the desk as he turned to face them. Tall and square faced, he had a thinning head of hair that rose in white waves at the front and then foundered into a black expanse at the rear. He was smartly dressed in a grey Armani suit and gaudy Versace tie with matching pocket handkerchief. The collar of his white shirt, however, appeared to be several sizes too small, as if he had gambled on not buying a new one in the belief that he would lose some weight. If so, it was a bet that he appeared destined to lose, his once sharp cheekbones sinking into his face like smudged lines on a charcoal drawing, a fleshy crevice forming in the cleft of his chin.

The guard handed him the file and the Polaroid. He glanced at each of them, then sat down. Swivelling to face them, he adjusted his cuffs, carefully covering his watch.

'Welcome to Rome, Signor Kirk.' He spoke in a thick accent, his eyes fixing them with a cold, mortuary gaze.

'You know him?' Allegra's voice was both angry and disbelieving.

Tom frowned as he tried to place the face, then gave a small shake of his head.

'Should I?'

'Should he?' the man asked Allegra, his face creased into a question.

'He's Giovanni De Luca,' Allegra replied unsmilingly. 'The head of the Banda della Magliana.'

Tom's eyes flickered in recognition. So much for tracking the Delian League down and the element of surprise. Instead, one half of it had come looking for them and sprung its own trap.

'Felix doesn't know me,' De Luca said, his flickering smile suggesting he was pleased that she had recognised him. 'But I had the pleasure of meeting his mother once.'

'My mother?' Tom breathed, not knowing whether to sound angry or astonished.

'A fundraising dinner many years ago. A beautiful woman, if I may say so. A terrible loss. Of course, it was only many years later that I heard of you.'

'Heard what, exactly?' Allegra asked, eyeing Tom with the same suspicious look she'd had back in Cavalli's house when she'd first met him.

'It's hard to be good at what Felix does without word getting out. He has a special talent.'

'Had,' Tom corrected him. 'I got out a few years ago.'

'And yet, from what I hear, you're still running.' He nodded towards the scanner.

'Is that what this is about?' Tom asked impatiently. His arms were beginning to ache and every gear change and bump in the road was making the cuffs saw a little deeper into his wrists.

'What's this?' De Luca waved the photo at him.

'We found it in Cavalli's car,' Tom explained. 'We think he was trying to sell it.'

'What do you know about Cavalli?' De Luca shot back, spitting the name out in a way that revealed more than he had probably intended.

Tom nodded slowly, immediately guessing at the truth.

'Why did you kill him?'

De Luca paused, then inclined his head in a small bow, as if acknowledging applause.

'Strictly speaking, the river killed him.'

'Did he work for you?'

'Pfff! He was one of Moretti's.'

Moretti. Tom recognised the name as the person Allegra had identified as supposedly heading up the *other* half of the Delian League. De Luca's supposed business partner.

'What had he done?' Allegra asked.

'I only kill for two reasons. Theft and disloyalty.' De Luca counted them off on his fingers as if he were listing the ingredients for a recipe. 'In Cavalli's case, he was guilty of both.'

'You mean he'd betrayed the League?' Tom asked.

'It seemed fitting to mark his treachery on the spot of an earlier treason,' De Luca nodded, confirming what they'd already guessed on the bridge.

The van turned sharply left. Allegra slid across the seat, pressing up against Tom.

'And Ricci?' Allegra asked.

'I took care of Cavalli to protect the League. But Moretti, the old fool, got it into his head that I was about to make a move on the whole operation.' De Luca's tone hardened, his jaw clenching. 'He had Ricci killed to warn me off. Argento was me evening the score.'

Tom nodded as the realisation dawned that far from being a conversation the careful echoing and symbolism of the various deaths had in fact been the opening shots of a very public, very acrimonious divorce.

'And now it seems my accountant in Monaco has disappeared,' he continued angrily. 'Well, if Moretti wants a war, I'm ready for him.' He struck his chest with his fist, the dull thud revealing that he was wearing a bullet-proof vest under his shirt.

'What did Jennifer Browne have to do with your war?' Tom demanded angrily.

'Who?' De Luca frowned.

'The FBI agent you had killed in Vegas.'

'What FBI agent?'

'Don't lie to me,' Tom shouted, his wrists straining against the handcuffs.

'Cavalli was going to sing, so I clipped his wings,' De Luca said in a low, controlled voice. 'Ricci and Argento – that's just business between Moretti and me. But I had nothing to do with killing any FBI agent. I've never even heard of her.'

'She was closing in on the Delian League, so you had her taken out,' Tom insisted.

'Is that what this is about? Is that why you're here?' De Luca picked up the FBI file and glanced at its monogrammed cover with a puzzled shrug. 'Well then, maybe somebody did us a favour. Either way, I never ordered the hit.'

'Well, somebody in the League did,' Tom insisted. 'And I'll take you all down to find them, if I have to.'

There was a pause. De Luca blew out the sides of his cheeks, clearly mulling something over. Then, with a shrug, he nodded.

'Yes. I expect you probably would.'

Tom felt the needle before he saw it, a sharp stab of pain in his neck where the guard had stepped forward and pulled the trigger on an injection gun. Allegra was next, her head slumping forward as he felt the room begin to spin and darken. The last thing he was aware of was De Luca's voice, deepening and slowing as if being played back at half speed.

'Do give my best to your mother.'

FORTY-SEVEN

Sotheby's auction rooms, Quai du Mont Blanc, Geneva
19th March – 1.32 p.m.
Short, perhaps only four feet high, she had braided hair that fell across her forehead and down her neck. Dressed in a simple tunic that hung from her body in smooth folds, a hunting strap ran down from her shoulder and across her breasts, pulling the material tight against their firm slope. Gazing straight ahead, she wore a slight smile, lips parted as if she was about to speak. Her arms were cut off at the elbows.

'Statue of the goddess Artemis; fourth century BC,' Archie murmured to himself as he looked down from the marble sculpture to the auction catalogue and scanned through the entry again. 'Believed to be from a settlement near Foggi. Private Syrian collection.'

This last detail made Archie smile. Even if Tom hadn't asked him to investigate this lot, the fact that it had supposedly come from a Syrian family would have made him suspicious anyway. The simple truth was that, while the contents of most major European and American collections were well documented, little, if anything, was known about the majority of Middle Eastern and Asian private collections. Anyone trying to disguise the fact that an artefact was looted, therefore, was far more likely to tie it back to some obscure family collection where they could convincingly claim it had been languishing for the last eighty years, than to risk the awkward questions that a European provenance might trigger.

He stepped back and pretended to study some of the other lots, ignoring the call on his phone which he guessed, from the New York prefix, was the lawyer they'd met at Senator Duval's funeral still trying to arrange a meeting with Tom. Next time, he'd know better than to hand out his card so readily, he thought to himself with a pained sigh.

Looking up, he caught sight of Dominique de Lecourt standing near the entrance. Seeing her now, blonde hair cascading on to her delicate shoulders, it struck him that her pale, oval face mirrored something of the goddess Artemis's cold, sculpted and remote beauty. There was a parallel too, between the statue's simple tunic and her tailored linen dress, and perhaps even an echo of the carved hunting strap in the rearing stallion that he knew Dominique had had tattooed on her shoulder when younger. But any resemblance was only a fleeting one, the illusion shattered by her Ducati biker jacket and the way her blue eyes glittered with a wild freedom that the marble sculpture would never taste.

She was too young for him, although that hadn't stopped him thinking about what might have been from time to time. Still only twenty-five, in fact. Not that her age had prevented her from successfully running Tom's antiques business, having helped him transfer it from Geneva to London after his father died. This was her first time back here since then, and he could tell she was finding it difficult, however much she was trying to hide it.

She had been close to Tom's father – far closer, in fact, than Tom himself. The way she told the story, he had saved her from herself, offering her a job rather than calling the cops when he'd caught her trying to steal his wallet. With it had come a chance to break free from the spiralling cycle of casual drugs and petty crime that a childhood spent being tossed between foster homes had been steering her towards; a chance she'd grabbed with both hands. All of which made what they were about to do that much more ironic.

He nodded at her as Earl Faulks turned to leave the room, leaning heavily on his umbrella. Even if the auctioneer hadn't accepted the carefully folded five-hundred-euro note to finger him as the lot's seller, Archie would have guessed it was him. It wasn't just that he had returned four times during the viewing period that had marked him out, but the questioning look he had given anyone who had strayed too close to the statue. It rather reminded Archie of a father weighing up a potential boyfriend's suitability to take their teenage daughter out on a date.

Seeing Archie's signal, Dominique set off, bumping into Faulks heavily as they crossed.

'*Pardon,*' she apologised.

'That's quite all right,' Faulks snapped, a cold smile flickering across his face before, with a curt nod, he limped on.

'Go,' she whispered as she walked past Archie, their hands briefly touching as she handed him Faulks's PDA.

Turning to face the wall, Archie deftly popped off the rear cover, removed the battery and then slipped out the SIM card. Sliding it into a reader connected to an Asus micro laptop, he scanned its contents, the software quickly identifying the IMSI number, before girding itself to decrypt its Ki code.

Archie glanced up at Dominique, who had moved back

towards the entrance and was signalling at him to hurry. Archie gave a grim nod, his heart racing, but the programme was still churning as it tried to break the 128-bit encryption, numbers scrolling frantically across the screen.

He looked up again, and cursed when he saw that she was now mouthing that Faulks was leaving. Damn! He'd counted on him staying for the auction itself, although he knew that some dealers preferred not to attend their own sales in case they jinxed them. He looked back down at the computer. Still nothing. Dominique was looking desperate now. Back to the screen again.

Done.

Snatching the SIM card out of the reader, he hurried to the door, fumbling as he slid it back into Faulks's phone and fitted the battery and then the cover. He crossed Dominique, their hands briefly touching again as slipped her the micro-computer, leaving her the final task of programming a new card.

'He's outside,' she breathed.

Archie sprinted into the hall, down the stairs and through the main entrance. Faulks was settling back in the rear seat of a silver Bentley, his chauffeur already at the wheel and turning the ignition key.

'Excuse me, mate,' Archie panted, rapping sharply on the window.

The window sank and Faulks, sitting forward on his seat, fixed him with a suspicious look.

'Can I help you?'

'You dropped this.'

Faulks looked at the phone, patted his breast pockets, then glanced up at Archie.

'Thank you,' he said, his wary look fading into a grateful smile. Taking it with a nod, he sat back, the window smoothly sealing itself shut.

As Faulks's car accelerated away, Dominique appeared at Archie's shoulder.

'All sorted?' he puffed.

'We've got him.' She nodded, handing him the newly cloned phone.

FORTY-EIGHT

Nr Anguillara Sabazia, northwest of Rome
19th March – 8.34 p.m.

Tom's eyes flickered open. The room slowly came into focus. Allegra was lying on the tiled floor next to him. Still breathing.

Gingerly pulling himself upright, he sat with his back against the wall, trying not to vomit. The drugs had left him dizzy and with a bitter taste at the back of his throat. Worse still was the headache centred behind his right eye, the daggered pain ebbing and flowing with the hammer beat of his pulse. Within seconds he'd fainted back to sleep, vaguely aware of a dancing blue light licking the walls, of the whisper of running water, of the deadened echo of his own breathing, and of De Luca's warm breath on his neck. *Do give my best to your mother.*

'Tom?'

Allegra had rolled over on to her side to face him, her dark hair tumbling forward over her face. She looked worried and he wondered how long she had been calling his name.

He groaned as he sat up, his neck stiff where his head had fallen forward on to his chest.

'What time is it?' she asked.

He checked his watch, then remembered with a rueful grimace that it was still wrapped around Johnny Li's tattooed wrist.

'No idea.'

'*Merda.*' She rubbed her hands wearily across her face, then sat up next to him. 'Where do you think they've taken us?'

Tom looked around with a frown. They were at one end of a windowless room that had been almost entirely swallowed by what appeared to be a large swimming pool. Five feet deep, sixty feet long and thirty feet across, it was lined with white tiles, the water spilling with a gurgling noise over the edges into an overflow trench and washing through skimmers. The underwater lights cast a shimmering flicker on to the white-washed concrete walls.

Standing up, Tom walked unsteadily to the edge. His eyes adjusting, it took him a few moments to realise that the dark shapes lurking under the water's silvered surface were rows of antique vases and jars, each carefully spaced one from the other along the pool floor like vines anchored to a steep slope. Stiff and still, they reminded him of a Roman cohort arranged in a *testudo* formation, their shields held over their heads like a tortoise's shell, bracing themselves for an attack.

'It's a chemical bath,' he said, pointing at the blue drums that explained the slight burning sensation in his eyes.

'I've seen something like this before,' Allegra nodded, joining him. 'But not this big. Not even close.'

'Over there,' Tom pointed hopefully at a door on the far side of the pool.

They passed through into a large room, its tiled walls lined with glass-fronted cabinets that contained a rainbow array of paints and chemicals in differently sized and shaped tins and jars. Beneath these, running along each wall, were polished stainless steel counters loaded with microscopes, centrifuges, test-tube racks, scales, shakers and other pieces of laboratory equipment.

The centre of the room, meanwhile, was taken up by two large stainless steel benches and deep sinks. A trolley laden with knives, saws, picks, tweezers, drills and other implements had been drawn up next to them, as if in preparation for an imminent procedure. In the corner was a coiled hosepipe, the white tiled floor sloping towards a central drain as if to carry away blood.

'Cleaning, touching up, repairs, open-heart surgery . . .' Tom pursed his lips. 'This is a tombaroli restoration outfit.'

'On an industrial scale,' she agreed, Tom detecting the same instinctive anger in her voice as when she'd found the orphan vase fragment in Cavalli's car.

There was another unlocked door which gave, in turn, on to a third room, lit by a single naked bulb whose weak glare didn't quite reach to the corners. Here there was a more rustic feel, the ceiling supported by parallel lines of closely spaced wooden beams, semicircular iron-framed windows set into the stone walls at above head height and welded shut. A flight of stone steps led upstairs to another door. Predictably, this one was locked.

Shrugging dejectedly, Tom made his way back down. Allegra was waiting for him, silently pointing, her outstretched arm quivering with rage.

Looking around, he could see that the paved floor was covered in a foaming sea of dirty newspapers, wooden crates and old fruit and shoe boxes, some stacked into neat piles, others split open or listing dangerously where the cardboard had collapsed under their combined weight. He only had to open a few to guess at the contents of all the others – antique vases still covered in dirt, loose jumbles of glass and Etruscan jewellery, envelopes bulging with Roman coins, gold rings strewn on the floor. In the corner was what had once been an entire fresco, now hacked away from the wall and chain-sawed into laptop-sized chunks. Presumably to make them easier to move and sell.

'How could they do this?' Allegra breathed, her anger tinged by a horrified sadness.

'Because none of this has any value to them other than what they can sell it for. Because they don't care. Look.'

He nodded with disgust towards one of the open shoe-boxes. It was stuffed with rings and human bones, the tombaroli having simply snapped off the fingers of the dead to save time.

'You think this is where Cavalli got the ivory mask?' she asked, looking away with a shudder.

'I doubt it,' Tom sighed, sitting down heavily on the bottom step. 'Whoever owns this place must work for De Luca, and he certainly didn't look like he'd ever seen the mask before.'

'He may not have seen it, but he might have found out that Cavalli was ripping him off,' she suggested, sitting down next to him. 'Theft and disloyalty, remember? According to De Luca, Cavalli was guilty of both. Maybe Cavalli was trying to sell the mask behind the League's back.'

'So De Luca killed Cavalli, Moretti evened the score by murdering Ricci, and then De Luca struck back by executing Argento. He was right. We've stumbled into a war.'

'That must be why they both put the lead discs on the bodies.'

'What do you mean?'

'Remember I told you that the original Delian League was to have lasted as long as the lead its members had thrown into the sea didn't rise to the surface? The discs were to signal that this new alliance was fracturing.'

'None of which explains who ordered the hit on Jennifer or why.' He sighed impatiently.

'You don't think De Luca had anything to do with it?'

'I don't know. Maybe . . . No. I think he would have told me if he had.'

'Then who?'

Tom shook his head, still no closer to the truth. There was a long pause.

'She must have meant a lot to you,' Allegra said gently. 'For you to have come all this way. For you to be risking so much.'

'She trusted me to do the right thing,' Tom answered with a half smile. 'That's more than most have ever done.'

There was another, long silence, Tom staring at the floor.

'How did you two meet?'

He was glad that Allegra hadn't picked up on the obvious cue and said that she trusted him too. He wouldn't have believed her if she had. Not yet at least.

'In London,' he began hesitantly. 'She thought I'd broken into Fort Knox.' He smiled at the memory of their first bad-tempered exchange in the Piccadilly Arcade.

'Fort Knox!' She whistled. 'What did she think you'd . . .'

She broke off as the door above them was unbolted and thrown open. A man stood silhouetted in the doorway, his long shadow stretching down the stairs towards them. He was holding a hip flask.

'Let's go for a drive.'

FORTY-NINE

**Banco Rosalia head office, Via Boncompagni, Rome
19th March – 9.24 p.m.**
'So? How much are we down?' Santos sniffed, helping himself to a half tumbler of Limoncella from the drinks trolley.

Alfredo Geri looked up from his laptop, frowning slightly as he worked through the math. Five feet ten, he was wearing a grey suit, his tie yanked down, jacket trapped under the wheel of his chair where it had fallen on to the floor and he'd run over it. His thin black hair was slicked down against his marbled scalp, his face gaunt and bleached a cadaverous shade of white by lack of sleep and sunlight. To his right, balancing precariously on a slumping battlement of stacked files, was a pizza box that he'd not yet had time to open.

'Now I've had a chance to look properly . . . eight . . . maybe nine?'

'Eight or nine what?' Santos snapped. He sat down heavily at the head of the table, a blanket of scattered paper stretching along its polished surface like an avalanche over a valley floor. 'It's a big number. Show it some respect.'

'Eight or nine hundred million. Euro.'

'Eight or nine hundred million euro.' Santos closed his

eyes and sighed heavily, then gave a rueful smile as he kicked back. 'You know, the strange thing is that a few months ago losing just fifty million would have felt like the end of the world. Now, it feels like a rounding error.'

He reached for his tin of liquorice, shook it, then popped the lid.

'It's the CDOs that have killed us,' Geri continued, putting his half-moon glasses back on and hunching over his screen. 'The entire portfolio's been wiped out. The rest is from currency swings and counterparty losses.'

'I thought we were hedged?'

'You can't hedge against this sort of market.'

'And the League's deposits and investments?' Santos asked hopefully.

'Antonio, the bank's entire capital base is gone,' Geri spoke slowly as if trying to spell out complicated directions to a tourist. 'It's all gone. Everything.'

Santos sniffed, then knocked the Limoncella back with a jerk of his wrist.

'Good. It makes things easier. This way I only need to worry about myself. Where did I come out in the end?'

'I've liquidated what I can,' Geri sounded almost apologetic. 'Most of it at a loss, like I told you when we spoke. But the bulk of your portfolio would take weeks if not months to sell.'

'How much?' Santos snapped.

'Three, maybe four million.'

'That barely gets me a chalet,' Santos said with a hollow laugh. 'What about the money market positions?'

'Already included, minus what you had to sell to fund your fun and games in Las Vegas last week,' Geri reminded him in a reproachful tone.

A long pause.

'Fine,' Santos stood up. 'It is what it is and what it is . . .
is not enough. I need the painting.'

'You've found a buyer?'

'The Serbs are lined up to take it off my hands for twenty
million,' Santos said with a smile. 'I'm flying out to meet
them later tonight.'

'And the watches?'

'I've got one already and another on its way. I'll get the
third on the night from De Luca or Moretti. They always
wear theirs.'

'They won't let you get away with it,' Geri pointed out,
closing his file.

'They won't be able to stop me if they're dead.' Santos
shrugged, moving round to stand behind him.

'For every person you kill, the League will send two more.
You can't kill them all. Eventually they'll find you.'

'How?' Santos shrugged, stepping even closer until he
could see the liver spots and tiny veins nestling under Geri's
thin thatch. 'The world's a large place. And you're the only
other person who knows where I'm going.'

'Well, you know I'll never tell them,' Geri reassured him,
shoulders stiff, staring straight in front of him.

'Oh, I know.' Santos smiled.

In an instant, he had locked his left arm around Geri's
throat and pulled him clear of the table. Geri lashed out with
his legs, catching the edge of his file and sending it cart-
wheeling to the floor, paper scattering like feathers. Then
with his right hand, Santos reached round and grabbed Geri's
chin.

With a sharp jerk, he snapped his neck.

FIFTY

Nr Anguillara Sabazia, northwest of Rome
19th March – 9.56 p.m.

'Drink?'

Fabio Contarelli had turned in the passenger seat to face them, battered hip flask in hand. In his mid forties, short and pot-bellied, he had the warm, jovial manner of someone who prided himself on being on first-name terms with everyone in his village, and who the local butcher had come to favour with the best cuts. Shabbily dressed, his weather-worn face was brown and cracked like a dried river bed, although his fern green eyes shone as if he was permanently on the verge of playing a practical joke. There was certainly little there to suggest that he had been respon-sible for the horrors Allegra and Tom had witnessed in the basement of his house.

'*No*,' she refused, then watched as Tom did the same. Contarelli shrugged and took a swig himself, turning back to face the road as the mud-flecked Land Cruiser danced over the pot holes.

'How long have you been a tombarolo?' Tom asked.

'Since I was a boy.' Contarelli said proudly. He spoke fast

and mainly in Italian, with a booming voice that was too big
for his body. 'It's in the blood, you see. I used to come out
to these fields with my father. In those days the earth would
be littered with fragments of pottery and broken statues
surfaced by the farmers' ploughs. That's when I realised there
was another world under there.' He gestured longingly out
of the window towards the earthquake-scarred landscape
now shrouded by night. 'I sold what I found in the market,
used the money to buy some books, got smarter about what
pieces were and how much they were worth, climbed through
the ranks. Now I'm a *Capo di Zona* and it's the only life I
know.'

'And you always go out at night?'

'It depends on the site.' He shrugged, lighting a cigarette
from the smouldering stub of the one which had preceded
it, his fingernails broken and dirty. He seemed to be
enjoying himself. 'For some of the larger ones, we offer
the landowner a share in the profits. Then my boys turn
up in the day with a bulldozer and some hard hats. If
anyone asks, we tell them we're working on a construction project. If they ask again, we pay them off. Or shut
them up.'

Allegra felt her anger rising, its delirious scent momentarily blinding her to the danger they were in and to the
armed man seated in the back with her and Tom. She'd
seen enough already to know that this wasn't just tomb
robbing. It was cultural vandalism, Contarelli's brutal
methods probably destroying as much as he found. The
fact that he was now happily boasting about it only made
it worse.

'So you've never been caught?' Tom asked quickly, his
worried glance suggesting that he could tell she was about
to snap.

'The Carabinieri need to find us before they can catch us,'

he explained with a grin. 'They do their best, but there are thousands of tombs and villas buried out here and they can't be everywhere at once. Especially now the politicians are table-thumping about immigration, drugs and terrorism. You know, a few years ago, I even cleared out three graves in a field next to the police station in Viterbo. If they can't stop us there, right under their snouts, what are their chances against us out here?'

He laughed, slapping the knee of the driver next to him in merriment.

'Why do you still do it?' Allegra snapped. 'Haven't you made enough money?'

'I don't do it for the money, my dear. Not for a long time now. Archaeology is my sickness, my addiction,' he explained, his eyes shining, his hands conducting an unheard symphony. 'The thrill of finding a tomb, the smell of a freshly opened chamber, the adrenaline rush as you crawl inside, the fear of being caught . . .'

'What you do is not archaeology,' Allegra snapped. 'It's rape. You take innocence and corrupt it, turning beauty into a bauble for the rich to decorate their mantelpieces with.'

'I bring history back from the dead,' he shot back, his face hardening. 'I restore artefacts from thousands of years of neglect. I provide them with a home. A home where they will go on display and be appreciated, rather than languish in some museum's basement storeroom. Now tell me, is that rape?'

The same tired old excuses, the same self-serving justifications.

'What about *your* basement and the fresco we saw there, hacked into pieces?' she retorted. 'Or the fingers ripped from the dead, or the remains of tombs that have been gouged clean like a back-street abortionist scraping out a womb. Is that archaeology?'

Contarelli, face now like thunder, eyed her coldly, then turned to face the front.

'Stop the car,' he ordered the driver tonelessly. 'We'll walk from here.'

FIFTY-ONE

19th March – 10.31 p.m.
They had parked at the end of a rutted track and then set
out across the fields on foot, Contarelli leading the way, his
two men at the rear. One of them had a pair of infra-red
binoculars that he held to his face every few minutes to scan
the horizon, presumably on the lookout for a possible
Carabinieri patrol. Tom and Allegra, meanwhile, had been
roped together by their wrists; Tom's tied behind his back,
Allegra's fixed in front of her so that she could follow behind.

Contarelli was grasping a *spilloni*, a long metal spike that
he had explained was used to identify a site's size and
entrance. He was still smoking, Tom noted, although he had
turned the cigarette around so that the lit end was inside his
mouth, to mask its glow when he inhaled. For the same
reason no one was using a flashlight, relying instead on the
low moon to light their path.

'The most important thing is to be able to read the land,'
Contarelli expounded, having decided, it seemed, to focus all
his attention on Tom after Allegra's outburst. 'You see how
the grass is drier there?' He pointed out a patch of ground
that, as far as Tom could see, didn't look any different from

the rest of the field. 'The earth above a hollow space has less moisture. And those brambles there –' he gestured to his right – 'when they grow tall and yellowish like that, it means that their roots are leaning on a buried wall.'

Tom nodded, struggling to keep up – Contarelli was proving to be surprisingly nimble over the rough terrain, although unlike Tom he didn't have to cope with his arms being forced up behind his back every time he stumbled.

'Wild fig trees are a give-away too,' he continued. 'And fox and badger tracks can often lead you straight to the entrance.'

'Where are you taking us?' Tom demanded, the hopelessness of their situation growing with every step. Over this rough ground, roped together, they had no chance of escaping.

'Don De Luca told me you were interested in understanding what we do.' Contarelli shrugged, turning to face him.

'I think I've got the general idea, thanks.' Tom gave a tight smile. 'We can make our own way back from here.'

Contarelli gave one of his booming laughs and strode on, leaving one of his men to prod Tom forward.

'It takes us two nights to break into a tomb normally. On the first night we clear away the entrance and let whatever's inside oxidise and harden. Then on the second night we come back and take what we can before dawn. Usually I never come back a third time. It's too risky. But I've made an exception for you.'

He stopped and signalled at someone standing beneath a low hillock covered in trees. The man was leaning wearily on a shovel and had clearly been waiting for them. As they approached him and the dark passage he had uncovered, he waved back, jumping down to greet them.

'It's an Etruscan burial chamber,' Allegra breathed.

Contarelli turned, smiling.

'You see,' he said with a pained sigh, as if he was wearily scolding a small child. 'That's the type of cleverness that's got you both killed.'

Before Tom could move, a plastic hood was placed over his head by one of the men standing behind him and he was forced to his knees. Working quickly, they deftly passed a length of duct tape several times around his neck, sealing the bag against his skin.

He felt himself being lifted and then dragged along the tomb's short corridor into the Stygian darkness of the burial chamber. Moments later, Allegra was thrown down on to the damp earth next to him, struggling furiously.

'Compliments of Don De Luca,' Contarelli intoned from somewhere above them, his disembodied voice echoing off the tomb's domed roof.

For a few moments Tom could hear nothing apart from the rattle of his own breathing and Allegra's muffled shouts as her heels scrabbled in the dirt. But then came the muted sound of steel against stone.

They were filling the entrance in.

FIFTY-TWO

19th March – 11.06 p.m.

They didn't have long, Tom knew. Each breath used a little
more of the oxygen sealed within the bag. He could already
feel the plastic rubbing against his face, warm and moist;
hear it crinkling every time he inhaled, growing and shrinking
like a jellyfish's pulsing head. In a few minutes the air would
all be gone and then the CO_2 levels in his blood would rise,
shutting down first his brain's cerebral cortex and then the
medulla.

It was a cruel death – light-headedness, followed by nausea,
then unconsciousness. And finally oblivion. But then that
was hardly a surprise, given that they were here at the orders
of the same man who had, by his own admission, ordered
Cavalli to be slowly choked by the Tiber's strong current and
Argento to be partially decapitated and left to bleed out like
a slaughtered lamb.

Lying next to him, Allegra had stopped struggling but was
still shouting, using up her air far more quickly than she
should. He'd have to get to her first.

He shuffled back towards her, feeling for her with his
hands, which were still tied behind his back. Touching her

arm, he bent forward and pulled himself round with his feet until he made contact with the hood's slippery surface. She seemed to guess what he was doing, because she went quiet and bent towards him until he was able to feel the outline of her mouth.

Digging his finger hard into the shallow depression formed between the hard edges of her teeth, he gouged the thick plastic with his nail, weakening its surface until it suddenly gave way. There was a loud whistling noise as Allegra sucked air greedily through the small hole.

But the effort had cost Tom more than he'd expected. He felt light-headed, almost as if he was floating outside of himself. He didn't have long before he went under. Thirty seconds at most. He shuffled down, bending his head towards where he guessed Allegra's hands had been retied behind her back so that she could feel for his mouth. With her longer nails, it took far less time for her to rupture the plastic, the chamber's stale air tasting sweet to Tom's starving lungs.

'You okay?' Tom called through the darkness when his head had cleared, the plastic hood both muffling and amplifying his voice.

'Not really,' she answered, coughing.

'Where are your hands?'

Feeling for her wrists, he carefully picked away at the knot, the rope resisting at first, until little by little he was able to loosen it and then undo it completely. Sitting up, Allegra returned the favour. As soon as he was free they felt for each other in the darkness and hugged with relief – relative strangers brought unexpectedly close by the intimacy of fear.

'Which way's the entrance?' Tom asked as he broke away and ripped the remainder of the plastic hood from his neck.

'We should be able to find it if we feel our way along the walls,' she replied. 'Perhaps if we . . . what's this?'

A light clicked on, forcing Tom to shield his eyes as it was pointed at him. Allegra snatched it away with an apology. Unless it had fallen from Contarelli's pocket, it appeared that he had left them a torch. Perhaps he had anticipated that they might free themselves? Perhaps he was trying to help them escape? The thought filled Tom with hope.

He glanced around excitedly, noting the low domed roof above them and the earthen floor littered with pottery fragments. Lying discarded in the corner was a bundle of rags that Tom suspected marked what was left of the tomb's original occupant.

'That way –' Allegra pointed towards the low tunnel that led to the entrance.

He crawled hopefully down it, but soon found his path blocked. As the shovelling sound earlier had suggested, the entrance had been filled in. And not just with earth, but with a massive stone plug that they must have brought there with this single purpose in mind.

'We should have left the bags on,' Allegra said in a shaky voice. 'I'd rather suffocate quickly than starve down here.'

'I wouldn't worry about starving,' Tom said with a grim smile. 'I'd say we have six hours of air, eight max.'

'That's reassuring.' She gave a short laugh, then frowned as her torch picked out a dull metal object lying near the entrance.

It was a Glock 17. Tom picked it up and checked the magazine. It contained two bullets.

Contarelli, it seemed, was offering them a way out after all.

FIFTY-THREE

Avenue Krieg, Geneva, Switzerland
20th March – 12.02 a.m.

'This can't be it,' Dominique whispered.

Normally Archie would have agreed with her – a half-empty building with a broken lift, shabby communal areas, half the light bulbs blown and the name plate hanging loose, certainly didn't seem to fit with what he'd seen of Faulks. But the porter he'd bribed in the Sotheby's loading bay had been adamant that this was the right address, floor and suite number for the company who'd sold the Artemis. In fact, he'd proved it.

'He showed me the bloody receipt,' Archie grunted as he tried to force the final locking pin out of the way. 'Galleries Dassin is registered here.'

'It just doesn't feel right,' she said, shaking her head. 'We should have spoken to Tom first.'

'I've been trying to get him on the blower all day,' Archie reminded her sharply, his tone reflecting both his irritation at being second-guessed and his concern. It wasn't like Tom to be out of touch this long. Not deliberately. 'Besides . . .' With a final effort, the pin fell into place and the lock clicked open. '. . . We're in now. We might as well have a butcher's.'

Pulling their masks down over their faces, they slipped inside and gently closed the door behind them. The suite consisted of a large open-plan space with perhaps four desks in it, a small kitchen, a meeting room, and what Archie guessed was the owner or manager's personal office.

'Still sure this is the right place?' Dominique whispered as her torch picked out bookcases overflowing with legal and tax reference books, stacks of paperwork secured by treasury tags, filing cabinets, printers and shredders, and a series of insipid paintings of a yacht sailing across the lake. Archie sighed. He hated to admit it, but it looked as though she might be right after all.

'I'll have a quick shifty in there,' Archie suggested, nodding towards the manager's office. 'You have a look through this lot.'

The office was dominated by a vast, monolithic desk whose primary purpose could only have been to intimidate anyone standing on the other side of it. Behind this ran thick-set, mahogany shelves loaded with books, photo frames and various stress-busting executive toys. Archie couldn't help himself but set off the Newton's Cradle, his eyes dancing to the metronomic click-click-click of the balls as they swung back and forth. Glancing up with a smile, he absent-mind-edly picked up one of the photo frames, then frowned. Rather than be confronted by Faulks's patrician scowl as he had expected, he instead found himself staring at a heavily over-weight man in swimming trunks trying to pour himself into a wetsuit.

Replacing it with a shudder, Archie turned his attention to the two filing cabinets lurking in the corner. Opening the drawers in turn, he walked his fingers along the tabs until he found one marked Galleries Dassin.

'I've got something,' he called in a low voice, carrying it to the entrance. Dominique looked up from where she had been leafing through the papers arranged on one of the desks. *'Galleries Dassin,'* he read, flicking through a few of the pages. *'Registered address, 13 Avenue Krieg.* That's here. *Fiduciary owner, Jérome Carvel.'* He glanced up at the door and saw the same name picked out on it in black letters. 'That's him.'

'What's a fiduciary owner?' Dominique asked.

'Someone who deals with all the administrative bollocks, as opposed to the beneficial owner, who calls the shots and makes the serious wonga and who in this particular instance is . . .' He'd found a shareholder contract and flipped to the signature page, then looked up with a grim smile. 'Earl Faulks. Carvel's a front.'

'Why bother?'

'Fuck knows. But if I had to guess, to hide . . .' Archie paused, struck by a thought. 'Who bought the Artemis again?'

Dominique had approached the auctioneer after the sale and expressed an interest in buying the statue from its new owner. Sensing the opportunity to make another fee, the auctioneer had volunteered their name and offered to broker the deal.

'It was a commission bid for Xenephon Trading.'

Archie vanished back inside the office, returning a few moments later clutching another file.

'Xenephon Trading,' he read. *'Fiduciary owner, Jérome Carvel. Beneficial owner . . . Earl Faulks.'* He looked up at her triumphantly.

'He bought it from himself?' Dominique exclaimed. 'That makes no sense. Even if he'd negotiated special rates, he'd still be paying six to ten per cent commission on both sides of the deal.'

'Are those the invoices?' Archie nodded at the sheaf of papers she'd been sorting through.

'Last month's auction.' She nodded.

'Any where Xenephon is the buyer?' Archie went to stand next to her.

Gripping her torch in one hand and flipping the pages over quickly with the other, she quickly counted them up. 'There's one here. Two . . . three . . . four . . . five. And look who's on the other side of the deal here and here: Galleries Dassin.'

'Who's Melfi Export?' Archie tapped his finger on the page with a frown. 'They show up a lot too.'

Without waiting for an answer, he disappeared back into the office, returning a few moments later with a third file and a solemn expression.

'*Melfi Export. Fiduciary owner, Jérome Carvel. Beneficial owner . . . Earl Faulks*. It's the same story – he's selling with one company and buying with another. It makes no sense.'

'He must be getting something out it,' she pointed out.

'Well, I don't see what, apart from a shit-load of paper-work.' He slapped the pile of invoices with a shrug. Dominique turned to him with a smile.

'That's it.'

'What?'

'The paperwork. He's doing it for the paperwork.'

'What the hell are you talking about?'

'Maybe it's a laundering scam,' she said excitedly. 'First he puts an item up for auction. Then he buys it back under another name. Finally he sells it on to a real buyer, only this time with a manufactured provenance, courtesy of an official auction house invoice and valuation certificate.'

'It's not just about provenance,' Archie said with a slow nod. 'Arms dealers get around embargoes by selling weapons down a network of shell companies and middlemen, so that by the time the shipment gets to the intended customer, no one can tie the final transaction back to the original seller. It's called triangulation. Faulks could be pulling the same stunt here to cover his tracks.'

FIFTY-FOUR

Nr Anguillara Sabazia, northwest of Rome
20th March – 1.13 a.m.

They had both run out of conversation a while ago. Now they were sitting in silence, locked into their own thoughts, hugging their knees for warmth. The torch nestled on the ground between them in a puddle of light, their bodies huddled around it as if to shield it from the wind. Tom had the ominous feeling that once its fragile flame finally expired, they wouldn't long survive it.

He'd faced death before, of course. But never with the resigned acceptance and powerlessness he felt now. The walls were rock solid, the floor packed firm, the domed roof unyielding, the entrance sealed. They had no tools, no way of communicating with the outside world, no answers. Nothing except for the two bullets that lay side by side in the torch's pale wash, like bodies awaiting burial.

'How did you know?' Allegra's voice broke the cloying silence.

'Know what?'

'When we first met at Cavalli's and you handed me the

gun,' she reminded him. 'How did you know I wouldn't just shoot you?'

'I didn't.'

'Then why did you trust me?'

'I didn't.' He shrugged.

'Then what . . .?'

'I took the clip out before I gave you the gun.' Tom grinned. 'You couldn't have shot me if you'd wanted to.'

'Why you . . .' Allegra's face broke into a wide smile as she reached across to punch Tom's shoulder.

'Ow.' He winced, his arm still bruised from where she'd hit him that morning.

'Still sore from being beaten up by a girl?' she said, the clear bell of her laughter both unexpected and strangely uplifting in the darkness.

'You landed a couple of lucky shots.' Tom gave a dismissive shake of his head. 'Another few seconds and I . . .'

He paused. Allegra was holding up her hand for him to be quiet, her chin raised like a foxhound who has caught a scent.

'What's that?'

Tom listened, at first not hearing anything, but then making out what seemed to be the faint rattle of an engine.

'They're coming back,' Allegra exclaimed, turning excitedly towards the entrance tunnel.

'Maybe to finish the job,' Tom said grimly, hauling her back and loading the gun.

They sat there, the ground now shaking with a dull throb, the occasional sound of a muffled voice reaching them. Readying himself, Tom took aim at the stone plug that was blocking the entrance, determined to take Contarelli, or whichever of his men he sent ahead of him, down with them.

Ten or so minutes later the massive stone began to move,

dirt and moonlight trickling through the crack. The sound of voices was clearer now, someone swearing in Italian, another one groaning under the strain. Then, with a final effort, the stone was rolled free. It fell on to its side with a leaden thump.

A harsh, lightning strike of light flooded down the entrance corridor, washing over them and making them blink. On its heels came the thunder of what Tom realised now was a helicopter, the hammer chop of its rotors echoing off the walls.

For a few moments nothing happened. Then a figure appeared at the tunnel entrance, a black silhouette against the floodlit backdrop.

'Tom Kirk? Allegra Damico? *Andiamo,*' he said, reaching towards them.

They swapped a look, Tom slowly lowered the gun.

'What's going on?' Allegra shouted through the noise.

'I don't know,' Tom called back. 'But it beats being in here.'

Crawling forward, they emerged gratefully into the night, brushing the earth from their clothes and hands as they stood up. But whatever relief they felt at escaping was soon tempered by the realisation that their three liberators were all dressed in black paramilitary clothing – ski masks, fatigues, bullet-proof vests, field boots, guns strapped to their thighs. Two of the men were also equipped with night-vision goggles which they kept trained on the horizon, their Beretta PS12-SDs held across their chests, safety's off.

'Go,' the man who had helped them to their feet ushered them towards the black Augusta Bell 412EP which had landed about thirty feet away, its spotlight trained on the tomb's entrance, the wash of its rotors back-combing the grass. A fourth man was waiting for them in the cockpit.

'Get in,' the first man shouted over the roar of the engine, handing them each a set of headphones. 'Don't worry. We'll put everything back here so they won't know you've gone.'

Slamming the door, he stepped back and gave the pilot the thumbs-up. Throttling up, the helicopter lurched unsteadily off the ground, dipped its rotors, and then climbed at a steep angle into the sky. In a few minutes, the tomb had faded from view, swallowed by the night.

'Military?' Allegra's voice hummed in Tom's ear, worried but with a curious edge.

'I don't know,' he replied, glancing round. 'Their equipment's standard Italian army issue. Could be special forces or some sort of private militia?' He nodded at the back of the pilot's head. 'You could try asking him, but I don't think he'll tell us.'

'Right now, I'm not sure I even care,' she said with a relieved shrug. 'The further we can get . . .' Her voice tailed off into a puzzled frown as she noticed the envelope that had been left on the bench opposite. It was addressed to both of them. Swapping a look with Tom, she ripped it open and glanced inside, then emptied the contents into her lap: about twenty thousand euro secured in a neat bundle, a set of car keys, and five black-and-white photographs of a fire-ravaged apartment attached to an official press release from the Monégasque Police.

'What does it say?' Allegra frowned, handing it to him.

'They're looking for two missing people,' Tom quickly translated. 'An Irish banker, called Ronan D'Arcy and his housekeeper, Determination Smith. It says no one's seen them since D'Arcy's apartment caught fire two days ago. Looks like somebody wants us to take a closer look.' His eyes narrowed as he studied the third photograph again, a small object having caught his eye. Had the police noticed that yet, he wondered?

'De Luca?' she suggested. 'Remember he told us that his accountant in Monaco had disappeared?'

'Why have Contarelli bury us, only to dig us up a few hours later?' Tom asked with a shake of his head.

'But who else would have known where to find us?'

Tom shrugged. She had a point, although right now he was less concerned with who had rescued them than why, and what they wanted.

The pilot's voice broke into their conversation with a crackle.

'What's our heading?'

'What?'

'My orders are to take you anywhere within operational range,' the pilot explained.

'Anywhere?' Tom asked in surprise. He'd assumed that whoever had set them free was planning to have them brought to him.

'Anywhere,' the pilot confirmed. 'As soon as we land, you're free to go.' He reached back and handed them two Swiss passports made out in false names. 'What's the heading?'

Tom paused before answering, flicking through the forged documents. He reckoned a full tank would last them 600 kilometres. More than enough to leave De Luca, Gallo and the murderous madness they seemed to have stumbled into far behind. Allegra seemed to be having the same thought, because she pulled her headset off and yelled into his ear so she couldn't be overheard.

'What do you want to do?'

'If we want out, then this is it,' he called back. 'A chance to walk away while we still can.'

'Walk away to what? Until I can prove what Gallo's up to, I've nothing to walk away to.'

Tom slipped his headset back on.

'Can we make it to Monte Carlo?' he asked.

'Of course,' the pilot confirmed. 'What do you need?'

Tom paused before answering.

'A suit for me. Three buttons and a double vent. A dress for the lady. Black. Size 8.'

PART THREE

'I fear the Greeks, even when they bear gifts'
Virgil, *The Aeneid*, Book II, 48

FIFTY-FIVE

Over the Ligurian Sea, fifty kilometres south-east of Monaco
20th March – 2.21 a.m.

Rigged for black, they had headed west, hitting the coast just north of Civitavecchia and then hugging it as far as Livorno, sawing in and out of the jagged shoreline to stay under the radar. Once there, they had struck out across the sea, the city's bright lights fading behind them to a gossamer twinkle, until there was nothing but them and the water's empty shadow and the echo of the rotors as they skimmed low across the waves.

Occasionally the moon would emerge from behind a cloud, and for a few moments Allegra could see their spectral reflection in the swell, a ghost ship carried on neon whitecaps. Then, just as quickly, it vanished again and the darkness would open beneath them once more, an endless abyss into which they seemed to be falling without moving.

Allegra glanced over at Tom, but like her he seemed to be enjoying the flight's noisy stillness, his dirt-smudged face pressed to the window, alone with his thoughts. She wondered if, like her, he could still feel the plastic against

his skin, moist and warm, still feel his fingernails lifting as
he scrabbled at the chamber's earthen walls.

She hated to admit it, but she had been scared back there.
Not danger scared, where adrenaline kicks in and instinct
takes over before you even have a chance to think. Dying
scared, where there is time for the mind to wander long and
lonely corridors of fear and uncertainty. The sort of fear that
she imagined lingered in the portentous shadows of a
surgeon's forced cheerfulness or a radiologist's brave smile.

Perhaps this explained why she found something strangely
comforting about the engine's noise now, its animal roar
having settled into a contented purr that was a welcome
contrast to the ticking contemplation of death that she had
endured in that tomb. A reminder that she was alive. That
she had escaped.

Not that she was sure what they had escaped to, exactly,
or who had helped them. Clearly somebody had their reasons
for wanting them alive and continuing their investigation.
Less clear was who that might be. De Luca, perhaps; if she
was right about D'Arcy working for him. But then, as Tom
had suggested, it seemed unlikely that he would order
Contarelli to kill them, only to dispatch a search-and-rescue
team a few hours later. But if not him, who? The FBI? Tom
had told her that he had worked with them before. Was this
them protecting their best chance of finding Jennifer's killer?
She shook her head ruefully. The truth was, there was no
way of telling.

More certain was her growing trust in Tom. He would
never stop, she knew, never rest until he had brought the
Delian League down and punished whoever had killed his
friend. Part of her almost felt jealous of this fierce loyalty.
Did she have anyone who would have done the same for
her? Probably not. The realisation strengthened her resolve.
If she didn't follow this through to the end, wherever it

led her, no one else would. And then Gallo would have won.

Tom suddenly tapped the window.

'Monte Carlo.'

The city had appeared out of the night, a stepped pyramid of lights that clung to the steep mountainside with concrete claws, its jaws open to the sea. The helicopter banked to the left and climbed over the yachts anchored in the harbour before swooping back towards the heliport, a narrow cantilevered shelf that hung over the water. It landed with a bump and then dusted off as soon as their feet had hit the tarmac, climbing steeply until the clatter of its blades was nothing but a warm whisper on the wind.

The heliport was shut for the night, but someone had seen to it that the gate set into the hurricane fence had been left unlocked. The keys left for them in the envelope opened an X5 parked on the street outside the deserted terminal building. Inside, Allegra found a bag of casual clothes and two suit carriers – one containing Tom's shirt and suit, the other a knee-length black dress that they had clearly managed to lay their hands on in the hour or so it had taken them to fly here. Shoes, underwear, cufflinks, comb, make-up – they'd thought of everything, and she knew without even looking that it would all fit. These people, whoever they were, knew what they were doing.

'Ladies first?' Tom offered, closing the door after her and then turning his back.

It was only when she had undressed that she realised how filthy she was; her face, arms and clothes were covered in stains, dirt and small cuts and grazes that she had unconsciously picked up somewhere between Li's oily workshop, Cavalli's foam-filled car, Contarelli's gruesome basement and the empty tomb. Grabbing some wipes, she quickly cleaned herself up as best she could, applied some make-up, and then wriggled into the dress. She checked herself in the mirror before she got out. Not bad, apart from her hair, which would need six months and several very expensive haircuts to get it looking even half decent. But it had served its purpose.

She got out and swapped places with Tom, hoping that his raised eyebrows were a sign of silent appreciation. Five minutes later and he too was ready to go.

'Want to drive?' Tom offered, holding out the keys. 'Only this time you have to promise not to crash into anything.'

She refused with a smile.

'What's the fun in that?'

The casino was only a short drive from the heliport, although, in a country of only 485 acres, everything was, almost by definition, close to everything else. It was still busy, a succession of Ferraris and Lamborghinis processing slowly across the Place du Casino to give the tourists enough time to gawp. Turning in by the central fountain, its bubbling waters glowing like molten glass in the floodlights, they waited in line behind a Bentley Continental for the valet to take their car.

The casino itself was an elaborate, baroque building, its façade dominated by two flamboyant towers either side of the main entrance and encrusted with statues and ornate architectural reliefs. The floodlights had given it a rather gaudy appearance, clothing it in amber in some places and gold in others, while a lush green copper roof was just about visible through the gaps between the towers. A central clock, supported by two bronze angels, indicated it had just gone three.

'You still haven't told me why we're here,' Allegra complained as Tom led her into the marble entrance hall to the ticket office.

He glanced across with an indulgent smile as he paid their entrance fee, as if this was a somehow rather foolish question.

'To play blackjack, of course.'

FIFTY-SIX

Casino de Monte Carlo, Monaco
20th March – 3.02 a.m.

There was a compelling logic to the casino's layout: the further inside you ventured, the more money you stood to lose. Although a simple conceit, it had, over the years, led to the evolution of a complex and intuitive ecosystem whereby those at the bottom of the food chain rarely strayed into the territory of the higher, predatory mammals.

This could be easily observed in the way that the outer rooms were mainly inhabited by sunburnt British and German tourists, their clothes creased from having been kept at the bottom of a suitcase for the best part of a week in anticipation of a 'posh' night out, their modest losses borne with thinly disguised resentment. The middle rooms, meanwhile, were populated by immaculately dressed Italian and French couples – 'locals' who had driven up on a whim and who seemed to play the tables with an almost effortless familiarity. The inner rooms, finally, had been overrun by Russians; for the most part overweight men dressed in black and clutching cigars as they would a bayonet, accompanied by dagger-thin blonde women half their age wearing white to better show off their tans. Here they bet with an indifference that verged on boredom, the roulette table lavished with chips, each spin of the wheel a desperate plea to feel something, anything, in a life blunted by having forgotten what it means to want something but not be able to buy it.

As they walked through from the Salle Europe, Tom found his thoughts wandering. He had tried to resist it as long as he could, but it was hard not to be drawn back to the Amalfi, not to let the fairground flash of the slot machines and the piano play of the roulette ball grab him by the throat and catapult him back through time, as if he had stumbled into some strange parallel world.

It was almost as if he was watching a film. The echo of the shot being fired, Jennifer crumpling to the floor, the smell of blood and cordite, that first, disbelieving scream. A film that he could play, pause, forward and rewind at any time, although it would never allow him to go further back than the crack of the gunshot. That's when everything had started.

'Tom?' The mirrored room slowly came back into focus and he saw Allegra's hand laid in concern on his shoulder. 'Are you okay?'

'I'm fine.' He nodded, the scream still silently ringing in his ears even though what struck him most about this place now, on closer inspection was less its similarity to the Amalfi than its differences.

Here, they played Chemin de Fer not Punto Banco, for example. The poker tables were marked in French not English. The roulette wheel had one zero, not two. And the air was seared with the bittersweet tang of a century and a half of fortunes being lost and made. Small differences on their own, perhaps, but pieced together and set amidst the jewelled chandeliers, stained-glass windows and ornate sculptures that adorned the casino's soaring rococo interior, they breathed a soul into this place that Kezman could never hope to buy, and revealed the Amalfi in all its silicone-enhanced artifice.

'Deal me in.' Tom sat at an empty blackjack table and placed a five-thousand-euro chip on the box in front of him.

The croupier looked up and smiled. In his early forties, he was a tall precise man, gaunt and with a pianist's long, cantilevered fingers.

'Monsieur Kirk. Very good to see you again.'

He dealt him a king and a five.

'You too, Nico.'

'I was sorry to hear about your loss.' For a moment Tom thought he meant Jennifer, before realising he must be referring to his father. That was almost three years ago now. It showed how long it had been since he was last here.

'Thank you. *Carte.*'

'You don't twist on fifteen,' Allegra whispered next to him. 'Even I know that.'

'Seven,' the croupier intoned. 'Twenty-two.' He scooped the cards and Tom's chip off the baize.

'See?' Allegra exclaimed.

'I've come for my gear,' Tom said in a low voice, placing another five-thousand-euro chip down. 'Is it still here?'

'Of course.' Nico nodded, dealing him an ace and a seven.

'Eighteen. You need to stick again,' Allegra urged. Tom ignored her.

'*Carte.*'

The croupier deftly flicked an eight over to him.

'Twenty-six.'

Allegra tutted angrily.

'You don't like losing, do you?' Tom said, amused by the expression on her face.

'I don't like losing stupidly,' she corrected him.

'Perhaps madame is right,' the croupier ventured. 'Have you tried the Roulette Anglaise?'

'Actually, I was hoping to bump into an old friend here. Ronan D'Arcy. Know him?'

The croupier paused, then nodded.

'He's been in a few times. Good tipper.' A pause. 'Ugly business.'

'Very ugly,' Tom agreed. 'Any idea where I can find him?'

Nico shrugged, then shook his head.

'No one's seen him since the fire.'

'Where did he live?'

'Up on the Boulevard de Suisse. You can't miss it.'

'Can you get me in?'

The croupier checked again that no one was listening, then nodded.

'Meet me in the Café de Paris in ten minutes.'

'I'll need a couple of phones too,' Tom added. 'Here –' He threw another five-thousand-euro chip down. 'For your trouble.'

'*Merci, monsieur*, but four should cover everything.' He slid a one-thousand-euro chip back, then signalled at the floor manager that he needed to be relieved.

'You lost both those hands on purpose, didn't you?' Allegra muttered as they made their way back towards the entrance.

'He charges a ten-thousand-euro fee.'

'Fee for what?'

'For looking after this –' He held up the chip that the croupier had returned to him in change. Two numbers had been scratched on to its reverse. 'Come on.'

Reaching the main entrance lobby, Tom led her over to the far side of the galleried space, where a mirrored door on the right-hand side of the room gave on to a marble stair-case edged by an elaborate cast-iron balustrade. They headed down it, the temperature fading, until they eventually found themselves in a narrow corridor that led to the men's toilets on one side and the women's on the other.

Checking that they hadn't been followed, Tom opened the small cupboard under the stairs and removed two brass stands joined by a velvet rope and an *Hors Service* sign. Pinning the sign to the door, he cordoned the toilet entrance off and then disappeared inside, reappearing a few moments later with a smile.

'It's empty.'

'Is that good?' she asked, an impatient edge to her voice as she followed him inside.

The room was as he remembered it: four wooden stalls painted a pale yellow to his right, six porcelain urinals separated by frosted-glass screens to his left. Unusually, the centre of the room was dominated by a large white marble counter with two sinks set on each set of a double-sided arched mirror. The walls were covered in grey marble tiles.

'Six across, three down.'

He showed her the numbers scratched on to the chip and then turned to face the urinals and began to count, starting in the far left corner and moving six tiles across, then dropping three tiles down.

'I make it this one,' he said, stepping forward and pointing at a tile over the third urinal.

'Me too,' Allegra agreed with a curious frown.

Snatching up the silver fire extinguisher hanging just inside the door, he swung it hard against the tile they had picked out. There was a dull clunk as it caved in.

'It's hollow,' Allegra breathed.

Tom swung the extinguisher against the wall again, the hole widening as the tiles around the opening cracked and fell away until he had revealed a rectangular space. Throwing the extinguisher to the floor, he reached into the space and hauled out a large black holdall.

'How long's that been here?'

'Three or four years?' he guessed. 'Nico paid off the builder the casino hired to re-tile this room. It was Archie's idea. A precaution. Enough to get us operational again if we ever had to cut and run. He chose here and a few other places around the world where we had people we could trust.'

Allegra leaned forward as he unzipped the bag.

'What's inside?'

'Batteries, tools, drill, borescope, magnetic rig, backpack,' he said quickly, sorting through its contents. 'Money, guns,' he continued, taking one of the two Glocks out, checking the magazine was full and placing it in his pocket.

'And this?' Allegra asked, frowning as she took out a small object the size of a cigarette packet.

'Location transmitter. Three-mile radius,' He pulled out the receiver, slotted a fresh battery in place and then turned it on to show her. 'Stick it on, if you like. At least that way I won't lose you.'

'Don't worry, you won't get rid of me that easily.' She smiled, tossing it back.

'Good. Then you can give me a hand with this up the stairs. Nico will be waiting by now.'

FIFTY-SEVEN

Boulevard de Suisse, Monaco
20th March – 3.35 a.m.

Barely ten minutes later, they pulled in a little way beyond
D'Arcy's building. Nico had been right – you couldn't miss
it. Not only was a police car parked outside on the narrow
one-way street, but the upper stories of the otherwise cream
apartment block were scorched and coated with ash, like a
half-smoked cigarette that had been stood on its filter and
then left to burn down to its tip.

Tom gave her a few minutes to struggle out of her dress
and heels and into the casual clothes that had been left for
them in the car, and then rapped impatiently on her window.
She lowered it and he thrust the second Glock and a couple
of spare clips through the gap.

'Ready?'

'Are there actually any bullets in this one?' she asked,
eyebrows raised sceptically.

It wasn't that she minded carrying a gun. In fact, she quite
liked its firm and familiar presence on her hip, like a dance
partner's hand leading her through a rehearsed set of steps. It
was just that she preferred to know what she was dealing with.

'Let's not find out.' He winked.

The building was called the Villa de Rome, an appropriate and perhaps not entirely coincidental name if they were right about D'Arcy's involvement with De Luca and the Delian League. Although old, it betrayed all the signs of a recent and rather ill-judged refurbishment, the entrance now resembling that of a two-star hotel with ideas above its station – all rose marble, smoked glass and gold leaf.

'*Bonsoir,*' a junior officer from Monaco's small police force rose from behind the reception desk and greeted them warmly, relieved, it seemed, at the prospect of a break in his vigil's lonely monotony.

'Thierry Landry. Caroline Morel,' Tom snapped in French, each of them flashing the special passes that Nico had produced for them. 'From the palace.'

'Yes, sir, madam,' the officer stuttered, his back straightening and heels sliding almost imperceptibly closer together.

'We'd like to see D'Arcy's apartment.'

'Of course.' He nodded eagerly. 'The elevator's still out, but I can escort you up the stairs to the penthouse.'

'No need,' Tom insisted, stepping deliberately closer. 'We were never here. You never saw us.'

'Saw what, sir?' The officer winked, then froze, as if realising that this was probably against some sort of royal protocol. To his visible relief, Tom smiled back.

'Exactly.'

Leaving the officer saluting to their backs, they climbed the stairs in silence, the fire's charred scent growing stronger and the floor getting wetter as water dripped through from the ceiling like rainwater percolating into an aquifer. There was a certain irony, Allegra reflected, in how the fire brigade had probably caused more damage to the flats below D'Arcy's than the blaze they were meant to be protecting them from. She couldn't help but wonder if there wasn't a warning there for them both: were they causing more harm by trying to fix things than if they had just let matters run their natural course?

On the third floor, Tom stopped and swung his backpack off his shoulder. Reaching inside, he took out a small device that he stuck on to the wall at about knee height, then turned on.

'Motion sensor,' he explained, holding out a small receiver that she guessed would sound if anyone broke the transmitter's infrared beam.

They continued on, emerging half a minute later on the top landing, the fire's pungent incense now so heavy that she could almost taste the ash sticking to the back of her throat. Tom flicked his torch on, the beam immediately settling on the door to D'Arcy's apartment that had been unscrewed from its hinges and placed against the wall.

'Quarter-inch steel and a four-bar locking mechanism,' Tom observed slowly. 'Either he knew his attackers or someone let them in.'

They stepped inside the apartment on to a sodden carpet of ash and charred debris, weightless black flecks fluttering through their torch beams like flies over a carcass. The walls had been licked black by the cruel flames, and the ceiling almost entirely consumed, so that she could see through it to the roof's steel ribs and, beyond them, the sky. The furniture, too, had been skeletonised into dark shapes that were both entirely alien and strangely familiar, although the fire, ever capricious, had inexplicably spared a single chair and a large section of one wall, as if to deliberately emphasise the otherwise overwhelming scale of its devastation.

It was an uncomfortable, dislocating experience, and Allegra had the strange impression of having stepped on to a film set – an imagined vision, rendered with frightening detail, of some future, post-apocalyptic world where the few remaining survivors had been reduced to taking shelter where they could and eking out an existence amidst the ashes.

'This looks like where it started.' She picked her way over the charred wreckage to a room that looked out over the harbour. The fire here seemed to have been particularly intense, the steel beams overhead twisted and tortured, opaque pools of molten glass having formed under the windows, the stonework still radiating a baked-in heat that took the edge off the chilled sea breeze. There was also some evidence of the beginnings of a forensic examination of the scene: equipment set up on a low trestle table, mobile lighting arranged in the room's corners.

'Probably here,' Tom agreed, pointing his torch at a dark mound that was pressed up against what was left of a book-case. 'As you'd expect.'

'What do you mean?'

Tom reached into his backpack and pulled out one of the photographs that had been left for them in the helicopter.

'What do you see?'

She studied it carefully, then ran her torch over the burnt bookcase with a frown. As far as she could tell they looked the same. There certainly didn't seem . . . She paused, having just noticed a rectangular shape on the photo that the torch-light revealed to be a small metal grille set into the wall at about head height.

'What's that?' she asked with a frown.

'That's what I wondered too,' Tom muttered. 'Probably nothing. But then again . . .' He stepped closer and rubbed gently against a section of the wall. Through the damp layer of soot, a narrow groove slowly revealed itself.

'A hidden door,' Allegra breathed.

'A panic room.' Tom nodded. 'The grille must be for an air intake that would have been concealed by the bookcase. D'Arcy hasn't disappeared. He never even left his apartment.'

'Can you open it?'

'Half-inch steel, at a guess.' Tom rapped his knuckles against the door with a defeated shrug. 'Electro-magnetic locking system. Assuming they've cut the mains power, the locking mechanism will release itself as soon as the batteries run out.'

'Which is when?'

'Typically about forty-eight hours after they kick in.'

'Which is still at least twelve hours away,' she calculated, thinking back to the time of the fire given in the missing persons report. 'We can't hang around here until then.'

'We won't have to,' Tom reassured her. 'Here, give me a hand clearing this away.'

Reaching up, they ripped what was left of the bookcase to the floor, the charred wood crisping as they grabbed it, the dust making them both cough.

'There would have been an external keypad, but that must have melted in the fire,' Tom explained as the panic room's steel shell emerged through the soot. 'But there's usually a failsafe too. A secondary pad that they conceal inside the room's walls in case of an emergency. That should have been insulated from the heat.'

Stepping forward, he carefully ran his hands across the filthy steel walls at about waist height.

'Here.'

He spat into his hand and wiped the dirt away in a series of tarred smears to reveal a rectangular access panel that he quickly unscrewed.

'It's still working,' Allegra said with relief as she shone her torch into the recess and made out the keypad's illuminated buttons and the cursor's inviting blink.

Tom reached into his bag and pulled out a small device that looked like a calculator. Levering the fascia off the panic room's keypad to reveal the circuit board, he knelt down next to it and connected his device. Immediately the screen lit up, numbers scrolling across it in seemingly random patterns until, one by one, it began to lock them down. These then flashed up on the keypad's display, hesitantly at first, and then with increasing speed and confidence, until the full combination flashed up green: 180373.

With a hydraulic sigh, the panic room's door rolled back.

FIFTY-EIGHT

20th March – 3.44 a.m.

Allegra approached the open doorway, then staggered back.

'*Cazzo!*' She swore, her hand over her mouth. Peering through the opening, Tom understood why.

The emergency lighting was on, the room soaked in its blood-red glaze. D'Arcy was lying slumped in the corner and had already begun to bloat in the heat, the sickly sweet stench of rotting meat washing over them. Head lolling against his chest, his eyes were bulging as if someone had tried to pop them out on to his cheek, his stomach ballooning under his white shirt, the marbled skin mottled blue-green through the gaps between the buttons.

Breathing through his mouth, and trying to ignore the way D'Arcy's black and swollen tongue had forced his jaws into a wide, gagging smile, Tom stepped inside the cramped space. Allegra followed close behind.

'The smoke would have killed him,' Tom guessed, pointing out some plastic sheeting hanging loose from the air vent which it looked as though D'Arcy had tried to seal shut with bandages and plasters raided from a first-aid kit. 'Then he must have started to cook in the heat.'

'*Cazzo*,' she breathed to herself again.

Glancing round, it seemed pretty clear that D'Arcy had taken to using the room for storage rather than survival, with filing boxes stacked to the ceiling against the far wall, and a large server array providing some sort of data back-up facility to whatever computers he guessed must have once stood on the desk outside. Clearly, like most people who had these types of rooms installed, D'Arcy had drawn comfort from knowing it was there should he want to use it, without ever really expecting that he would ever need to.

'Help me lift one of these down.'

Mindful of not tripping over D'Arcy's outstretched legs, he lifted down a box and opened it up. Inside were four or five lever-arch files, neatly arranged by year, containing hundreds of invoices.

'Renewal fees for a burial plot in the Cimitero Acattolico in Rome,' Allegra read, opening the most recent file and then turning the pages. 'Private jet hire. Hotel suites. Yacht charter agreements. It's expensive being rich.'

'Anything linking him to De Luca?' Tom asked, hauling a second box down.

'Nothing obvious. Trade confirmations, derivatives contracts, settlement details, account statements . . .' She flicked through a couple of the folders.

'This one's the same,' Tom agreed, having heaved a third box to the floor.

'Look at this, though,' Allegra said slowly, having come across a thick wedge of bank statements. 'Every time his trading account went over ten million, the surplus was trans-ferred back to an account at the Banco Rosalia.'

'The Banco Rosalia?' Tom frowned. 'Wasn't that where Argento worked?'

'Exactly. Which ties D'Arcy back to the other killings.'

'Except there's nothing here that links his death to either Caesar or Caravaggio,' Tom pointed out. 'Why would Moretti have broken the pattern?'

'Maybe he didn't. Maybe D'Arcy locked himself in here before Moretti could get to him,' she suggested.

Tom nodded, although he wasn't entirely convinced. Compared to what he'd heard about the other murders, this one seemed rushed and unplanned. Different.

'What do you know about the Banco Rosalia?' he asked.

'Nothing really.' She shrugged. 'Small bank, majority owned by the Vatican. I met the guy who runs it at the morgue, ID-ing Argento's body. '

'We should take the disks.' Tom pointed at a stack of DVDs that he guessed were server backups. 'If the bank's involved, the money trail might show us how.'

'What about him?' She motioned towards D'Arcy's distended corpse.

'We'll re-seal the door and leave him for the cops to find when it opens tomorrow,' he said with a shrug. 'There's nothing he can tell them that we –' He broke off, having just caught sight of D'Arcy's wrist.

'What's up?'

Tom knelt down and gingerly lifted D'Arcy's arm.

'His watch,' he breathed as he tried to get at the fastening. The cold flesh had risen like dough around the black crocodile-skin strap, his blackened fingers leaving dark bruise-like marks on D'Arcy's pale skin.

'What about it?'

'It's a Ziff.'

'A Ziff?'

'Max Ziff. A watch-maker. A genius. He only makes three, maybe four pieces a year. They sell for hundreds of thousands. Sometimes millions.'

'How can you tell it's one of his?' She crouched down next to him.

'The orange second hand,' he explained, the catch coming free and the strap peeling away, leaving a deep welt in the skin. 'That's his signature.'

'I've seen one of these before,' she frowned, reaching for it.

'Are you sure it was a Ziff?' he asked with a sceptical look. Not only were there so few of them around, but they were so unobtrusive that most people never noticed them when they saw them. In fact that was half the point.

'It wasn't *a* Ziff. It was the *same* Ziff,' she insisted. 'It was in Cavalli's evidence box. White face with no make on it, steel case, roman numerals, orange second hand and . . .' she flipped it over '. . . Yes. Engraved Greek letter on the back. Only this is delta. Cavalli's was gamma.'

'Are you sure it . . .?' he asked again.

'I'm telling you, it was identical.'

Tom shook his head in surprise.

'It must have been a special commission. He normally only makes one of anything.'

'Then we should talk to him,' Allegra suggested. 'If it's unusual, he might remember who ordered it and where we can find them?'

'We'd have to go and see him. He doesn't have a phone.'

'Where?'

'Geneva. We could drive there in a few hours and Archie could –' A sharp electronic tone broke into the conversation. Tom's eyes snapped to the door. 'Someone's coming.'

They leapt towards the exit, Allegra pausing only to hit the close button and snatch her hand out of the way as the door slammed shut. Working quickly, Tom stuffed the keypad back into the recess and screwed the access panel on, rubbing soot over it so that the area blended in with the rest of the wall.

'Outside,' Allegra mouthed, dragging him on to the balcony, the air cool and fresh after the panic room's putrid warmth. Moments later, his back pressed against the stone, he heard the unmistakeable sound of someone crunching through the ash and debris, entering the room and then stopping. Reaching into his backpack for his gun, Tom flicked the safety off. Allegra, standing on the other side of the doorway, did the same.

'It's Orlando,' a voice rasped in Italian. Tom frowned. He sounded strangely familiar. 'No, it's still shut . . .' A pause as he listened to whatever was being said at the other end, Tom barely daring to breathe in the silence. 'They've cleared away what was left of the bookcase, so they must know it's there . . .' Another pause, Tom still trying to place a voice that he was now convinced he'd heard only recently. If only he could remember when and where. 'I'll make sure we have someone here when it opens. It's the least they can do for us. Otherwise there's someone in the morgue . . . we've got an agreement . . . As soon as they bring the body in . . . Don't worry, everything's already set up. I'll be back before they land.'

The call ended and the footsteps retreated across the room towards the stairs. A few minutes later, the motion sensor beeped again and Allegra let out a relieved sigh. Tom, however, was already halfway across the room, heart thumping.

'Where are you going?' she called after him in a low voice. 'Tom!' She grabbed him by the arm and pulled him back. 'He'll hear you.'

Tom spun round, his eyes blazing, a tremor in his voice that he barely recognised as his own.

'It's him,' he spat angrily. 'I recognised his voice.'

'Who?'

'The priest,' Tom said through gritted teeth, all thoughts of Cavalli and the League and following up on the Ziff watch having suddenly left him. 'The priest from the Amalfi. The one sent to handle the Caravaggio exchange.'

FIFTY-NINE

20th March – 3.52 a.m.

Barrelling through the doorway, Tom took the stairs as quickly as he dared, Allegra on his heels. Nothing made sense any more. Nothing, except that he couldn't let him get away. He connected whatever had happened here to both the killings in Rome and Jennifer's death. He could lead Tom to whoever had ordered the hit.

A few minutes later, they emerged breathlessly into the ground-floor lobby.

'Which way did he go?' Tom barked at the officer, whose smile had quickly faded as he caught sight of the expression on Tom's soot-smudged face.

'Who?' he stuttered.

'The man who just came down ahead of us,' Tom snapped impatiently.

'No one else has been in since you went up,' the officer replied in an apologetic voice, as if he was somehow at fault.

'He must have come in another way,' Allegra immediately guessed. 'Probably jumped across from a balcony next door.'

They stepped through the sliding glass doors just as the garage entrance on the adjacent building rattled open. A blood-red Alfa Romeo MiTo chased the echo of its own engine up the slope from the underground car park, Tom glimpsing the driver as he quickly checked for traffic before accelerating down the street.

'Is everything okay?' the officer called after them with a worried cry as they sprinted to their car.

'Are you sure it's him?' Allegra asked as she buckled herself in, bracing an arm against the dash as the car leapt away.

'I remember every voice, every glance, every face from that night,' Tom insisted in a cold voice. 'He was as close to me as you are now. It was him. And if he's here, whoever sent him might be too.'

They caught up with the Alfa near the casino, the priest being careful, it seemed, to stay well within the speed limit. Dropping back to a safe distance, Tom followed him down the hill and through the underpass back towards the port, where workmen were busy disassembling a temporary dressage arena and stables under floodlights. Pulling in, they watched as he parked up and made his way down to the water, where a launch was waiting for him between two top-heavy motor cruisers.

'Drive down to the end,' Allegra suggested. 'We'll be able to see where he's going.'

With a nod Tom headed for the harbour wall and then got out, pausing to grab a set of night-vision goggles out of his bag. Putting them on, he tracked the small craft as it cut across the waves to an enormous yacht moored in the middle of the bay.

'*Il Sogno Blu*,' Tom read the name painted across its bows. 'The Blue Dream. Out of Georgetown.' A pause. 'We need to get out to it.'

Allegra eyed him carefully, as if debating whether she should try and talk him out of it. Then, with a shrug she pointed back over his shoulder.

'What about one of those?'

They ran down the ramp on to a pontoon where three small tenders had been tied up. The keys to the second one were attached to a champagne cork in a watertight storage compartment under the instrument panel. A few minutes later and they were slapping across the waves towards the yacht.

'This will do,' Tom called over the noise of the outboard as they approached. 'If we get any closer they'll hear us. I'll swim the rest.'

She killed the engine, then went and stood over him as he took his soot-stained tie off and loosened his collar.

'You don't know who's onboard or how many of them there are,' she pointed out, the wind whipping her hair.

'I know that someone on that ship helped kill Jennifer.' He kicked his shoes off and stood up, looping the night-vision goggles over one arm. 'That's enough.'

'Then I'm coming with you,' she insisted.

'You need to stay with the boat,' he pointed out, handing her both the phones the croupier had given him and D'Arcy's watch. 'Otherwise it'll drift and neither of us will make it back.'

She eyed him angrily.

'I thought we were in this together.'

'We are. But this is something I have to do alone.'

'I could stop you,' she reminded him in a defiant tone, standing in front of him so that he couldn't get past.

A pause, then a nod.

'You probably could.' A longer pause. 'But I don't think you will. You know I have to do this.'

There was a long silence. Then Allegra stepped unsmilingly to one side. With a nod, Tom squeezed past her to the stern and lowered himself into the water.

'Look, I'm not stupid,' he said, with what he hoped was

a reassuring smile. 'I'll be careful. Just give me twenty minutes, thirty max. Enough time to see who's on board and what they're doing here.'

Lips pursed, she gave a grudging nod.

Turning, Tom kicked out for the yacht with a powerful stroke, the waves rolling gently underneath him. He was lucky, he knew. On a rougher day, they might well have tossed him from crest to crest like a dolphin playing with a seal. Even so, it took him five, maybe even ten minutes to cover the hundred and fifty yards he'd left himself, his clothes dragging him back, a slight current throwing him off his bearing.

Up close, the yacht was even larger than it had appeared from the shore – perhaps 400 feet long, with sheer white sides that rose above him like an ice shelf, the sea lapping tentatively around it, as if afraid of being crushed. Even though it was anchored, the yacht's shape made it look as if it was powering through the waves at eighteen knots, its arrowed bow lunging aggressively over the water, its rear chopped off on a steep rake, as if it had been pulled out of shape. Tom counted five decks in all, their square portholes looking as if they must have been dynamited out of the ship's monolithic hull, capped by a mushrooming radar and comms array that wouldn't have been out of place on an aircraft carrier.

The launch had been moored to a landing platform that folded down out of the stern. Swimming round to it, Tom hauled himself on board and then carefully climbed across on to the ship itself. The landing platform was deserted, although he could see now that when lowered it revealed a huge garage and electric hoist, with room to store the launch itself, together with a small flotilla of jet-skis, inflatables and other craft.

Quickly drying himself on one of the neatly folded towels

monogrammed with the yacht's name, he buttoned his jacket and turned the collar up to conceal as much of his white shirt as he could. Then he slipped his NV goggles over his head and turned them on. With a low hum, night became day, albeit one with a stark green tint. The outline of the deck's darkest recesses now revealed themselves as if caught in the burst of a permanent firework.

Treading stealthily, Tom made his way up a succession of steep teak-lined staircases to the main deck, which he had noticed on the swim across was the only one with any lights on. Finding the port gangway empty, he made his way forward along it, keeping below the windows and checking over his shoulder that no one was coming up behind him. Two doors had been left open about halfway along, the glow spilling out on to the polished hardwood decking and making his goggles flare. Switching them off, he edged his head round the first opening. It gave on to a walnut-panelled dining room, the table already set with china and crystal for the following morning's breakfast. In the middle of the main wall he recognised Picasso's *Head of a Woman*, taken from a yacht in Antibes a few years ago.

The second open doorway revealed the main sitting room. Hanging over the mantelpiece was a painting that Tom recognised as the *View of the Sea at Scheveningen*, stolen from the Van Gogh Museum in Amsterdam. This room, too, had been set up, although in readiness for what looked like cocktails rather than breakfast: champagne cooling in an ice bucket, an empty bottle of '78 Château Margaux standing next to a full decanter, glasses laid out on a crisp linen cloth.

Turning the goggles back on, he continued along the gangway, wondering if he had chanced his luck long enough up here and whether he should head down below instead. But before he could do anything, a door ahead of him opened. A man stepped out, talking on his phone. Tom froze in the shadow of a bulkhead. It was the priest, his mouth twisted into a cruel laugh, but recognisably the same man he'd faced in the casino – medium build, white, wavy hair, ruddy cheeks.

Even as Jennifer's image filled his mind, he felt the anger flood through him, sensed his chest tightening and his jaw clenching. Before he knew it, he was clutching his gun, her name on his lips, and death in his heart.

SIXTY

Il Sogno Blu, **Monaco**
20th March – 4.21 a.m.

It hadn't taken Allegra long to decide to ignore Tom's instructions and follow him on board. There'd been something dead in his eyes, something in the way he'd deliberately patted his pocket to check that his gun was still there, that had suggested he would need her help – not to deal with whoever was on board, but to protect him from himself.

Having approached from behind so that the wind would carry the engine's breathless echo away from the yacht, Allegra had pulled alongside the launch and lashed the tender to it. Then she had paused for a few moments, waiting for an angry shout and for an armed welcoming party to materialise. But none came.

Climbing across the launch and on to the landing platform, she made her way up to the main deck, pressing herself flat against one of the aluminium staircases when a sentry walked whistling past above her. Unlike Tom, she had no night-vision equipment, so had to feel her way through the darkness, the distant flicker of the steeply banked shore providing only the faintest light by which to navigate. Even so,

Tom was proving relatively easy to track, the deck still damp wherever he had paused for more than a few seconds.

Moving as quickly as she dared, she edged forward, ducking under windows and darting across the open doorways until she had almost reached the sundeck area which took up the entire front third of this level. At its centre was a helipad that she realised parted to reveal a swimming pool.

In the same instant she saw Tom ahead of her, crouched in the shadows of the side rail, his gun in his hand. She followed his aim and saw a man standing at the bow, looking out to sea, talking into his phone. Leaping forward, she placed her hand on Tom's shoulder. He spun round to face her, a strange, empty expression on his face as if in some sort of trance.

'Not now,' she whispered. 'Not here.'

For a few moments it was almost as if he didn't recognise her, before his face broke with surprise, and then a flash of anger.

'What . . .?'

She held her finger to her lips, then pointed above them towards the top deck. An armed guard was leaning back casually against the railings above them, blowing smoke rings. Tom blinked and then glanced across at her, his eyes betraying a flicker of understanding.

She motioned for him to follow her, the second door she tried opening into a small gymnasium.

'Are you trying to get yourself killed?' she hissed as soon as the door had shut. Their shadows danced off the mirrored walls, the exercise equipment's skeletal frames looming menacingly around them as if they were limbering up for a fight.

'I . . .' he faltered, staring at the gun in his hand as if he wasn't quite sure how it had got there. 'You don't understand.'

'You're right, I don't understand . . .' She broke off at the sound of someone approaching with a squeak of rubber soles, the noise growing and then slowly fading away. 'You said you were just going to see who was here. Not get yourself killed.'

'It's him,' Tom said in a low voice, almost as if he was trying to convince himself. 'He set her up!'

'*He* doesn't matter. What's important is finding out who sent him.'

'I saw him and I . . .' Another long pause, until he finally looked up, his lips pressed together as if he was trying to hold something in. 'You're right. I wasn't . . .'

With a curt nod, she accepted what she assumed was as close as she was going to get to an apology. 'Let's just get off this thing before they find us.'

Checking that the gangway was still empty, Allegra led him back towards the stern. But they were only about halfway along it when the echo of a barked order and the sound of running feet forced them to dive through the open sitting-room door and crouch behind the sofa, guns drawn. Three men tore past the doorway, the approaching thump of rotor blades explaining the sudden commotion.

'Someone's landing,' Allegra breathed.

'Which must be what all this is for,' Tom said, pointing at the carefully prepared drinks and glasses. 'We need to . . . What the hell are you doing?'

'Inviting us to the party,' she said with a wink. Having taken out both the phones Tom had handed her earlier, she used one to dial the other and then slid it out of sight under the coffee table. 'At least until the battery runs out.'

With the phone hidden and still transmitting, they made their way back along the gangway, then down the stair-case to the landing platform, the helicopter's low rumble now a fast-closing thunder. As it landed, they cast off, using the engine noise as cover to throttle up and spin away towards the harbour and the relative sanctuary of their waiting car.

SIXTY-ONE

Il Sogno Blu, **Monaco**
20th March – 4.56 a.m.

Santos uncorked the decanter and poured the Margaux into four large glasses. It pained him to share a bottle as good as this at the best of times, but to split it at this time of the night with two former members of the Serbian special forces, whose palates had no doubt been irretrievably blunted by eating too much cabbage and drinking their own piss while out on exercise, seemed positively criminal. Then again, they would recognise the Margaux for what it cost, even if they couldn't taste why it was worth it. And that was half the point in serving it.

'Nice boat,' Asim whistled. 'Yours?'

He was the older of the two and clearly in charge, squat and square headed, with a five-mil buzz-cut and a bayonet scar across one cheek.

'Borrowed from one of my investors,' Santos replied, sitting down opposite them. 'How was your flight?'

'No problem,' Dejan, the second Serb, replied.

Compared to Asim, he was tall and gaunt, with curly black hair that he had slicked back against his head with some sort of oil. One of his ears was higher than the other, which caused his glasses to rest at a slight angle across his face.

'Good,' Santos replied. 'You're welcome to stay the night, of course.'

'Thank you, but no,' Dejan declined, Santos noting with dismay that he had already knocked back half his glass as if it was tequila. 'Our orders are to agree deal and return.'

'We do have a deal then?'

'Fifteen million dollars,' Asim confirmed.

'You said twenty on the phone,' Santos retorted angrily. 'It's worth at least twenty. I wouldn't have invited you here if I'd known it was only for fifteen.'

'Fifteen is new price,' Asim said stonily. 'Or you find someone else with money so quick.'

There was a pause as Santos stared angrily at each of the Serbs in turn. With Ancelotti's team of forensic accountants due to start on his books any day, he was out of options. And from their obvious confidence, they knew it. He glanced across at Orlando, who shrugged helplessly.

'Fine. Fifteen,' Santos spat. 'In cash.'

'You understand the consequences if you are not able to deliver . . .'

'We'll deliver,' Santos said firmly, standing up.

'Then we look forward to your call,' Dejan shrugged, draining his glass. 'Tomorrow, as agreed.'

Shaking their hands, Santos showed them to the door, waited until their footsteps had melted into towards the engine whine of the waiting helicopter, then swore.

'We could find another buyer,' Orlando suggested.

'Not at this short notice, and the bastards know it,' Santos said angrily. 'It's tomorrow night or never.'

'De Luca and Moretti agreed to the meet?'

'I told them that things had got out of hand,' Santos nodded. 'That business was suffering. Then offered to broker a settlement. They didn't take much convincing. Usual place. No weapons, no men. It'll be our only chance to get the watches and the painting in the same room.'

'As long as we can get to D'Arcy's.'

'We only need three,' Santos reminded him. 'We've got Cavalli's already and Moretti and De Luca should both be wearing theirs. D'Arcy's is back-up.'

'They'll come after you. They'll come after us both.'

'They'll have to find me first.' Santos shrugged. 'Besides, life's too short to waste it worrying about being dead.'

'Amen,' Orlando nodded, topping up their glasses.

SIXTY-TWO

Main harbour, Monte Carlo
20th March – 5.03 a.m.

'Are you sure that was him?'

'I'm telling you, it's Antonio Santos,' she breathed, certain she was right but still not quite able to believe it. 'The Chairman of the Banco Rosalia. He said exactly the same thing about life being too short when he was identifying Argento's body.'

'It wouldn't exactly be the first time a Vatican-funded bank has been a front for the mafia,' Tom conceded with a shrug.

'Do you think he ordered the hit on Jennifer?'

'The priest clearly works for him and, by the sound of it, he had access to the Caravaggio too,' Tom nodded darkly.

'But why would he have done it?'

'My guess is that she found something during that raid on the dealer in New York. A bank statement or an invoice or a receipt. Something that implicated the Banco Rosalia or that tied him back to the League. Something worth killing her for.'

'Even if we could prove that, he's got a Vatican passport,' she reminded him with a shake of her head. 'He can't be prosecuted.'

'Maybe if we can get to the painting before him, he won't have to be.'

'What do you mean?'

'I mean the Serbs will take care of him for us if he doesn't deliver,' Tom explained in a grim voice.

There was a pause as she let the implications of this sink in.

'At least now we know why D'Arcy's murder didn't match any of the other killings,' she said. 'It had nothing to do with the League's vendetta. Santos killed him for his watch.'

'They link everything,' Tom agreed.

'Moretti, De Luca, D'Arcy . . .' She counted the watches off on her fingers.

'Cavalli,' Tom finished the list for her.

'That must have been what Gallo was looking for when he killed Gambetta,' Allegra said with an angry shake of her head. 'He's been working for Santos all along.'

'But why? How can a watch help get to a painting?'

'Even if we knew, we still don't know where the painting is.'

'Ziff's our best hope,' Tom said slowly. 'He'll know why Santos needs them.'

'Will he see us?' Allegra asked.

'Oh, he'll see us,' Tom nodded. 'But that doesn't mean he'll tell us anything.'

SIXTY-THREE

Near Aosta, Italy
20th March – 8.33 a.m.

It was a six-hour drive to Geneva, the road snaking up into the hills behind Monte Carlo and then along the motorway into Italy, before turning north and plunging into the Alps. They'd had no trouble at the border, their Swiss passports earning little more than a cursory once-over from the duty officer and then a dismissive flick of his hand as he waved them through. Even so, Tom was certain that he'd caught him giving them the finger as they'd accelerated away. So much for European harmony.

Allegra had soon drifted off, leaving Tom to take the first shift, although she had at least managed to share what she remembered about Santos's immaculate dress sense, compulsive liquorice habit and cold-eyed charisma before her tiredness had finally caught up with her. Eventually, about three hours in, Tom had turned off at a service station near Aosta on the A5, hungry and needing to stretch his legs before swapping over.

'I need a coffee,' Allegra groaned as he shook her awake. 'We both do.'

'Where are we?'

'Not far from the Mont Blanc tunnel.'

The service station was bright and warm, something indistinct but resolutely cheerful playing in the background. A busload of school children on a ski trip had turned up just before them and they were besieging the small shop. Desperately rooting through their pockets for change, they were noisily pooling funds to finance a hearty breakfast of crisps, coke and chocolate. As soon as the onslaught had cleared, the teachers swooped in behind them to pick over the bones of whatever they hadn't stripped from the shelves and apologise to the staff.

While Allegra queued for the toilet, Tom got them both a coffee from the machine and managed to locate a couple of pastries that had somehow survived the raid. Then he called Archie.

'Where the fuck have you been?' Archie greeted him angrily. 'I've been trying to call since lunchtime yesterday.'

'I had to swap phones. It's a long story.'

'Then make it a good one. Dom was worried. We both were.'

'We think Jennifer was killed because she was investigating a mafia-controlled antiquities smuggling ring called the Delian League,' Tom explained, mouthing Archie's name to Allegra as she returned.

'*We*? Who the bloody hell is "we"?'

Tom sighed. He could see this was going to be a long conversation. But there was no avoiding it. Step by step, he ran through the events of the last day or so – his encounter with Allegra at Cavalli's house, their trip to see Johnny Li, the abortive attempt to steal a car, their interrogation of Aurelio, their capture by De Luca and subsequent escape from the tomb, their trip to the casino and their discovery of D'Arcy's panic room. And finally, the conversation they had just overheard between Santos and the Serbs. Archie was an impatient listener, interrupting every so often with questions or a muttered curse until Tom had finished. Then it was his turn to explain how it seemed that the Artemis Tom had asked them to look into had in fact been bought by a company controlled by the same person who had sold it in the first place.

'Our guess is that it's part of an elaborate laundering scam to manufacture provenance,' Archie added. 'You ever heard of an antiquities dealer called Faulks?'

'Faulks,' Tom exclaimed, recognising the name that Aurelio had mentioned. 'Earl Faulks?'

'You know him?' Archie sounded vaguely disappointed.

'Aurelio mentioned his name,' Tom explained. 'Where he is now?'

'His car had Geneva plates, so I'm guessing he's based here.'

'See if you can find him. When we've finished with Ziff, I'll call you. We can pay him a visit together.'

'Everything okay?' Allegra asked as he ended the call. From her expression, Tom guessed that she'd overhead the tinny echo of Archie's strident tone.

'Don't worry. That's standard Archie,' Tom reassured her with a wink. 'He's only happy when he's got something or someone to complain about.' He held out the car keys. 'Here – it's your turn to drive.'

SIXTY-FOUR

Lake Geneva, Switzerland
20th March – 10.59 a.m.

A couple of hours later, they drew up at the lake's edge. A yacht was skating across the water's glassy surface, its sail snapping in the breeze. In the distance loomed the jagged, snow-covered teeth of the surrounding mountains, their reflection caught so perfectly by the water's blinding mirror that it was hard to know which way was up. It was a strangely disorientating illusion. And one that was broken only when the yacht suddenly tacked left, its trailing wake corrugating the water.

Getting out, they walked up to the gates of a large three-storey red-brick building with steep gabled roofs. Set high up and back from the road behind iron railings, it appeared to be empty; grey shutters drawn across the mullioned windows, walls choking with ivy, the gardens wild and over-grown. Even so, there were faint signs of life – tyre tracks in the gravel suggesting a recent visit, roving security cameras patrolling the property's perimeter, steam rising from an outlet.

'The Georges d'Ammon Asylum for the Insane?' Allegra

read the polished brass nameplate and then shot Tom a questioning, almost disbelieving look.

'Used to be,' Tom affirmed, rolling his shoulders to try and ease the stiffness in his back and neck. 'That's why Ziff bought it. He thought it was funny.'

'What's the joke?'

'That anyone who spends their life watching the seconds tick away is bound to go mad eventually. He thought that at least this way, he wouldn't have far to move.' A pause. 'Swiss humour. It takes some getting used to.'

Tom pressed the buzzer. No answer. He tried again, holding it down longer this time. Still nothing.

'Maybe he's out,' Allegra ventured.

'He never goes out,' Tom said with a shake of his head. 'Doesn't even have a phone. He's just being difficult. Show him the watch.'

With a shrug, she held D'Arcy's watch up to the camera. A few seconds past, and then the gate buzzed open.

They made their way up the steep drive, the gravel crunching like fresh snow underfoot, the building's institutional blandness further revealing itself as it slowly came into view.

'How long has he been here?'

'As long as I've known him,' Tom replied. 'The authorities shut it down after some of the staff were accused of abusing the inmates. They found two bodies under the basement floor, more bricked up inside a chimney.'

Even as he said this, Allegra noticed that the spiked railings girdling the property were angled back inside the garden – to keep people in, not out. She shivered, the sun's warmth momentarily eclipsed by the shadow of a large plane tree.

'How many watches does he make a year?' she asked, changing the subject.

'New? Not many. Maybe three or four.' Tom shrugged. 'His main business is upgrades.'

'What sort of upgrades?'

'It depends. Retrofitting manufactured components with handmade titanium or even ceramic ones, improving the balance wheel and mainspring design, engraving certain parts of the movement, adding new features, modifying the face . . . The only way you'd know it was one of his is from the orange second hand that he fits to everything he touches.'

'So you buy a watch that tells the time perfectly well and then pay him more money to take it apart and rebuild it to do exactly the same thing?' she asked incredulously.

'Pretty much.' Tom grinned. 'People do it with sports cars.'

'But that's to make them go faster. A watch either tells the time or it doesn't. It can't do it better.'

'That's not the point. It's not what it does but the way it does it. The ingenuity of the design. The quality of the materials. The skill with which it's been assembled. It's like people. It's what you can't see that really counts.'

'Some people, maybe.'

The front door was sheltered under an ornate cast-iron canopy at the top of several shallow steps. It was open and they stepped inside, finding themselves in a large entrance hall lit by a flickering emergency exit sign.

Her eyes adjusting to the gloom, Allegra could see that the room rose to the full height of the building, an oak staircase zig-zagging its way up to each floor capped off by a glass cupola far overhead. To their right was what had clearly once been the reception desk, the yellowing visitors' book still open at the last entry, a gnarled claw of desiccated flowers drooping over it as if poised to sign in. Up on the wall was a large carved panel lauding the generosity and wisdom of the asylum's founder and marking its opening in 1896. Next to this, another panel commemorated those who had served as directors over the years, the final name on the list either incomplete or deliberately defaced, it was hard to tell. To the left, a straitjacket had been left slung over the back of a wheelchair at the foot of the staircase, its leather straps cracked, the buckles rusting. Behind it was a grandfather clock, its face shrouded by a white sheet.

Allegra had the strange feeling that she was intruding, that the building was holding its breath, and that as soon as they left the straitjacket would deftly fasten itself, the doors would swing wildly in their frames, the clock chime and silent screams rise once again from the basement's dank shadows.

'Up here,' a voice called, breaking the spell.

She looked up through the darkness and saw a man peering down at them over the second-floor banisters. Swapping a look, they made their way up to him, the wooden staircase groaning under their unexpected weight, their footsteps echoing off the flaking green walls.

'So you've come to visit at last, Felix?' Ziff grinned manically, thrusting his hand towards them as they stepped on to a landing lit by sunshine knifing through the gaps and cracks in the shuttered windows. He spoke quickly and with a thick German accent, his words eliding into each other.

'A promise is a promise.' Tom smiled, shaking his hand. 'Max, this is Allegra Damico.'

'Friend of yours?' Ziff asked without looking at her.

'I wouldn't have brought her here otherwise,' Tom reassured him.

Ziff considered this for a few seconds, then gave a high-pitched, almost nervous laugh, that flitted up and down a scale.

'No, of course not. *Wilkommen.*'

Ziff stepped forward into the light. He was tall, perhaps six foot three, but slight, his reedy frame looking as though it would bend in a strong wind, dyed black hair thinning and

cropped short. His features were equally delicate, almost femi-
nine, his face dominated by a neatly trimmed moustache that
exactly followed the contours of his top lip and had been dyed
to match his hair. He was wearing a white apron over green
tweed trousers, gleaming brown brogues and an open-necked
check shirt worn with a yellow cravat. His sleeves were rolled
up so she could see his thin wrists, the slender fingers of his
right hand tapping against his leg as if playing an unheard
piece of music, the left gripping an Evian atomiser. Strangely,
given his occupation, he wasn't wearing a watch.

She shook his hand, his skin feeling unnaturally slick, until
she realised that he was wearing latex gloves.

'I was so sorry to hear about your father.' Ziff turned back
to Tom, gripping him firmly by the elbow and leaning in
close. 'How have you been?'

'Fine,' Tom nodded his thanks. 'It's been a while now.
Almost three years.'

'That long?' Ziff let him go, his head springing from side
to side in bemusement. 'You know me: I try not to keep
track. I find it too depressing,' He licked the corner of his
mouth absent-mindedly, then repeated his shrill laugh.

The sight of a round mark on the wall behind him where
the clock that had once hung there had been removed
made Allegra wonder if perhaps Ziff hadn't been joking
when he had told Tom his reasons for buying this place.
Maybe he really did believe that a life spent watching time
leak irresistibly away would condemn him to insanity, and
that by removing a clock here and covering another there,
he might in some way avoid or at least delay his fate.

Ziff seemed to guess what she was thinking, because he
glanced up at the ghostly imprint of the missing clock behind
him.

'Time is an accident of accidents, signorina.' He gave her
a sad nod.

'Epicurus,' she replied, recognising the quote.

'Exactly!' His face broke into a smile. 'Now tell me, Felix. What accident of accidents brings you here?'

SIXTY-FIVE

20th March – 11.14 a.m.
Ziff led them through a set of double doors into a sombre corridor, its grey linoleum unfurling towards a fire escape at its far end. Several gurneys were parked along one wall, while on the other wall patients' clipboards were still neatly arranged in a rack with the staff attendance record chalked up on a blackboard – further confirmation that the building's former occupants had left in a hurry and that Ziff had made little effort to clean up after them.

He stopped at the first door on the left, sprayed its handle with the atomiser, then opened it to reveal one of the asylum's former wards. Here, too, it seemed that nothing had been touched, until Ziff flicked a power switch and Allegra suddenly realised that all the beds were missing and that in their place, lined up between the floral curtains dangling listlessly from aluminium tracks, were pinball machines. Sixteen of them in all, eight running down each side of the room, backboards flashing, lanes pulsing, drop targets blinking and bumpers sparking as they happily flickered into life. Allegra read the names of a few as she walked past – 'Flash Gordon', 'Playboy', 'Close Encounters of the

Third Kind', 'The Twilight Zone' – their titles evocative of a distant, almost forgotten childhood. Every so often one of them would call out a catchphrase or play a theme song, and this seemed to set the other machines off, their sympathetic chorus building to a discordant crescendo before dying away again.

'They're all vintage,' Ziff explained proudly, stepping slowly past them like a doctor doing his rounds. 'Each one is for a private commission I've completed. A tombstone, if you like. So I don't forget.'

'How many have you got?' Allegra asked, pausing by 'The Addams Family', and then jumping as it blasted out a loud clickety-click noise.

'About eighty,' he said after a few seconds' thought. 'I've almost run out of bed space.'

'Which one's your favourite?'

'Favourite?' He looked horrified. 'Each one is unique, each different. If you were to try and choose one over the others . . .' He tailed off, as if afraid the machines might overhear him.

He stopped by a battered wooden desk marooned in the middle of the ward. Its top was covered in red felt, worn and stained in places with oil. A large magnifying lamp was clamped to one edge and it was on casters, prompting Allegra to wonder if Ziff wheeled it from room to room, moving around the different wards as the mood took him.

He sat down, a steel tray in front of him containing the disembodied guts of a Breguet, a 20x loupe and several jeweller's screwdrivers. Other tools had been carefully laid out in the different drawers of a small wheeled cabinet to his right, as if in preparation for surgery – case openers, tweezers, screwdrivers, watch hammers, pliers, brushes, knives – each sorted by type and then arranged by size.

'Show me,' Ziff said, pushing the tray out of the way and

putting on an almost comically large pair of black square-framed glasses that he secured to his head with an elastic strap.

Allegra handed him the watch and he angled the magnifying lamp down over it, peering through the glass.

'Oh yes.' His face broke into a smile. 'Hello, old friend.'

'You recognise it?'

'Wouldn't you recognise one of your own children?' Ziff asked impatiently. 'Especially one as special as this.'

'What do you mean?' Tom shot back eagerly.

'Each of my watches is normally unique,' Ziff explained. 'A one-off. But in this case, the client ordered six identical pieces. And paid handsomely for the privilege, from what I remember.'

'Six?' Allegra repeated excitedly. They knew of four already. That left two others still unaccounted for.

'They're numbered,' Ziff continued, pointing at the delta symbol delicately engraved on the back of the case. 'Platinum bezel, stainless-steel case, ivory face, self-winding, water resistant to thirty metres, screw-down crown . . .' He balanced it in his hand as if weighing it. 'A good watch.'

'Who was the client?' Tom asked.

Ziff looked at him with an indulgent smile, slipping his glasses up on to his forehead where they perched like headlights.

'Felix, you know better than that.'

'It's important,' Tom insisted.

'My clients pay for their confidentiality, the same as yours,' Ziff insisted with a shrug.

'Please, Max,' Tom pleaded. 'I have to know. Give me something.'

Ziff paused before answering, his eyes blinking, then slipped his glasses back on to his nose and stood up.

'Do you like pinball?'

'We're not here to play pinball,' Tom said sharply, although Ziff didn't seem to pick up on his tone. 'We're here to . . .'

'"Straight Flush" is a classic,' he interrupted, crossing over to the door. 'Why don't you have a game while you're waiting?'

'Waiting for what?' Tom called after him, but Ziff was already out of the room, the sprung door easing itself shut behind him.

Allegra turned towards the machine he had pointed out. It appeared to be one of the oldest and most basic in the room, the salmon-coloured back-board illustrated with face-card caricatures, the sloping yellow surface decorated with playing cards that Allegra guessed you had to try and illuminate to create a high-scoring poker hand. She frowned. It wasn't an obvious recommendation, compared to some of the more modern, more exciting games in the room, but then again she had detected an insistent tone in his voice. A tone that had made her wonder if there was something there he wanted them to see. Something other than the machine itself.

'Can you open it?' she asked, pointing at the metal panel on the front of the machine that contained the coin slot.

'Of course,' Tom squatted down next to her with a puzzled frown, reaching into his coat for a small pouch of lock-picking tools.

'He said that each machine was for a job he'd completed. A tombstone so he wouldn't forget,' she reminded him as he deftly released the lock and opened the door, allowing her to reach into the void under the playing surface. 'I just wondered . . .'

Her voice broke off as her fingers closed on an envelope of some sort. Pulling it out, she opened it, the flap coming away easily where the glue had dried over the years. It contained several sheets of paper.

'It's the original invoice;' she exclaimed with an excited smile. 'Six watches. Three hundred thousand dollars,' she read from the fading type. 'A lot of money, thirty years ago.'

'A lot of money today.' Tom smiled. 'Who was the client?'

'See for yourself.'

Allegra handed him the sheet, her eyes blazing with excitement.

'E. Faulks & Co,' Tom read, his face set with a grim smile. 'And there's a billing address down at the Freeport. Good. I'll ask Archie to meet us there. Even if Faulks has moved we should be able to find –'

'That's strange,' Allegra interrupted him, having quickly leafed through the rest of the contents of the envelope. 'There's another invoice here. Same address, only twelve years later.'

'But that would make seven watches.' Tom frowned. 'Ziff only mentioned six.'

Before she could even attempt an explanation, she heard the whistled strains of the overture from *Carmen* echoing along the corridor outside. Snatching the invoice from Tom's hand, she slipped it back in the envelope, shoved it inside the machine and shut the door.

"Magnets,' Ziff announced as he sauntered in, excitedly waving several sheets of paper over his head. 'I knew they were down there somewhere.'

'What?'

'Magnets,' Ziff repeated with a high-pitched giggle, his glasses hanging around his neck like a swimmer's goggles. 'See.'

Picking D'Arcy's watch up, he held it over the tray containing the watch he was working on. Two small screws leapt through the air and glued themselves to the bezel.

'Each watch has a small electro magnet built into it powered by the self-winding mechanism,' he explained, opening the file and pointing at a set of technical drawings as if they might mean something to either of them. 'They were all set at slightly different resistances.'

'What for?'

'Some sort of a locking mechanism, I think. They never said exactly what.'

Allegra swapped a meaningful glance with Tom. So this was why Santos needed the watches. Together, they formed a key that opened wherever the Caravaggio was being stored.

'Normally I destroy the drawings once a job is completed, but this was the first time I had used silicon-based parts and I thought they might be useful. Turns out it was just as well.'

'What do you mean?'

'The client lost one of the watches and asked for a replacement. The epsilon watch, I think. Without these I might have struggled to replicate it.'

Allegra took a deep breath. That explained the second invoice. More importantly, it meant that there were seven numbered watches out there somewhere. Each the same and yet subtly different. Each presumably entrusted to a different key member of the Delian League.

'By the way, what was your score?' Ziff jerked his head towards the 'Straight Flush' pinball machine he had pointed out earlier.

'Ask us tomorrow,' Tom answered with a smile.

SIXTY-SIX

Free Port compound, Geneva
20th March – 12.02 p.m.

The Free Port was a sprawling agglomeration of low-slung warehouses lurking in the shadow of the airport's perimeter fence. Built up over the years, it offered a vivid snapshot of changing architectural fashions, the older buildings cinder grey and forbidding in their monolithic functionality, the newer ones iPod white and airy.

For the most part, its business was entirely legitimate, the facilities providing importers and exporters with a tax-free holding area through which goods could be shipped in transit or stored, with duty only being paid when items officially 'entered' the country.

The problem, as Tom was explaining to Allegra on the drive down there, lay in the Free Port's insistence on operating under a similar code of secrecy to the Swiss banking sector. This allowed cargo to be shipped into Switzerland, sold on, and then exported again with only the most cursory official records kept of what was actually being sold or who it was being sold to. Compounding this was Switzerland's repeated refusal to sign up to the 1970 Unesco Convention on the illicit trade in cultural property. Not to mention the fact that, under Swiss law, stolen goods acquired in good faith became the legal property of the new owner after five years on Swiss soil.

Taken together these three factors had, over the years, established Switzerland's free ports as a smuggler's paradise, with disreputable dealers exploiting the system by secretly importing stolen art or looted antiquities, holding them in storage for five years, and then claiming legal ownership.

To their credit, the Swiss government had recently bowed to international pressure and both ratified the Unesco Convention and changed its antiquated ownership laws. But so far the Free Port's entrenched position at the crossroads of the trade in illicit art and antiques seemed to be holding surprisingly firm. As Faulks's continuing presence served to prove.

They turned on to La Voie des Traz, the road choked with lorries and vans making deliveries and collections at the different warehouses, fork lifts shuttling between them as they loaded and unloaded with a high-pitched whine. For a moment, Tom was reminded of his drive into Vegas a few nights before, the vast buildings lining both sides of the street like the casinos studding the Strip.

'There's Archie and Dom –' Tom pointed at the two figures waiting in the car park of the warehouse mentioned on the invoice.

'Everything all right?' Archie bellowed as they got out.

'Tom!' A tearful Dominique tore past him and wrapped her arms around Tom's neck. 'I'm so sorry about what happened to . . . I'm so sorry.'

'Yeah,' Archie coughed awkwardly, lowering his eyes.

Even now, no one could bring themselves to say Jennifer's name, he noticed. Afraid of upsetting him. Afraid of what he might do or say.

'This is Allegra Damico,' Tom said, turning to introduce her.

She nodded hello, Tom realising from their forced hand-shakes and awkward greetings that they were all probably feeling a bit uncomfortable. Dom and Archie at Allegra stepping inside their tight little circle, Allegra at being so quickly outnumbered, with only Tom providing the delicate thread that bound them all together.

'How was Max?' Archie asked. 'Still bonkers?'

'Getting worse,' Tom sighed. 'Although we did manage to find out why Santos needs the watches.'

'They contain small electro-magnets that open some sort of lock,' Allegra jumped in. 'Presumably to wherever the painting's being kept.'

'Faulks commissioned seven of them,' Tom continued. 'So as well as the four we know about, there are three more out there somewhere, which might give us a chance to get to the painting before Santos.' He glanced sceptically at the squat, square building behind them, its exterior clad in rusting metal sheeting. 'So, this is it?'

'It's scheduled for demolition later in the year,' Archie nodded. 'Faulks and a few other tenants who are due to move out at the end of the month are the only people left inside.'

'He's got a suite of rooms on the third floor,' Dominique added. 'He's due back at around four for a meeting with Verity Bruce.'

'The curator of antiquities at the Getty?' Allegra frowned in surprise. 'What's she doing here?'

'Having lunch at the Perle du Lac any time now and then doing the usual rounds of the major dealers.'

'How do you . . .' Allegra's question faded away as she saw the phone in Dominique's hand.

'We cloned his SIM. I've got it set up to mirror his calendar entries and record every call he makes.'

'Does that mean you know where they're meeting tonight?' Tom asked hopefully.

'The time's blocked out but there's no details.'

'Well, if they're due back here at four that gives us . . . just under four hours to get inside, have a look around and get out.'

'I've rented some space on the same floor as Faulks.' Archie held out a key. 'Bloke on the desk thought I was loopy, given they're shutting down, but it's ours for the next two weeks.'

They signed in, the register suggesting that they were the only people there. The guard was all smiles, the momentary flurry of activity clearly a welcome respite from the silent contemplation of empty CCTV screens. To Archie's obvious amusement he seemed to take a particular shine to Dominique.

'You're well in,' he grinned as they made their way to the lift.

'Lucky me.'

'Archie's got a point,' Tom said. 'Why don't you stay down here and keep him busy.'

She gave Tom an injured look.

'Please tell me you're joking.'

'Just until we can get inside.'

She glared at Archie, who was trying not to laugh, then turned wearily back towards the reception as they got into the lift.

'Great,' she sighed as the doors shut.

A few moments later and they stepped out on to a wide cinder-block corridor that led off left and right. The floor had been painted grey, the evenly spaced neon tubes overhead reflecting in its dull surface every fifteen or so feet. A yellow line ran down its centre, presumably to help the fork-lifts navigate safely along it, although the gouges and marks along the greenwashed walls suggested that it had not been that effective. Steel doors were set into the walls at irregular intervals, the relative distance between them giving some indication as to the size of the room behind each one. As was usual in the Free Port, they were identified only by numbers, not company names.

They followed the signs to corridor twelve and then stopped outside room seventeen.

'This is it,' Archie confirmed.

'You know seventeen is an unlucky number in Italy,' Allegra observed thoughtfully.

'Why?'

'In Roman numerals it's XVII, which is an anagram of VIXI – I lived. I'm now dead.'

'She's a right barrel of laughs, isn't she?' Archie gave a flat sigh. 'Do you do bar mitzvah's too?'

'Give her a break, Archie,' Tom warned him sharply. 'She's part of this now.'

The offices were secured by three locks – a central one, common to every door, and two heavy-duty padlocks that Faulks must have fitted himself at the top and bottom. Working quickly, Tom placed a tension wrench in the lower-half of the key hole and placed some light clockwise pressure on it. Then he slipped his pick into the top of the lock and, feeling for each pin, pushed them up out of the way one by one, careful to maintain the torque on the tension wrench so that they wouldn't drop back down. In little over a minute, all three locks had been released.

Grabbing the handle, Tom fractionally eased the door open and looked along its frame, then shut it again.

'Alarmed?' Archie guessed.

'Contact switch,' Tom said, glancing up at the camera at the end of the corridor and hoping that Dominique was working her magic.

'Can't you get round it?' Allegra asked.

'The contact at the top of the door is held shut by a magnet,'

Tom explained. 'If we open the door, the magnet moves out of range and the switch opens and breaks the circuit. We need another magnet to hold the switch in place while we open the door.'

'I'll go and get your gear out the car,' Archie volunteered.

'Can't we just use this?' Allegra held up D'Arcy's watch, her eyebrows raised into a question. 'It's magnetised, isn't it?'

Tom turned to Archie with a questioning smile.

'Yeah well, I can't think of everything, can I?' Archie sniffed grudgingly.

Taking the watch from her, Tom again eased the door open and then held the back of the watch as close as he could to the small surface-mounted white box he had noticed previously. Then, exchanging a quick, hopeful look with both Archie and Allegra, he pushed the door fully open. For a few moments they stood there, each half-expecting to hear warning tones from the alarm's control panel. But the sound never came.

They were in.

SIXTY-SEVEN

Restaurant Perle du Lac, Geneva
20th March – 12.30 p.m.

'You found it!'

Faulks leant on his umbrella to stand up as the maitre d'
escorted Verity along the terrace to the table. She was wearing
a black dress and a denim jacket and clutching a red Birkin
to match her shoes. Half her face was masked by a pair of
dark Chanel sunglasses, a thick knot of semi-precious stones
swaying around her neck.

'Earl, darling,' she gushed. They air-kissed noisily. 'Sorry
I'm late. Spanish air traffic control was on strike again. *Quelle
surprise!* I just got in.'

'Allow me.' He stepped forward and pushed her chair in for
her, then handed her a napkin with a flourish. The maitre d',
looking put out at having been so publicly supplanted, retreated
in stony silence.

'What are we celebrating?' She clapped her hands excitedly as the waiter stepped forward and poured them both a
glass of the Pol Roger Cuvée Sir Winston Churchill that Faulks
had specially pre-ordered.

'I always drink champagne for lunch.' He shrugged casually. 'Don't you?'

'Oh, Earl, you're such a tease.' She took a sip. 'You know this is my favourite. And as for the view –' she gestured beyond the terrace towards the lake, its jewelled surface glittering in the sun – 'you must have sold your soul to get such a perfect day.'

'You're half right.' He winked.

She turned back to him with a suspicious smile, pushing her sunglasses up and shielding her eyes from the sun with a hand.

'Are you trying to soften me up?'

'As if I'd dare!' He grinned. The waiter materialised expectantly at their table. 'I recommend the pigeon breast.'

Their order taken, the waiter backed away. There was a lull, the delicate chime of Verity's long painted nails striking her glass echoing the clink of cutlery from the neighbouring tables, until she fixed him with a casual look.

'Do you have it?'

There. The question he'd been waiting for. Faulks was impressed. It had taken her a full three minutes longer to ask this than he'd thought it would. She'd obviously come here determined to play it cool.

'I have it,' he confirmed. 'It arrived yesterday. I unpacked it myself.'

'Is it . . .?' Her voiced tailed off, as if she didn't trust herself to put what she felt into words, her carefully planned strategy of feigned indifference falling at the first hurdle, it seemed.

'It's everything you dreamt it would be,' he promised her.

'And you have a buyer?' she asked, her voice now betraying a hint of concern. 'Because after the kouros, the trustees have asked for a review of our acquisitions policy. They're even talking about establishing some sort of unofficial black-list. It's madness. The lunatics are taking over the asylum.'

'I have a buyer,' he reassured her. 'And provided you value the mask at the agreed figure, he will happily donate it to the Getty as we discussed.'

'Of course, of course,' she said, seeming relieved.

'What about Director Bury?' It was Faulks's turn to sound concerned. 'Have you spoken to him?'

'That man is a disgrace,' Verity snorted. 'How he ever came to . . .' She broke off, and took a deep breath, trying to compose herself. 'Well, maybe I shouldn't complain. Better a riding school pony on a lead rope than an unbroken Arab who won't take the bit.'

She drained her glass, the waiter swooping in to refill it before Faulks had time to even reach for the bottle.

'So he said yes?'

'If it's in the condition you say it is and I confirm that it's by Phidias, he'll submit the acquisition papers to the trustees himself. Bury may be incompetent, but he's not stupid. He realises that this could make his own reputation as much as mine. And he knows that if we don't take it, someone else will.'

'My buyer has promised me the money by the end of the week if you green-light it. It could be in California by the end of the month.'

'I just wish we hadn't arranged all these meetings today,' she sighed. 'Four o'clock seems like a long way away.'

'Then I've got some good news for you,' Faulks smiled. 'I bumped into Julian Simmons from the Gallerie Orientale on the way in and he wants to cancel. We should be able to head over there by around three.'

'Two and a half hours.' She checked her watch with a smile. 'I suppose that's not too long to wait after two and a half thousand years.'

SIXTY-EIGHT

Free Port Compound, Geneva
20th March – 12.32 p.m.

'What a shithole,' Archie moaned.

Tom had to agree. Withered carpet, wilting curtains, weathered windows, a stern row of steel-fronted cupboards lining the right-hand wall. There was something irredeemably depressing about the room's utilitarian ugliness that even the unusual table at the centre of the room – a circular slab of glass supported by a massive Corinthian capital – couldn't alleviate. Sighing, he opened one of the cupboards and then stepped back, open-mouthed.

'Look at this.'

The shelves were overflowing with antiquities. Overwhelmed by them. Vases, statues, bronzes, frescoes, mosaics, glassware, faience animals, jewellery . . . packed so tightly that in places the objects seemed to be climbing over each other like horses trying to escape a stable fire. The strange thing was that, while there was nothing here of the casual brutality with which Contarelli had treated the objects in his care, Tom couldn't help but wonder if the sheer number and variety of what had been hoarded here, and what it said about the likely scale and sophistication of the Delian League's operation, wasn't actually far more horrific.

'This one's the same,' Allegra said, her voice brimming with anger.

'Here too,' Archie called, opening the one next to her.

There was a gentle knock at the door. Using D'Arcy's watch again, Tom let Dominique in.

'You escaped?' Archie grinned.

'No thanks to you,' she huffed angrily. 'I don't know what you said to him to convince him to rent us some space, but he's been giving me some very strange looks. Luckily he had to go and do his rounds or I'd still be . . .' She broke off, having just caught sight of the open cupboards. 'I guess we're in the right place.'

'You're just in time,' Tom said. 'We were about to have a look next door.'

They stepped through into the adjacent room, the lights flickering on to reveal another Aladdin's cave of antiquities, although here stored with rather less care – a wooden Egyptian sarcophagus sawn into pieces, straw-packed chests with Sotheby's and Christie's labels still tied to them with string, vases covered in dirt, cylinder seals from Iraq wrapped in newspaper, bronze statues from India propped up against the wall, Peruvian ceramics . . . In the middle of the room, raised off the floor, a quarter-ton Guatemalan jaguar's head glowered at them through the slats of its wooden crate.

'He's got shit here from all over,' Archie noted, taking care to look where he was treading. 'And fakes too.' He pointed at two identical Cycladic statues of a harp player. 'The original's in Athens.'

But Tom wasn't listening, having seen the large safe at the far end of the room. He tried the handle, more in hope than expectation. It was locked.

'Over here.'

Allegra was standing at the threshold of a third room, much smaller than the others, but no less surprising. For where they had been flooded with antiquities, this was drowning in documentation – Polaroids, invoices, valuation certificates, consignment notes, shipping manifests, certificates of authenticity, remittance notes. All carefully filed away by year in archive boxes.

The photographs, in particular, told their own grim story. One set picked at random showed an Attic kylix covered in dirt and in pieces in the boot of a car, then the same object cleaned and partially restored, then fully restored with all the cracks painted and polished, and finally on display in some unnamed museum, Faulks standing next to the display case like a proud father showing off a newborn child.

'Like Lazarus raised from the dead,' Allegra murmured, peering over Tom's shoulder.

'Only this time with the evidence to prove it,' Dominique added. She'd found several long rectangular boxes crammed with five-by-eight-inch index cards. Written on each one in Faulks's looping hand was a meticulous record of a particular sale he'd made – the date of the transaction, the object sold, the price paid, the name of the customer. 'The Getty, the Met, the Gill brothers, the Avner Klein and Deena Carroll collection . . .' she said, flicking through the first few cards. 'This goes back fifteen, twenty years . . .'

'Insurance,' Archie guessed. 'In case anyone tried to screw him.'

'Or pride,' Tom suggested. 'So he could remind himself how clever he was. He just never counted on anyone finding it.'

'Does it matter?' Dominique snapped her fingers impatiently.

'It's quarter to one. That means we've only got just over three hours until Faulks gets back.'

'Just about enough time to get his safe open,' Tom said with a smile.

SIXTY-NINE

20th March – 12.46 p.m.

Five feet tall and three feet across, the safe had a brutish,
hulking presence, its dense mass of hardened steel and poured
concrete exerting a strange gravitational pull that almost
threatened to fold the room in on itself. A five-spoke gold-
plated handle jutted out of its belly, the Cyclops eye of a
combination lock glowering above it, the whole crowned
with an elaborate gilded copperplate script that proudly spelt
out its manufacturer's name. Under the flickering lights its
smooth flanks pulsed with a dull grey glow, like a meteorite
that had just fallen to earth.

With Dom having volunteered to fetch Tom's equipment,
Tom, Allegra and Archie stood in a line in front of it, like
art critics at an unveiling.

'How do you know the watches are inside?' Allegra
asked.

'I don't. But I don't see where else he would keep them.'

'He certainly wasn't wearing one,' Archie agreed.

'Can you open it?' She was trying to sound positive,
but she couldn't quite disguise the sceptical edge to her
question.

'It's a Champion Crown,' Tom said, rubbing his chin wearily.

'Is that bad?'

'Two-and-one-eighth-inch thick composite concrete walls with ten-gauge steel on the outside and sixteen-gauge on the inside. A five-inch-thick composite concrete door secured by twenty one-and-a-half-inch active bolts. Internal ball-bearing hinges. Sargent & Greenleaf combination dial with a hundred million potential combinations . . .' Tom sighed. 'It's about as bad as it gets.'

'Don't forget the sodding re-lockers,' Archie added with a mournful sigh.

'Re-lockers?' Allegra looked back to Tom with a frown.

'The easiest way to crack a safe is to drill through the door,' Tom explained. 'That way you can use a borescope, a sort of fibre-optic viewer, to watch the lock wheels spin into position while you turn the dial, or even manually retract the main bolt.'

'Only the manufacturers have got smart,' Archie continued. 'Now they fit a cobalt alloy hardplate around the lock mechanisms and sprinkle it with tungsten carbide chips to shatter the drill bits. Sometimes the bastards even add a layer of steel washers or ball bearings too. Not particularly hard, but they spin round when the drill bit touches them, making them a bugger to cut through.'

'The answer used to be to go in at an angle,' Tom picked up again. 'Drill in above or to the side of the hardplate and get at the lock pack that way. So the high-end safes now have a re-locker mechanism. A plate of tempered glass that shatters if you try to drill through it, releasing a set of randomly located bolts which lock the safe out completely. Some of them are even thermal, so that they trigger if you try and use a torch or plasma cutter.'

'So you can't open it?' Given what she'd just heard, it seemed like a fair, if depressing conclusion.

'Everything can be opened, given the right equipment and enough time,' Archie reassured her. 'You just need to know where to drill.'

'Manufacturers build in a drill point to most types of safes,' Tom explained, running his hand across the safe's metal surface as if trying to divine its location. 'A specific place where locksmiths can more easily drill through the door and, for a safe like this, a hole in the glass plate to get at the lock. They vary by make and model, and if you get it wrong . . .'

'You trigger the re-lockers.' Allegra nodded in understanding.

'Drill-point diagrams are the most closely guarded secret in the locksmithing world,' Archie sighed, before turning to face Tom. 'We'll have to get them off Raj.'

'Who's Raj?' She asked.

'Raj Dhutta. A locksmith we know. One of the best.'

'It's too late for that.' Tom shook his head. 'Even if he could get it to us in time, it would still take hours to drill through the hardplate with the kit I've got.'

'Then your only option is a side entry.' Archie dragged three crates out of the way to give them access to the safe's flanks.

'And then in through the change-key hole,' Tom said.

'You what?' Archie gave a disbelieving, almost nervous laugh.

'It'll take too long to drill back through into the lock pack. It's the only way in the time we've got.'

'What's a change-key hole?' Allegra asked with a frown. Hardplate. Re-locker. Change-key. Part of her wondered if they were deliberately tossing in these terms to confuse her.

Dominique interrupted before Tom could answer, breathing heavily as she hauled Tom's equipment bag behind her.

'Did you get lost?' Tom asked, surprised it had taken her so long.

'I got out at two by mistake,' she panted. 'I was banging on the door like an idiot until I realised that I was on the wrong floor. They all look the same.'

'And there was me thinking your new boyfriend was showing you his torch,' said Archie, grinning.

'I'll bet it's bigger than yours,' she retorted, screwing her face into an exaggerated smile.

'Stop it you two,' Tom said as he knelt down and unzipped the bag, and then carefully lifted out the magnetic drill rig.

'What about all that?' Allegra asked, nodding towards the paperwork in the third room.

'What about it?' Archie frowned.

'It's evidence. Proof of every deal the Delian League has ever done. We can't just leave it.'

'Why not?'

'Because this isn't just about Santos and Faulks. There's enough in there to bring the whole organisation down and implicate everyone who has ever dealt with them.'

'Have you seen how much of that shit there is?' Archie snorted.

'We could photograph some it,' she suggested. 'We've got three hours. That's more than enough . . .'

'Two hours,' Dominique corrected her.

'What?' Tom's head snapped round. 'You said . . .'

'According to his calendar, Faulks just cancelled his last meeting,' she explained, holding up her phone. 'That means he could be here any time after three.'

'Shit,' Archie swore, then shot Tom a questioning glance. 'Can you do it?'

'No way.' Tom shook his head emphatically, running his fingers distractedly through his hair. 'It's a three-hour job. Two and a half if we're lucky.'

'Then we need to buy you some more time,' Archie said. 'Find a way to keep Faulks away from here until we've finished.'

There was a long, painful silence, Tom glaring at the safe door as if it was somehow to blame for the change in Faulks's schedule, Dominique flexing her fingers where they'd gone stiff from dragging the bag.

'Come on,' Archie snorted eventually. 'Nothing? Anyone?'

'Can you get to the surveillance cameras?' Allegra asked.

'The patch panel's probably next to the server room down-stairs,' Dominique said with a nod. 'Why?'

'It's just . . . I might have an idea. Well, it was your idea really.'

'My idea?' Dominique looked surprised, the brusque tone she'd reserved for Allegra up until now softening just a fraction.

'Only it'll never work.'

'Perfect!' Archie grinned. 'The best ideas never do.'

SEVENTY

Free Port, Geneva
20th March – 3.22 p.m.
'What did you think?' Verity asked, fixing her lipstick in the mirror.

'Which one?'

The Bentley tacked into the warehouse car park, the chassis leaning gracefully into the bend.

'Sekhmet. The Egyptian lion goddess.'

'Oh, that one,' Faulks sniffed, looking disinterestedly out of the window.

'Don't go all shy on me.' Verity glanced across, wiping the corner of her mouth where she had smudged it slightly. 'What did you think?'

'I don't like to bad-mouth the competition,' Faulks gave a small shake of his head as the car glided to a halt.

'Liar!' Verity laughed. 'You thought it was a fake, didn't you?'

'Well, didn't you?' He threw his hands up in exasperation. 'And not even a very good one. The base was far too short.'

'Are we here?' Verity glanced up at the warehouse's rusted façade with a dubious expression.

'Don't sound so disappointed,' Faulks laughed. 'Most people don't even know I have this place, let alone get to come inside.'

'In that case I'm honoured.' She smiled.

'Anyway, I'm moving. They're knocking it down. It's a shame, really. I've been here almost since I started. Grown quite attached to it over the years.'

'I never took you for a romantic, Earl,' she teased.

'Oh, I'm an incurable romantic,' he protested. 'Just as long as there are no pcople involved.'

Logan stepped round and opened her door. But as Verity went to get out, Faulks placed his hand on her arm.

'Can you give me five minutes? I just want to make sure everything's set up.'

'Of course.' She sat back with an indulgent smile although there was no disguising the impatience in her voice. 'There are a few calls I need to make anyway.'

Nodding his thanks, he led Logan inside where they both signed in.

'New tenants, Stefan?' Faulks asked, surprised to see four names above his.

The guard checked that no one else was listening then leaned forward with a grin.

'Just until the end of the month,' he whispered excitedly. 'They're making a porno and wanted somewhere . . . discreet. You should see the two girls they've got! The director said I could go and watch them shoot a couple of scenes later this week.'

Faulks mustered a thin smile.

'How nice for you.'

They rode the lift to the third floor and traced a familiar path round to corridor thirteen, stopping outside Faulk's suite. Unlocking the door, he stepped inside and then stopped.

'That's funny,' he muttered.

'What?' Logan followed him inside, immediately alert.

'The alarm's off. I was sure I'd . . .'

Logan drew his gun and stepped protectively in front of him.

'Wait here.'

Treading carefully, he stepped over to the door to the middle room, eased it open and then peered inside. His gun dropped.

'Boss, you'd better come'n see.'

Faulks stepped past him with a frown, the tip of his umbrella striking the floor every second step, then froze.

It was empty. Gutted. Stripped clean. The crates, the boxes, the vases, the statues, the safe – everything had gone.

He felt suddenly faint, the room spinning around him, his heart pounding, the blood roaring in his ears. Turning on his heels, he limped back into the first room and threw one of the cupboards open with a crash. Empty. The next one was the same. And the one after that, the metal doors now clanging noisily against each other like shutters in a storm as he jumped from one cupboard to the next. They were all empty.

'You've been fuckin' turned over,' Logan growled.

Faulks couldn't speak, could barely breathe, felt sick. He staggered to the table, his legs threatening to give away under him at any minute, the open cupboard doors still swaying around him as if they were waving goodbye.

What about the files?

Somehow he found the strength to limp through to the third room, Logan following behind, his warning to be careful echoing unheard off the bare walls. Faulks stopped on the threshold, supporting himself against the door frame, not needing to go inside to see that this room too had also been stripped bare.

He had the strange sensation of drowning, of the air being squeezed from his lungs, the pressure clawing at his eardrums, pressing his eyes back into his head. And then he was falling, legs tumbling away from underneath him, back sliding down the wall as the floor rose up to grab him, umbrella toppling on to his lap. Gone. Gone. Everything gone.

'Earl?' He heard Verity's voice echoing towards him. 'You said five minutes, so I thought I'd come up. Is everything okay?'

SEVENTY-ONE

Free Port, Geneva
20th April – 3.36 p.m.

'He's gone inside.' Archie let himself back into the room with a relieved smile. 'I've left Dom watching the stairs. How are you getting on?'

'Any minute now,' Tom replied, the air thick with the smell of oil, burnt steel and hot machine parts.

Allegra had been right. Her idea had had no reason to work. And yet, like all good ideas, there had been an elegance and simplicity to it that had at least given it a fighting chance of success.

'Dominique said all the floors look the same,' Allegra had reminded them. 'If she's right, then maybe we could try and trick Faulks into getting off on the second floor.'

'It could work,' Tom had said, immediately catching on. 'We could rig the lift, swap over the wall signs and door numbers and then use the forklift to move all his furniture downstairs so that when he goes inside his first thought will be that he's been robbed.'

'I'll reroute the camera feed so the guard can't see us,'

Dominique had suggested. 'And we could fix the alarm cover panel to the wall so it at least looks the same.'

'What about the cupboards?' Archie had reminded them. 'We haven't got time to unload them all.'

'Check out some of the other empty offices,' Tom had suggested. 'There's bound to be a couple of spares lying around. As long as they look vaguely similar, he'll be too shocked to notice. And by the time he does, we'll be long gone with whatever's inside.'

Tom's safe-cracking kit was surprisingly simple. A 36-volt Bosch power drill, like you would buy at any normal hardware store. A tungsten-carbide-tipped drill bit shaped for steel cutting. A twenty-millimetre diamond-core drill bit, routinely used in the construction industry. And finally a Fein electromagnetic drill rig to hold the power drill in place and control the pressure.

The method was relatively straightforward too. First fix the rig on to the side of the safe over the chosen breach point with the magnets. Then clamp the power drill into the rig. Then equip the tungsten carbide drill bit, and lower the drill to bore a centring hole in the steel. Finally swap it for the diamond-core drill bit and punch through.

The tricky part was applying the correct combination of drill speed and pressure at the right time. Puncturing the safe's steel casing, for example, required drilling at about 2000 rpm with only medium to low pressure applied by the rig. Getting through the composite material underneath, however, demanded high pressure and low revs, maybe 300 rpm. Even then Tom had to go easy, the diamonds clogging in the angled mild steel plates that had been embedded in the concrete. With only one power drill, that meant he had to be careful not to blow the motor, and he was forced to stop at regular intervals and allow it to cool.

'How are you getting on with the photos?' Tom called, adding some lubricant.

'I've got a system going –' Allegra poked her head into the room – 'I won't get them all, but I'll get enough.'

'Anything that might tell us where the League are meeting tonight?'

'No, but I'll keep looking.'

At last the drill punched through, the motor racing wildly.

'That's it,' Tom called, fumbling for the off switch and then heaving the rig out of the way.

'Here –' Archie handed him a small monitor that he taped to the side of the safe and then connected to the borescope. The screen flickered with light, indicating it was working.

'Ready?' Tom looked up with a hopeful smile at Allegra, who had run across to join them. She nodded silently as he blew against the hole to cool the scorched metal and then slipped the cable inside.

'Look,' she gasped almost immediately. The outline of a white face was framed on the small screen like a human skull, the grainy image looking like it was being broadcast up through the depths from a long-lost shipwreck. 'It's the ivory mask. Cavalli must have sent it here before he was killed.'

'They must have been working together,' agreed Tom. 'Cavalli supplying the antiquities and Faulks providing the buyers. That way, they didn't have to split the profits with the Delian League.'

'Faulks doesn't have to split anything with anyone now that Cavalli's dead,' Allegra observed wryly.

'Pretty convenient,' Tom agreed. 'It wouldn't surprise me if . . .' He broke off, a sudden thought occurring to him. Of course. It had been so simple. So easy. And once Faulks had realised how much the mask was worth, so necessary.

'Oi, you two,' Archie interrupted. 'Holmes and bloody Watson. Do you mind if we get a move on?'

Tom winked at Allegra, then nodded. He was right.

Looking back to the screen to get his bearings, he bent the cable towards the left and found the back of the safe door. Then he slowly moved it along until he was roughly behind the combination dial.

'There it is,' Archie said sharply.

'There what is?' Allegra leant closer with a frown.

'The key-change hole,' Archie explained. 'Every combination safe comes with a special key that you insert in that hole when the safe's open to change the code.'

'How big is the hole?'

'Not very,' Tom said, jaw clenched in concentration.

'Not big enough,' Archie muttered under his breath. 'That's the problem.'

They watched the image silently, the camera's proximity making the tiny hole look surprisingly large on the screen, the cable catching on its edge as Tom tried to nudge it inside.

'Shit,' he hissed, the cable slipping past yet again. 'It keeps sliding off.'

'Try from the other side,' Archie suggested.

'I've done that,' Tom snapped, smearing oil across his forehead as he wiped the sweat away.

Dominique came in, out of breath from having run up the stairs.

'How much time have we got?' Tom barked without looking up.

'About as much time as it takes them to look out the window and realise they're only two floors up. How are we doing?'

'Shit,' Tom swore as the camera skated past the hole again.

'That well.' She pulled a face.

'Why don't you try coming in from underneath?' Archie suggested. 'You might catch against the upper lip.'

'I don't see why that will . . .' Tom glanced up at Archie with a sheepish smile. It had worked first time.

The screen now showed a fuzzy image of the lock mechanism – four wheels, each with a notch that had to be aligned so that the locking gate could fall into them.

'Someone's going to have to turn the dial for me,' Tom said, carefully holding the cable in place so that it didn't pop out. Allegra immediately stepped forward and crouched down to next to him.

'Which way?'

'Clockwise. You need to pick up all the wheels first.'

Allegra turned the lock, the picture showing the drive cam turning and then gathering up each of the four wheels one by one until they were all going round.

'Slowly,' Tom said, as he saw the notch on the first wheel at the bottom right of the screen moving upwards.

'Stop!' Archie called as the notch reached the twelve o'clock position. Fifteen. 'Now back the other way.'

Allegra turned the dial back, again slowing as the notch appeared on the second wheel and then stopping when Archie called to her. Seventy-one. Then came sixteen.

'The last number's ten,' Tom guessed.

'How do you know?' Dominique asked with a frown.

'Fifteen seventy-one to sixteen ten,' Tom explained with a smile. 'Caravaggio's dates.'

As Tom pulled the borescope out of the hole, Allegra turned the dial to the final number and then tried the gold-plated wheel in the middle of the door. It turned easily, the handle vibrating with a dull clunk as the bolts slid back. Standing up, she tugged on the door, the airtight seal at first resisting her until, with a swooshing noise, it swept open.

The safe had a red velour interior and four shelves

containing an eclectic assortment of items that Faulks had presumably felt deserved the extra security – twenty or so antique dinner plates, a set of red figure vases, notebooks, some files, a few maps. And of course, the ivory mask.

Tom's attention, however, was drawn to a rectangular black velvet box, monogrammed with a by now familiar symbol: the clenched fist and entwined snakes of the Delian League. It opened to reveal a cream silk interior moulded to house six watches. Two of the spaces were occupied.

'Epsilon and zeta,' Allegra said, taking them out and turning them over so that they could see the Greek letters engraved into their backs.

'Which gives us the three we need,' Tom said, sliding D'Arcy's watch into place and then snapping the case shut. 'Let's just see if there's anything in here that tells us where they're meeting tonight.'

'What about this?' Archie asked, carefully sliding out the small packing crate containing the ivory mask, its delicate face cushioned by the straw that poked through its eyes and parted lips in a way that reminded Tom of the Napoleonic death mask he and Archie had discovered the previous year.

'Leave it,' Tom said with a shake of his head, glancing up from the handful of notes and maps he had pulled from the safe and was now leafing through.

'Leave it? Are you joking? This thing's worth a bloody fortune.'

'Not to us, it isn't. Besides, the less we take, the more chance that Faulks won't even realise we've been here.'

SEVENTY-TWO

Free Port, Geneva
20th March – 3.46 p.m.

Faulks's initial shock had given way to a bewildered incredulity. It was impossible. The stock. His best stock. The documentation. The safe. Everything gone. Spirited away. Everything. Thousands of items. Tens of millions of dollars. How had they got in? How had they got away without being seen?

'Earl, I don't understand. What's going on? What is this place?' Verity sounded nervous, like someone who'd witnessed a gangland killing and was now worried about being dragged into testifying.

'Did you tell anyone you were coming here?' Faulks spun round to face her, jabbing his umbrella at her accusingly.

'Of course not,' she insisted hotly. 'How could I? I've never been here before.'

He glared at her, his disbelief having slipped into anger, although not with her in particular. With everyone. With everything. She gave a sharp intake of breath, her eyes widening in understanding.

'Oh my God, Earl, have you been robbed?'

He closed his eyes, took a deep breath, exhaled and then opened them again, part of him almost expecting to find that everything was still there after all and that this had just been a terrible dream. Logan reappeared and jerked his head to indicate that they needed to talk. Alone.

'Give me a minute, Verity,' Faulks said, following Logan back out into the first room and closing the door behind him.

'Well?'

'The guard downstairs hasn'a seen nothing,' Logan said in a low voice. 'Nor had th' one on the night shift when we called him.'

'Not unless they're both in on it together,' Faulks pointed out.

'Aye well, I'd know if he was.' Logan gave him a tight smile.

Looking down, Faulks noticed that the Scotsman's knuckles were grazed and that there was a faint spray of blood on his collar. He felt a little better.

'What about the surveillance footage?'

'Backed up remotely. I've asked for a copy. It'll be here in an hour.'

'Anyone else in the building?'

'Just the people who moved in today.'

Faulks snorted.

'Well, there you go then.'

'There's only four o' them and they signed in at twelve thirty,' Logan pointed out with a firm shake of his head. 'Shiftin' all tha' would have tak'n them days.'

'And he didn't hear the alarm go off?'

'No.'

'Bastards must have disabled it,' Faulks hissed, striding over to the control panel next to the main entrance and smacking it angrily, taking some pleasure in the sharp stab of pain as it spread across his palm. 'What's the point in paying for . . .'

He broke off as the keypad fell away from the wall and crashed on to the floor. Frowning, he bent down to pick it up, then noticed the two pieces of black tape that had been securing it to the wall.

'Jesus,' he swore, tossing the panel to Logan. 'It's a dummy. We're in the wrong goddamned room.'

Turning, he limped back out on to the corridor. Ignoring the lift, he made his way to the fire escape and leaned over the banisters, following the staircase as it snaked its way down to the floor below and then . . . to the ground floor.

With Logan at his shoulder, Faulks climbed the staircase as fast as he could, then stepped out on to the empty corridor and turned towards his offices. Here the nature of the deception became abundantly clear – all the signs and door numbers were missing, having presumably been removed and re-attached on the floor below to confuse him.

He flung the door to his offices open. Apart from the cupboards down the right-hand wall, the room was empty and almost unrecognisable without its furniture, carpet or curtains.

And standing at its centre was a woman.

SEVENTY-THREE

'Where's Archie?' Tom asked as he threw his bag into the boot and slammed it shut.

'With Allegra,' Dominique panted, sliding into the passenger seat next to him.

There was a brief lull as they waited, Tom tapping his fingers nervously on the window sill.

'Did you sweep the safe clean?'

'He won't know we've been in there,' she reassured him. 'Not unless he moves the crates and sees where I've taped over the drill hole in the side.'

'Good.'

'So what now?'

'I'm not sure,' Tom admitted. 'We still don't know where they're meeting.'

'What was that piece of paper you took out of the safe, then?'

'Something else that I thought might come in useful.' He craned his neck for a view of the entrance. 'What's taking them so long?'

'Do you want me to go back inside?'

'Let's just give them another –'

'Look, here he comes!' Dominique pointed with relief as Archie exited the building and jogged over to the car.

'Yeah, but why's he on his own?' Tom frowned, his eyes still fixed on the building's entrance.

Archie threw the door open and climbed in.

'Close one.' He sighed with relief. 'Nearly bumped into Faulks coming up the stairs. I think he's finally twigged.'

'Where's Allegra?' Tom asked in an urgent voice.

'Allegra?' Archie looked around, only now, it seemed, noticing that she was not in the car. 'I thought she was with you?'

'Well, she's not,' Tom shot back.

'When did you last see her?'

'Upstairs. She was helping me pack up my kit. I handed her the . . .'

He paused, a sudden thought occurring to him. Flinging the door open, he raced round to the back of the car and popped the boot.

'What are you looking for?' Archie asked as he rooted through his bag.

'This,' Tom said, holding up the receiver for the location beacon.

He turned it on. A faint pulse of light confirmed what he had already guessed. The transmitter was showing us being about fifty yards directly in front of him.

'She's still inside.'

'What the hell's she doing?' Archie's voice was caught somewhere surprise and admiration.

'Playing the only card we have left.'

SEVENTY-FOUR

Free Port, Geneva
20th March – 3.50 p.m.
'Who the hell are you?' Faulks paused on the threshold, wary of another trick.

'Everything's here,' she reassured him. 'I just wanted to make sure I got your attention.'

'Congratulations. You've got it,' he snarled, motioning at Logan to grab her, while he checked the cupboards and stuck his head into the next room.

Unbelievably, everything did indeed seem to be there, the empty desolation of a few minutes ago quickly replaced by a warm wave of relief. And a cold current of anger.

'Who are you?' he repeated.

'Lieutenant Allegra Damico. An officer with the TPA.'

A pause, Faulks giving a thin smile at her laboured breathing as Logan tightened his grip on her arm which he had bent behind her back.

'What do you want?'

'I have some information for the Delian League.'

'Who?'

'I think we're a little beyond that,' she said, nodding in the direction of the documentation in the small room.

'Earl, are you in here?'

Faulks's head snapped round at the sound of Verity's approaching voice.

'Damn,' he swore, then turned back to Allegra with an impatient shrug. He didn't have time for this. Not today of all days. Not now. But after the lengths she'd gone to . . . there was no telling what she knew or who she'd told. He had to be sure. The League had to be sure. 'You're right. We're way beyond that.'

Stepping forward, he grabbed the end of his umbrella and swung its handle hard against her temple. Groaning, she went limp in Logan's arms.

'Take her to the back and keep her quiet,' he hissed. 'When we're finished here, load her up with the rest of the shipment.'

Turning on his heel, he walked back out on to the corridor. Verity was marching towards him, her face drawn into a thunderous scowl, hands clenched like an eagle swooping to snatch a rabbit out of long grass.

'Earl, I don't know what you're playing at, but . . .'

'Verity, I can't begin to tell you how sorry I am,' he apologised, arms outstretched, palms upturned, his brain working hard. 'There's been a terrible mistake. Terrible. And it's entirely my fault.'

'The only mistake was me agreeing to come here,' she retorted angrily. 'Abused, accused, abandoned . . .'

'We were on the wrong floor!' He laughed lustily, hoping that it didn't sound too forced. 'Can you believe it? It's old age. It must be. I'm losing it.'

'The wrong floor?' she repeated unsmilingly.

'The landlord needed access to my old offices to begin the demolition planning, so they've moved me up here,' he explained, with what he hoped was a convincingly earnest wide-eyed look. 'I'm so used to going to the second floor after all these years, that I didn't even think about it. I'm so sorry.'

'So everything's here?' She glanced past him with a sceptical frown.

'Absolutely.' He gave an emphatic nod. 'Thank God, because for a terrible moment I thought . . .'

'I know. Me too.' She let out a nervous, hesitant laugh. He forced himself to join in.

'Can you ever forgive me?'

'That depends on what's inside.' She flashed him a smile.

Ushering her in, he led her through to the middle room, Verity murmuring with appreciation at some of the items she could see stacked there.

'Good God, Earl, this is wonderful.'

'Even better, it's all for sale,' he reminded her with a smile as he crouched next to the safe, flicked the dial and heaved it open.

'Is that it?' Verity breathed over his shoulder, pulling on a pair of white cotton gloves.

'That's it.' Sliding the shallow box out, he carefully placed it on top of one of the neighbouring packing crates. Removing his jacket, he lay it over another crate so that its scarlet lining covered it. Then he gingerly removed the mask and set it on top of the lining, the pale ivory leaping off the red material. Finally he stepped back and ushered her forward.

'Please.'

Approaching slowly as if she was afraid of waking it, Verity pulled on a pair of white cotton gloves and carefully picked the mask up. She raised it level with her face, eyes unblinking, the colour flushing her throat and cheeks, her breathing quickening, hands trembling. For a moment, it seemed she might kiss it. But instead, she gave a long sigh of pleasure and lowered it unsteadily back into its straw bed, her shoulders shaking.

'So? What do you think?' Faulks asked, after giving her a few moments to compose herself.

Verity made to speak, but no sound came out, her lips trembling, tears welling in her eyes. She looked up at him, her hand waving in front of her mouth as if she was trying to summon the words out of herself.

'It's so beautiful,' she breathed eventually. 'It's like . . . it's like gazing into the eyes of God.'

'Attribution?'

'Assuming the dating is right . . .'

'Oh, it's right.'

'Then Phidias. Phidias, Phidias, Phidias!' Her voice built to an ecstatic crescendo. 'We would have heard of any other sculptor from that period of this quality.'

'Then I hope you won't mind confirming that to my buyer?' Faulks pulled out his phone and searched for a number. 'Or the valuation you'll put on it once he donates it to you?'

'Of course,' she enthused, snatching the phone from him as soon as it started ringing. 'What's his name?'

SEVENTY-FIVE

Over Milan, Italy
20th March – 6.27 p.m.

Darkness. The smell of straw. A dog barking.

Coming round, Allegra lifted her head and then sank back with a pained cry. There was something above her preventing her from sitting up. Something smooth and flat and . . . wooden. She moved her hands gingerly across it, sensing first its corners and then the constrictive press of the walls at her side. It was a box. She was lying in a wooden box.

The last thing she remembered was Faulks, wild-eyed, raising his umbrella above her like an executioner's axe and then . . . darkness. Darkness, the smell of straw, a dog barking, something hard and uneven underneath her, her head throbbing where he'd struck her. And in the background a low, incessant drone, a rushing whistle of air, a bass shudder.

A plane. She was on a plane. Lying in a wooden box in the hold of a plane.

She nervously patted her inner thigh, and then sighed with relief. The location transmitter was still there – taped to her skin at the top of her leg where they only would have found it if they had stripped her down.

She'd taken a big risk, she knew. A risk that Tom would never have agreed to. But as soon as it had become clear that there was nothing in either Faulks's papers or the safe that was going to give them even the slightest hint as to where the League was meeting that night, she'd known what she had to do. Grab the transmitter and some tape out of the bag. Hold back amid the confusion of their hurried retreat as Faulks pounded along the corridors towards them. And then try to talk or shock him into delivering her to the League himself. It was that or give up on getting to the painting before Santos could hand it over to the Serbs. It was that, or admit that they couldn't stop him.

'Stop' was a euphemism, she knew, for what the Serbs would do to him if he failed to deliver the Caravaggio. The strange thing was that, after the horrors she'd witnessed and endured over the past few days, she felt remarkably sanguine about his likely fate. Especially when the alternative was that, armed with his diplomatic immunity and the proceeds of the Caravaggio's sale, Santos would escape any more conventional form of justice.

Tom had said that the radius of the transmitter was three miles. No use at thirty thousand feet, but if he'd realised what she was doing when she hadn't come back down, and then followed her signal to the airport, he should have been able to work out where she was heading and take another flight to the same destination where he would hopefully be able to pick up her signal again when she landed. At least, that was had been her rough, ill-conceived plan.

For now, all she had was darkness and the sound of her own breathing. Its dull echo, in fact, that seemed to be getting louder and louder as the box's walls closed in, pressed down on her chest, her lungs fighting for air.

Suddenly she was back in the tomb. The entrance blocked, the earth cold and clammy underneath. She called out, her fists pounding against the sides, her feet drumming against the end, twisting her body so that she could lever her back up against the lid.

There. Above her head. Two small, perfectly round holes in the wood that she hadn't been able to see before. She inched forward on her stomach, pressed her face to them, drinking in the narrow rivulets of air and light with relief, her heart rate slowing.

She looked down, struck by a sensation of being watched.

In the dim light, a pair of lifeless eyes stared back up at her, cold lips parted in a hard smile, nose sliced off.

She was lying on top of a statue. A marble statue. But to Allegra the statue might as well have been a corpse, and the box a coffin, and the rumble of the engines the echo of loose earth being shovelled back into her grave.

SEVENTY-SIX

Cimitero Acattolico, Rome
20th March – 10.22 p.m.

'I've lost her,' Tom barked.

'What do you mean, you've lost her?' Archie grabbed the receiver from him and shook it. 'She was just there.'

'Well, she isn't now,' Tom shot back, his anger betraying his concern.

Until now, Allegra had proved surprisingly easy to track, her signal leading them from the Freeport to the cargo terminal at Geneva airport, where they had observed Faulks's driver overseeing several large crates being loaded on to a plane bound for Rome. It hadn't taken much imagination to deduce that she had been placed inside one of them. They had therefore immediately booked themselves on to an earlier flight to ensure that they would already be in position to pick up the signal again by the time her plane landed.

Watching through his binoculars from the airport perimeter fence, Tom had been able to tell that this was a well-established smuggling route for Faulks, the Customs officers welcoming him off the plane on to a remote part of the airfield with a broad smile as a black briefcase had swapped hands.

The cargo had then been split, some heading for the warm glow of the main terminal, the rest to a dark maintenance hangar into which Faulks had driven, the doors quickly rolling shut behind him. Then for two, maybe three hours nothing. Nothing but the steady pulse of her location transmitter on the small screen cradled in his lap. A pulse that had served as a taunting reminder of the fading beat of Jennifer's heart-rate monitor in the helicopter over the desert. A pulse which they had carefully followed here, only to see it flatline.

Sheltered by regimented lines of mourning cypresses and Mediterranean pines, the Cimitero Acattolico nestled on the slope of the Aventine Hill, in the time-worn shadow of the Pyramid of Caius Cestius and the adjacent Aurelian walls. Even by moonlight, Tom had been able to see that it was populated by an eclectic tangle of stone monuments, graves and family vaults, separated by long grass woven with wild flowers. These elaborate constructions were in stark contrast to the trees' dark symmetry: pale urns, broken columns, ornate scrollwork and devotional statuary bursting in pale flashes through the gaps in their evenly spaced trunks, as if deliberately planted there in an attempt to prove the superiority of human creativity over natural design.

If so, it was increasingly obvious to Tom that this was an argument that nature was winning, decades of neglect having left monuments eroded by pollution and tombs cracked open by weeds and the cruel ebb and flow of the seasons. In one place, a pine tree had shed a branch, the diseased limb collapsing on to a grave and smashing its delicately engraved headstone into pieces. In another, the ground had risen up, snapping the spine of the vault that had dared to surmount it. And now it seemed to have swallowed Allegra's signal too.

'Where was the last reading from?' Dominique asked, ever practical.

'Over there –' Tom immediately broke into a loping run, vaulting the smaller graves and navigating his way around the larger tombs. Then, just as he was about to emerge into one of the wide avenues that cut across the cemetery, he felt Archie's hand grab his shoulder and force him to the ground.

'Get down,' he hissed.

Three men had emerged from the trees ahead of them, their machine guns glinting black in the moonlight, torch beams slicing the darkness. Moving quickly, they glided over to a large family vault, their boots lost in the long grass so that they almost appeared to be floating over the ground. As Tom watched, they ghosted up its steps and vanished inside.

'She must be in there,' Tom guessed, standing up.

The vault was a small rectangular building designed to echo a Roman temple, a few shallow steps leading up to the entrance, a Doric frieze carved under the portico, white Travertine walls decorated with columns that gave the illusion of supporting the tiled roof. The entrance was secured by a handsome bronze door that the elements had varnished a mottled green. A single name had been carved over it: *Merisi*. Tom pointed at it with a smile as they crept towards it.

'What?' Dominique whispered.

'Merisi was Caravaggio's real name.'

They paused, straining to hear a voice or a sound from inside. But nothing came apart from the silent echo of darkness.

With a determined nod at the others, Tom carefully eased the door open with one hand, his gun in the other. This and three other 'clean' weapons had been sourced by Archie from Johnny Li while they had been watching the hangar at Rome airport. The price had been steep – the money he claimed Tom still owed him, plus another ten for his trouble. Archie had only just stopped cursing about it, although Johnny had at least held his half of their earlier bargain and returned Tom's watch.

Inside, a thin carpet of dirt and leaves covered the black-and-white mosaic floor and lay pooled in the room's dark corners. At the far end stood a black marble altar with the name *Merisi* again picked out in bronze letters above a date – 1696. In front of this were two high-backed prayer stools, once painted black and upholstered in a rich velvet, but now peeling and rotted by the cold and the damp. Above the altar, suspended from the wall, was a crucifix, one arm of which had broken off so that it hung at an odd angle.

The room was empty.

'Where the hell have they gone?' Archie exclaimed, rapping the walls to make sure they were solid.

Tom examined the floor with a frown.

'How did they expect to bury anyone in here?'

'What do you mean?' Dominique frowned.

'It's a family vault. There should be a slab or something that can be lifted up.'

'No inscriptions either,' Archie chimed in. 'Not even a full set of dates.'

'And the one that's here doesn't fit,' Dominique pointed out. 'This graveyard wasn't used until the 1730s. No one would have been buried here in 1696.'

'It could be a birth year,' Tom suggested, crouching down in front of the altar. 'Maybe the second date has come away and . . .'

The words caught in his throat. As he'd rubbed the marble, his fingers had brushed against the final number, causing it to move slightly. He glanced up at the others to check that they had seen this too, then reached forward to turn it, the number spinning clockwise and then clicking into place once it was upside down so that it now read as a nine.

Archie frowned. '1699? That doesn't make no sense either?'

'Not 1699 – 1969,' Tom guessed, turning each of the

previous three numbers so that they also clicked into place upside down. 'The year the Caravaggio was stolen.'

There was the dull thud of what sounded like a restraining bolt being drawn back from somewhere in front of them. Then, with the suppressed hiss of a hydraulic ram, the massive altar began to lift up and out, pivoting high above their heads, stopping a few inches below the coffered ceiling.

They jumped back, swapping a surprised look. Ahead of them, a flight of steps disappeared into the ground.

SEVENTY-SEVEN

20th March – 10.37 p.m.
The steps led down to a brick-lined corridor set on a shallow
incline. It was dimly lit, the sodium lighting suspended from
the vaulted ceiling at irregular intervals forming pallid pools
of orange light that barely penetrated the cloying darkness.
In places the water had forced its way in, the ceiling flowering with calcite rings that dripped on to the glistening concrete
floor.

Treading carefully, their guns aiming towards the darkness into which the three armed men who had preceded
them down here had presumably disappeared, they crept
down the tunnel. Tom had the vague sense that they were
following the contour of the Aventine as it rose steeply to
their right, although it was hard to be sure, the passage
tracing a bewildering course as it zig-zagged violently
between the graveyard's scattered crypts and burial cham-
bers. Eventually, after about two hundred yards, it ended,
opening up into a subterranean network of interlinking
rooms supported by steel props.

'It's Roman,' Dominique whispered, stooping to look at a
small section of the frescoed wall which hadn't crumbled

away. 'Probably a private villa. Someone rich, because this looks like it might have been part of a bath complex.' She pointed at a small section of the tessellated floor which had given way, revealing a four-foot cavity underneath, supported by columns of terracotta tiles. 'They used to circulate hot air through the *hypercaust* to heat the floors and walls of the *caldarium*,' she explained.

They tiptoed through into the next room, their path now lit by spotlights strung along a black flex and angled up at the ceiling, the amber glow suffusing the stone walls. Dominique identified this as the *balneum*, a semicircular sunken bath dominating the space.

Picking their way through the thicket of metal supports propping the roof up, they arrived at the main part of the buried villa, the tiled floor giving way to intricate mosaics featuring animals, plants, laurel-crowned gods and a dizzying array of boldly coloured geometric patterns. Here, some restoration work appeared to have been done: the delicate frescoes of robed Roman figures and carefully rendered animals showed signs of having been pieced back together from surviving fragments, the missing sections filled in and then plastered white so that the fissures between the pieces resembled cracks in the varnish on an old painting.

An angry shout echoed towards them through the empty rooms.

'You think Santos is already here?' Dominique whispered.

'Allegra first,' Tom insisted. 'We worry about Santos and the painting when she's safe.'

They tiptoed carefully to the doorway of a small vaulted chamber. The walls here had been painted to mimic blood-red and ochre marble panels, while the ceiling had been covered in geometric shapes filled with delicately rendered birds and mischievous-looking satyrs. And crouching on the floor with their backs to them, checking their weapons and speaking in low, urgent voices, were the three men they'd seen earlier.

Tom locked eyes with Archie and Dominique; both of them nodded back. On a silent count of three, they leapt inside and caught the three men completely cold.

'*Tu*?' one of the men hissed as, one by one, Archie taped their hands behind their backs and then gagged them.

It was Orlando – the priest from the Amalfi. Tom returned his hateful glare unblinkingly. Strangely, the murderous rage that had enveloped him in Monte Carlo had vanished; he felt almost nothing for him now. Not compared to Santos. Not with Allegra's life at stake.

'I'll watch them,' Dominique reassured him, waving the men back into the corner of the room with her gun.

'You sure?'

'Go.'

With a nod, Tom and Archie continued on, a bright light and the low rumble of voices drawing them across an adjacent chamber decorated with yellow columns, to the next room where they crouched on either side of the doorway.

Edging his head inside, Tom could see that they were on the threshold of the most richly decorated space of all, the floor covered in an elaborate series of interlocking mosaic medallions, each one decorated with a different mythological creature. The frescoes, meanwhile, looked almost entirely intact and mimicked the interior of a theatre, the left-hand wall painted to look like a stage complete with narrow side doors that stood ajar as if opening on to the wings. To either side, comic and tragic masks peered through small windows that revealed a painted garden vista.

'Look,' Archie whispered excitedly. Tom followed his gaze and saw that a large recess, perhaps nine feet high, six across and three deep, had been hacked out of the far wall. And, hanging within this, behind three inches of blast-proof glass, was the Caravaggio. It was unframed, although its lack of adornment seemed only to confirm its raw, natural power.

'That's Faulks,' Archie whispered.

At the centre of the room, over a large mosaic of a serpent-headed Medusa, was a circular table inlaid with small squares of multicoloured marble. The man Archie had pointed out was clutching an umbrella and standing in front of three other men who were seated around the table as if they were interviewing him.

'The guy on the left is De Luca,' Tom breathed, recognising the badger streak running through his hair and the garish slash of a Versace tie. 'And the one in the middle who's speaking now . . .' He broke off, his chest tightening as he realised that this was the face of the man he'd overheard on the yacht in Monaco. The same man who'd ordered Jennifer's death. 'That's Santos.'

'Which must make the other bloke Moretti,' Archie guessed, nodding towards a short man wearing glasses who was seated on the other side of Santos. Completely bald across the top, his scalp gleaming under the lights, he had a bristling wire-wool moustache that matched the hair clinging stubbornly to the back and sides of his head. He was wearing a grey cardigan and brown corduroy trousers, looking more like someone's grandfather than the head of one of the mafia's most powerful families.

Tom nodded but looked past him, distracted by the gagged and bound figure he could see slumped in a chair to Faulks's left. It was Allegra. Still alive, thank God, although there was no telling what they might have done to her. Or what they might still be planning.

'She wants to speak to us,' Faulks protested. 'She said she had a message.'

'Of course she does,' Santos shot back in English, his tone at once angry and mocking. 'She's working on the Ricci and

Argento cases.' He glanced across at De Luca. 'I thought you said you'd taken care of her?'

De Luca shrugged, gazing at Allegra with a slightly dazed look.

'I thought I had.'

'She managed to locate and break into my warehouse,' Faulks retorted. 'Who knows what else she's found out.'

'She broke in and, from what you've told us, took nothing apart from your pride,' Santos reminded him. 'You should have taken care of her in Geneva. You have no business here.'

'In case you've forgotten, I have two seats on this council.' Faulks spoke in a cold, deliberate tone. 'I have as much right to be here as anyone. If not more.'

'An accident of history that you delight in reminding us of,' De Luca said dryly.

Santos took a deep breath, attempting what Tom assumed was intended to be a more conciliatory tone.

'This meeting was called by the Moretti and De Luca families –' he nodded at the two men either side of him in turn – 'as representatives of the founding members of the Delian League, to resolve their recent . . . disagreements. Disagreements that, as we all know, have led to two former members of this council not being here with us tonight.'

'We had nothing to do with D'Arcy's death,' Moretti insisted angrily.

'Cavalli was a traitor who deserved what he got,' De Luca retorted, both men standing up and squaring off.

'Enough!' Santos called out. Muttering, they both sat down. Santos turned back to face Faulks. 'They asked me here to help mediate a settlement. I let you know we were meeting as a courtesy. But, as I told you when we spoke, there was no need for you to come.'

Faulks looked at them, then nodded sullenly towards Allegra.

'Then what am I meant to do with her?'

'What you should have done already.'

'I dig bodies up, not bury them,' Faulks said through gritted teeth.

'Then I'll finish what you are too weak to begin,' Santos snapped, taking his gun out from under his jacket and aiming it at Allegra's head.

SEVENTY-EIGHT

20th March – 10.54 p.m.

A shot rang out. Santos fell back with a cry, clutching his arm.

'Sit the fuck down. Don't nobody move,' Archie bellowed.

Tom pushed past him to Allegra, pulling the gag out of her mouth, then slicing her wrists free.

'Are you okay?' he breathed as she fell gratefully into his arms.

She nodded, gave him a weak smile. Turning, Tom scooped Santos's weapon off the floor and quickly searched the others.

'I'm bleeding,' Santos shrieked.

'It's a graze. You'll live,' Tom snapped.

'Pity,' Archie intoned behind him. Looking up, Faulks's eyes widened in shocked recognition, although the others didn't seem to notice his expression.

'You have no idea what you've done,' Santos hissed though clenched teeth, holding his arm to his chest. 'You're both dead men.' He snatched a glance towards the entrance.

'Who are you?' Moretti demanded.

'He's Tom Kirk,' De Luca said slowly, greeting Tom with a half-smile. 'Also risen from the dead, it seems.'

'Kirk?' Moretti gasped.

'Tom Kirk?' Faulks gave a disbelieving smile, his face turning grey.

Tom frowned, confused. Some people, criminals especially, knew who he was, or at least who he had been. But that didn't usually warrant this sort of reaction.

'What do you want?' Santos demanded.

'The same as you,' Tom said simply. 'The Caravaggio.'

'You're robbing us?' De Luca seemed to find this almost amusing.

'I'm borrowing it,' Tom corrected him.

'You'll never get it out of there,' Faulks scoffed. 'Not without destroying it.'

'Even with these?' Tom asked, holding up the monogrammed case he'd taken from Faulks's safe. The dealer went pale, his eyes bulging. 'Here, you might as well collect them all up,' said Tom, tossing Allegra the box. 'Although it is only the three watches I need, isn't it?'

Moretti and De Luca swapped a dumbfounded look.

'How did you know?' De Luca asked as Allegra loosened his watch and then Moretti's, before finding the sixth in Santos's top pocket. 'Did your . . .'

'Santos has struck a deal to sell your painting,' Tom explained. 'We overheard him negotiating the terms yesterday in Monte Carlo. He let slip about the watches.'

Santos rose from his seat.

'*Stronzata*,' he spat, his face stiff with anger.

'Bullshit. Really?' Tom smiled. 'Dom?' he called out.

A few moments later Dominique appeared, ushering Santos's three sullen-faced men ahead of her. Eyes narrowing, Santos slumped back into his seat as she forced them on to the ground and made them sit with their hands on their heads.

'These men work for Santos. We found them next door. You were the only people standing between him and the fifteen million dollars his Serbian buyers have promised him for the painting.'

'He's lying,' Santos seethed, his eyes fixed on Tom. 'It's a trick. We all know to come to this place alone. I would never break our laws.'

'Can you open it?' Tom called across to Allegra, who was crouching in front of the case.

'There are six plates,' she said, pointing at the brass roundels set into the wall under the painting. 'Each one's engraved with a different Greek letter.'

Opening the box, she took out the first watch and carefully matched it to the corresponding plate, the case sinking into the crafted recess with a click. Then she repeated the exercise with another two watches and stood back, glancing across at Tom with a hopeful shrug. For a moment nothing happened. But then, with a low hum, the thick glass slid three feet to the right, leaving an opening that she could step through.

'I'll give her a hand,' Archie volunteered, handing Tom his gun. He followed her through the gap into the narrow space behind the glass, and then helped her lift the unframed painting down. Carrying it back through with small, shuffling steps, they leaned it gently against the wall.

Tom stepped closer. He recognised the scene. It was exactly as he remembered it from the Polaroid Jennifer had shown him in her car. But there was no comparing that flat, lifeless image to the dramatic energy and dynamism of the original. The angel swooping down from heaven like an avenging harpy, the boy's taunting face creased with a cruel laughter, Mary's exhaustion and exultation, the fear and anticipation of the onlooking saints. Light and darkness. Divine perfection and human fallibility. Life and death. It was all there.

'Let's take it off the stretchers so we can roll it up,' Archie suggested.

'Be careful with it,' Moretti warned him.

Tom fixed him with a questioning look, detecting a proprietary tone.

'Is it yours?'

'Not any more,' he admitted. 'We donated it as a gesture of good faith when the League was founded. The De Luca family contributed this villa.'

'I'll return it,' Tom reassured him. 'You have my word.'

'Then why take it?' De Luca demanded.

Tom paused before answering, not wanting to give Santos the pleasure of hearing him stumble over his words.

'You know the FBI officer I asked you about, the one who was shot in Vegas three nights ago?' De Luca nodded with a puzzled frown. 'A few weeks back she got a tip-off about one of your US-based distributors. An antiquities dealer based in New York. Under questioning, he volunteered Luca Cavalli's name.'

'I knew Luca,' Moretti frowned. 'He was careful. He would never have revealed his name to someone that far down the organisation.'

'He didn't,' Tom agreed. 'Faulks did.'

'What?' Faulks gave a disbelieving laugh.

'Remember that photo of the ivory mask we came across in Cavalli's car?' Allegra glanced up at De Luca from where she was helping free the painting from the wooden stretchers. 'We found it in Faulks's safe. It's worth millions. Tens of millions.'

'My guess is that Cavalli had been secretly bringing you pieces for years,' Tom said, turning to stand in front of Faulks, whom he noticed had slid his chair a little way back from the others. 'Pieces his men had dug up and that he had deliberately not declared to the League, so that you could sell them on and share the profits between you. But then one day he unearthed something really valuable, didn't he?

Something unique. And you just couldn't help yourself. You got greedy.'

'Cavalli sent me the mask, it's true,' Faulks blustered, looking anxiously at De Luca and Moretti. 'A wonderful piece. But my intention was to split the proceeds with the League in the usual way after the sale. And not just the mask. I have the map showing the location of the site where he found it. Who knows what else might be down there?'

'Can you prove any of this?' De Luca challenged Allegra, fixing her with an unblinking, stony-faced stare.

'Who told you that Cavalli had betrayed you?' Tom shot back.

De Luca paused, then pointed a wavering finger towards Faulks. 'He did.'

'I had no choice,' Faulks protested. 'It's true that Cavalli wanted me to deal with him direct. But when I refused he threatened to go public with everything he knew. What I told you was the truth. He was planning to betray you. He was planning to sell us all out. You know yourself that your informants backed me up.'

'The FBI had Cavalli's name,' De Luca acknowledged, turning his gaze back to Tom. 'They wanted the authorities here to arrest him.'

'Cavalli was ripping you off, but I doubt he was going to go public with anything,' Tom said with a shrug, thinking back to the moment in front of Faulks's open safe when this had all clicked into place. 'The simple truth is that Faulks wanted him out of the way so he could have the mask for himself. So he came up with a plan. First feed Cavalli's name to the New York dealer. Then sell the dealer out to the FBI to make sure he would talk. Finally accuse Cavalli of betraying you, knowing your police informants would confirm that the FBI was investigating him and that you would think he was collaborating.'

'This is crazy,' Faulks spluttered. 'I've never . . .'

'The clever thing was the way he set both sides of the League against each other,' Allegra mused, rising to her feet. 'He knew that Don Moretti would retaliate once you'd killed Cavalli, leaving him free to sell it for himself, while you were busy fighting each other.'

'That was never my intention,' Faulks pleaded angrily. 'Cavalli was a threat. I was simply acting in the best interests of the League. As I have always done.'

'Of course, while all this was going on, Santos was busy taking out a contract on my friend,' Tom continued, turning to face him. 'My guess is . . .'

'How much more of this do we have to listen to?' Santos interrupted, his palms raised disbelievingly to the ceiling. 'I've never –'

'*Basta*,' De Luca cut him off angrily. 'You'll have your chance.'

Santos sat back with a scowl, muttering to himself.

'My guess is that, when she searched the dealer's warehouse, she found something implicating the Banco Rosalia and started kicking the tyres,' Tom continued. 'When Santos realised that she was on to him, he had her taken out, using the prospect of recovering your Caravaggio to lure her to Las Vegas where he had a gunman waiting.'

'She was a threat to us all,' Santos blurted out defiantly.

'You mean this is true? You killed an FBI agent without our permission?' De Luca jumped to his feet, violence in his voice now.

'I did what I had to do to protect the League,' Santos protested. 'I'd do the same again.'

'At first we thought everything was connected,' Allegra admitted. 'It was only later that we realised that the Rome murders and the ivory mask had nothing to do with Jennifer's assassination, or with D'Arcy, who was killed for his watch.'

'The irony is that it was Faulks' tip-off about the dealer in New York that unknowingly led to the FBI looking into the Banco Rosalia in the first place,' Tom said with a rueful smile. 'Without that, Jennifer would probably still be alive, and Santos wouldn't be preparing to explain to his Serbian friends why he hasn't been able to deliver the painting.'

'No, Kirk,' Santos said with a cruel smile. 'The biggest irony is that –'

A single gunshot cut him off. Tom's head snapped towards the doorway. A uniformed policeman in a bullet-proof vest was standing there, gun pointed towards the roof, five, maybe eight armed police filtering into the room either side of him, machine guns braced against their shoulders.

Tom snatched a look at Allegra. Ashen faced, she mouthed one word.

Gallo.

SEVENTY-NINE

20th March – 11.13 p.m.
'Colonel Gallo, thank God you're here!' Santos rose gratefully from his seat and stepped towards him, switching back
to Italian.

'Sit down,' Gallo ordered him back.

'I've been kidnapped. Held against my will. Shot!' He held
out his bloodied arm, his voice rising hysterically.

'Sit down, Santos, or I'll shoot you again myself,' Gallo
warned him in an icy tone.

'This is an outrage,' Santos insisted. 'In case it's slipped
your mind, Gallo, I have diplomatic immunity. You have
no legal right to detain me here. I demand to be released
immediately.'

'No one is going anywhere,' Gallo fired back. 'Get their
weapons.' Two of his men shouldered their machine guns
and quickly patted everyone down, tossing whatever they
found into the far corner of the room. Santos sank into his
chair. Gallo turned to Allegra. 'Lieutenant Damico, are you
hurt?'

'N-n-no,' Allegra stammered, bewildered. This was the

man she'd been running from; the man she'd seen execute Gambetta and then pin the crime on her; the man who had supposedly supplied Santos with Cavalli's watch. And yet, this same man was now holding Santos at gunpoint and asking if she was okay.

'Good.' Gallo twitched a smile. 'Then maybe you can tell me what the hell is going on down here?'

Again she looked for signs of the person who had been haunting her thoughts for the past few days. But it was almost as if she'd imagined the whole thing.

'There's a secret organisation called the Delian League,' she began haltingly. 'An alliance between the different mafia families to co-ordinate their antiquities smuggling operations and split the profits. Don De Luca and Don Moretti head it up. This man –' she pointed at Faulks – 'was responsible for selling whatever was smuggled out of the country to dealers and collectors around the world. Santos provided the financial backing and laundered the profits for them through the Banco Rosalia.'

'And this?' Gallo kicked the rolled up painting.

'The missing Caravaggio *Nativity*.'

'You're joking!' Placing his gun down next to him, Gallo knelt and unrolled the first few feet of the canvas before glancing up, shaking his head in wonder. 'My God, you're not.'

Without warning, Santos flew forward off his chair, snatched Gallo's gun up and before anyone had time to move, aimed it at his forehead.

'Back off,' he snarled as the armed police belatedly aimed their weapons at him. 'Put your guns on the floor or I'll kill him right here.'

The police ignored him, a few even taking a step closer. Santos immediately took shelter behind Gallo, pressing the gun to his temple.

'You know I'll do it,' he hissed, his lips hovering over Gallo's ear. 'Tell them to back the fuck off.' From the wild look in his eyes, Allegra could tell that he meant it.

'Stand down,' Gallo ordered in a strangled voice, clearly sensing this too. 'Stand down, that's an order.'

One by one, the officers lowered their guns, placing them at their feet, and then backed away. Santos's three men immediately re-armed themselves, Orlando leaping to Santos's side, the other two covering off the rest of the room.

'Now get them out of here.'

Gallo said nothing.

'Now!' Santos roared, striking him on the back of his head with the heel of his gun.

'Fall back the way you came in,' Gallo ordered grudgingly, clutching his skull. 'Tell them what's happening.'

'Yes, tell them everything,' Santos called after them. 'And tell them that if anyone else comes down here, I'll kill everyone in this room, starting with the colonel.'

There was a pause as Santos waited for the room to empty, a few of the retreating officers glancing nervously behind them in anticipation of perhaps being shot from behind. But the attack never came, and the sound of their leaden footsteps soon faded away. Allegra glanced at Tom, who gave her a grim smile. They were on their own.

'Get the painting,' Santos barked. 'Time to go.'

With Orlando standing guard, the two other men heaved the rolled-up canvas on to their shoulders and staggered towards the entrance. Still holding Gallo's neck in the crook of his arm, the gun pressed to his head, Santos backed across the room.

'I'll be seeing you soon, Antonio,' Moretti called after him. 'Sooner than you think.'

Santos paused, then shoved Gallo into Orlando's arms and grabbed two grenades from the bag looped around Orlando's neck.

'I doubt it,' he said, smiling as he pulled the pins out and lobbed one, then the other, into the middle of the room.

EIGHTY

20th March – 11.16 p.m.

The first grenade landed at Tom's feet. Without thinking, he snatched it up, and with a deft snap of his wrist, flicked it through the gap in the glass-fronted display case where the painting had been hanging. Hitting the wall, it bounced a short way along the bottom and then exploded.

The room jumped around them, smoke and dust avalanching through the opening, bits of plaster peeling off the walls like the bark on a cork tree, a terrible, angry roar lifting them off their feet and knocking the wind out of them. But, as some primitive, instinctive part of Tom's brain had no doubt intended, the two-inch-thick armoured glass absorbed the brunt of the blast, its surface cracking but holding firm.

There was to be no such reprieve from the second grenade, however. Having struck the marble table it bounced into Moretti's lap. He looked up, his eyes beseeching, mouth gaping as De Luca dived out of the way. Then it went off, cutting Moretti in half and sending a meteor shower of shrapnel across the room.

Tom looked up from where he had thrown himself to the

floor, barely able to see through the thick smoke that seemed to have blown in like a sea fog. Ears ringing, he staggered to his feet and made his way unsteadily towards where he had last seen Allegra and the others, tripping over De Luca, who had lost a shoe and whose arm was hanging limply at his side, blood leaking from a deep gash to his head. The two halves of Moretti's body were lying next to him, although the way they had landed made it look as if his legs were growing out of his head. It was a gruesome sight.

Coughing, he knelt by Allegra's side. She seemed okay if a little disorientated, Moretti having clearly absorbed the worst of the explosion. But both Archie and Dominique were injured – Archie clutching the side of his face, the blood soaking through his fingers, while a shard of hot metal had embedded itself in Dominique's thigh.

'Are you okay?' Tom called, knowing that he was shouting but still barely able to hear himself.

'We'll be fine,' Archie said through gritted teeth. 'Just go and shoot the bastard.'

With a nod, Tom jumped across to the pile of guns discarded by Gallo's men, grabbing one for himself and tossing another to Allegra, who was now back on her feet.

'Let's go,' she said, her eyes filled with the same diamond-tipped determination he'd seen when she'd engineered their escape from the car park.

They sprinted back through the various decorated rooms towards the bath complex and the vaulted tunnel that led outside.

'Wait!' Allegra called as he turned towards the entrance. 'Can you feel that?'

He paused, and then realised what she meant. A fresh breeze was tickling his cheek, the air sweet and rich compared to the otherwise brackish atmosphere. Santos must have found another way out.

Turning to her right, she led him down a narrow tunnel that rose in total darkness up a steep incline. Feeling his way along the brick walls, Tom followed closely behind, the breeze getting stronger, until they found themselves in a square chamber. Above them, an iron ladder climbed towards a patch of star-flecked sky. At the foot of the ladder, a body was lying on a bed of rubble. It was Gallo.

'He's alive,' Allegra said, kneeling next to him and pressing her fingers against his neck. Tom wasn't sure if she sounded relieved or disappointed. 'Santos must have thrown him back down the hole.' She pointed at the colonel's arm, which was bent up at an unnatural angle where he had dislocated his shoulder in the fall.

Tom flew up the ladder, emerging under the disapproving glare of an angel that had escaped damage when Santos had smashed through the gravestone she had been guarding. Hauling himself clear, he reached down to help Allegra climb out, the flickering blue lights on the other side of the cemetery indicating where Gallo's men had congregated around the entrance to the Merisi tomb.

'Which way?'

Allegra's question was almost immediately answered by the sound of an engine being started. They ran to the cemetery wall, Allegra giving Tom a leg up, Tom then reaching down and hauling her up behind him. As he jumped down on to the pavement, an ambulance surged out of the darkness, headlights blazing, Santos hunched over the wheel.

Stepping into the road and taking careful aim, Tom unloaded a full clip into the ambulance's onrushing windscreen. Allegra, still perched on the wall, did the same. But they both missed, forcing Tom to leap out of the way at the last minute as the ambulance veered past, followed the road round and then disappeared into the night.

'*Merda*,' Allegra swore.

'I had him,' Tom panted as he clambered back up alongside her. 'I was aiming right at him.'

'Well, you missed. We both did.'

'That's impossible.' Tom shook his head, popping out the magazine and checking it. 'He was coming straight towards me. He could only have been thirty feet away. Less.'

A sudden thought came to him. An impossible thought. And yet . . . it was the only explanation. Ignoring Allegra's calls, he jumped down and raced back to the stern angel guarding the shattered gravestone. Peering through the opening to check that no one was coming up behind him, he lowered himself inside and then slid down the ladder.

'Don't move!'

Hearing the voice, Tom turned and saw that Gallo was conscious now, propped up against the wall and being attended by a medic. Four armed policemen were eyeing Tom suspiciously, their machine guns raised.

'It's okay,' Gallo rasped. 'He's with us. Her too.'

Tom looked up and saw that Allegra was climbing down towards them. The policemen relaxed, allowing their weapons to swing down across their stomachs.

'What the hell is going on?' Tom demanded angrily.

'What do you mean?' said Gallo, wincing as the medic prodded his shoulder.

'I mean this –' Stepping forward, Tom smashed his forearm into the bridge of a policeman's nose and wrenched the machine gun from the man's grasp as he staggered back, howling in pain.

'Tom, what are you doing?' Allegra gasped as he swung the weapon towards Gallo and flicked the safety off.

'Ask him,' he replied tonelessly, before pulling the trigger.

The gun jerked in his hand, the muzzle flash lighting the narrow tunnel like a strobe light, hot shell casings pinging off the walls, the noise crashing around them with a deafening echo that seemed to feed off itself and last long after the final shot had been fired.

Gallo returned Tom's accusing glare through the smoke. Unharmed.

'Blanks?' Allegra's face turned from horror to understanding, to confusion as she looked from Tom to Gallo.

Pushing the medic roughly out of the way, Gallo heaved himself to his feet.

'We need to talk,' he growled.

'*You* need to talk,' Tom corrected him.

'Fine, but not here.'

EIGHTY-ONE

Ponte Sant' Angelo, Rome
20th March – 11.55 p.m.

With his men forming a cordon at either end of the bridge, Gallo led them out to the middle, then turned to face them, his arm strapped across his chest where the medic had popped his shoulder back into its socket.

'This will do.'

'Where have you taken Archie and Dom?' Tom asked angrily.

'To hospital,' Gallo reassured him. 'My men will take you to them when we've finished.'

'The same men who attempted a rescue armed with blanks?' Allegra snorted. She didn't believe a word he said any more.

He gave a heavy sigh.

'It's complicated.'

'Is that your idea of an apology?' she shot back.

'There are forces at work here. Powerful forces.'

'What the hell are you talking about?' Tom's tone was caught between irritation and impatience. 'I want an explanation, not a palm reading.'

Gallo paused, turning to face down the river so that his back was to them.

'Santos is connected. Very well connected,' he began. 'It seems that, over the years, the Banco Rosalia has done a lot of favours for a lot of people.'

'What sort of people?' Allegra pressed.

'People he helped to evade tax and launder money. People who had relied on him to help fund their political campaigns. People who had profited from the sale of tens of millions of dollars in looted antiquities. *Important* people. People who couldn't risk Santos going down and taking them with him.'

'So these . . . people – they're why you helped him get away?' Allegra's voice was heavy with an air of resigned disgust. 'They're why you watched him try to kill us.'

'He wanted it to look as though he'd had to shoot his way out,' said Gallo. 'I didn't know he was going to throw . . . that was . . . wrong.'

'*Wrong?*' Tom repeated with a hollow laugh.

'How long has he had you on a leash?' Allegra asked. 'Since Cavalli was killed? Before?'

'I didn't even know who Cavalli was until I was put on to the Ricci case,' Gallo turned to face them again, pressing his back against the parapet. 'I don't think Santos did either. But when Argento was killed, Santos grew worried that I might somehow connect the murders back to him or the Delian League. So he made some calls.'

'Who to?' Tom asked.

'I've already told you –' Gallo shrugged – 'People. All I know is that, when my orders came, they came from the top. The very top. Protect Santos. Keep a lid on things. Stop the case spiralling out of control.'

'What about Gambetta?' Allegra said sharply. 'Did they tell you to kill him too?'

'I did what I had to do,' Gallo said defiantly. 'Santos had

offered us a deal. Cavalli's watch in return for keeping a lid on everything he knew and a promise to leave the country by the end of the week. Gambetta was an old fool who was never going to keep quiet about evidence going missing or how clever he'd been in linking all the murders together. He was a necessary sacrifice.' A pause. 'He's not the first person to have died for his country.'

'A necessary sacrifice?' Allegra shook her head in disgust, a fist of anger clenching her stomach. 'This has nothing to do with patriotism. This is about rich, powerful people doing whatever it takes to protect themselves. This is about murder. You killed Gambetta for doing his job.'

'You don't understand,' Gallo shot back. 'I had my orders. The things Santos knows . . . this was a matter of national security. He was to be protected at all costs. I had no choice.'

'You had a choice,' Allegra insisted. 'You just chose not to make it. You killed a man and framed me for it.'

'I was trying to protect you.'

'From what?'

'Santos found out you were asking questions about the Delian League. He wanted you dealt with. Why else do you think De Luca picked you up? I thought that if I blamed you for the killing and got your face in the papers, I might find you before he did. I was never planning to . . . Look, maybe it was wrong of me. But you'll get a full retraction, an apology, your choice of assignments –'

'You disgust me. You and whoever it is that can decide that an old man should die to stop someone like Santos being caught.'

'I love my country,' Gallo insisted. 'I did what I had to do to protect it, and I'd do the same again. Anyway, I tried to put things right.'

'How? With that little show you and Santos put on tonight?'

'By saving you.'

'What are you talking about?' Tom challenged him. 'Saving us from what?'

'Who do you think dug you out of that tomb?'

'That was you?' Allegra swapped a glance with Tom, almost not wanting to believe him. Anything to avoid feeling that she might in some way owe him something.

'How did you find us?'

'I had a back-up team watching Eco. They picked you up coming out of the gallery and followed you to where De Luca snatched you up and then out to Contarelli's farm-house. I sent my men in as soon as I could. Luckily, they weren't too late.'

'Luckily,' Allegra repeated in a sarcastic tone, the thought of the plastic bag slick and tight against her lips still making her stomach turn.

'So it was you that fed us the information about D'Arcy?'

'I knew that he worked for De Luca,' Gallo nodded. 'So when I heard about the fire and that he'd gone missing, I realised it was probably connected. The problem was that I didn't have the jurisdiction to investigate. Luckily for me, I'd seen enough of Allegra to know that, if I gave her the option, she'd follow up the lead herself rather than walk away.'

There was a long silence, Gallo glancing at each of them in turn with a look that threatened to veer into an apology, although Allegra knew that he'd never allow himself to actually say anything.

'So what happens to Santos now?' she asked eventually.

'He sells the painting and leaves the country. As long as he never comes back, we forget about him and move on. Let him become someone else's problem.'

'And the Banco Rosalia?'

Gallo laughed.

'The Banco Rosalia is bankrupt. That's why he had to make a move for the painting. It was his last chance to get out with something before the news broke. Not that it ever will. The government and the Vatican have already agreed to jointly underwrite the losses and quietly wind the business down to avoid any bad press. No one will ever know a thing.'

Allegra shook her head angrily, her jaw clenching and throat tightening. The hypocrisy and injustice of a world where a murderer like Santos was allowed to go free to protect a cabal of corrupt politicians and God-knows who else, while Gambetta was . . . it made her feel dirty.

'What about De Luca and Faulks? Aren't you going to charge them?' Tom asked hopefully.

'What with?' Gallo shrugged. 'We know what Faulks does, but we've never had any proof that he's broken an Italian law on Italian soil. And as for De Luca . . .'

'Colonel!' He was interrupted by an officer signalling urgently from the end of the bridge. 'We've found them.'

EIGHTY-TWO

Via Appia Antica, Rome
21 March – 12.29 a.m.

Sirens blaring, they swept through the city, outriders clearing their path, people pointing and staring. Twenty minutes later they reached the Via Appia Antica where curious faces were replaced by the sombre countenance of the Roman funerary monuments that, like foxes pinned down by their headlights, momentarily reared out of the darkness, only to slink away as soon as they had raced past.

'A local patrol unit ran their plates as they came past,' Gallo explained over the noise of the engine as soon as he had finished his call. 'They came up registered to a vehicle stolen last week in Milan. When they tried to stop them, the driver lost control and rolled it into a tree.'

Peering through the seats in front of her, Allegra could see a faint glow on the horizon, a red hue with a blue-edged tint. She looked across to Tom, who gave her an encouraging smile and then reached for her hand. She understood what he was trying to tell her. That this was nearly all over. That they'd almost won.

There were two fire crews on the scene but they were

holding back, their flaccid hoses lying uncoiled at their feet.

'The fuel tank could go at any moment and there's no danger of it spreading,' one of the crew explained to Gallo. 'We're just going to let it die down a bit.'

Allegra led Tom to the edge of the semi-circle of policemen and passers-by that had formed around the burning ambulance like kids at a bonfire, the heat from the flames searing her cheeks. Deep ruts in the verge showed where the vehicle had careered off the road and into a ditch, a partially uprooted tree explaining why it hadn't continued on into the field that lay on the other side of the hedge. One of the wheels was on fire and still slowly turning.

Abruptly, the fuel tank exploded, the ambulance jerking spasmodically, the noise of breaking glass and the tortured shriek of expanding metal coming from somewhere inside it. Sparks flitted though the air around them like fireflies.

Allegra glanced at Tom and followed his impassive gaze to the body that must have been thrown clear before the fire had broken out. It was the priest, Orlando. From the way he was lying it didn't look like he would be getting up again. She turned back to the ambulance, straining to see through the swirling flames and smoke, and caught the charred outline of a body in the driver's seat, head slumped forward, hands still gripping the wheel.

'Santos?' she asked Tom.

Tom shrugged and then turned away.

'If you want it to be.'

EIGHTY-THREE

The Getty Villa, Malibu, California
1st May – 11.58 a.m.
One thing was certain – they had all been asked here to witness something special. The clue, as always, had been in the expense lavished on the engraved invitations, the quality of the champagne served at the welcoming reception and the bulging gift bags positioned next to the exit.

When it came to what was going to be announced, however, opinions were more divided. Opinions that, as the minutes passed, grew ever more outlandish and unlikely, until some were confidently predicting that the entire collection of the British Museum was even now being loaded into containers to be shipped to California, and others that it was the Getty itself that was relocating to Beijing. As guesswork was layered on to conjecture, so the noise grew, until what had started as a gentle breeze of curious voices had grown into a deafening storm over which people were struggling to make themselves heard.

Then, without warning, the lights dimmed and three people stepped out onto the stage, one of them wearing sunglasses. The noise dropped as abruptly as if they had passed into the eye of a hurricane, leaving an eerie, pregnant silence.

The shortest person, a man, approached the lectern and gripped its sides, seemingly comforted by its varnished solidity. A large screen behind him showed a close-up of his face – pink, fleshy and sweating.

'Ladies and gentlemen,' Director Bury began nervously, licking the corners of his mouth. 'Ladies and gentlemen, it is my pleasure to welcome you here today. As many of you know, our founder had a simple vision. It was that art has a civilising influence in society, and should therefore be made available to the public for their education and enjoyment.' He paused, his voice growing in confidence as a polite round of applause rippled through the crowd. 'It is a vision that continues to inspire us today as we seek to collect, preserve, exhibit and interpret art of the highest quality. More importantly, it is a vision that continues to inspire others into the most extraordinary acts of generosity. Acts of generosity that have led us today to what I believe is the single most important acquisition in the museum's history. Dr Bruce, please.'

He retreated a few steps, glistening and exultant, and led the clapping as Verity stepped forward. Saying nothing, she waited for the applause to die down, and then nodded. The stage was immediately plunged into darkness. For a few moments nothing happened, people craning their necks to see over or between the rows in front of them, hardly daring to breathe. Then a single spotlight came on, illuminating the jagged outline of a carved face. An ivory face. Behind them the screen was filled with its ghostly, sightless eyes.

Still Verity said nothing, the silence of anticipation giving way to an excited murmur, a few people standing up to get a closer look, one man at the front clapping spontaneously, others turning to each other and muttering words of confusion or shocked understanding. Little by little the noise grew,

until the room was once again gripped by a violent, in-
coherent storm that was only partially muted by the sound
of Verity's voice and a second spotlight revealing her face.

'Thanks to the incredible generosity of Myron Kezman, a
man of singular vision and exquisite taste whose philan-
thropy shines through these dark economic times,' she called
over the clamour, waving at a beaming Kezman to step
forward, 'the Getty is proud to announce the acquisition of
the Phidias Apollo, the only surviving work of possibly the
greatest sculptor of the classical age.' She paused as the
applause came again, unrestrained and exultant. 'As you can
see, it is a uniquely well-preserved fragment of a chryselephantine sculpture of the Greek god Apollo. Dated to
around 450 BC, it shows –'

'Verity Bruce?' A man in the front row had interrupted
her. Standing up, he moved to the stage.

'If you don't mind, sir, I'll take questions at the end,' she
said through a forced smile, eyeing him contemptuously.

'My name is Special Agent Carlos Ortiz, FBI,' the man
announced, holding out his badge. 'And if you and Mr Kezman
don't mind, you'll be taking my questions downtown.'

The audience turned in their seats as the doors at the back
of the auditorium flew open. Four dark-suited men entered
the room and fanned out.

'What is this?' she called out over the crowd's low, confused
muttering, her expression caught somewhere between
incredulity and indignation.

'I have a warrant for your arrest, along with Mr Myron
Kezman and Earl Faulks,' Ortiz announced, the sight of the
piece of paper in his hand raising the audience's muttering
to a curious rumble. Kezman said nothing, his indulgent
smile having faded behind the blank mask of his sunglasses
as two further agents had taken up positions either side of
the stage.

'On what charges?' Director Bury challenged him, advancing to Verity's side.

'Federal tax fraud, conspiracy to traffic in illegal antiquities and illegal possession of antiquities,' Ortiz fired back. 'But we're just getting started.'

'This is outrageous,' Verity erupted, shielding her face from the machine-gun flash of press cameras. 'I have done nothing –'

She was interrupted by a commotion at the back of the room as a man tried to make a run for the exit, only to be brought down heavily by the outstretched leg of another member of the audience.

'It seems Mr Faulks is not as confident in his innocence as you appear to be in yours,' Ortiz observed wryly as two of his men pounced on Faulks's prone figure and hauled him to his feet. 'Cuff them.'

Verity and Kezman's shouted protests were drowned out by the hyena howl of the crowd as they leapt from their seats and surged forward to feast.

Amidst the commotion, a man and a woman slipped out, unobserved.

EIGHTY-FOUR

1st May – 12.09 p.m.
'How's your foot?' Allegra laughed as they made their way out into the Outer Peristyle's shaded cloister. A light salt breeze was blowing in from the Pacific and tugging at her hair, which was now its original colour once again.

'He was meant to trip over it, not step on it,' Tom grinned, pretending to limp over the marble floor.

'Do you think they'll let him cut a deal?'

'Unlikely, given what you copied in his warehouse and the tape.'

'What tape?' Allegra asked with a frown.

'Dominique recorded the three of them discussing the mechanics of the whole on using the phone she and Archie cloned.'

They stepped between two of the fluted columns and made their way down a shallow ramp into a large rectangular courtyard. Running almost its entire length was a shallow reflection pool, its rectangular white stone basin curving at both ends like a Venetian mirror.

'What do you think they'll do with the mask?' Allegra asked as they navigated their way along a labyrinthine arrangement of box hedge-lined gravel paths to the pool's edge.

'Ortiz told me that the Italian government has drawn up a catalogue of forty artefacts acquired by or donated to the Getty over the past twenty years that they want returned. The mask is at the top of the list.'

'That's a start,' she said, sitting down next to him.

'The Greek and Turkish governments are talking about doing the same. And that's just the Getty. There are other museums, galleries, private collections . . . the fall-out from this will take years to clear.

'But nothing will change,' she sighed. 'When the Delian League finally falls, others will just see it as an opportunity to step in and fill the vacuum.'

'You can't stop the supply,' Tom nodded. 'Contarelli was right about that. The tomb robbers are fighting a guerrilla campaign and the police are still lining up in squares and using muskets. But if the publicity makes museums, collectors and auction houses clean up their act, it might choke the demand. And with less buyers, there'll be less money and less incentive to dig. In time, things might just change.'

There was a silence, Allegra playing with the water and letting it slide through her fingers like mercury.

'They buried Aurelio yesterday,' she said, without looking up.

'I didn't know that . . .?'

'Some kids found his body washed up on the Isola Tiberina.'

'Murdered?'

'They don't think so.'

Tom placed his hand on her shoulder. She glanced up and then quickly looked down again, her eyes glistening.

'I'm sorry.'

'I think he was too.' She shook the water from her fingers and then wiped them on her skirt.

'What's happened to Gallo?'

'Promoted, I expect.' She gave a hollow laugh. 'To be honest, I don't care. Him, the people he was protecting . . . they all disgust me.'

'But he kept his part of the deal?' Tom checked.

She nodded. 'All charges dropped. A formal apology. My pick of assignments. He even had my parking tickets cancelled.'

'So you'll stay?'

'I'll think about it,' she said. 'Not everyone's like him. Besides, I want to see Contarelli's face when I raid his place.' Tom grinned. 'What about you?'

'Me?' He gave a deep sigh. 'Archie's meeting me in New York for Jennifer's funeral. The FBI only released her body last week, After that . . . Who knows? I never like to plan too far ahead. Which way's the sea?'

They stood up and walked through to the other side of the colonnade, following some steps down to a path.

'By the way, did you hear about the Caravaggio?' Allegra asked as they headed up a slope to their right.

'Destroyed?' A hint of surprise in Tom's voice.

She shook her head.

'There wasn't any trace of it in the ambulance.'

'And Santos?'

'The DNA from the body at the wheel matched the sample the Vatican provided for him,' she said with a shrug. 'So that's case closed, I guess.'

'Except you think he's still alive,' Tom guessed.

'I think if he's got any sense, he'll stay dead,' she said, the muscles in her jaw flexing with anger. 'Moretti's people are looking for him and the word is that De Luca's put a five-million-dollar ticket on his head.'

They reached a large lawned area and walked to its far wall where there was a view out over the treetops to the sea, white caps rolling in neat parallel lines towards the beach.

'There's one thing I still can't figure out,' Allegra said, hitching herself on to it to face Tom, who was shielding his eyes from the sun. 'Why did Faulks have two watches?'

'What do you mean?'

'De Luca, D'Arcy, Moretti and Cavalli only had one watch each. Why did Faulks have two in his safe?'

'He said he had two seats on the council,' Tom reminded her. 'Presumably to act as a counterweight between D'Arcy and De Luca on one hand and Cavalli and Moretti on the other. The watches went with the seats, I guess.'

'Except the League was formed by putting De Luca's and Moretti's two organisations together,' she said slowly. 'That must have meant that they would each have had their own dealer at one stage.'

'So what are you saying? That one of the watches used to belong to someone else?' Tom frowned as he considered this.

'De Luca did say that Faulks's two seats were an accident of history,' she said. 'What if the other dealer left? Faulks would have taken over his seat and his watch.'

'Unless the other dealer never handed the watch back. That might explain why Faulks had to go and get a replacement made.' Tom suggested. 'You could be right. Maybe when you see him you can ask him. Which reminds me . . .'

He took a piece of paper from his pocket and deliberately ripped it in half and then half again.

'What's that?' she asked, as he continued to rip it into ever smaller pieces.

'You remember when we went through the papers in Faulks's safe? Well, I found a map. The one showing where Cavalli found the mask.'

'Wait!'

She reached out to grab his hand, but he threw the pieces up into the air before she could get to him.

'Tom!' she shouted angrily. 'Have you any idea what else could be down there?'

He gave her a rueful smile.

'Not everything's ready to be found, Allegra.'

Above him, the scraps of paper fluttered like butterflies in the sunlight, before a gust of wind lifted them soaring into the sky and carried them out to sea, like a flock of birds at the start of a long migration south.

EIGHTY-FIVE

Central Square, Casco Viejo, Panama
1st May – 6.36 p.m.

Antonio Santos, his arm in a sling, stood to one side and pressed the muzzle of his gun against the door at about head height.

'Who is it?'

'DHL,' a muffled voice called back. 'Package for Mr Stefano Romano?'

'Leave it outside.'

'I need a signature,' the voice called back.

Santos paused. He was expecting a couple of deliveries this week under that name, and it would be a shame if they got returned. On the other hand, he needed to be careful until he was certain that he had shaken everyone off the trail.

'Who is it from?' he asked, slowly sliding his face across to the peep hole.

A bored-looking man was standing on the landing dressed in a brown uniform. He appeared to be trying to grow a beard and was chewing gum. Santos's last question had prompted him to roll his eyes and blow a bubble that he popped with his finger.

'It's from Italy,' he replied, glancing at the stamps and then turning it over so that he could read the label on its back. 'Someone called Amarelli?'

Grinning, Santos tucked his gun into the back of his trousers, unbolted the door and threw it open.

'Amarelli liquorice from Calabria,' he explained, signing the form and eagerly ripping the box open. 'The best there is.' He flicked open a tin of Spezzata and crammed two pieces into his mouth, chewing them noisily. 'Want to try some?' he mumbled, thrusting the tin at the courier, who waved them away with a muttered word of thanks. 'I've looked everywhere, but no one seems to stock it here. Lucky for me they do mail order.'

'Lucky for me too, Antonio,' the courier replied. 'Or I'd never have found you.'

His eyes widening as he realised his mistake, Santos immediately kicked the door shut and reached for his gun. But the man was too quick, stamping his foot in the jamb and then shouldering the door open, sending Santos reeling backwards. Swinging his gun out from behind him, Santos lined up a shot, but before he could pull the trigger a painful punch to the soft inside of his arm sent it rattling across the tiled floor, while a forearm smash to his neck sent him crashing to his knees. He made a choking noise, his hands wrapped around his throat, his breathing coming in short, animal gasps.

Quickly checking that no one had heard them, the man eased the front door shut and then dragged Santos by his feet towards the kitchen. Once there he cuffed him, and then attached his wrists to a steel cable that he looped over the security bars covering the window.

'Wait. What's your name?' Santos croaked as he was forced to his feet.

'Foster,' the man replied as he tugged down hard on the

cable, the metal fizzing noisily as it passed over the bars until Santos's hands were stretched high above his head, forcing him to stand on the balls of his feet to stop the cuffs biting into his wrists, his injured arm burning.

'Please, Foster, I'll pay you,' he wheezed. 'Whatever they're paying you, I'll double it.'

'You know how this works.' The man eyed him dispassionately. 'Once I've taken a job, there's no backing out. It's why people hire me. It's why you hired me.'

'I don't even know you.'

'Sure you do.' Foster tied the cable to a radiator, twanging it to check that it was under tension. 'Las Vegas? The Amalfi? That *was* you, wasn't it?'

'The Amalfi?' Santos breathed, whatever colour he had left in his face draining away. 'Please,' he whispered. 'There must be another way. Let me go. I'll disappear. They'll never know.'

'I'll know,' the man replied. 'And I can't have your life on my conscience. Now, open wide.'

'What?'

Santos gave a muffled shout as a grenade was forced into his mouth. The ribbed metal casing smashed two of his teeth as Foster wedged it between his jaws, making sure that the safety handle was at the back so that its sharp edges cut into the corners of Santos's mouth like a horse bit. Santos began to gag on the oily metal, his eyes wide and terrified.

'The person who sent me wanted you to know that he is a reasonable man. A civilised man. So, if you were to feel able to apologise . . .?'

Santos nodded furiously, the pain in his arms now making him feel faint.

'Good!' Foster reached forward, pulled the pin out and placed on the counter. Then he took out a mobile phone, dialled a number and positioned it next to the pin. 'He's listening now –' Foster nodded at the phone. 'So when you're ready, just spit the grenade out and say your piece.

EPILOGUE

'Know thyself'
Inscription on the Temple of Apollo at Delphi

EIGHTY-SIX

Tarrytown, New York
2nd May – 4.03 p.m.
This was how everything had started.

A funeral. Black limos lining the road. A sea of un-familiar faces. Secret service agents patrolling the grounds. Guests seated in a horseshoe. The coffin draped with the Stars and Stripes. The service droning towards its muted conclusion.

For a moment it seemed to Tom that time had stood still. That he must have imagined everything. That any moment now Jennifer would appear out of the rain and, silhouetted against the headlights of the car behind her, wave at him to run up and see her.

Except today there was no rain, clear blue skies and the crisp spring sunlight conspiring to lift the congregation's sombre mood. Today there was no choreographed ceremony or martial display, the service playing out with a discreet inti-macy of its own invention. Today people were there not because of some misplaced sense of duty or to cut a deal, but out of love. And today, rather than be exiled to some sodden, windswept slope, Tom was sitting amongst them.

Same start. Different ending.

'Thanks for coming,' Tom whispered to Archie as FBI Director Green stepped forward and handed Jennifer's parents the neatly folded flag. Her father took it with a proud nod, clutching it to his chest, his left arm hugging her mother into his collar, her shoulders shaking. Next to them both, Jennifer's sister and her boyfriend were clasping each other's hands.

'You know what? I'll miss her,' Archie sighed, medical gauze still taped to his left cheek. 'Never thought I'd say that about an FBI agent, but I really will.'

'I'm sure she would have said the same about you,' Tom smiled.

'How was Allegra when you saw her?'

'Still angry.'

'Do you think she'll stick with it? With being a copper, I mean?'

'I'm not sure. I don't think she knows herself yet.'

The service ended and the congregation broke up. Some remained seated, alone with their thoughts; others lingered in small groups, swapping memories or phone numbers as old acquaintances were renewed; a few paused at the grave's edge, peering down at the earth-speckled coffin and maybe passing on a final thought.

Tom had a sudden urge to go and introduce himself to Jennifer's parents, to share his memories of her and hear theirs, to let them know the part she'd played in his life and he in hers. But there seemed little point. They had no idea who he was. The truth was, he was as much a stranger here as he had been at his grandfather's funeral.

'Come on. Let's go.'

He got up and made eye contact with FBI Director Green on the other side of the coffin. He too was preparing to leave, it seemed, but the sight of Tom caused him to mutter some instructions to his security detail and then step towards him. Tom met him halfway.

'Kirk.'

'Mr Director.'

'I thought you might like to know that Santos was killed yesterday. In Panama.'

Tom nodded slowly, a weight that he had scarcely been aware of slowly lifting from his shoulders.

'How?'

'Hard to tell really. There wasn't much left of him. My people tell me a grenade.'

'Dangerous things, grenades.' Tom nodded. 'What about the shooter? This isn't over yet.'

'We're still working on it.' Green shrugged. 'As soon as we get a firm lead, I'll let you know.'

'And the ballistics results? I know someone who . . .'

'We'll find him. And when we do, I promise you that he'll feel the full force of . . .'

'Not if I get him first.'

'Be careful, Kirk. I can't protect you if you do something . . .'

'Excuse me, but are you Tom Kirk?' Jennifer's father had appeared in front of them. A tall man, he was immaculately dressed in a pale grey suit and a black woven silk tie, his eyes sore, a slight tremor in his voice.

'Yes, yes I am,' Tom stammered, feeling both surprised and strangely awkward. 'I'm so sorry . . .'

'I think . . . I think she would have wanted you to have this.'

Biting his lip to hold back his tears, he pressed the triangular shape of the folded flag into Tom's uncertain hands and then, with a tight nod at Green, fell back to his sobbing wife's side.

Tom and Green stood there silently, only a few feet apart, the material strangely warm against Tom's chest. Green glanced around, as if to check that no one was watching, then thrust out his hand.

'Thank you,' he said.

Tom hesitated for a few moments, then shook it.

The next instant he was gone, caught up in a flurry of dark suits, Ray-Bans and clear plastic ear-pieces as he was bundled towards his car.

'You think he let you escape from the FBI building on purpose?' Archie murmured.

'I think I did exactly what he'd hoped I would,' said Tom. 'Come on. Let's get out of here.'

'Mr Kirk? Mr Kirk?'

A voice called out as they turned to leave. Tom's eyes narrowed, unable to place the man navigating his way through the crowd, although he recognised his jowly face and the metronomic sway of his gut from somewhere.

'Larry Hewson, from Ogilvy, Myers and Gray,' the man introduced himself enthusiastically.

'I'm sorry, I don't . . .' Tom frowned.

'We met at your grandfather's funeral. I'm the Duval family . . .'

'Attorney, yes,' Tom suddenly remembered. 'How did you . . .?'

'Your associate was kind enough to suggest that I might find you here,' Hewson explained.

Tom fixed Archie with a questioning stare.

'My associate?'

'He kept bloody calling.' Archie shrugged. 'I didn't think he'd actually show up.'

'There's the small matter of your grandfather's will,' Hewson continued. 'As I explained to you when we last met, he specified that I was to pass on to you something that your mother had given him shortly before her death.'

'Yes, I remember.'

'This time I've brought all the paperwork with me. If you wouldn't mind just signing here –' Hewson produced a sheet of paper and a pen and then held up his briefcase so that Tom could lean against it as he signed. 'Excellent,' he exclaimed, popping the briefcase's brass catches and taking out a small wooden box and an envelope that he handed to Tom with a flourish. 'Then I will be on my way.'

With a nod, he filed away the signed sheet of paper and strode off towards his waiting car, a phone snapping to his cheek.

'What is it?' Archie asked in a curious voice.

'A letter from my mother,' Tom replied, the sight of his name written in faded black ink strangely familiar from hoarded postcards.

The envelope opened easily, revealing a white card dated to the year before she'd died, across which she'd scribbled a brief message:

Darling Tom
One day, when you're older, you might want some answers. And if you're reading this, it probably means I'm not there to give them. So what's inside this box might help. Whatever you find, don't think too badly of me. I always loved you. I still do.
Love Mummy

Tom turned away from Archie, his eyes hot and stinging, his throat tightening, and opened the box.

All of a sudden, the events of the past few weeks came flooding back into sharp focus. De Luca's strange familiarity on meeting him, Faulks's open-mouthed surprise at the mention of his name, Santos's veiled questions.

Because inside, nestling on a black velvet background, was a watch.

A watch with an ivory face and an orange second hand.

NOTE FROM THE AUTHOR

The Nativity with St Francis and St Lawrence (also known as *The Adoration*) was painted by the Italian master Michelangelo Merisi da Caravaggio in 1609 during his self-imposed exile from Rome after killing a man in a duel. The six square metre work was stolen from the Oratory of San Lorenzo in Palermo, Sicily on 16th October 1969. Working under the cover of darkness, the thieves cut the work from its frame with razor blades and escaped in a lorry. In 1996, Francesco Marino Mannoia, an informant and former member of the Sicilian mafia, claimed he had stolen the painting as a young man on the orders of a high-ranking mobster. Other sources, however, have pointed the finger at amateurs who acted after seeing a TV programme about the painting the previous week and then sold it on to the local Sicilian mafia when they realised that they couldn't fence it. At one point it is said to have ended up in the hands of Palermo boss Rosario Riccobono (throttled in 1982 at a barbecue lunch organised for that purpose by the Corleonesi family) before passing on to Gerlando 'The Rug' Alberti, commander of the Porta Nuova district in Palermo. Other rumours that the work was damaged in the theft or even destroyed in an earthquake in

1980 have also circulated from time to time, as have stories of supposed sightings abroad. Today, however, the *Nativity* remains one of the most famous unrecovered stolen paintings in the world. It is listed by the FBI as one of its top ten art crimes and they have estimated its value at $20 million, although the likely auction value is far, far greater.

Tomb-robbing has often been called the second oldest profession. Italy, with over forty UNESCO World Heritage sites, is a particular target, but it is a plague that increasingly affects other countries such as Peru, Guatemala, Mexico, China, Thailand, Turkey, Egypt and Greece, where poverty, poor security, the buried remains of a rich civilisation and seemingly insatiable demand from unscrupulous dealers and collectors have conspired to rapidly destroy thousands of years of our shared archaeological and historical heritage for profit. On 13th September 1995, Swiss police raided four bonded warehouses in the Geneva Free Port and seized a large number of illegally excavated antiquities. The premises were registered to a Swiss company called Editions Services, which police later traced to Giacomo Medici, a man later described as 'the real "mastermind" of much of [Italy's] illegal traffic in archaeological objects.' According to the Carabinieri, the warehouses contained over ten thousand artefacts worth around $35 million at the time, including hundreds of pieces of ancient Greek, Roman, and Etruscan art and a set of Etruscan dinner plates alone worth $2 million. Accompanying these were files, binders and boxes containing sales records and correspondence between Medici and dealers and museums around the world, and thousands of photographs, some of which illustrated the journey of single pieces from the ground, to their restored state, to the display cabinets of some of the world's largest museums. As a result of these findings, Medici was sentenced to ten years and fined ten million euro in 2004 for dealing in stolen ancient artefacts.

Evidence from the Geneva raid was also used to bring charges against American antiquities dealer Robert Hecht, Jr. and former J. Paul Getty Museum curator of antiquities Marion True for conspiracy to traffic in illegal antiquities, with True claiming that she was being made to carry the burden for practices which were known, approved, and condoned by the Getty's Board of Directors. Their trial continues. In September 2007, the Getty signed an agreement with the Italian culture ministry to return forty major works of ancient art. Similarly in 2006, the New York Metropolitan Museum of Art agreed to give legal ownership of the famous Euphronios krater (sold to it by Robert Hecht in 1972) back to the Italian government. The Museum of Fine Arts in Boston and the Princeton University Art Museum have also returned items. Since the destruction of the Medici smuggling ring and the more stringent acquisition policies put in place by museums and collectors in the light of these events, the latest information suggests that illegal digging is down by half. The Carabinieri art squad also claim that the quality of seized objects has collapsed. Whether this is just a temporary lull, or sign of a more permanent shift, remains to be seen.

The Phidias ivory mask was recovered by Italian police in London in 2003. A unique life-size ivory head of Apollo, the Greek god of the sun, from a fifth century BC chryselephantine statue, it is one of the world's rarest and most important looted antiquities. Many experts believe that it was carved by the classical sculptor Phidias, considered to have perhaps been the greatest of all Ancient Greek sculptors. Responsible for many of the marble reliefs on the Parthenon, Phidias also carved two legendary chryselephantine (Greek for gold and ivory) statues: the Athene Parthenos and the statue of Zeus at Olympia, one of the seven wonders of the ancient world, which was taken to Constantinople and destroyed in a palace fire in AD 475. The Apollo ivory mask was seized from the London antiquities dealer Robin Symes, after he was presented with evidence that the statue had been illegally excavated and smuggled out of Italy. It was originally discovered in 1995 by notorious tombarolo (tomb robber) Pietro Casasanta near the remains of the Baths of Claudius, north of Rome. Chryselephantine statues were built around a wooden frame, with thin carved slabs of ivory attached to it to represent the skin and sheets of gold leaf for the garments, armour, hair, and other details. Such statues were incredibly rare, even in ancient times, and historians believe that all seventy-four of Rome's chryselephantine statues vanished when it was sacked by Alaric, chief of the barbarian Visigoths, in AD 410. Although dozens of fragments are known to have survived, only one other life-size figure has been found in Italy (now in the Apostolic Library in the Vatican). A badly fire-damaged set of statues of Apollo and Artemis can also be seen at the Archaeological Museum at Delphi. The Phidias Apollo is currently the star attraction at an exhibition of looted artefacts that have been returned to Italy at the Quirinale Palace in Rome.

The Getty kouros, supposedly from the sixth century BC, was bought by the Getty from a Swiss dealer in 1983 for a reported $7–9 million. A kouros is a statue of a standing nude youth that did not represent any one individual person, but the ideal of youth itself. Used in Archaic Greece as both a dedication to the gods in sanctuaries and as a grave monument, the standard kouros stood with his left foot forward, arms at his sides, looking straight ahead. The Getty kouros has always attracted controversy, for while scientific tests have shown that the patina on the surface could not have been created artificially, a mixture of earlier and later stylistic features and the use of marble from the island of Thassos at an unexpected date, have caused some to doubt its authenticity. These doubts were compounded when several of the other pieces bought with the kouros were shown to be forgeries, and when a letter accompanying it, supposedly written by German scholar Ernst Langlotz in 1952 indicating that the kouros came from a Swiss collection, was also revealed as a forgery, since it bore a postal code that only came into use in the 1970s. In 1992, the kouros was displayed in Athens, Greece, at an international conference called to determine its authenticity. However, the conference failed to resolve the issue, with most art historians and archaeologists denouncing it, and the scientific community believing it to be authentic. To this day, the statue's authenticity remains unresolved and it is displayed with the inscription: 'Greek, *530 BC, or modern forgery.*'

For more information on the author and on the fascinating history, people, places and artefacts that feature in *The Geneva Deception* and the other Tom Kirk novels, please visit www.jamestwining.com.